倍斯特出版事業有限公司
Best Publishing Ltd.

U0066425

新制多益
聽力滿分

神準5回全真試題 ✚ 解題策略

TOEIC

韋爾 ◎ 著

四大特色

1 圖表題強化：眼、耳同步處理聽力和視覺訊息
大幅改善視覺圖像入眼時，大腦預期影像與聽力訊息不同的問題，強化拆解出題者心理，
眼耳一致，完全答對所有圖表題。

2 影子跟讀設計：聽力「理解力」和「專注力」雙軌提升實力
獨家「影子跟讀」設計讓讀者打好聽力「專注力」基礎，改進海量試題盲點，進而精準聽好
所有考點。

3 主題式單字記憶：一石二鳥，神準記憶「聽力」和「閱讀」中循環主題單字
改善考生常規學習下，背了又忘的窘境，反覆聆聽主題音檔，一次性連
鎖記憶相關字彙，一本搞定聽力和閱讀循環出題字彙。

4 試題強力篩選：最省時達到考試成效
時間花在刀口上，精練挑選過的試題，即刻抓住考試脈絡，五回試題寫
完後就能獲取佳績。

MP3

作者序

　　儘管之前有著寫新多益書籍和其他考用書籍的經驗、腦海中盛滿各式各樣的英文對話和原文書，我並未預期能夠在這麼短的時間內完成這本書。當時內心浮現「在短時間內，要獨自完成五回聽力模擬試題的英文撰寫和出題，且還要順利錄完音」，是一項很大的挑戰。在這當中我與有些朋友、之前撰寫新多益書籍的合著作者以及曾經來信的考生，常有信件往來，在當中也形塑著我寫完這本書。寫完後突然發現其實五回能納入的主題不多，跟當初要寫書時的忐忑心情反差很大。

　　在之前所撰寫的新多益書籍出版前，記得我的合著作者莊琬君老師曾詢問我會不會覺得試題出得太簡單？有些題目一看就可以看出答案了。當時我回答：有一點唉！書籍出版後，我曾詢問周遭的朋友，不過他們英文都很好所以會覺得題目很簡單。後來我思考，認為詢問的對象應該要是各程度的考生才正確，因為書籍主要是要協助大多數的考生考到某個分數段，而非替學校或語言機構篩選出語言資優班的學生或是針對英文本身就很好的學生設計的（某些本身英文程度就很好的考生，可以直接裸考或是寫一兩回官方試題就應考了）。當然，適度難度的題目是必要的，可以區隔出某些考生的「層」度差異，但是在出題比例上過多的過難題目就失去模擬試題的效用了。

　　在這些來回思考中、翻閱之前書籍的出題後，我在這次出題上比較小心，秉持著避免納入過難的題目進入，和官方出題難度較為一致，相信這是讀者在乎的部分。所以在試題的難度上會包含「簡易」、「適中」、「稍難」和「難」四種的綜合，相信這樣會比較符合考生的需求。這本書的所有題目和先前出版的《全新制新多益聽力：金色證書（附MP3）》題目完全不同，是全新的題目，我想這對需要很多試題演練又不希望買到已經寫過的題目的考生來說是很重要的。撰寫期間我也遇到一位朋友，問我有沒有寫過有別於其他新多益的單字書，因為他看了很多單字書卻很難記憶起來。在聊天的過程中，我有了新的想法。

　　對於多數的考生來說，單字是基礎，而市面上的單字書琳瑯滿目，有的編排精美或是搭配了學習法或主題等等，但是對於考生來說還是很容易在備考中又忘記某些單字。因為如果僅僅是寫個對話或獨白很容易，但是要將書籍內容呈現生活化且在聽力part 3和part 4都融入閱讀中也會考到的主題單字和外國人常使用的道地慣用語，這部分確實促成和增加了撰寫這本書的難度。而在新多益的這兩部分的聽力原文中均融入了這些元素，此舉讓學習者能熟悉在**「閱讀」**或**「聽力」**中都會**循環出現的字彙**且這些**「單字」**都符合官方所公佈的主題，深刻學習印象並做出聯想，進而一次記下更多主題字彙，考生等於藉由這本書也同時準備了「閱讀測驗」的相關字彙。另外這樣的設計對於仰賴「聽力」來學習的學習者，更是一大幫助，藉由零碎時間聽這些音檔，在聽完當天的其他時段，藉由回憶對話中深刻的片段強化回想相關字彙的記憶連結，就聯想到相關的字彙或唸出聽力單字和片段。例如在藥局的主題中一次就記下**「藥錠」**、**「膠囊」**、**「粉末狀藥物」**和**「藥膏」**等相關英文字彙，而非從單字書中硬記、暫時記下這些字的片段式學習。其中納入一些有趣的主題（所有對話等話題均為杜撰，且以倍斯特的各行業的公司搭配新多益官方提供的主題做設計，旨在提供給考生更多元的學習話題），當然還是有嚴肅的主題提供考生學習，希望提升學習成效讓考生備考時不會感到枯燥。此外，還有加入生活化的**字彙**和**道地慣用語**，像是空服主題中加入了**「值勤名單」**、**「販賣部」**、**「對講機」**等，這些對讀者來說會有興趣知道的單字或是跟自己工作本身相關的字彙，在坊間常見的7000單或10000單是不太會收錄的字，有些考生就會覺得陌生了。像是考生一定知道phone，但是出現interphone，或是知道restaurant但是換成canteen卻又要多花時間去猜想這個字，若在寫閱讀測驗的其他題型或聽力測驗中出現，就阻礙了的閱讀速度或答題，這可能是教科書裡面的英文字和實際在生活或工作中常使用的單字上的落差。雖然在撰寫當中也覺得空服部分的主題有趣，不過為了平衡每個主題的份量，還是有限制這部分的主題量，不然就要成為空服的書籍了。

　　能否答對試題和高分的關鍵，就是「同義轉換」的能力。聽力每題的答題時間有限，所以需要靈活的反應力、迅速聽懂「聽力訊息」，對應到「題本的改寫選項」，迅速判斷出答案，甚至提前「預測」出答案（在聽力段落邊播放就能提前答題，而非等到全數聽力訊息都播畢才開始答題組中接續的數個題目），且不會影響答接續試題的心情，進而獲取高分。書籍中除了「同義轉換」的規劃外，在解析中仔細剖析考點，強化考生應對新制題型中考查考生對「綜合訊息」、「推測文意」、「暗示性」和「圖表題」題型的答題能力。

　　最後是關於其他考用書著作中其他考生的來信，這部分讓我思考著將「影子跟讀法」的學習」更細節地列入這本書籍的「使用說明頁面」，讓讀者能更清楚學習方式。一方面是有些考生想要學好聽力，但是卻不知道從何下手。另一方面，許多考生確實卡在某個分數段，寫了許多試題卻沒有在下次應考時反應在考試分數上（這部分在上本的聽力書有提過），我認為紮實地藉由影子跟讀法提升聽力專注力是解決之道，且這部分連帶影響到聽力理解力的提升，所以如果你寫了很多試題卻仍卡關了，建議好好練習一下「聽力耳」相信學習成效會很顯著的，在考取金色證書後，猛然驚覺自己在觀看歐美影集不需要字幕，真的是一舉兩得。最後祝考生獲取心中的理想成績。

韋爾 敬上

使用說明
INSTRUCTIONS

強力篩選試題，濃縮式精煉聽力，不需要海量試題
掌握出題規律性，即刻具備應考實力

‧ 在寫一定數量的試題後，大概能掌握常見的出題，像是詢問說話者身處何處等等，而不管**主題**或**問法**為何，**在出題上其實還是有其規律性**，可以歸納成主要的提問，即【6W1H】，或是歸類成 ❶ 每個話題的主題和目的 ❷ 說話者身處的地點 ❸ 針對聽到的訊息進行推測 ❹ 細節性考點 ❺ 所發生的問題或狀況 ❻ 接下來可能會發生的事情 ❼ 被要求的事情／建議／提到的事情 ❽ 解決之道 ❾ 新題型的「圖表題」和「掌握說話者意圖」題型。

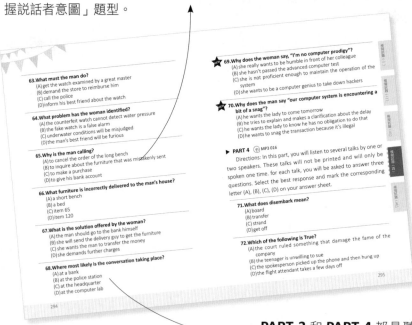

‧ **PART 3** 和 **PART 4** 都是聽力訊息輪流搭配上述出題模式，掌握規律性後就能迅速上手，立即攻略新多益聽力。

提高同義詞轉換實力
總是能將聽力訊息對應到關鍵考點
答題力提高 100%

· 聽力訊息稍縱即逝，除了掌握出題規律外，高分的考生都能具備一定程度的同義轉換能力，即能在聽到「一個聽力詞彙或語句」後能迅速對應到**「選項的改寫」**所以能即刻理解並快速畫卡。

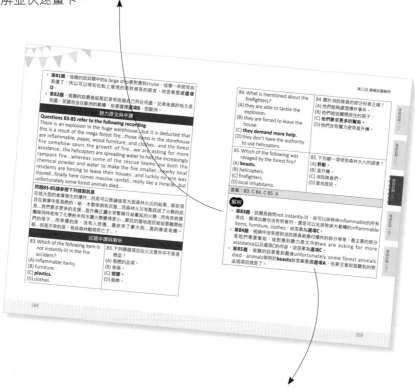

· 書籍中的出題和解析中包含了更多掌握同義轉換的要訣並詳細列於解析中，且以更靈活的出題模式讓考生演練是否都掌握這些考點，應試中更無往不利。

強化整合答題能力
無懼任何出題陷阱和「結合數個聽力訊息考點」的出題
迅速拆解各式題型
・包含 ❶ 將聽到的訊息轉換成「**形容詞**」的同義轉換 ❷ 要「**理解慣用語**」才能選對的試題 ❸ 需要綜合訊息後才理解的新聞類話題 ❹ 包含「**較為進階**」的計算 ❺ 在所提供的聽力訊息有限的情況下，要搭配「**刪去法**」的答題 ❻ 部分要理解某些「**進階字彙**」才能答的試題 ❼ 區別近似或重疊性的聽力訊息，且容易誤選的試題，詳細釐清題目到底問什麼 … 等等。

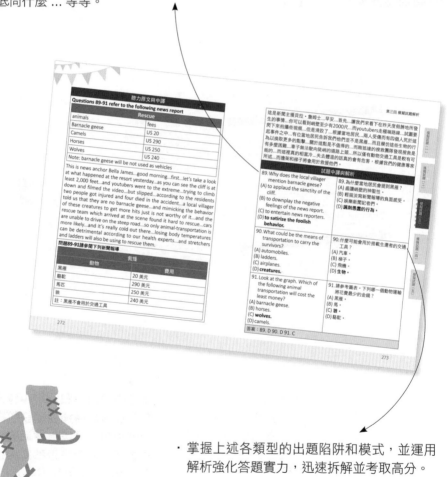

・掌握上述各類型的出題陷阱和模式，並運用解析強化答題實力，迅速拆解並考取高分。

「影子跟讀學習法」

- 「影子跟讀學習法」是個很好的聽力訓練方式且能提高學習者的「專注力」。這個方法更能有效提升寫海量試題但仍卡在某個分數段的考生使用。當「聽力專注力」和「理解力」都同步提升時，就能突破某個分數段。

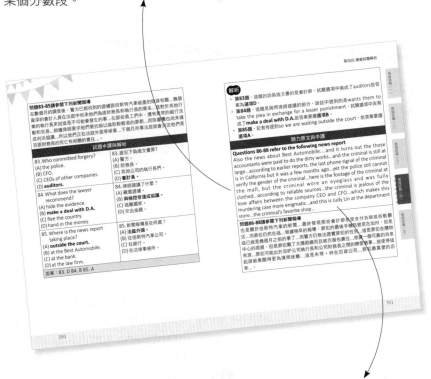

- 專注力夠也能有助於回想剛聽到到訊息，更不會造成混淆訊息或誤選的方式發生。反之，**專注力不夠很容易會憑腦海中印象或聽到的 GIST 去答題**（聽力訊息中確實出現過該訊息），但題目並不是問那個。

・關於影子跟讀的練習的方法的話，可以將 **Part 3** 和 **Part 4** 內容都拆成**數句**或**數個小節**。【**STEP 1**】。以**模擬試題（四）** **Part 4** 其中一篇**簡短獨白**為例，如下方的標示：❶-❽，然後依據自己本身程度來練習（反覆聆聽）。

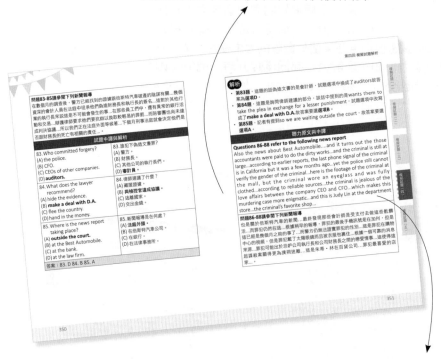

・❶After months of investigation, the police have found evidence linking to the conspiracy of the Best Automobile bankruptcy...❷several senior accountants are admitting in court that they forged the signatures of both the CFO and CEO...❸which is deemed impossible to CEOs of other businesses...❹and there are abnormal bank activities and transactions in those employees...

· ❺the defense attorney wants them to take the plea in exchange for a lesser punishment...❻and the jury hasn't yet reached a verdict...❼so we are waiting outside the court...❽and next month a criminal court will determine whether or not they are responsible for the death of the CFO...

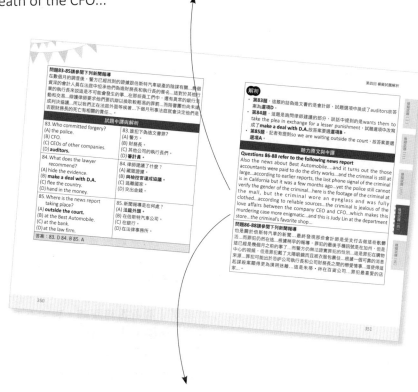

· 區分好後，第二個步驟是【跟著原稿讀】（可以根據自己程度調整，跟得上的可以直接跳過這個步驟），學習者必須要先跟得上音檔的語速，然後看著原稿以同樣的速度跟讀，當音檔開始唸第一句時，以同樣速度跟著唸整個段落。【STEP 2】

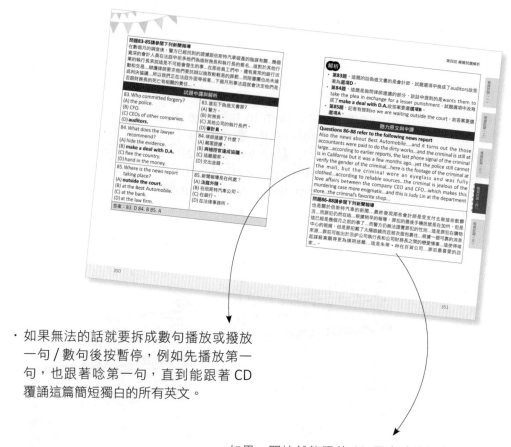

· 如果無法的話就要拆成數句播放或撥放
一句／數句後按暫停，例如先播放第一
句，也跟著唸第一句，直到能跟著 CD
覆誦這篇簡短獨白的所有英文。

· 如果一開始就能跟著 CD 同步唸這個段落，甚至
整個單元的段落，恭喜你，你已經具備了「初步
的跟讀基礎」。跟讀其實牽涉到的層面很廣。這
僅是加強聽力專注力的第一步，接下來，第三個
步驟是【看著書籍原稿，聽完至少一句或數句後
再開始跟讀】【STEP 3】

· 學習者必須要掌握能夠拉長一句到數個句子的長
度做跟讀練習，才能真的強化聽力和口譯能力。

- 能拉長越多越好。例如：播放音檔，但這時候不是同步跟著讀，等 CD 唸到 ❷ 時，你開始唸 ❶ 的內容，CD 唸到 ❸ 時，你接續唸 ❷ 的內容，一直到這個段落結束。如果你都能跟上的話代表你能夠練習【拉長一句或數句後的跟讀練習】，你可以接續練習拉長兩句等地接續練習，最後能夠拉長到五句。如果也都能達到這個標準時，其實你聽力已經大有進展，代表在聽完一段話時，你腦海中會記住對方剛講的五句話，所以專注力提升的同時，面對聽力試題，其實不太可能會沒辦法答題，也不會需要寫一堆試題。（不過要注意的是，一直演練同一篇，其實效度會不準，因為你會記憶起段落的內容，所以要找更多的聽力音檔來進行練習 ...）

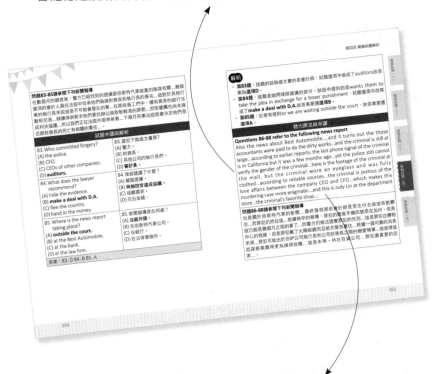

- 最後一個步驟是【不看原稿，僅聽音檔】，這個練習常見於較高階的學習者，也是以上述的練習步驟進行練習，如果無法一字不差的進行跟讀，即代表聽得不夠清楚，也會反映到理解聽力內容的部分。【STEP 4】

目次
CONTENTS

- 【倍斯特空服：討厭對講機】難道我就不能在經濟艙裡頭倒倒水就好嗎？

- 【倍斯特空服：選中廣告刊版的模特兒】還是有人不想獲選的

- 【野生國家公園】難道研究人員的生活就是 ...「賭」嗎？

- 【倍斯特主題樂園】小孩無故打翻飲料，我還是要替他裝滿啊！

- 【倍斯特主題樂園】想要詢問您關於申請主題樂園的打工申請？

- 【超級業務員】倒要看看別人是怎麼達到業績的

- 【工作】工作的獨立自主性和消費者需求

- 【面試】Interview 忘了在面試時，稱讚面試官的房裡相關的

物品

- 【動物庇護之家 ：烏龍報導】刊登報紙，澄清之前的誤會
- 【動物庇護之家 ：新聞獨家消息】無尾熊要分娩了，希望能有獨家消息
- 【倍斯特海產貿易公司】跟潛水客議價 ... 嗯！頗刺激的！
- 【倍斯特海產貿易公司】老闆期望你最好下週就要能上手
- 【倍斯特海產貿易公司】開車駛向碼頭，等等在海產餐廳要點什麼呢？

PART 4 簡短獨白

- 【倍斯特商場】購物中心搶案，歹徒也沒多強啊！
- 【沙漠露營】沙漠環境保育營，不是蓋你，浣熊又派上用場了！
- 【叢林探險】或許該丟些三明治和貝果啊！ ... 或是我的餅乾（誤）
- 【叢林探險】那些鱷魚以及巨蟒 ... 牠們會對於我的鮪魚三明治有興趣嗎 ... ？

- 【倍斯特水族館】章魚到底最渴望的事情是什麼呢？有請專家告訴我們吧！
- 【倍斯特水族館】章魚善良到讓我避開了目睹這血腥的狩獵場景
- 【倍斯特汽車大廠】政府拒絕給予紓困金，因為這是公司經營不善的結果
- 【倍斯特汽車大廠】檢控官也對於貪汙罪和內線交易、公司海外的帳戶的部分開啟了新的調查案 ...
- 【倍斯特汽車大廠】投資客對於重組公司感到興趣
- 圖表題：公司行程表
- 【消防局】消防救援，除了大黃蜂入侵外，又多了好多事情啊！

PART 1　照片描述

PART 2　應答問題

PART 3　簡短對話

- 【研究】致電國家公園研究申請
- 【倍斯特空服：長途飛勤的組員值勤名單】我想我們就只能憑緣分遇見了

- 【倍斯特空服：販賣部 (canteen)】現實生活中沒有 photoshop 這軟體的
- 【倍斯特資優學院招生】父母的望子成龍
- 【倍斯特資優學院招生】面試開始了，小孩的表現會是！？
- 【非洲之旅】掃興的是，不是每個成員都能去
- 【非洲之旅】為期 14 天的旅程，「故事編輯」總會在名單上
- 【非洲之旅】賽倫蓋地相當的悶熱 … 但願我能有杯椰子水！
- 【倍斯特水族館：應徵者來電】應徵者詢問招聘的回覆
- 【倍斯特水族館：訂場地】員工將電話轉接給公司經理
- 【倍斯特旅行社】從會計部意外得知每個人的薪資
- 【醫療】手術同意書，還有好多事項喔！
- 【倍斯特水族館：顧客電話訂票】無法給票嗎？我想要跟你的經理談談 …

PART 4　簡短獨白

- 【倍斯特健身房】四種口味的高蛋白棒，健身者的需求一次滿足
- 【叢林探險】首次在巨大竹筏上的廚藝「初」體驗
- 【叢林探險】先前的視頻有數百萬的點擊率 … 哈雷路亞！
- 【叢林探險】戴著這副時髦的眼鏡在這煮中餐真的有點不搭
- 【晨間新聞】暴雪來襲，已經達到了教育部的停課標準
- 【倍斯特古董店】從船骸中找到綠水晶

- 【倍斯特有機農場】你該吃的更健康才是，猝死這個現代化疾病不是開玩笑的
- 【倍斯特馬戲團】馬戲團中大象的「眼淚」...（唉）！
- 【倍斯特航空】駕駛員在飛機橫跨太平洋時睡著了 ... 這 ... 還能搭嗎！
- 【倍斯特設計公司】錄取的居然大多是毫無工作經驗的求職者

PART 1　照片描述
PART 2　應答問題
PART 3　簡短對話

- 【倍斯特空服：説謊話】可別拿紅酒來滅火啊！
- 【倍斯特空服：模擬機艙】什麼？ ... 我不會拿到負面的評論了吧！
- 【倍斯特花店】我們確實備有室內耕種的薰衣草和康乃馨
- 【倍斯特花店】花朵提早運至真的如釋重負了
- 【倍斯特跨國海產公司】居然一下就錄取了，可是有這麼容易嗎？

- 【倍斯特跨國海產公司】跟當初說的全然不同，去拿午餐盒吧（唉）！
- 【倍斯特跨國海產公司】招聘手冊和網站介紹原來在騙人啊！
- 【倍斯特水族館：談價格】議價沒這麼容易，不過確實還有很多細節要談
- 【倍斯特水族館：見面勘場】勘場的驚喜，水族館有個城堡啊！
- 【倍斯特水族館：見面勘場】跟老闆通電話並草擬了一份合約
- 【倍斯特房屋仲介】這樣不會造成房價貶值吧！
- 【倍斯特房屋仲介】媲美國王湖的景色，如何能拒呢！
- 【國家公園】居然還要有一位「嚮導」陪同前往

PART 4　簡短獨白

- 【叢林探險：廚具】高級烹飪廚具跟村民的石板相比似乎有點相形見絀
- 【叢林探險：廚具】居民的木製長柄勺也太好
- 【倍斯特汽車大廠】財務長捲款而逃
- 【倍斯特汽車大廠】執行長因為涉及內線交易而被拘留
- 【消防局】倉庫爆炸和大型的森林火災 ... 所幸出現奇蹟
- 【倍斯特珠寶展】一票難求的珠寶展，有四種類型的珠寶
- 【晨間新聞】居民暗諷飛簷走壁博點閱，又不是黑雁！

- 【倍斯特海產貿易公司】靠窗的餐桌，偏好在三樓的座
- 【倍斯特海產貿易公司】哇！餐廳贈送精緻的冰淇淋城堡和蛋糕
- 【倍斯特海產貿易公司】在加工廠，第一個任務是要分類好一百隻魷魚
- 【倍斯特旅行社】駱駝騎乘服
- 【倍斯特手錶】居然送了手錶仿冒品，有安全疑慮時還真的輕忽不得
- 【倍斯特傢俱行】傢俱訂購，公司客服一一搞定後續延伸問
- 【倍斯特銀行】銀行交易出現異常，不會是駭客吧！

PART 4　簡短獨白
- 【倍斯特航空】任何負面的新聞，都會對公司造成影響呢！？
- 【倍斯特馬戲團】老虎被逼的狗急跳牆了！
- 【叢林探險：廚具】客座評審要品嚐了，不知道結果會是！
- 【叢林探險：廚具】居然成了烹飪競賽的贏家
- 【倍斯特汽車大廠】偽造簽名和異常的銀行活動和交易
- 【倍斯特汽車大廠】案情變得更撲朔迷離
- 【倍斯特珠寶展】新聞發佈到現在，終於見到「珠寶問世」
- 【下午新聞播報】颱風的三個路徑預測，其中一個預測和國際新聞預測吻合

- 【倍斯特博物館】數以千計的觀光客都會跟活現的火山和湖泊形成的模型拍照
- 【倍斯特電視】價值連城的城堡主人來電視節目中參加通告

Part 1　照片描述
Part 2　應答問題
Part 3　簡短對話

- 【國家公園】真的傾盆大雨，不過還有好多室內活動可供選擇唷！
- 【倍斯特飾品店】這個紫色的水晶有特別的力量
- 【倍斯特動物庇護之家：動物葬禮】向動物庇護之家確認葬禮日期
- 【倍斯特旅行社：replacement】辭職 ... 嗯，還真阿莎力呢
- 【倍斯特巧克力工廠】巧克力嚐到不想再嚐了！
- 【倍斯特巧克力工廠】開會時最好還是提個問題吧！
- 【倍斯特巧克力工廠】切蛋糕慶祝升遷
- 【倍斯特巧克力工廠】別困惑了，好好接受升遷喜悅吧！
- 【倍斯特房屋仲介】真的是，很會跟買家應對！

- 【倍斯特房屋仲介】先看看周遭環境、再慢慢進入主題吧！
- 【倍斯特房屋仲介】買家也做足了功課，要考驗銷售員功力了！
- 【倍斯特研究中心】法庭判定血液樣本受到汙染，所以這不能用於呈堂的證據
- 【倍斯特藥局】藥錠、膠囊、粉末狀藥物還是藥膏呢？

Part 4 簡短獨白

- 【獨自旅行】中國夜市美食趣 ... 鴕鳥蛋還是烤山羊呢？
- 【晨間新聞】雨季的道路交通就是一團亂 ... 而且還有「蛇」竄出來
- 【倍斯特博物館】博物館的恐龍拼圖競賽 ... 獎項是 ... ！？
- 【旅行社合辦活動】海灘上的寶藏狩獵活動開跑了 ... 連「螃蟹」也要來搶食嗎？
- 【倍斯特馬戲團】許多大學學生的懇求後，馬戲團承諾要改善
- 【書評】怪透了 ... 評論一本完全不驚悚的驚悚暢銷書籍 ...（暈）
- 【倍斯特牙醫診所】超強牙齒美白療程，接下來幾週可以大吃特吃一番
- 【倍斯特航空】上手後，飛機盤旋在幾千公尺高空並不是什麼新奇的事情了
- 【倍斯特天文館】天文館的工作，雜七雜八的事情還真多呢！
- 【倍斯特服飾店】服飾店裁員兩樣情！

- 【空服話題】考生可以多揣摩這類別的相關出題，對答題的幫助很大。
- 【面試類話題】考生要注意訊息點出現重疊的部分，說話者均有這方面的經驗，專注力一定要夠，迅速區隔出男女雙方的差異處，攻略這類試題。
- 【Part 4】包含了各類型考題，都需要較靈活的思維才能答好，考生可以於寫完試題後，多聆聽這類的話題。

模擬試題（一）

▶ Listening Test 1 ◉ MP3 001

In the Listening Test, you must demonstrate your ability to understand spoken English. This section is divided into four parts and will take approximately 45 minutes to complete. There are four parts, and directions are given for each part. Do not mark the answers in your test book. Use the answer sheet that is provided separately.

▶ PART 1

Directions: For each question, you will listen to four short statements about a picture in your test book. These statements will not be printed and will only be spoken one time. Select the statement that best describes what is happening in the picture and mark the corresponding letter (A), (B), (C), (D) on the answer sheet.

Example   Sample Answer

A ● C D

Statement (B), "**Some people are wearing backpacks**", is the best description of the picture. So you should select answer (B) and mark it on your answer sheet.

1.

(A)　(B)　(C)　(D)

2.

(A)　(B)　(C)　(D)

3.

(A) (B) (C) (D)

4.

(A) (B) (C) (D)

5.

(A)　(B)　(C)　(D)

6.

(A)　(B)　(C)　(D)

▶ **PART 2** 🎧 MP3 002

Directions: For each question, you will listen to a statement or a question followed by three possible responses spoken in English. They will not be printed and will only be spoken one time. Select the best response and mark the corresponding letter (A), (B), or (C) on your answer sheet.

7. Mark your answer on your answer sheet.
8. Mark your answer on your answer sheet.
9. Mark your answer on your answer sheet.
10. Mark your answer on your answer sheet.
11. Mark your answer on your answer sheet.
12. Mark your answer on your answer sheet.
13. Mark your answer on your answer sheet.
14. Mark your answer on your answer sheet.
15. Mark your answer on your answer sheet.
16. Mark your answer on your answer sheet.
17. Mark your answer on your answer sheet.
18. Mark your answer on your answer sheet.
19. Mark your answer on your answer sheet.
20. Mark your answer on your answer sheet.
21. Mark your answer on your answer sheet.
22. Mark your answer on your answer sheet.
23. Mark your answer on your answer sheet.
24. Mark your answer on your answer sheet.
25. Mark your answer on your answer sheet.
26. Mark your answer on your answer sheet.

27. Mark your answer on your answer sheet.

28. Mark your answer on your answer sheet.

29. Mark your answer on your answer sheet.

30. Mark your answer on your answer sheet.

31. Mark your answer on your answer sheet.

▶ **PART 3** 🎧 MP3 003

Directions: In this part, you will listen to several conversations between two or more speakers. These conversations will not be printed and will only be spoken one time. For each conversation, you will be asked to answer three questions. Select the best response and mark the corresponding letter (A), (B), (C), (D) on the answer sheet.

---

32. Where most likely is the conversation taking place?
    (A) on the airplane
    (B) at the boarding gate
    (C) at the airport
    (D) at the training center

---

33. What is the language that the two customers use?
    (A) German
    (B) Greek
    (C) Russian
    (D) Chinese

---

34. Which of the following language cannot be seen written on the woman's resume?
    (A) German
    (B) Spanish

(C) Russian
(D) Greek

---

35. Where most likely is the conversation taking place?
   (A) at the desert
   (B) at the boarding gate
   (C) at the airport
   (D) at the training center

---

 36. Why does the woman say, "I'm nobody's competition"?
   (A) because she is a nobody
   (B) because she wants to clarify and not getting clashed with others
   (C) because she doesn't want to compete
   (D) because she is not competent enough

---

37. What is not the woman's concern?
   (A) long hours of shooting
   (B) squeeze the laughter
   (C) please the cameraman
   (D) getting picked on by the boss

Oasis	
Drinks	**price**
coconut juice	US 35
mango juice	US 50
camel milk	US 45
coke	US 40

38. Where most likely is the conversation taking place?
  (A) at the zoo
  (B) in the office
  (C) at the research center
  (D) at the wild national park

39. What is the target of the lions?
  (A) a newborn giraffe
  (B) a male giraffe
  (C) a female giraffe
  (D) a gazelle

40. Look at the graph. What is the most expensive drink at the oasis?
  (A) coconut juice
  (B) camel milk
  (C) coke
  (D) mango juice

41. What is not mentioned about the drink?
  (A) the kid expected a refill
  (B) the kid didn't get rejected
  (C) It was spilled by the kid who did not under parental watch
  (D) It was deliberately spilled by the kid

42. Why should the woman give the kid a refill?
  (A) because she is pressured by the colleague
  (B) because she loves the kid
  (C) because it's the company policy
  (D) because the juice doesn't cost the company a dime

43. Why does the woman say, "the more the merrier"?
  (A) to be supportive of the company culture stuff
  (B) to show her preference for the Christmas

(C) to spread the happy seed
(D) to satirize the refill thing

44. Where most likely is the conversation taking place?
    (A) at the engagement party
    (B) at the mall
    (C) at the coffee shop
    (D) at the Disneyland office

45. How will the woman apply for the job?
    (A) fake the background check
    (B) call the HR personnel
    (C) register on-line
    (D) fill in the application form on the scene

46. What was the man's job last summer?
    (A) the manager
    (B) the waiter
    (C) an outdoor vendor
    (D) an indoor operator

47. Where most likely is the conversation taking place?
    (A) at the office
    (B) at the department store
    (C) at the Halloween Party
    (D) at the music studio

 48. Why does the woman say, "how you are gonna pull that off"?
    (A) to solidify her viewpoint
    (B) to question another woman
    (C) to lessen another woman's confidence
    (D) to steal the perks from another woman

 49. Why does the man say, "I love what you think"?
    (A) because they used to be an acquaintance

(B) because the woman makes the prediction that he will love purple

(C) because he is in love with her

(D) because what the woman says actually resonates

50. Why does the man say, "without any knowledge in that field"?

(A) to criticize his boss

(B) to indicate the situation and that's why there is a clash

(C) to degrade the reputation of the investor

(D) to show that there is a need for his boss to learn things

51. Why does the man's friend recommend him?

(A) to please the boss and let go of the ego

(B) to ignore the boss whenever he can

(C) to quit the job as fast as he can

(D) to think of a way that makes both parties pleased

52. What does the man say about the concept?

(A) It's written by the unprofessional

(B) it will affect the overall sales

(C) it's only important to the boss

(D) it's relatively important to the consumers

53. According to the man, what is not on the interviewer's desk?

(A) a plastic plane

(B) a statuette

(C) tickets for transportation

(D) photos of ships

54. According to the woman, what is the item she complimented?

(A) a statuette

(B) a plane ticket

(C) a plastic plane

(D) a desk

55. Why does the woman say, "you don't have to overdo it to make it a little bit too phony."?

(A) she knows too well that the man will blow it
(B) to remind him that doing repetitively can do more harm than good
(C) to kindly remind the man and hopefully help him in the next interview
(D) to let him know that being too fake is not good

56. Why does the woman say, "I've straightened this out"?

(A) because it was a misunderstanding
(B) because the misunderstanding is cleared up
(C) because it is hard to convince others
(D) to elucidate and clear the doubts

57. Why does the man say, "I'm not buying it"?

(A) to strengthen his stance
(B) to clarify that he already explained
(C) because he doesn't want to buy it
(D) to show his disbelief

58. Where most likely is the conversation taking place?

(A) at an animal shelter house
(B) at the news building
(C) at the newspaper
(D) at the information center

59. Where most likely is the conversation taking place?

(A) At the delivery room
(B) At an animal shelter house
(C) At the doctor's house
(D) At the news building

60. **When is possibly the time that the mother koala is going to give birth?**
   (A) October
   (B) September
   (C) November
   (D) December

61. **What is the woman's previous profession?**
   (A) A news reporter
   (B) A stay-home mom
   (C) An animal lover
   (D) A veterinarian

62. **Where most likely is the conversation taking place?**
   (A) at the dock
   (B) at the processing plant
   (C) at the aquarium
   (D) at the river bank

63. **Why does the woman say, "take it or leave it"?**
   (A) because she has to leave soon
   (B) to bully those divers
   (C) to show her strong stance and be firm
   (D) because the seafood doesn't worth more money

64. **Why does the man say, "leave us with no profit"?**
   (A) to plead the negotiator
   (B) perhaps a technique employed by a shrew negotiator
   (C) because the margins are small
   (D) to confront the negotiator

65. **Who might be the speaker that assigns Jason to Cindy?**
   (A) the boss
   (B) the HR

(C) the diver
(D) the sales rep

66. What could be the job title for the new hire?
(A) the diver
(B) the assistant
(C) the HR personnel
(D) the manager

67. Where is the gift housed at?
(A) in the container
(B) at the business lunch building
(C) at the aquarium
(D) at the beach

68. Where most likely is the conversation taking place?
(A) at the dock
(B) on the car
(C) at the restaurant
(D) at the aquarium

69. Why does Cindy not recommend dolphin meat?
(A) because it doesn't taste good
(B) because the chef is a lousy dolphin cooker
(C) because it is harmful to human body
(D) because it is against human nature

70. Who could be the demographic that consumes sea mammals?
(A) tourists
(B) divers
(C) buyers
(D) the boss

▶ PART 4   MP3 004

Directions: In this part, you will listen to several talks by one or two speakers. These talks will not be printed and will only be spoken one time. for each talk, you will be asked to answer three questions. Select the best response and mark the corresponding letter (A), (B), (C), (D) on your answer sheet.

71.Who most likely are the listeners?
(A) policemen
(B) photographers
(C) department employees
(D) audiences

72.According to the reporter, which cannot be found on the ground?
(A) unfinished burgers
(B) French fries
(C) precious metal
(D) coke

73.Why does the woman say, "not so tough are you"?
(A) to demonstrate the spirit of the reporter
(B) to get the applause for tackling down the criminal
(C) to respond in a mocking, humorous way
(D) to show other criminals that they need to be tougher

74.What is the purpose of this camp?
(A) tackle rattlers in the wild
(B) get the water by traveling long distance
(C) appreciate things and know about environmental conservation
(D) prepare more cotton candy

75. Why does the woman say, "I really shouldn't have fallen on deaf ears"?

(A) because it is the lesson she now learns

(B) because she has a hearing problem and she doesn't want to admit it

(C) because she never thought knowledge could be useful and someone told her before

(D) because her phone doesn't work

76. Which of the following can be the cure for dealing with the rattler?

(A) cotton candy

(B) raccoons

(C) rats

(D) rabbits

77. Which of the following items was received by the monkey?

(A) bagels

(B) banana

(C) cookies

(D) peach

78. Which of the following is not what the reporter jokes to throw at the python?

(A) bananas

(B) cookies

(C) sandwiches

(D) peach

79. Which of the following will be used to grieve the monkey?

(A) sandwiches

(B) peach

(C) cookies

(D) bananas

80. Where most likely is the news report taking place?
  (A) on a ship
  (B) on a canoe
  (C) on a cruise
  (D) on a raft

81. Why does the man say, "I just never saw it coming"?
  (A) because he didn't see the torrent
  (B) because he wasn't experienced to see the torrent
  (C) because he didn't expect it to show up
  (D) because he didn't have a cloth to change

82. Which of the following do not pose any danger to them?
  (A) pythons
  (B) crocodiles
  (C) torrents
  (D) tuna sandwiches

83. What will be provided to the octopus?
  (A) a crab
  (B) the flounder
  (C) a clam
  (D) a lobster

84. Which of the following is the activity that the octopus most desires to do?
  (A) solve a difficult puzzle
  (B) use instruments
  (C) use magical coloration
  (D) endless crabs to eat

85. What is the essence of the octopus?
  (A) aggressive
  (B) greedy

(C) dazzling
(D) pleasurable

Best Aquarium/profile of the octopus (Adam)	
description	food
least enjoyed	Pacific eels
one of the favorites	Pacific huge clams
most enjoyed	Australia large crab
relative enjoyed	Boston lobsters

86. **Look at the graph. What is Adam's most favorite food?**
    (A) Pacific eels
    (B) Pacific huge clams
    (C) Australia large crabs
    (D) Boston lobsters

87. **What is not mentioned about the lobster?**
    (A) it is larger than the octopus
    (B) it has no clue that the octopus is nearby
    (C) it's kind enough to let the reporter not see what's cruel
    (D) its body is fastened by the tentacles of the octopus

88. **What can be inferred from the fate of the lobster?**
    (A) escaped
    (B) injured
    (C) alive
    (D) dead

89. **Who is the person that the reporters are waiting for?**
    (A) the CEO
    (B) the spokesperson
    (C) the employees
    (D) the local residents

90. Why did the government refuse to grant bail money?
    (A) because it will lose lots of votes from the local residents
    (B) because the company refuses to pay the payment of employees
    (C) because there are lots of voice against that
    (D) because the company was wrongly operated

91. Whose money won't be used to aid the company, according to the government?
    (A) investors
    (B) taxpayers
    (C) employees
    (D) the CEO

92. Which of the following is not mentioned as the possible reason that makes the company unable to function?
    (A) corruption
    (B) embezzlement
    (C) insider trading
    (D) indignation

93. Who is parading on the street?
    (A) the CEO
    (B) the prosecutors
    (C) the employees
    (D) the indignant wage earner

94. Who cannot get away with the Commission's scrutiny?
    (A) the CEO
    (B) the president
    (C) The offshore accounts
    (D) the protestors

Best Automobile	
description	date
rent the jet	July 9 2022
have the talk with senators	July 19 2022
invite investors	August 9 2022
have the talk at Bahama	August 19 2022

95. Look at the graph. How soon will the company return to normal if the restructuring works?
(A) July 9 2022
(B) July 19 2022
(C) August 9 2022
(D) August 19 2022

96. Who took a vehicle to Florida?
(A) the reporter
(B) investors
(C) legislators
(D) the spokesperson

97. Which of the following can be the trigger to social turbulence?
(A) restructuring the company
(B) investors ganging together
(C) large discharge
(D) news not verified

98. Where most likely is the line recording taking place?
(A) in the school
(B) in the dormitory
(C) in the forest
(D) near the fire department

99.Which of the following creatures is not mentioned in the talk?
(A) large sting wasps
(B) chameleons
(C) an amphibian
(D) a viper

100.According to the fire fighter, which of the following task will be ignored?
(A) remove the nest of bees
(B) remove the nest of birds
(C) remove the snake near the pond
(D) dispel the monkeys

第一回
模擬試題解析

 **Part 1**

聽力原文與中譯	
1. (A) Some people are sitting on the rock. (B) Crabs are evading because of the approaching dog. (C) Waves are coming towards beachgoers. (D) **A dog is lying on the sandy beach.**	1. (A) 有些人正坐在岩石上頭。 (B) 因為狗的靠近，螃蟹正逃離。 (C) 海浪正朝著海灘愛好者打來。 (D) **有隻狗正躺在沙灘上。**

答案：(D)

 解析

這題很明顯可以看出是有隻狗正躺在沙灘上，所以答案要選**選項D**。

聽力原文與中譯	
2. (A) There are no price tags on the vending machine. (B) All beverages are made in one shape. (C) **There is a special card to highlight the new product.** (D) The choices of beverages are few and far between.	2. (A) 在販賣機上頭，商品沒有標價。 (B) 所有的飲料都是同樣的規格。 (C) **一個特製的卡片用於凸顯新的產品** (D) 飲料的選擇是稀少的。

答案：(C)

 解析

如圖片所示，可以看到的是販賣機中的飲料且形狀是各式各樣的，每一排的飲料均有標價，而新商品有個卡片式的new跟其他一般商品區隔出來而其同義表達即是選項C的描述，所以答案要選**選項C**。

聽力原文與中譯	
3. (A) Some people are reading next to the bookcase. (B) The door is fully closed. (C) **The library houses a variety of books on various shelves.** (D) Books on the bookcases are slim picking.	3. (A) 有些人正在書櫃旁閱讀書籍。 (B) 門是完全關上的。 (C) **圖書館的不同書架上儲藏了不同種類的書籍。** (D) 在書櫃上的書是寥寥可數的。

答案：(C)

 解析

這題有許多陷阱的部分，但是實際上圖片中圖書館有的是各式各樣的藏書，書籍陳列於各式的書架上，所以答案要選**選項C**。

聽力原文與中譯	
4. (A) **There is a balcony adjacent to the library building.** (B) The library is a dome-like building. (C) Flowers are in full blossom on trees. (D) People are gathering outside the library.	4. (A) **在圖書館的建築物旁有個陽台比鄰在旁。** (B) 圖書館是個像是圓頂型的建築物。 (C) 花朵在樹上盛開著。 (D) 人們聚集在圖書館外頭。

答案：(A)

解析

這題一樣有許多的陷阱和干擾選項，但是同圖片所示，在設計上有個陽台緊連著圖書館的入口處的樓上，所以答案要選**選項A**。

聽力原文與中譯	
5. (A) Lobsters are served on the beach dining tables. (B) There are no deck chairs on the beach. (C) **Some people are wading into the water.** (D) The tree has few leaves left on the branch.	5. (A) Lobsters are served on the beach dining tables. (B) There are no deck chairs on the beach. (C) **Some people are wading into the water.** (D) The tree has a few leaves left on the branch.

答案：(C)

解析

這題可以看到岸旁有海灘，有些人在水裡戲水，故答案要選**選項C**。

聽力原文與中譯	
6. (A) The door is open. (B) **English characters on the wall form the map of the globe.** (C) A waiter is preparing dishes on the kitchen countertop. (D) There is a cat on the sofa.	6. (A) 門是打開的。 (B) **牆上的英文字組成了一幅全球地圖。** (C) 在廚房吧台上服務生正準備菜餚。 (D) 沙發上有隻貓。

答案：(B)

解析

這題的話可以看到，牆上有許多英文字，而這些英文字剛好組成了一幅世界地圖，故答案要選**選項B**。

PART 2

聽力原文與中譯	
7. The snowstorm is going to hit the town in the afternoon. (A) **Why didn't anyone inform me?** (B) Afternoon is great. (C) I studied that in the high school.	7. 暴風雪將於下午時分時侵襲小鎮。 (A) **為什麼沒有人通知我？** (B) 下午的時候很棒。 (C) 我在高中時研讀過那個。

答案：(A)

 解析

這題是描述一個事件或現象，答案有可能是任何聽到這事件的反應，不論是好或壞，也有可能是**反問對方**，故答案要選**選項A**。

聽力原文與中譯	
8. Why aren't aquarium operators answering the phone? (A) That's their jobs. (B) **They are eating pizzas in the dining area.** (C) We have to hire more people.	8. 為什麼沒有水族館接線生接電話呢？ (A) 那是他們份內工作。 (B) **他們正在用餐區吃披薩。** (C) 我們需要雇用更多的人力。

答案：(B)

 解析

這題是「為什麼」開頭的問句，答案要選符合事件的合理原因，故答案要選**選項B**。

聽力原文與中譯	
9. How did the interview go? (A) The building looks terrific. (B) Adjacent to the business building. (C) **I don't want to talk about it.**	9. 面試進行的如何了？ (A) 那棟建築物看起來很棒。 (B) 鄰近商業大樓。 (C) **我不想要談論這個。**

答案：(C)

 解析

這題是詢問面試結果，較簡易的答案會直接是面試結果的好或壞，但也可能是**現在不想要談論這件事**，故答案要選**選項C**。

聽力原文與中譯	
10. Should we redecorate the living room? (A) More interior designers are needed. (B) We should invite more kids in the living room. **(C) But that would cost too much money.**	10. 我們應該要重新裝修客廳嗎？ (A) 需要更多的室內設計師。 (B) 我們應該要邀請更多孩子到客廳裡。 **(C) 但是那會花費太多錢。**

答案：(C)

 解析

這題是「應該」的描述句，要選的答案會是跟描述相關的內容，不論是反駁或是贊同，也要注意別被有其他**應該**的句型影響而誤選了其他答案，故答案要選**選項C**。

聽力原文與中譯	
11. How to get ahead over other applicants? **(A) donate lots of money to the school.** (B) if the weather is cloudless. (C) The school wants to recruit more students this year.	11. 如何才能領先其他申請者呢？ **(A) 捐贈很多錢給學校。** (B) 如果天氣是晴朗無雲的話。 (C) 學校今年想要雇用更多的學生。

答案：(A)

 解析

這題是問「如何」的句型，要思考下，答案要選能讓自己申請上的原因或方法，其中一個可能就是**選項A**，故答案為A。

聽力原文與中譯

12. Why don't we go to the hiking trail without a guide? (A) **that would be thrilling!** (B) we really have to learn how to read a map first. (C) the guide is too heavy.	12. 我們為什麼不自個兒走健行小徑，不需要嚮導呢？ (A) **那令人感到興奮呢！** (B) 首先我們真的必須要學習如何閱讀地圖。 (C) 那位嚮導太笨重了。

答案：(A)

 解析

這題也是詢問為什麼，答案可能有好幾種，像是可是這樣不太好等等，也可能是選項A，比較接受挑戰或冒險精神的旅伴會講的，故答案為**選項A**。

聽力原文與中譯

13. When will the perks be given? (A) The HR personnel is not ready. (B) **After Christmas.** (C) CFO will take most money.	13. 津貼會於何時發放呢？ (A) 人事專員尚未準備好。 (B) **在聖誕節過後。** (C) 財務長將會拿到最多金錢。

答案：(B)

 解析

這題是詢問「何時」，答案很明顯要選一個時間點，故答案為**選項B**。

聽力原文與中譯

14. Why don't you purchase a fake watch for Hawaii diving? (A) I am a licensed diver. (B) There are plenty of large crabs there. (C) **then you will probably find me on the news.**	14. 為何你不在夏威夷潛水時購買偽造的手錶呢？ (A) 我是位有證照的潛水員。 (B) 那裡有許多大型的螃蟹。 (C) **那麼你可能就會發現我上了新聞。**

答案：(C)

解析

這題也是詢問為何的問題，答案有可能是不願這麼做的原因，更高階的回答就會是像選項C這樣的表達，故答案要選**選項C**。

聽力原文與中譯	
15. Who is making the call to get theater tickets? (A) After July. (B) At the debut, celebrities will be there. (C) **Most likely the house owner.**	15. 誰致電去訂購戲院的門票呢？ (A) 在七月過後。 (B) 在首映時，名人們都會在那裡。 (C) **最可能是房屋的主人。**

答案：(C)

解析

這題是詢問關於誰，要選人物，故答案為**選項C**。

聽力原文與中譯	
16. Will your son be joining us at the birthday party? (A) The birthday cake looks delicious. (B) **He doesn't get invited.** (C) He already consumes 500 calories for the day.	14. 你的兒子會與我們一同參加生日派對嗎？ (A) 生日蛋糕看起來美味。 (B) **他並未獲得邀請。** (C) 他今天已經攝取500卡路里了。

答案：(B)

解析

這題答案有可能是有或沒有，比較隱晦一些的表達就會像是**選項B**，類似可是他沒有受邀等等的。

聽力原文與中譯

17. You are going to the kissing both for the charity, right? (A) The girls look equally the same. (B) **Unless Mary is there.** (C) The charity has lots of money.	17. 你會去這次慈善會舉辦的親吻亭對吧？ (A) 女孩們看起來都一個樣。 (B) **除非瑪莉也在那兒。** (C) 慈善會有許多錢。

答案：(B)

 解析

這題的答案可能是會去或不會去，更難的出題會像是選項B這樣的表達，用除非或如果...，而符合條件的情況才有可能去參加，故答案為**選項B**。

聽力原文與中譯

18. What is the problem with your coffee machine? (A) Perhaps an on-line coffee machine is better. (B) It's not even two years. (C) **I can't grind any coffee beans.**	18. 你的咖啡機出了什麼問題呢？ (A) 或許線上販賣的咖啡機更佳。 (B) 它甚至還使用不到兩年呢！ (C) **我無法研磨任何的咖啡豆。**

答案：(C)

 解析

這題的話要直接選擇問題點是哪裡出問題了，答案很明顯是**選項C**。

聽力原文與中譯

19. We have these kind of figurines in the zoo, don't we? (A) **Are you kidding? Those are bestsellers.** (B) I don't like the job there, so boring. (C) The elephant figurine is very expensive.	19. 在動物園裡頭，我們有這種款式的小雕像，對吧！ (A) **你在開玩笑嗎？那些是暢銷商品。** (B) 我不喜歡那裡的工作，無聊透頂。 (C) 大象的小雕飾非常昂貴。

答案：(A)

解析

這題的答案有可能是有或沒有這類商品，較有難度的回答會是選項A這樣的反問之後再做描述，故答案為**選項A**。

聽力原文與中譯	
20. When does Mark have to prepare the meat for the lion? (A) The zoo closes at 9 p.m. (B) He can't speak animal languages. (C) **At whatever time he pleases.**	20. 馬克何時必須要準備給獅子的餐點呢？ (A) 動物園於下午九點鐘關閉。 (B) 他無法說動物語言。 (C) **任何他高興的時刻都可以。**

答案：(C)

解析

這題是詢問時間點，正常來說較簡易的回答都是給時間點，較為有難度的回答會像是選項C這樣的表達，故答案為**選項C**。

聽力原文與中譯	
21. Which smartphone should I pick? (A) The owner of the cellphone is really nice. (B) **perhaps sky blue.** (C) My phone is not even two years old.	21. 我該選擇哪款智慧型手機呢？ (A) 手機的主人人真的很好。 (B) **或許天空藍吧！** (C) 我的手機甚至使用不到兩年。

答案：(B)

解析

這題是關於選擇，答案很明顯是**選項B**，某個顏色的機款。

聽力原文與中譯

22. Should I go through the resumes or leave those on the HR managers' desk. (A) We don't have enough folders for those resumes. (B) **The boss wants to see those in person.** (C) Every manager deals with different kinds of documents.	22. 我應該要逐一看過履歷表呢？還是將那些放在人事經理的桌上就好呢？ (A) 我們沒有足夠的資料夾來盛裝那些履歷表。 (B) **老闆想要親自看那些。** (C) 每位經理處理不同類型的文件。

答案：(B)

 解析

這題的敘述提供了兩個選項，較難的出題則不會在選項中有這兩個，而是第三個選擇，故答案要選**選項B**。

聽力原文與中譯

23. Didn't you get the romance novel in the bookstore? (A) What is your favorite novel? (B) The bookstore clerk is really rude. (C) **Unfortunately, it was sold out.**	23. 你怎麼沒有拿取書店裡的浪漫小說呢？ (A) 你最喜愛的小說是什麼呢？ (B) 書店的店員真的無禮。 (C) **不幸的是，它銷售一空了。**

答案：(C)

 解析

這題的答案有可能是沒拿的理由，也可能是像選項C這樣的表達，類似可是它賣完了，故答案為**選項C**。

24. Why can't we get the gelato at the tourist attractions? (A) Tourists all love hot meals. (B) The flavors are kind of limited. (C) **It's against the law there.**	24. 我們為什麼不在旅遊勝地購買義式冰淇淋呢？ (A) 遊客們都喜愛熱食。 (B) 冰淇淋的口味有點偏限。 (C) **在當地這是違法的行為。**

答案：(C)

 解析

這題是詢問為什麼，所以要選擇解釋的原因，答案很明顯是**選項C**。

25. You have been to Italy, is that correct? (A) The flight is delayed again. (B) My boss will go there next July, isn't that great? (C) **For different reasons.**	25. 你曾到過義大利，對吧？ (A) 飛機航班又再次延遲了。 (B) 我的老闆將於下個月份，七月到那裡，很棒對吧！ (C) **為了不同的理由去的。**

答案：(C)

 解析

這題有可能是是或否的答案，也可能是類似選項C這樣，省略是的，表達出是因為不同理由去過幾次，故答案為**選項C**。

26. How fast can you pack; the train is in an hour? (A) **according to the record, 5 minutes.** (B) I'm actually on my way to the train station. (C) The package is too heavy.	26. 你最快能打包好呢，火車將於一小時內啟航？ (A) **根據紀錄，五分鐘。** (B) 實際上我正朝著火車站走去。 (C) 這行李太過笨重了。

答案：(A)

解析

這題是要選擇一個時間點，故答案為**選項A**。

聽力原文與中譯	
27. The orchard owner is charging more fees this year. (A) Those watermelons are not selling really well. (B) **that's an extortion.** (C) most likely the house owner.	27. 果園的主人今年將收取更多的費用。 (A) 那些西瓜今年銷售的並不好。 (B) **這真是勒索啊！** (C) 最有可能是屋主。

答案：(B)

解析

這題要選聽到這個消息的反應，不論回應為好或壞，故答案要選**選項B**。

聽力原文與中譯	
28. Which software do we have to choose for the international trip? (A) I'm upgrading the seat for our trip. (B) **Definitely the most convenient one!** (C) But our smartphone can't download any software.	28. 對於國際旅遊的部分，我們該使用哪個軟體呢？ (A) 我正將我們旅行的座位進行升級。 (B) **當然是最便利的那款囉！** (C) 但是我們的智慧型手機無法下載任何軟體。

答案：(B)

解析

這題的話有可能是某一個軟體的名稱，也有可能是比較含糊的回答像是選項B，故答案為**選項B**。

29. Mark will give us the needed report at the crime scene. (A) The timing is odd, don't you think? (B) Guess what? the report is not carefully drafted. (C) At what time to be exact?	29. 馬克會給我們所需的犯罪現場的報告。 (A) 這個時機有點奇怪，你不覺得嗎？ (B) 你知道嗎？這份報告並未仔細撰稿。 (C) **確切的時間是幾點鐘呢？**

答案：(C)

 解析

這題要選的是聽者的反應，考生大多會預期是肯定句的表達，不過有時候答案會是詢問對方確切的時間點，這題要選**選項C**。

30. Who was chosen for the spokesperson of the hospital? (A) Those male models have an excellent chance to be selected. (B) The hospital toilets need to be maintained. (C) **Wait until the news announcement.**	30. 誰被選為醫院的發言人呢？ (A) 那些男性模特兒有極高的機會能雀屏中選。 (B) 醫院廁所需要維護保持。 (C) **等到新聞發佈。**

答案：(C)

 解析

這題要選的是人物，考生也會預期有人物的選項，不過較難的出題會是類似尚未決定或是要等到某個時間點才會知道人選，故答案要選**選項C**。

第一回 模擬試題解析

模擬試題（一）

模擬試題（二）

模擬試題（三）

模擬試題（四）

模擬試題（五）

聽力原文與中譯

31. Mr. Clarke is not happy, so he hires me to do the unhappy job for him.
(A) Unfortunately, we don't have any vacancies.
(B) **Seriously, I thought he liked our concept.**
(C) I bet he is very unthoughtful and pretentious.

31. 克拉克先生並不快樂，所以他雇用我來替他做不快樂的事情。
(A) 不幸的是，我們沒有任何空缺了。
(B) **真的嗎？我以為他喜歡我們的構想呢！**
(C) 我敢打賭，他一定非常不體貼且自命不凡。

答案：(B)

 解析

這題有些難，要選聽者的回應，仔細從平常生活中的對話回推，就能直接選出正確答案了，像是我還以為……，而現實生活中也確實有這樣的職務這樣一來就不會影響高層官員或老闆的形象，因為雇用了一個人當黑臉，所以正確答案為**選項B**。

Part 3

Questions 32-34 refer to the following conversation

Mary: I just hate the whole interphone thing...and I don't do well under stress

John: ok...why?

Mary: I kind of regretted writing the certificate of other languages...on the resume...what did I write? Greek, German, or Russian...

John: that was probably one of the reasons that got you hired.

Mary: can't I just serve water in the economy class cabin...
(interphone rings...)

Mark: hey...Mary...we have two customers from Moscow and they speak something that is all Greek to us...come here as quick as you can...

Mary: ...OK...I will...be..right there...

Mary: is there anything I have to do before going...like mopping the floor here...or pouring some wine...

John: just go...

Mary: ..you are not as supportive as you say you are...

問題32-34，請參考以下對話內容

瑪莉：我只是討厭整個對講機的事...而且在壓力下我無法有好的表現。

約翰：好的...為什麼呢？

瑪莉：我有點後悔在履歷上寫下其他語言的證照...我到底寫了什麼啊？希臘文、德文或是俄文...。

約翰：那或許就是妳獲得錄取的原因之一囉。

瑪莉：難道我就不能在經濟艙裡頭倒倒水就好嗎？
（對講機響了...）

馬克：嗨...瑪莉...我們有兩位顧客均來自莫斯科而且他們盡說些我們聽不懂的話...快點來這裡...越快越好

瑪莉：...好的...我馬上...就到...。

瑪莉：在我走之前，這裡還有什麼事我必須做的事情嗎？...像是在這拖個地...或是倒些酒...

約翰：快去吧...

瑪莉：你真的不像你說的那樣支持對方...。

試題中譯與解析

32. Where most likely is the conversation taking place? (A) **on the airplane.** (B) at the boarding gate. (C) at the airport. (D) at the training center.	32. 此篇對話最有可能發生在何處？ (A) **在飛機上。** (B) 在登機口。 (C) 在機場。 (D) 在訓練中心。
33. What is the language that the two customers use? (A) German. (B) Greek. (C) **Russian.** (D) Chinese.	33. 兩位顧客所使用的語言是什麼？ (A) 德文。 (B) 希臘文。 (C) **俄文。** (D) 中文。
34. Which of the following language cannot be seen written on the woman's resume? (A) German. (B) **Spanish.** (C) Russian. (D) Greek.	34. 下列哪一個語言沒有撰寫在女子的履歷上面呢？ (A) 德文。 (B) **西班牙文。** (C) 俄文。 (D) 希臘文。

答案：32. A 33. C 34. B

解析

- **第32題**詢問的是「**地點**」，從 **interphone**和 **economy class cabin**中可以推測出兩個人是空服員且在飛機上，兩人聊到對講機和當初在履歷表上所填的證照的事情，故答案要**選A**。
- **第33題**要綜合幾個訊息，**履歷表上所填的三種語言**Greek, German, or Russian和 最後提到的兩位乘客是來自**莫斯科**，所以可以推斷出乘客使用的可能是**俄文**，故答案要**選C**，D選項的中文則在對話中沒有提到。
- **第34題**，比上題更簡單，以刪去法刪除履歷表上所提到的三種語言，可以得知答案為**選項B**。

Questions 35-37 refer to the following conversation

Mary: I am feeling so grateful for getting chosen...

Cindy: the campaign model?

Mary: yep...I'm so excited...

Cindy: congratulations...and thank god I didn't get picked...imagine my relief...

Mary: why is that? I thought you wanted this...it's a great honor...

Cindy: I overheard some senior flight attendants saying that it's going to be filmed near the desert...sweltering hot desert...and you have to stand straight for hours...pretending that you are happy...manage to keep the smile on your face until the photographer is pleased about the shot...

Mary: ...OK

Cindy: ...to be honest...I'm nobody's competition...feeling pleased to know some of you guys got chosen...faking something is just not my strong suit...gotta go...I have to go to the training center...perhaps talk to you during the break...

問題35-37，請參考以下對話內容

瑪莉：我對於雀屏中選感到很感恩。

辛蒂：活動的模特兒嗎？

瑪莉：是的...我感到很興奮...。

辛蒂：恭喜...而且謝天謝地我沒有獲選...想像我真的鬆了口氣...。

瑪莉：為什麼呢？我以為你想要這個...這是個偉大的榮耀。

辛蒂：我從有些資深的空服員那裡偷聽到，拍攝地點靠近沙漠...悶熱的沙漠...而且有數個小時中你必須要站得很直...假裝你很快樂...設法維持你臉上的笑容，直到攝影師對於拍攝感到滿意...。

瑪莉：...好的。

辛蒂：...說真的...我不是任何人的競爭對手...對於知道你們有些人獲選感到高興...假裝一些事情真的不是我的強項...我必須要走到訓練中心了...或許在休息時在跟你聊了...。

試題中譯與解析	
35. Where most likely is the conversation taking place? (A) at the desert. (B) at the boarding gate. (C) **at the airport.** (D) at the training center.	35. 此篇對話最有可能發生在何處？ (A) 在沙漠。 (B) 在登機口。 (C) **在機場。** (D) 在訓練中心。
36. Why does the woman say, "I'm nobody's competition"? (A) because she is a nobody. (B) **because she wants to clarify and not getting clashed with others.** (C) because she doesn't want to compete. (D) because she is not competent enough.	36. 為何女子提及 "I'm nobody's competition"？ (A) 因為她是個無名小卒。 (B) **因為她想要澄清且不想要跟其他人起衝突。** (C) 因為她不想要競爭。 (D) 因為她的能力不足以競爭。
37. What is not the woman's concern? (A) long hours of shooting. (B) squeeze the laughter. (C) please the cameraman. (D) **getting picked on by the boss.**	37. 什麼不是女子所擔心的？ (A) 長時間的拍攝。 (B) 擠出笑容。 (C) 取悅拍攝者。 (D) **被老闆挑剔。**

答案：35. C 36. B 37. D

解析

- **第35題**，從一開始對話中提到的the campaign model和I overheard some senior flight attendants等，可以推斷出兩個人可能是剛入行的空服員，對話中最有可能發生的地點是在機場，所以要選**選項C**，選項D也有可能，不過根據對話中女子最後說的gotta go...I have to go to the training center，可以推斷出女子才正要去該地方，故可以排除掉選項D。

- 第36題，從the campaign model的部分可以推斷出許多人都想角逐但從對話中可以得知女子其實不感興趣，而且對女子來說也是件苦差事，更不想要捲入跟同事暗地裡相鬥的情況，所以講這句話其實有點是想表達不在意這件事、澄清和不想與人起衝突或被誤會是競爭對手等，以更隨意的口吻講出這句話，故答案要選**B**。
- 第37題，對話中有提到缺點的部分cameraman跟photographer是同義轉換，D選項的部分對話中沒有提到，故要選**選項D**。

聽力原文和對話

Questions 38-40 refer to the following conversation

Oasis	
Drinks	price
coconut juice	US 35
mango juice	US 50
camel milk	US 45
coke	US 40

Tom: 10 bucks for that male giraffe

Mary: seriously? Are we really doing this? Our life as researchers... gambling...

David: why not? it's funny...and exhilarating? There is strength in numbers...so I'm looting for the pride of lions to win...20 bucks

Mary: the giraffe hastens the speed...and is giving a fatal kick

David: ..my adrenaline rush...

Mary: the kick is amiss...lucky lions...I can't seem to decide...so hard

Tom: ...come on...giraffe...

David: ...lions are regrouping and are about to attack...

Tom: ...they can barely grasp the back of the giraffe...

David: ...they missed the opportunity...persistence is the key...keep doing it...

Tom: ...I think they are about to give up...they are unable to tackle the male giraffe...

David: ...what a disappointment....perhaps they should switch the target to the newborn giraffe or a gazelle

Tom: they should have thought about that...ha

問題38-40，請參考以下對話內容

綠洲	
飲料	價格
椰子汁	35 美元
芒果汁	50美元
駱駝牛奶	45美元
可樂	40美元

湯姆：10元賭雄性長頸鹿。

瑪莉：真的嗎？我們真的要這樣做嗎？難道我們研究人員的生活就是...賭嗎？

大衛：為何不呢？這很有趣...而且令人感到興奮？數量佔取優勢...所以我賭獅群的獅子們贏...20美元。

瑪莉：長頸鹿加快了速度...且給予了致命一擊。

大衛：我的腎上腺素大量分泌了...。

瑪莉：這擊失誤了...幸運的獅子...我無法下決定...太難了

湯姆：...拜託...長頸鹿...。

大衛：獅子正在重組而且正要攻擊...。

湯姆：他們幾乎抓不到長頸鹿的背後...。

大衛：...他們錯失了機會...毅力是關鍵...持續保持下去...。

湯姆：...我認為他們正要放棄了...他們無法擊倒雄性長頸鹿...。

大衛：...真令人失望...或許他們早該要將目標轉換成剛出生的長頸鹿或是瞪羚。

湯姆：他們早點想到那點...哈。

試題中譯與解析	
38. Where most likely is the conversation taking place? (A) at the zoo. (B) in the office. (C) at the research center. **(D) at the wild national park.**	38. 此段對話最有可能發生在何處？ (A) 在動物園。 (B) 在辦公室。 (C) 在研究中心。 **(D) 在野生國家公園。**

39. What is the target of the lions? (A) a newborn giraffe. (B) **a male giraffe.** (C) a female giraffe. (D) a gazelle.	39. 獅群的目標為何？ (A) 新生長頸鹿幼兒。 (B) **雄性長頸鹿。** (C) 雌性長頸鹿。 (D) 瞪羚。
40. Look at the graph. What is the most expensive drink at the oasis? (A) coconut juice. (B) camel milk. (C) coke. (D) **mango juice.**	40. 請參閱圖片。在綠洲裡最昂貴的飲料是什麼？ (A) 椰子汁。 (B) 駱駝奶。 (C) 可樂。 (D) **芒果汁。**

答案：38. D 39. B 40. D

解析

- 第38題，也是詢問「地點」的部分，而research center是干擾選項，雖然對話的人物都是研究人員，而他們最有可能是在野生國家公園做研究的研究人員，圖表題中也有綠洲販賣部分，而且也不太可能是動物園，動物園會將不同類型的動物隔開，故答案要選**選項D**。
- 第39題，從一開始男子選擇要賭的雄性長頸鹿到對話末提到應該將目標轉移成年輕的長頸鹿或者瞪羚，加上對話中未提及雌性長頸鹿是目標和they are unable to tackle the male giraffe等訊息，所以獅子的目標是雄性長頸鹿，答案要選**B**。
- 第40題，在表格中可以看到綠洲中販賣最貴的項目是芒果汁，故答案為**選項D**。

聽力原文和對話

Questions 41-43 refer to the following conversation

Cindy: that kid was running so fast and his drink spilled...he was unsupervised...

John: and?

Cindy: ..he came to me and expected me to give him a refill...of course I said no...

John: what? You didn't give him a refill...

Cindy: .should I...

John: ...of course...you should...Bestland is about creating a pleasurable experience for customers...now go and give him a new cup...no questions asked...

Cindy: ...ok...I still can't believe I blew that up...by saving the employer some cash...

John: ...doesn't that bother you...the frowned eyebrows of the kid...who is supposed to be happy here...

Cindy: ...I hate my job...kind of...here is the refill...I'm going there and give it to him...next time when another kid spills...I'm gonna yell...great...the more the merrier...since we have a refill policy...

John: ...ha

問題41-43，請參考以下對話內容

辛蒂：那個小孩跑得好快而且他的飲料打翻了...當時他沒有父母看管著...。

約翰：而且？

辛蒂：...他來找我，然後期待我要給他的空瓶飲料重新裝滿...當然，我回絕他...。

約翰：什麼？你沒有替他重新裝滿嗎？

辛蒂：我應該要嗎？...

約翰：...當然，你應該要...倍斯特樂園是關於替顧客創造一個愉快的體驗...現在快去且給他一杯新的飲料...別再問任何問題...。

辛蒂：...好的，我仍然無法相信我搞砸了...想說此舉替雇主省了一些錢...。

約翰：...那樣不會困擾到你嗎？...小孩皺著眉...而他在樂園裡頭本該是快樂的...。

辛蒂：...我恨我的工作...有點像是...這是我重新裝滿的飲料...我要走過去然後將飲料給他...下一次又有小孩打翻了...我應該要叫喊著...越多越好唷，既然我們有這個重新裝滿的政策。

約翰：...哈。

41. What is not mentioned about the drink? (A) the kid expected a refill. (B) **the kid didn't get rejected.** (C) It was spilled by the kid who did not under parental watch. (D) It was deliberately spilled by the kid.	41. 關於飲料的敘述，何者為非？ (A) 小孩期待飲料再重新裝滿。 (B) **小孩沒有被拒絕。** (C) 飲料是位沒有父母監督的小孩所潑灑出的。 (D) 飲料是小孩故意灑出來的。
42. Why should the woman give the kid a refill? (A) because she is pressured by the colleague. (B) because she loves the kid. (C) **because it's the company policy.** (D) because the juice doesn't cost the company a dime.	42. 為什麼女子應該要替小孩將飲料重新裝滿呢？ (A) 因為她受到同事的壓力。 (B) 因為她喜愛小孩。 (C) **因為這是公司的政策。** (D) 因為果汁不會花費公司一分錢。
43. Why does the woman say, "the more the merrier"? (A) to be supportive of the company culture stuff. (B) to show her preference for the Christmas. (C) to spread the happy seed. (D) **to satirize the refill thing.**	43. 為什麼女子提到「the more the merrier」？ (A) 對公司文化的東西表示支持。 (B) 顯示她對於聖誕節的偏好。 (C) 散佈快樂的種子。 (D) **諷刺重新裝滿這件事情。**

答案：41. B 42. C 43. D

解析

- **第41題**，僅有選項B的部分是錯誤的，小孩有提到要refill但女子拒絕他，故答案為**選項B**。選項C的部分，did not under parental watch等同於 **unsupervised**，要注意這個同義轉換。

- **第42題**，對話內容中可以推斷出這是公司的文化和政策，其實女子不太認同，故答案為**選項C**。（她沒有受迫於同事壓力，因為這是公司規定。她也沒有喜愛那個小孩。而果汁的refill等同增加公司的成本支出，由這幾點可以排除ABD。）
- **第43題**，女子會講這句話的部分其實很明顯是出於諷刺，故答案為**選項D**。

聽力原文和對話

Questions 44-46 refer to the following conversation

Mary: ...hey Jason...long time no see...I was going to ask you something while you were at the mall that day...but you were with a beautiful lady...so I didn't intrude...

Jason: ..ok...what would you like to ask...as long as it's not about marriage.

Mary: ...of course not...and I saw your engagement ring...quite dazzling...let's cut to the chase...I wanna to ask you about the application for Bestland..?

Jason: ok...don't worry about the process...it is very simple...you just have to fill in an on-line application form and go to the interview...

Mary: ...will there be any background checks?

Jason: I'm afraid that they will run those...but don't worry about it...I was an outdoor vendor last summer...it was fun...

Mary: ...thanks...for your time though...I'm going to fill the application in the coffee shop down the hall...I'll see you when I see you...

問題44-46，請參考以下對話內容

瑪莉：...嗨！傑森...很久不見了...那天在購物中心時，我本來要向你詢問一些事...但是那天你跟一個漂亮的女士在一塊...所以我不敢去打擾你...。

傑森：...好的...妳想要詢問什麼呢？...只要是跟婚姻無關的事都可以問...。

瑪莉：...當然不是囉...而我看到你的訂婚戒指了...相當眩人奪目...讓我們直接切入重點好了...我想要詢問你關於申請倍斯特打工的申請？

傑森：好的...別擔心申請的過程...這相當簡單...你只要填線上的申請表格然後去參加面試...。

瑪莉：...會有任何的背景調查嗎？

傑森：恐怕他們會有那些調查唷...但是別擔心...像我去年是戶外的攤販...很有趣...。

瑪莉：謝謝...你的時間...我正要去廳堂盡頭的咖啡廳填申請表...我就看到你時在跟你打招呼囉。

試題中譯與解析	
44. Where most likely is the conversation taking place? (A) at the engagement party. (B) **at the mall.** (C) at the coffee shop. (D) at the Bestland office.	44. 此段對話最有可能發生在何處？ (A) 在訂婚派對上。 (B) **在購物商場裡。** (C) 在咖啡店。 (D) 在倍斯特樂園的辦公室。
45. How will the woman apply for the job? (A) fake the background check. (B) call the HR personnel. (C) **register on-line.** (D) fill in the application form on the scene.	45. 女子將如何申請這份工作？ (A) 偽造背景調查。 (B) 致電給人事專員。 (C) **線上註冊。** (D) 在現場填申請表。
46. What was the man's job last summer? (A) the manager. (B) the waiter. (C) **an outdoor vendor.** (D) an indoor operator.	46. 男子去年夏天的工作是什麼？ (A) 經理。 (B) 服務生。 (C) **戶外販賣員。** (D) 室內操作員。

答案：44. B 45. C 46. C

 解析

- **第44題**，對話中有提到**engagement** ring但是發生的場景不在A處，這是干擾選項。對話中也不可能出現在選項C和D。咖啡店是女子才正要走過去的地方，用刪去法後，最有可能的答案只剩下一個，所以答案為**選項B**。
- **第45題**，對話中有提到背景調查但是沒提到造假的部分。對話中也沒有提到要打給人事專員和在現場填申請表。對話中提到的是在線上填申請的部分，選項C改成register online，是**fill in an online application form**的同義轉換，故答案為**選項C**。

- **第46題**，這題很簡單，就是男子所提到自己去年夏天的工作，故答案為**選項C**。

聽力原文和對話

Questions 47-49 refer to the following conversation

Mary: selling to that number is mission impossible...and I'm here to observe how you did it...

Cindy: ...watch and learn...that customer is wearing a lipstick and she looks great in purple...I'm gonna tell her that...

Mary: ...that's it...? That's nothing...even I can do that...

Cindy: ...I can't help but notice that you're wearing lipsticks...and you are going to look great in purple...

Customer: ...purple...me?

Mary: ...OMG...he is a guy...I just don't think how you are gonna pull that off...

Cindy: ...that's right...you heard me...purple...no doubt about it...and with Halloween coming up...a Vampire costume with a purple lipstick makes it look even more striking...I bet everyone at the party is going to notice you...and singing Adam's Cuckoo songs makes it even better...

Customer: ...I love what you think...I guess I will take it..

Cindy: ...thanks...you're really nice...

Mary: ...I can't believe that you did it...

Cindy: ...imagine my relief...

問題47-49，請參考以下對話內容

瑪莉：販售到那樣的數字是不可能的任務...而我今天就到此來觀察你是如何辦到的...

辛蒂：...看著學吧！...那個顧客目前有塗抹著唇膏，而且她用紫色的口紅看起來會很棒...我要去跟她講...。

瑪莉：...就這樣嗎...？這根本微不足道...甚至我也可以做到這樣...。

辛蒂：...我似乎無法不去察覺到你有擦口紅...而且你用紫色會很棒...。

顧客：...紫色...我嗎？

瑪莉：...我的天啊！...他是個男人...我不知道你要如何成事了...。

辛蒂：…是的…你聽到我講什麼了…紫色…這是無可否認的事…而隨著萬聖節即將到來…吸血鬼的服飾搭配紫色口紅讓人更為耀眼了…我打賭在派對的場合中每個人都會注意到你…而唱Adam's Cuckoo更搭了…。

顧客：…我喜愛你所想的…我想我要買它…

辛蒂：…謝謝…你人真的好好喔…。

瑪莉：…我不敢相信你辦到了…。

辛蒂：…想像我的如釋重負…。

試題中譯與解析

47. Where most likely is the conversation taking place? (A) at the office. (B) **at the department store.** (C) at the Halloween Party. (D) at the music studio.	47. 這段對話最可能發生在什麼地方？ (A) 在辦公室。 (B) **在百貨公司。** (C) 在聖誕派對上。 (D) 在音樂工作室。
48. Why does the woman say, "how you are gonna pull that off"? (A) to solidify her viewpoint. (B) **to question another woman.** (C) to lessen another woman's confidence. (D) to steal the perks from another woman.	48. 為何女子提及「how you are gonna pull that off」？ (A) 鞏固她的觀點。 (B) **質疑另一位女子。** (C) 削減另一位女子的自信。 (D) 從另一個女子身上偷取津貼。
49. Why does the man say, "I love what you think"? (A) because they used to be an acquaintance. (B) because the woman makes the prediction that he will love purple. (C) because he is in love with her. (D) **because what the woman says actually resonates.**	49. 為何男子提及「I love what you think」？ (A) 因為他們過去是熟識。 (B) 因為女子做了預測，知道男子會喜歡紫色。 (C) 因為他愛上她了。 (D) **因為女子所說的話實際上產生了共鳴。**

答案：47. B 48. B 49. D

解析

- **第47題**，從販賣口紅等可以推斷出最有可能的地點是百貨公司。而對話中有提到萬聖節和一首歌曲都不是對話中的場景，是干擾選項，故這題答案要選**選項B**。

- **第48題**，這題其實要從另一名女子來看，她先是訝異怎麼辦到的，然後看到身為超級銷售員的女子把對方認錯性別，才講了這句，有很大的成分是到底要怎麼圓場等等的，所以其實是質疑女子不可能談成這筆交易，很可能是道歉，所以答案為**選項B**。

- **第49題**，面對此狀況，該女子腦筋轉得很快，最後講了很多話，其實有講到男子心坎或產生共鳴或有同感等等的，男子才會講這句話，所以答案很明顯是**選項D**。

聽力原文和對話

Questions 50-52 refer to the following conversation

Jason: My boss isn't a professional.

Mark: why?

Jason: he is like an investor...without any knowledge in that field...

Mark: Dang that sucks...

Jason: ...but consumers care about that and for some reason...he wanted it removed....if this keeps moving forward...and I don't have the total autonomy...and it would be really hard to do the job...

Mark: ...unfortunately...we are living in a world where non-professionals manage professionals...and unless you are a boss...things won't change...perhaps you have to find another way to talk to him though...

Jason: ...and I'm praying that consumers can still understand the concept...if they don't sales will drop...and the whole R&D department also takes the blame...

Mark: ...you know what you need the most right now...a few more chicken wings and wine...that's tomorrow's thing...

問題50-52，請參考以下對話內容

傑森：我的老闆不是個專業人士。

馬克：為什麼呢？

傑森：他像是個投資客...在那個領域中完全不懂裡頭的任何知識...。

馬克：討厭...那樣糟透了。

傑森：...但是消費者在乎那部分而基於一些原因，他想要把那部分拿掉...如果情況持續是如此的話...而我也沒有全權的自主性...那麼在這份工作上就會真的很難進行...。

馬克：...不幸地是...我們正活在一個非專業人士控管著專業人士的世界中...而除非你是老闆了...事情沒辦法有什麼改變的...或許你必須要找其他的方式去跟他溝通...。

傑森：...而我正禱告，消費者仍然能夠了解概念...如果他們不瞭解的話，那麼銷售就會下降...那整個研發部門就會受到責難了...。

馬克：...你知道你現在最需要什麼了嗎？...更多的雞翅和酒...那是明天的事了...。

試題中譯與解析	
50. Why does the man say, "without any knowledge in that field"? (A) to criticize his boss. (B) **to indicate the situation and that's why there is a clash.** (C) to degrade the reputation of the investor. (D) to show that there is a need for his boss to learn things.	50. 為何男子提及「without any knowledge in that field」？ (A) 批評他的老闆。 (B) **指出此情況且這也是造成衝突的原因。** (C) 降低投資客的名聲。 (D) 顯示出他的老闆有學習新事物的需要性。
51. Why does the man's friend recommend him? (A) to please the boss and let go of the ego. (B) to ignore the boss whenever he can. (C) to quit the job as fast as he can. (D) **to think of a way that makes both parties pleased.**	51. 男子的朋友是如何建議他的？ (A) 取悅老闆且拿掉自負。 (B) 每當他想忽略老闆時。 (C) 盡快辭掉這份工作。 (D) **構想一個讓雙方都能滿意的解決之道。**

| 52. What does the man say about the concept?
(A) It's written by the unprofessional.
(B) it will affect the overall sales.
(C) it's only important to the boss.
(D) it's relatively important to the consumers. | 52. 男子對於概念的部分提到了什麼？
(A) 由非專業人士所撰寫的。
(B) 這將影響整體銷售。
(C) 這僅對於老闆來說是重要的。
(D) 這對於消費者來說相對是重要的 |

答案：50. B 51. D 52. B

解析

- **第50題**，如果說是要批評老闆其實不太完全，而老闆並非專業人士或許是老闆還有很多事情要去學，不過也不完全是男子講這句話的原因。最有可能的是他向友人傾訴，指出這樣的情況，然後說到非專業的人管理專業人士的情況，所以造成了溝通上的誤會跟衝突的部分，答案最可能是**選項B**。

- **第51題**，朋友並沒有建議他離職等等的，從perhaps you have to find another way to talk to him though可以得知朋友所要建議的是溝通，在溝通上找到一個平衡點或能讓對方也能理解的雙贏局面，自己也不用在苦惱老闆不懂的情況，這句也是D選項的同義轉換，故答案為**選項D**。

- **第52題**，這題要注意一些細節性資訊，ACD均是錯誤的描述或產生干擾的部分，最核心的部分是concept會影響到整體的銷售，選項並沒有直接表明消費者那塊或消費者當主詞的描述，而是更隱晦的表明概念，故答案是**選項B**。

聽力原文和對話

Questions 53-55 refer to the following conversation

Mary: so how did it go?

John: my interview...??

Mary: yep...did you compliment anything in the office?

John: ...I think I blew it....I was too nervous to say anything...there was a crystal ball on the table...pretty dreamy...

Mary: that's too bad...flattering something generally works...it means you admire the interviewer's taste.

John: there were also small figurines, pictures of boats, and plane tickets.

Cindy: I once complimented a plastic plane on an interviewer's desk...telling him how exquisite that is...and we ended up talking nothing relevant to the work...but his hobby and other things...three weeks later...I got the job

John: perhaps I should do the compliment thing in the following interview.

Mary: That's probably the first thing you do...after going into that room...say something like..."she (the ship) is a beauty"...but keep in mind that you don't have to overdo it to make it a little bit too phony.

問題53-55，請參考以下對話內容

瑪莉：面試進行的如何了？

約翰：我的面試嗎？

瑪莉：是的...你有稱讚辦公室的任何東西嗎？

約翰：我想我搞砸了...我太緊張而說不出任何東西...桌上放置著水晶球...相當夢幻...

瑪莉：那真不巧...奉承一些事情通常會成事...這意謂著欽佩面試者的品味。

約翰：桌上同時也放置著小型雕塑品、幾幅船畫和飛機票。

辛蒂：我曾經讚美面試者桌上的塑膠飛機...跟他說這多麼精緻啊...而我們最終聊著跟工作無關的事情...而是他的嗜好和其他事情...三週後...我獲得這份工作了。

約翰：或許我應該要在接續的面試中稱讚事情。

瑪莉：那可能是第一件你要做的事...在進那間房後...說些像是...「她（那艘船）真美」...但是要記得你不要使用過度...而變得有點太假了。

試題中譯與解析

53. According to the man, what is not on the interviewer's desk?	53. 根據男子所說的話，哪個物品不在面試官的桌上？
(A) **a plastic plane.**	(A) **塑膠的飛機模型。**
(B) a statuette.	(B) 雕像。
(C) tickets for transportation.	(C) 交通運輸的票。
(D) photos of ships.	(D) 船隻的照片。

54. According to the woman, what is the item she complimented? (A) a statuette. (B) a plane ticket. (C) **a plastic plane.** (D) a desk.	54. 根據女子所説的話，哪個項目是她曾稱讚過的？ (A) 雕像。 (B) 機票。 (C) **塑膠的飛機模型。** (D) 桌子。
55. Why does the woman say, "you don't have to overdo it to make it a little bit too phony."? (A) she knows too well that the man will blow it. (B) to remind him that doing repetitively can do more harm than good. (C) **to kindly remind the man and hopefully help him in the next interview.** (D) to let him know that being too fake is not good.	55. 為何女子提及「you don't have to overdo it to make it a little bit too phony」？ (A) 她很清楚那位男子會把事情搞砸。 (B) 提醒他重複此舉可能弊大於利。 (C) **善意提醒男子且希望能幫助到他下次的面試。** (D) 讓他了解到太假不是件好事。

答案：53. A 54. C 55. C

解析

- **第53題**，要注意的是選項中**男子和女子均有提到**在面試桌上面試官擺的東西，這題是詢問男子的部分，選項A是女子面試時所稱讚的部分，所以答案為**選項A**。選項B是figurine的改寫，選項C是飛機票的改寫，選項D也是改寫，但是均是男子面試時看到的桌上物品。
- **第54題**，這題是詢問女子的部分，很明顯答案為**選項C**。
- **第55題**，女子雖然建議他稱讚物品，但是也説了別過頭了。而女子講這句話的很主要原因是善意的提醒男子且希望真的能幫助到他，所以答案為**選項C**。

Questions 56-58 refer to the following conversation

Mark: you're the reporter that wrote a biased article about us...is that right?..by the look on your face...then...you're not welcome here...

Cindy: ...I admit it was a misunderstanding...I've straightened this out...and updated the latest information relating to the incident...

Mark: ...I'm not buying it...

Cindy: ...look...this is ABC newspaper...and the news is on the third page....a picture and a few hundred words that clarify the event...

Mark: ...ok...but...I'm not sure how people or animals getting hurt by the story...would feel right now...

Cindy: ...look...I've done my best to undo the wrongdoing...isn't that enough...?

Jason: ...it's ok...you can let her in...she doesn't seem like a malignant woman..

Mark: ...what?...

問題56-58，請參考以下對話內容

馬克：你是撰寫關於我們的偏見文章的記者嗎？對嗎？...從你臉上的表情...那麼...這裡不歡迎你...。

辛蒂：...我承認這是個誤會...我已經解釋清楚了...而且更新了關於這件事的最新資訊了...。

馬克：...我不相信...。

辛蒂：...瞧...這是ABC報紙...而這新聞在第三頁...一張圖片和幾百個文字澄清這個事件...。

馬克：好的...但是...我不確定，人們或動物因此故事而受到傷害的...現在會覺得如何呢...。

辛蒂：瞧...我已經盡我所能去補足過錯了...這樣還不夠嗎？

傑森：...沒關係...你可以讓她進來...她似乎不太像是個有惡意的女人...。

馬克：什麼？...。

試題中譯與解析

56. Why does the woman say, "I've straightened this out"? (A) because it was a misunderstanding. (B) because the misunderstanding is cleared up. (C) because it is hard to convince others. **(D) to elucidate and clear the doubts.**	56. 為何女子提到「I've straightened this out」？ (A) 因為這是個誤解。 (B) 因為誤解被澄清了。 (C) 因為這很難說服其他人。 **(D) 解釋和澄清疑惑。**
57. Why does the man say, "I'm not buying it"? (A) to strengthen his stance. (B) to clarify that he already explained. (C) because he doesn't want to buy it. **(D) to show his disbelief.**	57. 為什男子提到「I'm not buying it」？ (A) 強化他的立場。 (B) 澄清自己本身已經解釋過了。 (C) 因為他不想要購買。 **(D) 顯示他的不信任。**
58. Where most likely is the conversation taking place? **(A) at an animal shelter house.** (B) at the news building. (C) at the newspaper. (D) at the information center.	58. 這段對話最可能發生在什麼地方？ **(A) 在動物庇護之家。** (B) 在新聞大樓。 (C) 在報社。 (D) 在資訊中心。
答案：56. D 57. D 58. A	

解析

- **第56題**，這題有些困難，不過可以推想下女子有說了這是個誤會且事後自己有做出補償了，而講出這句話的原因是對方的不信任，所以強烈表明出自己已經解釋了，最主要的目的是讓男子了解自己有補救、欲解釋和澄清誤會的部分，所以答案為**選項D**。
- **第57題**，男子會講這句話的原因是表示自己的不信任，所以很明顯答案是**選項D**。
- **第58題**，對話中有提到動物，動物因此而受到傷害的部分，所以很可能對話的地點是在動物之家或動物庇護所，雖然文中也提到報紙刊登，但並非對話的地點，這題答案為**選項A**。

聽力原文和對話

Questions 59-61 refer to the following conversation

Jason: ..to be honest...where did you get this...?

Mary: ...a good reporter never reveals her sources...I have my own way...

Jason: ..it's true that one of the koalas is about to make a delivery...in October...

Mary: ...can I do a story?...I've already come up with some good ideas about the baby koala...it's going to be great...

Jason: ..since you are such an animal lover....I guess the answer is ok...

Mary: ...thanks...it's going to be huge for our newspaper...

Jason: ..but...the visiting of the baby should be at least a month after the baby is born...

Mary: why so late...?

Jason: ...there is a safety concern...and we are running out of the veterinarians.

Mary: ..I was an animal doctor for three years...I am sure that I can help out...

Jason: ...seriously...that's a relief...then you can come prior to that...

問題59-61，請參考以下對話內容

傑森：...説實話...你從哪裡得到這個資訊的...？

瑪莉：...一位好的記者不會揭露她的來源的...我有我的方式...。

傑森：真的有其中一隻無尾熊要分娩了...在10月...。

瑪莉：...我能做這個故事嗎？...我已經想好了一些關於無尾熊嬰兒不錯的想法...會很棒的...。

傑森：...既然你是如此愛好動物的人...我想答案是可以的...。

瑪莉：...謝謝...這對於我們報紙來說會是很重大的...。

傑森：但是...拜訪無尾熊嬰兒應該要於牠出生後的至少一個月後...。

瑪莉：為什麼這麼晚呢...？

傑森：...這是安全性的考量...而且我們正好缺乏獸醫。

瑪莉：我曾當動物醫生三年...我想我可以幫得上這個忙...。

傑森：...真的嗎？...那真的是如釋重負...那麼你可以在更之前來囉...。

試題中譯與解析

59. Where most likely is the conversation taking place? (A) At the delivery room. (B) **At an animal shelter house.** (C) At the doctor's house. (D) At the news building.	59. 此段對話最有可能發生在什麼地方？ (A) 在產房。 (B) **在動物庇護之家。** (C) 在醫生家。 (D) 在新聞大樓。
60. When is possibly the time that the mother koala is going to give birth? (A) **October.** (B) September. (C) November. (D) December.	60. 何時可能是母無尾熊生產的日期呢？ (A) **10月。** (B) 9月。 (C) 11月。 (D) 12月。
61. What is the woman's previous profession? (A) A news reporter. (B) A stay-home mom. (C) An animal lover. (D) **A veterinarian.**	61. 女子先前的職業是什麼？ (A) 新聞記者。 (B) 全職家庭主婦。 (C) 動物愛好者。 (D) **獸醫。**

答案：59. B 60. A 61. D

解析

- **第59題**，從對話內容推測對話最有可能是在動物庇護之家跟醫生的對談，故答案要選**選項B**。
- **第60題**，這題也有明確提到時間點是10月，只是make a delivery和give birth間的同義轉換，故答案為**選項A**。
- **第61題**，要注意這題是詢問女子先前的職業，後來在最後的對話中有提到這部分，答案要選獸醫，**選項D**。

聽力原文和對話

Questions 62-64 refer to the following conversation

Cindy: do you actually think that I'm dumb enough to believe that those lobsters are the good ones...

Diver: ok....so with this kind of lobsters...what exactly is the price that you deem is reasonable...

Cindy: US 7 dollars...

Diver: what? 7?..I can get better from other processing companies or buyers...

Cindy: 7 dollars and 50 cents...that's all I can offer...take it or leave it...

Diver: ...fine...what about the large crab...and shrimps...

Cindy: ...2 dollars per shrimp...and ten dollars for the crab

Diver: ...not if you buy five large bags of shrimps...

Cindy: ...that many...then I need a discount...

Diver: ...let me think...

Cindy: ...it's getting windy...I don't think other buyers are coming

Diver: ...giving you a discount would leave us with no profit...how about two octopuses for free

Cindy: ...fine...

問題62-64，請參考以下對話內容

辛蒂：你真的覺得我有笨到去相信那些龍蝦是好貨嗎？

潛水者：好的...，所以這樣的龍蝦...什麼樣的價格你才認為是合理的呢？

辛蒂：7美元...。

潛水者：什麼？7?...我可以從其他的加工廠或買家那裡獲得更好的價格。

辛蒂：7美元和50分錢...這是我所能提供的了...要或拉倒...。

潛水者：...好...那麼關於大型的螃蟹呢...還有蝦子呢？...。

辛蒂：每隻蝦子兩美元...然後螃蟹10美元。

潛水者：...除非你買下5大袋的蝦子...。

辛蒂：...那麼多呀...那麼我需要折扣...。

潛水者：...讓我想下...。

辛蒂：風越刮越大了...我不認為還會有買家會過來了。

潛水者：...給你折扣的話...那麼我們就毫無賺頭了...兩隻免費的章魚如何呢？

辛蒂：...好的...。

試題中譯與解析	
62. Where most likely is the conversation taking place? (A) **at the dock.** (B) at the processing plant. (C) at the aquarium. (D) at the river bank.	62. 這段對話最可能發生在什麼地方？ (A) **在碼頭。** (B) 在加工廠。 (C) 在水族館。 (D) 在河岸。
63. Why does the woman say, "take it or leave it"? (A) because she has to leave soon. (B) to bully those divers. (C) **to show her strong stance and be firm.** (D) because the seafood doesn't worth more money.	63. 為何女子提到「take it or leave it」？ (A) 因為她必須馬上離開。 (B) 去霸凌那些潛水客們。 (C) **顯示她強姿態且表示強硬的態度。** (D) 因為海產並不值更多錢。

64. Why does the man say, "leave us with no profit"?	64. 為何男子提到「leave us with no profit」？
(A) to plead the negotiator.	(A) 懇求協商者。
(B) perhaps a technique employed by a shrew negotiator.	**(B) 由精銳的協商者所採用的策略。**
(C) because the margins are small.	(C) 因為利潤很些微。
(D) to confront the negotiator.	(D) 面對協商者。

答案：62. A 63. C 64. B

 解析

- **第62題**，這四個選項都很有可能，不過從男子所說的I can get better from other processing companies or buyers...，可以排除海產加工廠，女子或海產加工廠等買家也是到此處來向他購買魚貨，所以不可能在加工廠。對話也不太可能出現在水族館。僅剩A和D選項，但是以漁貨和最後提到的章魚等部分，對話中較不可能出現在河岸，河岸抓得比較是小蝦小蟹，故答案為**選項A**。

- **第63題**，通常講這句話時比較是「要就要不要就拉倒」，通常是迫使對方接受、讓對方知道這是最後自己可以忍受的部分，這也是很強勢且堅決的表達，通常對方均會怕談不成而接受，故答案為**選項C**。

- **第64題**，這題有可能是真的會讓自己沒有利潤可言，也有可能是別讓對方砍價太多的說法等等，也是比較常在談價錢或是精銳的協商者所講的話，選項A, C和D僅表達了部分，並非全部，**選B**是最佳的。

聽力原文和對話

Questions 65-67 refer to the following conversation

Boss: since you are new here Jason...I'm assigning you to Cindy...you have to listen to whatever Cindy says...and not another word...and I want you to learn as fast as you can...probably be ready next week...

Jason: ...I will try my best...

Boss: Cindy might seem meek...but she is cut-throat when it comes to negotiating with those divers...she is back...

Boss: Cindy...this is our new recruit...Jason Clarke...he is now basically your assistant...and now you have to excuse me...I do have a business lunch I really have to go now...

Jason: ...hi...really nice meeting you...I heard lots of things about you...

Cindy: ...yesterday I got two free octopuses...they are adorable...I'm keeping them in our big aquarium...would you like to see them?

Jason: sure...

Cindy: ...follow me...

問題65-67，請參考以下對話內容

老闆：傑森，既然你是這裡新來的...我將你分配給辛蒂...你必須要聽任何辛蒂所説的...而且不能有異議...我想要你盡可能地學...越快越好...可能下週就要能上手...。

傑森：...我會盡我所能的...。

老闆：辛蒂可能看起來似乎溫和...但是當提到與那些潛水客議價，她是殘酷的...她回來了...。

老闆：辛蒂...這是我們的新聘員...傑森克拉克...他現在基本上是你的助理了...而現在要請你們見諒一下...我有個午餐會議我真的不走開不行了...。

傑森：...嗨...真的很高興見到妳...我聽説了很多有關於妳的事情。

辛蒂：...昨天我拿到兩隻免費的章魚...牠們很可愛...我將牠們放到我們的大型水族館裡頭...想要看看牠們嗎？

傑森：當然...。

辛蒂：...跟著我走吧！...。

試題中譯與解析

65. Who might be the speaker that assigns Jason to Cindy?	65. 誰可能是將傑森指派給辛蒂的説話者？
(A) **the boss.**	(A) **老闆。**
(B) the HR.	(B) 人事專員。
(C) the diver.	(C) 潛水客。
(D) the sales rep.	(D) 銷售業務。

66. What could be the job title for the new hire? (A) the diver. (B) **the assistant.** (C) the HR personnel. (D) the manager.	66. 什麼可能是新雇員的工作職稱呢？ (A) 潛水客。 (B) **助理。** (C) 人事專員。 (D) 經理。
67. Where is the gift housed at? (A) in the container. (B) at the business lunch building. (C) **at the aquarium.** (D) at the beach.	67. 禮物儲藏在何處呢？ (A) 在容器裡頭。 (B) 在商業午餐大樓。 (C) **在水族館。** (D) 在海灘。

答案：65. A 66. B 67. C

解析

- **第65題**，說話者最有可能是老闆，因為其他三個選項不太是能夠分派職務給一個資深人員的人，故答案為**選項A**。
- **第66題**，從前面提到的I'm assigning you to Cindy和後面的he is now basically your assistant可以得知答案就是助理，故答案為**選項B**。
- **第67題**，這題有比較隱晦，gift其實指的是two free octopus，housed at詢問的是地方，所以就是女子所說的I'm keeping them in our big aquarium，故答案為**選項C**。

聽力原文和對話

Questions 68-70 refer to the following conversation

Cindy: ...now we are driving to the dock...this is actually the time that those divers...

Jason: ...great...I'm expecting to see lots of sea creatures...

Cindy: ...we have to be careful though...some sellers are untrustworthy...there are just too many types of shrimps...lobsters...now is not the off-season...so I'm assuming that it's gonna be more divers and I believe that we can get a fairly reasonable price...ha...

Jason: ...it seems that I still have so many things to learn...

Cindy: ...don't worry about it...by the way what's your favorite seafood...? By noon...I'm taking you to the seafood restaurant...actually our largest buyer...you can order anything you want...sharks...clams...crabs...but definitely not dolphin meat...it contains mercury...

Jason: ...but why would someone eat dolphins?

Cindy: ...some tourists fancy that...

問題68-70，請參考以下對話內容

辛蒂：...現在我們開車駛向碼頭...實際上這時候真的是那些潛水客...。

傑森：...棒極了...我期待看到許多海洋生物...。

辛蒂：...我們必須要小心翼翼地...有些賣家很不值得信賴...而有太多樣的蝦子...龍蝦...現在不是淡季...所以我假定著會有很多潛水客，我相信我們可以拿到相當合理的價格...哈...。

傑森：...似乎我仍有很多事情要學習...。

辛蒂：...別擔心...順便一提的是，你最喜愛的海產是什麼呢？...中午的時候...我要帶你去一間海產餐廳...實際上我們最大的買家...你可以訂購任何你想要吃的東西...鯊魚...蚌類...螃蟹...但絕對不要點海豚肉...牠含有汞。

傑森：怎麼會有人吃海豚肉呢？

辛蒂：有些觀光客喜愛囉...。

試題中譯與解析

68. Where most likely is the conversation taking place? (A) at the dock. (B) **on the car.** (C) at the restaurant. (D) at the aquarium.	68.這段對話最可能發生在什麼地方？ (A) 在碼頭。 (B) **在車上。** (C) 在餐廳。 (D) 在水族館。

69. Why does Cindy not recommend dolphin meat? (A) because it doesn't taste good. (B) because the chef is a lousy dolphin cooker. (C) **because it is harmful to human body.** (D) because it is against human nature.	69. 為何辛蒂不建議吃海豚肉？ (A) 因為牠嚐起來不可口。 (B) 因為廚師是個糟透了的海豚烹飪者。 (C) **因為牠對於人體有害。** (D) 因為這違反人性。
70. Who could be the demographic that consumes sea mammals? (A) **tourists.** (B) divers. (C) buyers. (D) the boss.	70. 何者是攝食海洋哺乳類動物的目標族群？ (A) **觀光客。** (B) 潛水客。 (C) 買家。 (D) 老闆。

答案：68. B 69. C 70. A

解析

- **第68題**，這題要小心，因為有許多干擾選項，一開始說的駛向碼頭，所以不可能是對話發生的地點，還有對話中提到的要去海產餐廳也是干擾選項，答案最有可能是在車上談論這段話，所以答案為**選項B**。

- **第69題**，女子不推薦海豚肉的主因是it contains mercury，所以得知因為這是重金屬，以常理來判斷，這是對人體有危害的，故答案為**選項C**。雖然吃海豚肉也是違反人性或不合保育，但女子沒有說出這點，所以排除D選項。

- **第70題**，這題題目也有改寫過，demographic指的是客群，sea mammal指的是海豚，所以答案是**選項A**。

 **PART 4**

聽力原文與中譯

Questions 71-73 refer to the following news report

This is reporter...Cindy Lin...I'm here at Best Mall...one of the largest malls in the area...in a few minutes...this place is gonna be treated as the crime scene...let's take a quick look....on the second floor...apparently there were gun shot residues and blood on the scene...it's assumed that there were some struggles and the gun went off...and on the fifth floor...pearls and silver necklaces randomly scattered on the floor...and...unfinished burgers...from BFC...and French fries from Best burger king......we have no idea...wait...someone is screaming for help...I think it's best that we find a place to hide...our photographer is still shooting...of course we can't give them our cameras...it's the company's assets...and my smartphone...that's my personal property...I think that leaves me with no choice...I have no choice but to knock him with my microphone...not so tough are you?

問題71-73請參閱下列新聞報導

這是倍斯特記者...辛蒂‧林...我現在位在倍斯特購物中心...在這地區中其中之一的大型購物中心...在幾分鐘內...這個地方就會被視為是犯罪現場...讓我們很快看一下...在二樓...顯然在現場有槍擊的殘餘物和血液...可以假定出現場有些掙扎，且槍枝走火了...在五樓...珍珠和銀飾項鍊隨意散落在地面上...還有...吃剩的漢堡...BFC的...還有倍斯特漢堡王的薯條...我們沒有任何想法...等下...有人發出求救之喊...我想我們最好要找個地方躲藏...我們的攝影師仍在拍攝...當然我們不能將我們的相機交給歹徒...這是公司的資產...還有我的智慧型手機...這是我的個人財產...我想這樣我沒有選擇的餘地...我不得不以我的麥克風擊倒他...看來你也沒有多麼強悍？

試題中譯與解析

71. Who most likely are the listeners? (A) policemen. (B) photographers. (C) department employees. (D) **audiences.**	71. 新聞報導的聽者最可能是誰？ (A) 警察。 (B) 攝影師。 (C) 部門員工。 (D) **觀眾。**

72. According to the reporter, which cannot be found on the ground? (A) unfinished burgers. (B) French fries. (C) precious metal. (D) **coke.**	72. 根據新聞記者所述，在地面可能會發現什麼？ (A) 剩餘的漢堡。 (B) 薯條。 (C) 珍貴金屬。 (D) **可樂。**
73. Why does the woman say, "not so tough are you"? (A) to demonstrate the spirit of the reporter. (B) to get the applause for tackling down the criminal. (C) **to respond in a mocking, humorous way.** (D) to show other criminals that they need to be tougher.	73. 為什麼女子提及「not so tough are you」？ (A) 展示新聞記者的精神。 (B) 為了獲取擊倒罪犯的喝采。 (C) **以嘲諷幽默的方式回應。** (D) 向其他罪犯展示，他們要更難對付才是。

答案：71. D 72. D 73. C

解析

- **第71題**，這題最有可能的聽眾是電視機前的觀眾，所以要**選D**。
- **第72題**，這題是詢問細節的部份，precious metal指的是silver，所以要小心別誤選C，這樣一來排除了ABC是文章中有提到的部分，答案為**選項D**。
- **第73題**，最後一題稍難，不過可以推想下女子會講這句話的口吻，其他三個選項均不正確，僅有C較符合，女子在不得已的情況下拿了麥克風擊倒可能攻擊自己和攝影師等的歹徒，才講這句，沒想到一擊就倒，意謂著連她這樣的記者都能擊倒對方，帶有點嘲諷且以幽默的方式看到這起事件，故**答案為C**。

聽力原文與中譯

Questions 74-76 refer to the following news report

This is reporter...Cindy Lin...I'm here at Desert Camp...a meaningful activity for kids to learn the awareness of our environment and conservation...often things we take for granted...here you have to walk long miles to get the water you need...wait...what do you mean rattlers? Some students are pointing to me that there are several rattlers gathering near the place where we camp...are they venomous?...I'm gonna use my phone...but unfortunately...there are no signals...oh boy...that reminds me of a teacher in our biology class...I really shouldn't have fallen on deaf ears...oh my god...there are plenty of snakes...throw them...some rats...no rabbits...fine...I'm calling backups...once I am in the van...they are dead to me...we always have a few raccoons on our car...whoever takes down a few rattlesnakes will get more cotton candy...go...

問題74-76請參閱下列新聞報導

這是倍斯特記者...辛蒂‧林...我現在位在沙漠露營區...一個對於孩童們學習我們環境和保育意識有意義的活動...通常我們所認為理所當然的事情...在此你要長途跋涉才能獲取你所需的水源...等等...你所指的有響尾蛇是什麼意思？有些學生向我指著，有幾條響尾蛇在我們露營的地方聚集著...他們是有毒的嗎？...我來用我的手機看看...但是不幸的是...沒有訊號...噢！我暈...這讓我想到我們生物課的一位老師...我當時真的不該充耳不聞...我的天啊...這有許多蛇...丟牠們...丟些老鼠...不，丟些兔子...好吧...我來叫援軍...一旦我到了箱型貨車處...他們對我來說就如同死掉了一般...我們總是會帶幾隻浣熊在我們車上...誰擊倒幾隻響尾蛇的會拿到更多的棉花糖...快去吧！

試題中譯與解析

74. What is the purpose of this camp?
(A) tackle rattlers in the wild.
(B) get the water by traveling long distance.
(C) **appreciate things and know about environmental conservation.**
(D) prepare more cotton candy.

74. 此次露營的目的是什麼？
(A) 在野外應付響尾蛇。
(B) 長途跋涉取水。
(C) **珍惜事物且了解環境保育。**
(D) 準備更多的棉花糖。

75. Why does the woman say, "I really shouldn't have fallen on deaf ears"? (A) because it is the lesson she now learns. (B) because she has a hearing problem and she doesn't want to admit it. (C) **because she never thought knowledge could be useful and someone told her before.** (D) because her phone doesn't work.	75. 為什麼女子提及「I really shouldn't have fallen on deaf ears」？ (A) 因為這是她現在所學的一課。 (B) 因為她有聽力問題且她不想承認此事。 (C) **因為她從未想過知識會那麼有用且之前有人告訴過她。** (D) 因為她的電話沒有反應。
76. Which of the following can be the cure for dealing with the rattler? (A) cotton candy. (B) **raccoons.** (C) rats. (D) rabbits.	76. 下列哪一項能成為對付響尾蛇的良方呢？ (A) 棉花糖。 (B) **浣熊。** (C) 老鼠。 (D) 兔子。

答案：74. C 75. C 76. B

 解析

- **第74題**，這題是詢問目的，問中提及響尾蛇但制伏牠並非camp的目的，汲取水源也是事實的細節描述，不是目的，答案其實是一開始講到的環境意識和保育，所以答案為**選項C**。
- **第75題**，女子提到不該充耳不聞，最有可能的原因是，她想起生物課老師提過但當時自己不以為意，而在手機沒訊號無法查詢下，有感於當初自己沒留心，而自己未曾想到這個知識將來自己會用到且這麼重要，所以最可能的答案為**選項C**。
- **第76題**，這題很明顯答案會是**浣熊**，雖然女子有提到要丟些老鼠和兔子，但都並非擊倒響尾蛇的治療之方。

聽力原文與中譯

Questions 77-79 refer to the following news report

This is reporter...Jason Thornes....taking this trail isn't that hard...the air is incredibly fresh...quite soothing...and I'm bringing some bananas to feed those monkeys...wow they are not afraid of human contact...but they are intimidated by python contact...kidding...it's not that a python will suddenly appear and attack the monkeys...however, there are alarm calls...I'm gonna keep my composure...perhaps they are trying to scare me off...oh no...the python zeros in on the monkey...run...no fight back....apparently it can't fight back...I can't throw some bananas to the python can I, that would be so unfair...perhaps some sandwiches and bagels...or my cookies...kidding...but I really have to go...local inhabitants are taking me upstream to a more safer place...I'm gonna leave my peach here as a mourning for the monkey which took my banana a few minutes ago...

問題77-79請參閱下列新聞報導

這是記者...傑森・索恩...跋涉這樣的小徑並不是太難...空氣相當的新鮮...相當撫慰人心...我帶了一些香蕉來餵那些猴子...哇！他們不太懼怕跟人接觸...但是他們懼怕巨蟒接觸...開玩笑的...又不是突然之間就會有條巨蟒出現然後攻擊猴子...然而，還是有警戒呼叫存在...我正保持鎮定...或許他們試圖嚇跑我...喔...不好了...巨蟒對準了猴子...跑啊...別回擊...顯然，猴子無法回擊...我不該向巨蟒丟些香蕉，是嗎？...這樣就會很不公平...或許丟些三明治和貝果啊...或是我的餅乾...開玩笑的啦！...但是我真的要走啦...當地居民正帶我往上游走去更安全的地方...我正將我的桃子遺留在現場...哀悼那隻幾分鐘前拿我香蕉的猴子...。

試題中譯與解析

77. Which of the following items was received by the monkey? (A) bagels. (B) **banana.** (C) cookies. (D) peach.	77. 下列哪個物品是猴子拿走的？ (A) 貝果。 (B) **香蕉。** (C) 餅乾。 (D) 桃子。

78. Which of the following is not what the reporter jokes to throw at the python? (A) bananas. (B) cookies. (C) sandwiches. (D) **peach.**	78. 下列哪個項目不是新聞記者開玩笑說要丟巨蟒的？ (A) 香蕉。 (B) 餅乾。 (C) 三明治。 (D) **桃子。**
79. Which of the following will be used to grieve the monkey? (A) sandwiches . (B) **peach.** (C) cookies. (D) bananas.	79. 下列哪個項目用於哀悼猴子？ (A) 三明治。 (B) **桃子。** (C) 餅乾。 (D) 香蕉。

答案：77. B 78. D 79. B

解析

- **第77題**，這題要注意結尾提到猴子的部分as a mourning for the monkey which took my banana，所以知道猴子有跟他拿香蕉，故答案為**選項B**。
- **第78題**，他有開玩笑要向巨蟒丟東西，而沒提到的就是peach，故答案為**選項D**。
- **第79題**，最後提到的是I'm gonna leave my peach here as a mourning for the monkey，所以答案還是peach，答案為**選項B**。

聽力原文與中譯

Questions 80-82 refer to the following news report

This is reporter...Jason Thornes....continue our trip...the river is not as violent as most experts deem it is...and I'm not on a ship or a canoe...but on the crafted raft...it's amazing these villagers have the wisdom that was passed on to them and can still be really useful today....the downside of the raft is....oh...a huge torrent...I just never saw it coming...I guess I'm getting soaked and never thought I would get topless sooner...I might steal the show and get the most attention...which I want to avoid...other inhabitants on the raft are informing me that there are crocodiles beneath the river...I'm trying to find a lighter...it's getting dark...and I'm hungry...so do those crocodiles...and pythons...are they interested in my tuna sandwiches... ?

問題80-82請參閱下列新聞報導

這是記者...傑森·索恩...繼續我們的旅程...這條河並不是大多數的專家所認為的那樣，那樣的猛烈...而我並非在船上或者獨木舟上...而是在精心編織的筏上...令人吃驚的是這些村民們有這樣的智慧歷代相傳給他們且到今日都還是相當有用...乘坐竹筏的缺點是...噢...有巨大激流...我從沒預料到激流會來...我想我浸溼了而且沒想到我會這麼快就上裸...我可能會搶走風頭並且得到最多的關注...這也是我所想要避免的...在竹筏上的其他居民們向我告知，在河底下有鱷魚...我正試圖找尋打火機...天色正變暗...而且我餓了...所以那些鱷魚...以及巨蟒...牠們會對於我的鮪魚三明治有興趣嗎...？

試題中譯與解析

80. Where most likely is the news report taking place? (A) on a ship. (B) on a canoe. (C) on a cruise. (D) **on a raft.**	80. 這段新聞報導最有可能發生在何處？ (A) 在船上。 (B) 在獨木舟上。 (C) 在郵輪上。 (D) **在竹筏上。**
81. Why does the man say, "I just never saw it coming"? (A) because he didn't see the torrent. (B) because he wasn't experienced to see the torrent. (C) **because he didn't expect it to show up.** (D) because he didn't have a cloth to change.	81. 為何男子提及「I just never saw it coming」？ (A) 因為他沒有看到激流。 (B) 因為他沒有具有經驗到能看到激流。 (C) **因為他沒有料到激流會突然出現。** (D) 因為他沒有衣服可以更換。
82. Which of the following do not pose any danger to them? (A) pythons. (B) crocodiles. (C) torrents. (D) **tuna sandwiches.**	82. 下列哪個項目並未對他們造成威脅？ (A) 巨蟒。 (B) 鱷魚。 (C) 激流。 (D) **鮪魚三明治。**

答案：80. D 81. C 82. D

解析

- **第80題**，一開始有提到I'm not on a ship or a canoe...but on the crafted raft，故答案很明顯是**選項D**。
- **第81題**，這題也很容易，主要是男子沒有預料torrent的到來，故答案為**選項C**。
- **第82題**，這題也很容易，對他們的威脅中（包含野生生物和自然力量），最不可能的是三明治。

聽力原文與中譯

Questions 83-85 refer to the following news report

This is reporter...Cindy Lin...I'm here at Best Aquarium...I'm gonna ask some professional questions to our marine biologist...Susan...what might seem to be the most exciting thing that an octopus expects to do...solving a really hard puzzle...under the water...using tools to get what it wants...showcasing its magic...by using coloration...and make this place dazzling...or finding a shelter and outwit his opponent, the flounder....and she said...none...so what exactly is the thing octopuses aspire to do...Susan told us it's the all-you-can eat buffet of crabs...and finally I get her point...eating is still considered the most pleasurable thing to do for both animals and humans...and no exception...and Susan is handing me a large clam to feed the octopus... the camera is gonna capture its gluttonous nature and apparently...it doesn't care...

問題83-85請參閱下列新聞報導

這是記者...辛蒂 · 林...我現在位於倍斯特水族館...我要向我們的海洋生物學家...蘇珊詢問一些專業的問題...什麼可能是一隻章魚最期待做的事情呢？...解決一個極困難的謎...在水裡...使用工具得到其想要的東西...展示牠的魔法...藉由使用色彩變換...讓這個地方暈眩奪目般...或是找到庇護所且智勝牠的對手比目魚...而蘇珊回應...以上皆非...所以什麼事情才是章魚最期待做的事情呢？...蘇珊告訴我們答案是「免費的螃蟹自助餐吃到飽」...而我最後懂蘇珊說的了...吃東西對於動物和人們來說仍被視為是最愉悅的事情...而且毫無例外...而蘇珊遞給我一支大型蚌要餵食這隻章魚...相機正捕捉到章魚貪吃的天性而顯而易見的是...牠絲毫不在乎呢？

試題中譯與解析	
83. What will be provided to the octopus? (A) a crab. (B) the flounder. (C) **a clam.** (D) a lobster.	83. 什麼會提供給章魚？ (A) 螃蟹。 (B) 比目魚。 (C) **蚌。** (D) 龍蝦。
84. Which of the following is the activity that the octopus most desires to do? (A) solve a difficult puzzle. (B) use instruments. (C) use magical coloration. (D) **endless crabs to eat.**	84. 下列哪項活動是章魚最渴望做的呢？ (A) 解決困難的謎題。 (B) 使用工具。 (C) 使用魔術般的顏色變換。 (D) **數之不盡的螃蟹可供食用。**
85. What is the essence of the octopus? (A) aggressive. (B) **greedy.** (C) dazzling. (D) pleasurable.	85. 章魚的本性是什麼？ (A) 侵略性的。 (B) **貪婪的。** (C) 令人感到暈眩的。 (D) 令人感到愉悅的。

答案：83. C 84. D 85. B

解析

- **第83題**，由最後的Susan is handing me a large **clam** to feed the octopus，可以得知答案為**選項C**。
- **第84題**，可以看到有的選項有同義改寫，不過很明顯可以刪除掉ABC，而 endless crabs to eat是**all-you-can eat buffet of crabs**的改寫，故答案為**選項D**。
- **第85題**，這題的話要想到nature即是essence，而章魚的貪吃本性，其中 greedy對應到gluttonous，故答案為**選項B**。

Questions 86-88 refer to the following news report

Best Aquarium/profile of the octopus (Adam)	
description	food
least enjoyed	Pacific eels
one of the favorites	Pacific huge clams
most enjoyed	Australia large crab
relative enjoyed	Boston lobsters

This is reporter...Cindy Lin...I'm here at Best Aquarium...wondering whether the octopus is still remembering me...perhaps it doesn't...but perhaps it will remember me this time...I'm bringing the octopus the exceedingly large lobster...almost twice the size of the octopus' body to see if it can tackle...I'm starting to get nervous...the lobster has no idea the octopus is adjacent...and there is a underwater castle...the lobster is trying to occupy it as if the castle is his...own...but the pressing issue is the threat lurking in front of him...the tentacles of the octopus instantly attach to the lobster...it's being dragged into the lair of the octopus...I guess the end is inevitable...and I think the octopus is kind enough for not getting me seen the bloody scene...perhaps knowing that I am a female

問題86-88請參閱下列新聞報導

倍斯特水族館／章魚的檔案 （亞當）	
描述	食物
最不喜愛的	太平洋鰻魚
其中一個喜愛的	太平洋大型蚌
最喜愛的	澳洲大型螃蟹
相對來說喜愛的	波士頓龍蝦

這是記者...辛蒂・林...我現在位於倍斯特水族館...思考著章魚是否仍記住我呢...或許牠不記得了呢...但是或許牠這次會記得我呢...因為我帶給章魚一隻極大型的龍蝦...幾乎是章魚體積的兩倍大...看看牠是否能夠應付...我開始有點緊張...龍蝦對於章魚就在鄰近處絲毫沒有想法...而這裡有個水底下城堡...這隻龍蝦試圖要佔據這城堡彷彿這城堡是牠所擁有的...但是更迫切的議題是他前方所潛藏的威脅...章魚的觸手即刻附著在龍蝦上...龍蝦被拖進章魚的巢穴裡了...我想結果是無可避免的了...而我想章魚善良到不讓我看見這血腥的場景...可能知道我是位女性。

試題中譯與解析	
86. Look at the graph. What is Adam's most favorite food? (A) Pacific eels. (B) Pacific huge clams. (C) **Australia large crabs.** (D) Boston lobsters.	86. 請參考圖表。亞當最喜愛的食物是什麼？ (A) 太平洋鰻魚。 (B) 太平洋大型蚌。 (C) **澳洲大型螃蟹。** (D) 波士頓龍蝦。
87. What is not mentioned about the lobster? (A) it is larger than the octopus. (B) it has no clue that the octopus is nearby. (C) **it's kind enough to let the reporter not see what's cruel.** (D) its body is fastened by the tentacles of the octopus.	87. 關於龍蝦的敘述何者為非？ (A) 牠比章魚的體積還要大。 (B) 牠對於章魚在附近毫無線索。 (C) **牠善良到讓新聞記者不去目睹到血腥的畫面。** (D) 牠的身體被章魚的觸手繫住了。
88. What can be inferred from the fate of the lobster? (A) escaped. (B) injured. (C) alive. (D) **dead.**	88. 從新聞報導中可以推測出龍蝦的命運為何呢？ (A) 逃跑了。 (B) 受傷的。 (C) 活著的。 (D) **死亡了。**
答案：86. C 87. C 88. D	

解析

- **第86題**，可以從圖表中得知章魚的名稱是Adam，所以要找的是牠最喜愛的食物，試題中的most favorite food等於列表中的most enjoyed，故答案為Australia large crab，故**答案為C**。
- **第87題**，關於龍蝦的敘述何者為非，ACD均為錯誤的描述，故可以排除。而選項C是is kind enough for not getting me seen the bloody scene的改寫，故答案為**選項C**。
- **第88題**，這題是推測題，可以從敘述中向是the end is inevitable等，得知龍蝦死了，故答案為**選項D**。

聽力原文與中譯

Questions 89-91 refer to the following news report

This is Linda Wang...According to a reliable source...Best Automobile was unable to pay the paycheck of the employees last month...and the CEO is seeking for the government funds...we are here at the news conference waiting for the spokesperson of the Best Automobile...and clearly he is late...he is at the entrance...

Spokesperson: the rumor is true...and the government refused to grant bail money...saying that it's a result of the mismanagement of the company...using taxpayers' money to finance the company isn't fair to local residents...but we are doing what we can do and promise to pay the loans and the salary of the employees...that's all I have to say...

問題89-91請參閱下列新聞報導

這是琳達・王...根據可靠的消息來源...倍斯特汽車於上個月無法支付員工薪資...而執行長正要求政府資助...我們現在正在新聞記者會等待倍斯特汽車的發言人...而顯而易見的是他遲到了...他在入口了...

發言人：謠傳是真的...而政府拒絕給予脫困金...述說到這是公司經營不善的結果...使用納稅人的錢來資助公司對於當地居民來說是不公平的...但是我們已經做我們所能做的，並且承諾要償還負債和員工的薪資...這就是我所要說的了...。

試題中譯與解析

89. Who is the person that the reporters are waiting for? (A) the CEO. (B) **the spokesperson.** (C) the employees. (D) the local residents.	89. 新聞記者們在等的人是誰呢？ (A) 執行長。 (B) **發言人。** (C) 員工。 (D) 當地居民。
90. Why did the government refuse to grant bail money? (A) because it will lose lots of votes from the local residents. (B) because the company refuses to pay the payment of employees. (C) because there are lots of voice against that. (D) **because the company was wrongly operated.**	90. 為什麼政府拒絕給予紓困金呢？ (A) 因為政府將會失去許多當地居民的票。 (B) 因為公司拒絕支付員工薪資。 (C) 因為有許多的反對聲浪。 (D) **因為公司是不當經營。**
91. Whose money won't be used to aid the company, according to the government? (A) investors. (B) **taxpayers.** (C) employees. (D) the CEO.	91. 根據政府所述，誰的金錢不會用於救援公司呢？ (A) 投資客。 (B) **納稅者。** (C) 員工。 (D) 執行長。

答案：89. B 90. D 91. B

解析

- **第89題**，對話中很明顯有提到在等的對象是spokesperson，所以答案為**選項B**。
- **第90題**，這題是要找政府不願意的原因，而從對話中得知，這其實是公司mismanage的結果，對應到選項D的**was wrongly operated**，故答案為**選項D**。
- **第91題**，這題也是可以回到提到政府相關訊息的地方，有提到用納稅人的錢是不公平的，所以答案很明顯是**選項B** taxpayers。

Questions 92-94 refer to the following news report

This is Linda Wang...Also the news about the bankruptcy of Best Automobile...hundreds of protestors are on the street right now and demand to see the CEO...the police are responding to the event pretty seriously...an indignant employee tells us that there are plenty of lies and corruption within the company...which further impede the normal function of the company...and the prosecutors are also opening a case for the embezzlement and insider trading, the company's offshore accounts...not to mention that the president is under the SEC investigation...we can only hope that the entire incident will finally be put to rest...all the employees have a new start in life...

問題92-94請參閱下列新聞報導

這是琳達・王...以下也是有關於倍斯特汽車破產的新聞...現在數百位抗議者來到了街道上而且要求要見執行長一面...警方對於這個事件是相當嚴肅態度來看待...一位憤怒不平的員工告訴我們公司內部有許多謊言和貪汙...進一步地阻礙了公司正常的營運...而且檢控官也對於貪汙罪和內線交易、公司海外的帳戶的部分開啟了新的調查案...更別説倍斯特總裁正接受SEC調查中...我們只能希望整起事件最後能夠平息...在生活中,所有員工都能有個新的開始...。

92. Which of the following is not mentioned as the possible reason that makes the company unable to function? (A) corruption. (B) embezzlement. (C) insider trading. (D) **indignation.**	92. 可能導致公司無法運作的原因中,下列何者為非? (A) 貪汙。 (B) 盜用公款。 (C) 內線交易。 (D) **憤怒。**
93. Who is parading on the street? (A) the CEO. (B) the prosecutors. (C) **the employees.** (D) the indignant wage earner.	93. 誰在街道上遊行呢? (A) 執行長。 (B) 檢控官。 (C) **員工。** (D) 憤怒的薪資賺取者。

| 94. Who cannot get away with the Commission's scrutiny?
(A) the CEO.
(B) **the president.**
(C) The offshore accounts.
(D) the protestors. | 94. 誰無法擺脫證交所的審查呢？
(A) 執行長。
(B) **董事長。**
(C) 海外帳戶。
(D) 抗議者們。 |

答案：92. D 93. C 94. B

 解析

- **第92題**，在對話中有提到好幾個原因（題目是詢問哪個不是原因），故可以排除ABC選項。雖然有提到indignant employee，但是indignation不是原因，故可以得知答案為**D選項**。
- **第93題**，這題指的是protestors，而可以推斷出protestors一定是公司員工，不滿公司所為而上街抗爭，而D選項不是複數，抗爭的並非僅有他，故答案要選**選項C**較符合。
- **第94題**，這題要先理解到commission指的是SEC，而受到SEC調查的是the president，scrutiny其實是**investigate**的近似字，可以推斷出答案為**選項B**。

聽力原文與中譯

Questions 95-97 refer to the following news report

Best Automobile	
description	date
rent the jet	July 9 2022
have the talk with senators	July 19 2022
invite investors	August 9 2022
have the talk at Bahama	August 19 2022

After ongoing bad news and bombshells revolving around one of the car companies...Best Automobile....it seems that it is finally going to come to light...some investors are interested in restructuring the company and they are taking a private jet to the resort of Bahama to discuss further details...also noteworthy is the fact that legislators are worried that the layoffs are going to cause quite a lot of damage and instability of the society...so there might be some fortuitous signs for the future of the company...we have contacted the office and the spokesperson of the company...but the news needs further verification...and this is ABC news reporter Mark Cheng...at the airport...

問題95-97請參閱下列新聞報導

倍斯特汽車	
描述	日期
租借噴射機	July 9 2022
與議長們的談話	July 19 2022
邀請投資客們	August 9 2022
在巴哈馬的談話	August 19 2022

在一直持續的壞消息和突發事件，圍繞在其中之一的汽車廠，倍斯特公司...似乎最後露出的曙光...有些投資客對於重組公司感到興趣，而且他們搭乘了私人噴射機來到了巴哈馬度假勝地以討論進一步的資訊...也值得注意的是國會議員擔憂解雇可能會引起相當大的損害以及社會的不穩定...所以對於公司未來可能有些吉兆出現...我們已經聯繫了辦公室和公司發言人...但是新聞仍待進一步的證實...而這是ABC的新聞記者馬克・鄭...在機場的報導...。

試題中譯與解析	
95. Look at the graph. How soon will the company return to normal if the restructuring works? (A) July 9 2022. (B) July 19 2022. (C) August 9 2022. (D) **August 19 2022.**	95. 請參考圖表。如果重組成功的話，公司最快能於何時回到正軌？ (A) July 9 2022. (B) July 19 2022. (C) August 9 2022. (D) **August 19 2022.**
96. Who took a vehicle to Florida? (A) the reporter. (B) **investors.** (C) legislators. (D) the spokesperson.	96. 誰搭乘交通工具到佛羅里達洲？ (A) 新聞記者。 (B) **投資客們。** (C) 立法者。 (D) 發言人。
97. Which of the following can be the trigger to social turbulence? (A) restructuring the company. (B) investors ganging together. (C) **large discharge.** (D) news not verified.	97. 下列哪一項是引起社會動盪不安的原因呢？ (A) 重組公司。 (B) 投資客集結在一塊。 (C) **大量解僱。** (D) 還未經證實的新聞。
答案：95. D 96. B 97. C	

解析

- **第95題**，對話中有提到重組和與投資客交談的部分，其實公司最快能回復到正常的時間是和投資客交談後且談成，所以看到圖表可以看到最快也是 have the talk at Bahama，對應到對話訊息中的 to the resort of Bahama to discuss further details，所以答案為**選項D**。
- **第96題**，這題要理解的是took a vehicle和vehicle=交通工具=a private jet，故可以推斷出搭乘的是investors，故答案為**選項B**。
- **第97題**，在對話中legislators are worried that the layoffs are going to cause quite a lot of damage and **instability** of the society，這部分等同於試題的social turbulence，而**layoffs=large discharge**，故答案為**選項C**。

Questions 98-100 refer to the following line recording

An invasion of hornets is really a menace for pupils, so we are here to get rid of the hornets...the fire department is always as busy as ever...our fellows just did the inspection last week...and apparently there are other things that need to be taken care of...snakes...it's in the campus pond...which is used as the educational purpose...teaching children the biological concepts...a snake is chasing a tree frog...let's dismiss it...and there is a bird nest that needs to be removed...and naughty monkeys that break the window of the dormitory...I guess that we are a bit handful here...in this particular place...

問題98-100請參閱下列line的錄製訊息

大黃蜂的入侵對於小學學生來說真的是個威脅，所以我們來到這兒要移除掉大黃蜂...消防隊總是一如往常般的忙碌著...我們的同仁上週才做過檢查...而顯然這裡又有需要處理的事情了...蛇類...在這校園池塘裡...被用於教育性質的...教導小孩們生物學的概念...有條蛇正追逐著一隻樹蛙...讓我們忽略牠吧...這兒有個鳥的巢穴需要移除...還有搗蛋的猴子，破壞了宿舍的窗戶了...我想在這個特別的地方...我們有點忙不過來了呢！...。

試題中譯與解析	
98. Where most likely is the line recording taking place? (A) **in the school.** (B) in the dormitory. (C) in the forest. (D) near the fire department.	98. line視頻最有可能發生在何處？ (A) **在學校。** (B) 在宿舍。 (C) 在森林裡。 (D) 靠近消防部門。
99. Which of the following creatures is not mentioned in the talk? (A) large sting wasps. (B) **chameleons.** (C) an amphibian. (D) a viper.	99. 談話中沒有提到下列哪種生物？ (A) 大型螫人的黃蜂。 (B) **變色龍。** (C) 兩棲生物。 (D) 蛇。

100.According to the fire fighter, which of the following task will be ignored? (A) remove the nest of bees. (B) remove the nest of birds. (C) **remove the snake near the pond.** (D) dispel the monkeys.	100.根據消防員所述，下列哪項任務會被忽略呢？ (A) 移除蜂巢。 (B) 移除鳥巢。 (C) **移除在池塘邊出現的蛇。** (D) 驅散猴子。

答案：98. A 99. B 100. C

解析

- **第98題**，錄製訊息一開始就提到pupils可是還不能因此而判定，後面又提到it's in the campus pond更加可以判定談話的地點是在校園，故答案為**選項A**。也要小心別選成dormitory那只是學校的一部份。雖然講話的人是firefighter但地點也不是在消防隊。

- **第99題**，可以看到選項有出現了同義改寫的部分，large sting wasps = hornets, an amphibian = a frog, a viper = a snake，這幾個都在談話中出現過，所以答案為**選項B**。

- **第100題**，談話中依序講到遇到的情況，其中有提到let's dismiss it，這對應到了試題的**task will be ignored**，故答案為**選項C**。

模擬試題（一）
模擬試題（二）
模擬試題（三）
模擬試題（四）
模擬試題（五）

- 【非洲之旅話題】考生要注意一些「高階字彙」，出題中包含了字彙結合考題的部分，有些考生可能會因為不懂某些字而無法答題。另外，也要注意一些細節點。

- 【水族館話題】考生要注意「較進階」的圖表題的出題，需要思考下在回答，比起單純對著選項看圖表的答題更費神些。

- 【新聞報導和設計公司話題】要注意細節性資訊和區分是否為題目問的部分，很容易誤選或因為聽力理解力沒到位而選錯，要特別小心。

模擬試題（二）

▶ Listening Test 2 🎧 MP3 005

In the Listening Test, you must demonstrate your ability to understand spoken English. This section is divided into four parts and will take approximately 45 minutes to complete. There are four parts, and directions are given for each part. Do not mark the answers in your test book. Use the answer sheet that is provided separately.

▶ PART 1

Directions: For each question, you will listen to four short statements about a picture in your test book. These statements will not be printed and will only be spoken one time. Select the statement that best describes what is happening in the picture and mark the corresponding letter (A), (B), (C), (D) on the answer sheet.

Example   Sample Answer

A ● C D

Statement (B), "**Some people are wearing backpacks**", is the best description of the picture. So you should select answer (B) and mark it on your answer sheet.

1.

(A) (B) (C) (D)

2.

(A) (B) (C) (D)

3.

(A)　(B)　(C)　(D)

4.

(A)　(B)　(C)　(D)

5.

(A) (B) (C) (D)

6.

(A) (B) (C) (D)

► **PART 2** 🎧 MP3 006

Directions: For each question, you will listen to a statement or a question followed by three possible responses spoken in English. They will not be printed and will only be spoken one time. Select the best response and mark the corresponding letter (A), (B), or (C) on your answer sheet.

7. Mark your answer on your answer sheet.
8. Mark your answer on your answer sheet.
9. Mark your answer on your answer sheet.
10. Mark your answer on your answer sheet.
11. Mark your answer on your answer sheet.
12. Mark your answer on your answer sheet.
13. Mark your answer on your answer sheet.
14. Mark your answer on your answer sheet.
15. Mark your answer on your answer sheet.
16. Mark your answer on your answer sheet.
17. Mark your answer on your answer sheet.
18. Mark your answer on your answer sheet.
19. Mark your answer on your answer sheet.
20. Mark your answer on your answer sheet.
21. Mark your answer on your answer sheet.
22. Mark your answer on your answer sheet.
23. Mark your answer on your answer sheet.
24. Mark your answer on your answer sheet.
25. Mark your answer on your answer sheet.

26. Mark your answer on your answer sheet.

27. Mark your answer on your answer sheet.

28. Mark your answer on your answer sheet.

29. Mark your answer on your answer sheet.

30. Mark your answer on your answer sheet.

31. Mark your answer on your answer sheet.

▶ **PART 3** MP3 007

Directions: In this part, you will listen to several conversations between two or more speakers. These conversations will not be printed and will only be spoken one time. For each conversation, you will be asked to answer three questions. Select the best response and mark the corresponding letter (A), (B), (C), (D) on the answer sheet.

32.Which of the following is not the intended animals for the student's research?
(A) bison
(B) foxes
(C) wolves
(D) brown bears

33.What can be predicted about the outcome of the application?
(A) with the help of the employee there, she has nothing to worry about.
(B) she still has a shot.
(C) if other research teams are willing to make room for her, her application will be accepted.
(D) she will put it off by talking to the employee's supervision directly.

34. Why does the woman say, "you've gotta help me out here"?
    (A) because she really needs help
    (B) because saying that usually works
    (C) to plead the employee to see if there is still a chance
    (D) to sway the decision

35. Why does the man say, "are you also on that roster..."?
    (A) because he wants the woman to be on the same flight
    (B) because he wants the woman to be responsible
    (C) just a casual talk for people who are in the same industry
    (D) because the woman doesn't seem to like a long haul material

36. What is the man's profession?
    (A) an operator
    (B) a captain
    (C) a flight attendant
    (D) a ground crew

37. Why does the woman say, "I guess we will have to meet serendipitously"?
    (A) to show that their meeting is a serendipitous encounter
    (B) to end the unpleasant conversation
    (C) to demonstrate they are meant to be together
    (D) to leave the imagination for both parties

38. Why does the woman say, "there is no photoshop in real life"?
    (A) because she is not good at photoshop
    (B) because she wants to perfect the skill of photoshop
    (C) to remind her friend software things can't fix things in the real world
    (D) because she uses too many photo-editing software

39.Which of the following vocabulary is the synonym of overweight?
(A) obedient
(B) opaque
(C) greasy
(D) obese

40.Where most likely is the conversation taking place?
(A) at the restaurant
(B) at the office
(C) at the boarding gate
(D) on the airplane

41.What are the speakers talking about?
(A) interview the applicant and his family
(B) a brief talk of getting to know the applicant
(C) explanation for the son's personality
(D) a transparent glass wall

42.What is the father worried about?
(A) the tuition fee is expensive
(B) the son has to do the test individually
(C) the test being too difficult
(D) the test taking too long

43.What is required for the parents to do?
(A) help their son cheat
(B) calm their son
(C) go to the test room with him
(D) fill in the needed information

44.Which of the following is the device that interviewer uses?
(A) a TV
(B) a cellphone

(C) a camera
(D) a telephone

45. Which of the following is creatures that are grasped in the video?
(A) lobsters
(B) crabs
(C) bear cubs
(D) bears

46. What is the task given that requires brainstorming?
(A) answer questions after viewing the clip
(B) read the paragraph
(C) view the clip
(D) describe the drink

Bulletin board/African trip	
titles	O/X
All story editors	O
All photographers	X
All software programmers	X
Executives	O
All accountants	X
New recruits	X

47. Where most likely is the conversation taking place?
(A) at the travel agency
(B) at the National Park
(C) at a theater
(D) at an animation studio

48.What is the main purpose of this trip?
    (A) the benefit of the company
    (B) to make their work more believable
    (C) to relax after ongoing exhausted work
    (D) to breathe some new air

49.Look at the graph. Who will be going to this trip?
    (A) programmers
    (B) accountants
    (C) rookies
    (D) editors

50.How long does the entire trip take?
    (A) 10 days
    (B) 14 days
    (C) A week
    (D) 4 days

51.Why does the man say, "there is going to be a really tight deadline"?
    (A) because the budget is too short to shoot for a long time
    (B) because the story editors speed up to meet the deadline
    (C) because the time will be four months shorter
    (D) because the film company changes the date

52.Who will not be going to this trip?
    (A) story editors
    (B) the boss
    (C) programmers
    (D) photographers

53.Which of the following is not what speakers do during the trip?
    (A) walking long distance
    (B) animal riding

(C) taking the vehicle

(D) having an air travel

54. What is the function of the Zebra stripes?

(A) to make the flies sleepy

(B) to distract the flies

(C) to attract more flies

(D) to kill some flies

55. Which of the following animal is not seen in the conversation?

(A) meerkats

(B) zebras

(C) lions

(D) ostriches

56. Why does the woman make the phone call?

(A) to make a complaint

(B) to talk to the HR personnel

(C) to confirm the date of the interview

(D) to inquire a few things about the application

57. When will the applicant know the outcome?

(A) October

(B) November

(C) December

(D) January

58. Where is the place that the caller currently working at?

(A) at another Aquarium

(B) at the HR Department

(C) at the coffee shop

(D) at the restaurant

Best Aquarium	
descriptions	**time**
renovation	**July** 10 2021 – **Sep** 10 2021
exhibition	**Sep** 15 2021 – **Sep** 25 2021
Science Project Contest	**Sep** 27 2021 – **Sep** 30 2021
Wedding/governor Kim	**Oct** 20 2021

59.Why does the woman make the phone call?
(A) to purchase the Aquarium
(B) to book the Aquarium
(C) to lease the Aquarium
(D) to confirm the date of the wedding

60.Look at the graph. When could be the date that announces the champion of the Science Project Contest?
(A) July 10 2021
(B) Sep 30 2021
(C) Sep 27 2021
(D) Oct 20 2021

61.Look at the graph. When will the Aquarium finish its renovation?
(A) July 10 2021
(B) Sep 10 2021
(C) Oct 20 2021
(D) Sep 30 2021

62.Which of the following is the closest in meaning to "confidential"?
(A) confided
(B) confident
(C) revealed

(D) concealed

63. What is the problem?
   (A) the woman is forced to quit.
   (B) the woman knows her colleagues' payments
   (C) the woman doesn't want to go back to school
   (D) the woman finds the accountant untrustworthy

64. Why does the woman say, "it really is a hard lesson"?
   (A) because it is difficult
   (B) because now she knows
   (C) because she wants the lesson to be easy
   (D) because the realization of the whole thing makes her understand that

65. Where most likely is the conversation taking place?
   (A) at a dental clinic
   (B) outside the ER room
   (C) at a stem cell center
   (D) on a blood donation car

66. Which of the following organ is not mentioned in the conversation?
   (A) brain
   (B) stomach
   (C) kidney
   (D) gall

67. Why does the woman say, "I will breeze through the first few pages"?
   (A) because she doesn't want to read it
   (B) because the document is too lengthy
   (C) because the surgery is critical
   (D) because the nurse will roll her eyes at her

68. Why does the woman make the phone call?
  (A) to provide the service
  (B) to buy tickets
  (C) to have a fight with the worker
  (D) to have a chat with the manager

69. Why does the employee say, "I admire your enthusiasm"?
  (A) to compliment the customer
  (B) to make a heart-felt comment
  (C) to show her admiration
  (D) to sugarcoat and not irritate the customer

70. What information does the employee provide the woman with?
  (A) 9 digits social security number
  (B) a set of computer password
  (C) the use of credit card
  (D) how to use on-line service to book tickets

▶ **PART 4** 🎧 MP3 008

Directions: In this part, you will listen to several talks by one or two speakers. These talks will not be printed and will only be spoken one time. for each talk, you will be asked to answer three questions. Select the best response and mark the corresponding letter (A), (B), (C), (D) on your answer sheet.

71. What is being advertised?
  (A) the coach's muscle
  (B) strawberry
  (C) muscle-building bars
  (D) protein

72.How can listeners receive a price reduction?
   (A) follow the Instagram
   (B) buy to a certain number
   (C) talk to the gym coach
   (D) upload the pic to Instagram

73.Which of the following flavors is not mentioned in the advertisement?
   (A) coffee
   (B) chocolate
   (C) green tea
   (D) strawberry

74.Where is the video most likely taking place?
   (A) on a lager ship
   (B) on a canoe
   (C) on a small boat
   (D) at the river

75.Which of the following country's dish is not mentioned?
   (A) China
   (B) Germany
   (C) Korea
   (D) France

76.What is mentioned about the flagstone?
   (A) it's a valuable as the gold.
   (B) it's used to slice kimchi.
   (C) it can be used to bake food.
   (D) it has the same quality as the precious stone.

Best Kitchen Channel	
Dish	points
fried fish	25
barbecued crocodile meat	55
fruit salads	20
beef	45

77. Who most likely is the speaker addressing?
(A) students
(B) chefs
(C) audiences
(D) youtubers

 78. Look at the graph. Which finished dish earns the highest point?
(A) fish
(B) beef
(C) vegetables
(D) meat that we seldom consume

79. What is mentioned about red wine?
(A) it's from local inhabitants.
(B) it's a great blend with meat.
(C) it goes well with fruits.
(D) it will be the gift for followers.

Fashion & Design	
item	Fees for the youtuber
contact lenses	US 5 dollars
beach shorts	US 6 dollars
speedos	US 10 dollars
sunglass	US 8 dollars

80.Where most likely is the speaker?
(A) at the gym
(B) in the kitchen
(C) on the beach
(D) at the stream

 81.Look at the graph. Which is the most profitable for the youtuber?
(A) contact lenses
(B) beach shorts
(C) sunglass
(D) speedos

82.Which of the following is mentioned but not showcased in the video?
(A) sunglass
(B) contact lenses
(C) beach shorts
(D) speedos

Government's emergent aid/by helicopters	
time	Food and beverages
9:00 a.m.	Beef and pork
11:00 a.m.	Egg and butter
12:00 a.m.	milk
1 p.m.	Instant noodles

83. Who most likely are happy about the snowstorm?
(A) local residents
(B) students
(C) school principals
(D) officials at the Educational Bureau

84. Look at the graph. What will be provided to inhabitants at noon?
(A) beef
(B) egg
(C) instant noodles
(D) milk

85. Which of the following is not seen as a problem during the huge snow storm?
(A) electricity
(B) cars
(C) water
(D) food

86.Which of the following item is retrieved from an underwater creature?
(A) green crystal
(B) purple crystal
(C) pearls
(D) red crystal

87.According to the advertisement, which will attract fortune-seekers?
(A) red crystal
(B) pearls
(C) purple crystal
(D) green crystal

88.Which of the following item is currently out of stock?
(A) red crystal
(B) green crystal
(C) purple crystal
(D) yellow crystal

89.What kind of product is being advertised?
(A) fruits and vegetables
(B) vitamin tablets
(C) chicken soups
(D) diverse mushrooms

90.What will happen on the date prior to a major holiday?
(A) a cooking demonstration
(B) a free meal for the homeless
(C) cheaper prices of fruits
(D) quality chickens

91. What will be provided to visitors?
　(A) discounts
　(B) a cooking demonstration
　(C) a basket
　(D) free mushrooms

92. What is the main topic of the news report?
　(A) tourists happily view the performance with their kids
　(B) tourists applaud the authenticity of the show and upload enticing pics
　(C) a call for proper treatment of animals in the circus
　(D) a call for capturing an escaped young elephant instantly

93. What gadget is mentioned to record the show?
　(A) high-end cameras
　(B) telephones
　(C) cell phones
　(D) filming devices in the circus

94. What most likely will occur hours after the show?
　(A) tourists cheering for the performance
　(B) tourists uploading those click-baited photos
　(C) tourists finding an animal corpse outside the circus
　(D) tourists practicing using electrical guns

The Police Report	
Predicted Time	**Description**
8:42 a.m.	abnormality of the dashboard
8:45 a.m.	the plane losing control
8:46 a.m.	trying to remain at a certain height
8:47 a.m.	descended
8:48 a.m.	exploded

95.What is the main topic of the news report?
(A) a natural disaster
(B) a plane crash
(C) an anecdote told by a local villager
(D) the importance of the company's reputation

 96.Look at the graph. When did the plane land uncontrollably?
(A) 8:45 a.m.
(B) 8:42 a.m.
(C) 8:48 a.m.
(D) 8:47 a.m.

97.What could be the cause of the plane crash?
(A) a human error
(B) fowls
(C) a natural disaster
(D) an inexperienced pilot

98.Who most likely is the speaker addressing?
(A) jobseekers
(B) professors
(C) finalists
(D) experienced designers

99.Who could be the potential new hire?
   (A) experienced candidates with diverse portfolios
   (B) inexperienced interviewees with the great personality and potential
   (C) experienced candidates who have gone through three interviews
   (D) inexperienced interviewees without great portfolios

100.According to the manager, what will happen after going through four rounds of interviews?
   (A) getting hired
   (B) getting promoted
   (C) getting rejected
   (D) getting considered

第二回
模擬試題解析

 **Part 1**

聽力原文與中譯	
1. (A) A strict limit is set for people craving for the view. (B) **A reflection can be clearly seen.** (C) There are lots of people on the bridge. (D) The houses here are roofless.	1. (A) 對愛好此景的人有觀賞上的設限。 (B) **可以清楚地看到倒影。** (C) 許多人聚集在橋上。 (D) 這裡的房子是沒有屋頂的。
答案：(B)	

這題的話可以很清楚地看到橋上的倒影映在溪流上，故答案要選**選項B**。

聽力原文與中譯	
2. (A) No people are waiting to cross the road. (B) **The statue has been erected on the grass.** (C) There aren't any traffic lights in sight. (D) Flowers are in full bloom on the grass.	2. (A) 沒有人等著過馬路。 (B) **在草地上有雕像建立著。** (C) 視野所及沒有任何的交通號誌在。 (D) 在草地上的花朵正盛開。
答案：(B)	

解析

這題可以看到有個特別的雕像，但是題目並未描述特色，而是只大略地說明草地上有雕像，故要選**選項B**。

聽力原文與中譯

3.	3.
(A) There are two overpasses above pedestrians.	(A) 在行人上頭有兩個高架橋。
(B) **The statue has four stone elephants engraved onto it.**	(B) **雕像上有四個大象的雕飾在上頭。**
(C) People are forming different lines.	(C) 人們形成不同的隊列。
(D) There are flags fluttering over buildings.	(D) 在建築物上有旗幟飄揚著。

答案： (B)

解析

這題的話，在圖片的右側可以看到有柱子或雕像的物品，上頭有大象形狀的雕飾在上頭，故答案要選**選項B**。

聽力原文與中譯

4.	4.
(A) Lots of people are lining up outside the building.	(A) 在建築物外頭有許多人大排長龍。
(B) The revolving door is broken.	(B) 旋轉門是故障的。
(C) **Two statues have been. situated in the building.**	(C) **在建築物中，有兩個雕像佇立其中。**
(D) The security is sitting on a comfy chair.	(D) 保全正坐在舒適的椅子上。

答案： (C)

解析

這題可以看到在建築物內有兩個人形雕像，所以符合選項C的描述，故答案要選**選項C**。

5.

(A) **Several people are standing there appreciating these paintings.**

(B) These paintings are in consistent shapes.

(C) These paintings on the wall are slim pickings.

(D) There is a net preventing people from falling.

5.

(A) **有幾個人站在那裡欣賞這些畫。**

(B) 這些繪畫是一致的形狀。

(C) 這些牆上的繪畫寥寥可數。

(D) 有張網阻止人們跌落。

答案：(A)

 解析

這題也有些陷阱，不過可以看到的是有幾個人站在不同樓層的畫旁欣賞畫，所以答案要選**選項A**。

6.

(A) **There are face paints on the paintings.**

(B) Not all paintings are showcased in the human form.

(C) These paintings are significantly smaller than the people sitting next to them.

(D) All paintings are hung up on the wall.

6.

(A) **在畫上有臉部塗鴨。**

(B) 並非所有的畫都以人的形式展示出。

(C) 這些繪畫比起坐在一旁的人們顯得更小。

(D) 所有繪畫都掛在牆上。

答案：(A)

 解析

這題可以看到有很多幅畫，且畫吊掛在牆上，每幅畫都是人的臉，臉上有face paint之類的，故答案要選**選項A**。

PART 2

聽力原文與中譯	
7. Where is the warehouse? (A) The warehouse is exceedingly huge. (B) It can store many things. (C) **behind the maze.**	7. 倉庫在哪兒呢？ (A) 這間倉庫相當巨大。 (B) 它能夠儲藏許多東西。 (C) **在迷宮後方。**

答案：(C)

 解析

這題是詢問地點，要選擇有表達出位置的，故答案要選**選項C**。

聽力原文與中譯	
8. What is the groom's favorite dish? (A) **probably Boston lobsters.** (B) he doesn't know what that means. (C) in a night market.	8. 哪樣是新郎最喜愛的菜餚呢？ (A) **可能是波士頓龍蝦。** (B) 他不知道這意味著什麼。 (C) 在夜市裡頭。

答案：(A)

 解析

這題較為直接的答案是直接給考生項目或選項，故答案為**選項A**。

聽力原文與中譯	
9. How much does the maintenance cost you? (A) Unfortunately, we don't have the repair shop in town. (B) they don't have the best mechanics. (C) **zero. My insurance covers all.**	9. 維修費花你多少錢？ (A) 不幸的是，在小鎮裡頭，我們不需要維修店。 (B) 他們沒有最佳的機械工人。 (C) **零元。我的保險費負擔全額。**

答案：(C)

這題很直接的答案為給考生一個金額，也可能是較隱晦的答案這題答案要選**選項C**。

聽力原文與中譯	
10. How far is the distance from here to the King's Lake? (A) Probably 9 pounds. (B) **at a cursory glance. 19 kilometers.** (C) I'm not good at math.	10. 這裡到國王湖的距離有多遠呢？ (A) 可能是9磅重。 (B) **粗略估算下。19公里。** (C) 我數學不好。

答案：(B)

這題答案要選距離，答案也可能是先有其他描述再加上距離多遠，故答案為**選項B**。

聽力原文與中譯	
11. What did the realtor say about the corpse? (A) God. The property values will be affected. (B) The policemen did treat this as a crime scene. (C) **It's actually a prop from Halloween Party.**	11. 房仲人員怎麼説明屍體的部分？ (A) 天啊！地產的價值會受到影響。 (B) 警方曾把這裡視為犯罪現場。 (C) **這其實是萬聖節派對的道具。**

答案：(C)

這題要避免被其他干擾選項影響到，然後選個合理的解釋，故答案為**選項C**。

聽力原文與中譯

12. When can we dress as we please in school? (A) The principal is making a big deal about it. (B) **Every Friday.** (C) The campus cannot endure more color showing.	12. 我們何時能夠在學校裡頭隨我們高興的穿著呢？ (A) 校長正為此而小題大作一番。 (B) **每個星期五。** (C) 校園裡頭無法忍受更多的顏色展示著。

答案：(B)

 解析

這題要選一個時間點，故答案為**選項B**。

聽力原文與中譯

13. The fire needs to be dealt with ASAP. (A) I guess spreading some liquor is ok. (B) **Yes, call the fire department** (C) We have to invoke more rain...I told you	13. 大火需要立即處理。 (A) 我想撒些酒是可以的。 (B) **是的，打電話給消防局。** (C) 我告訴過你，我們必須要祈求更多的雨。

答案：(B)

 解析

這題要選回應或解決方案且要符合常理，故答案要選**選項B**。

聽力原文與中譯

14. Can you be the role model of our clinics? (A) Do I have to be pretty all the time? (B) The model looked in bad shape last year. (C) **I'm afraid not.**	14. 你可以當我們診所的模範模特兒嗎？ (A) 我必須要總是看起來很漂亮嗎？ (B) 去年的時候，那位模特兒看起來體態不佳。 (C) **我恐怕無法喔！**

答案：(C)

這題的答案很明顯是**選項C**，直接拒絕對方。

聽力原文與中譯	
15. Do you prefer to sit by the window or near the aisle? (A) Wow...the window is really dusty. (B) **As long as there is a seat, fine with me.** (C) You are being really difficult.	15. 你偏好靠窗的座位還是接近走道的？ (A) 哇！...這窗戶看起來相當多灰塵。 (B) **只要有座位我都無所謂的。** (C) 你真的是難伺候。

答案：(B)

這題也是二選一的答案，而通常答案是第三個選擇或只要有我都可以接受等等，故答案為**選項B**。

聽力原文與中譯	
16. We are asking for a direct verdict. (A) More witnesses are needed. (B) I think our attorney is not very professional. (C) **I hereby issue an injunction forbidding any production.**	16. 我們要求直接判決。 (A) 需要更多的目擊者。 (B) 我認為我們的律師並不是非常專業。 (C) **我因而宣佈發起一張禁制令禁制任何的產品生產。**

答案：(C)

這題要選法官所判決的一個結果，很明顯答案為**選項C**。

聽力原文與中譯

17. Can you pick me up at twelve? (A) You are not supposed to drive. (B) Twelve is my lucky number. Thanks. (C) **Twelve p.m. or twelve a.m.**	17. 你可以在12點時來接我嗎？ (A) 你不該開車的。 (B) 12是我的幸運號碼。謝謝。 (C) **午夜12點還是正午12點鐘呢？**

答案：(C)

 解析

這題答案可能是是或否，也可能是反問對方，也可能是確認一個時間點，故答案為**選項C**。

聽力原文與中譯

18. The food has to be ready for marine creatures. (A) Marine creatures are not friendly. (B) **That would require two hours top.** (C) Thank god. I'm not a big fan of seafood.	18. 給海洋生物的食物必須準備好了。 (A) 海洋生物不是很友善。 (B) **那將需要最多兩小時的時間準備。** (C) 謝天謝地。我不是海產的愛好者。

答案：(B)

 解析

這題要回答的是解釋所需的時間等等的，故答案為**選項B**。

聽力原文與中譯

19. Why are you a big fan of French dishes? (A) There are just a few things you can choose from. (B) French dishes are cheap in this restaurant. (C) **Because my mom is from France.**	19. 為什麼你是法國菜餚的愛好者？ (A) 可供你選擇的食物就只有這幾項。 (B) 在這間餐廳裡頭，法國菜餚是便宜的。 (C) **因為我的母親是來自於法國。**

答案：(C)

 解析

這題也是要選解釋或原因，故答案要選**選項C**。

聽力原文與中譯	
20. Where can I get to find the claw machine? (A) Oh...I really love the huge teddy bear. (B) **Every five blocks. I guess.** (C) I'm impressed by the guy.	20. 我在哪裡可以找到夾娃娃機呢？ (A) 噢！...我真的喜愛那隻泰迪熊。 (B) **我想，大概每五個街區。** (C) 那個男子令我印象深刻。

答案：(B)

 解析

這題有可能是提供一個明確的地點，也可能會是像選項B這樣的描述，故答案為**選項B**。

聽力原文與中譯	
21. Which countries will our sales reps be touring in their holiday? (A) They kind of fancy international countries. (B) **You can know the answer by viewing their IGs**. (C) Hope they enjoy their free time.	21. 我們的業務代表將會在假期期間旅遊哪個國家呢？ (A) 他們有點喜愛國際性的國家。 (B) **你可以從瀏覽他們的IG得知答案。** (C) 希望他們能夠享受他們自由的時間。

答案：(B)

 解析

這題也沒有明確提供一個答案，而是另一種的表達，故答案要選**選項B**。

聽力原文與中譯

22. Who is responsible for the canteen? (A) The flight attendants kind of like our food. (B) The roasted chicken will be served in an hour. (C) **The Italian guy with a chef hat**	22. 誰負責販賣部的？ (A) 空服員們有點喜歡我們的食物。 (B) 烤雞將於一個小時內上菜。 (C) **那位戴著廚師帽的義大利男子。**

答案：(C)

 解析

這題有明確的人物為誰，故答案要選**選項C**。

聽力原文與中譯

23. Haven't you been to China? (A) **No, but my mom did.** (B) I do love the koala there. (C) The panda looks so cute.	23. 你沒有到訪過中國嗎？ (A) **沒有，但是我媽媽曾去過。** (B) 我確實喜愛那裡的無尾熊。 (C) 貓熊看起來相當可愛。

答案：(A)

 解析

這題直接回答有或沒有，答案很明顯為**選項A**。

聽力原文與中譯

24. Have you given a thought about trying a rabbit meat? (A) **You mean the real rabbit...as the rabbit that roams on the grass?** (B) I can't find them in the kitchen...where are they? (C) but they are outrun by tortoises.	24. 你曾有過想嚐試下兔肉的念頭嗎？ (A) **你指的是真正的兔子...像是漫步在草地上的兔子嗎？** (B) 我在廚房裡頭找不到牠們...牠們去哪了呢？ (C) 但是牠們跑輸烏龜了。

答案：(A)

解析

這題也有些難度，沒有明確的回答，而是疑惑產生的反問句，故答案要選**選項A**。

聽力原文與中譯	
25. Would you mind pointing me in the right direction? (A) **Glad that I can help.** (B) Geography concepts are hard to recite. (C) God. You are weird.	25. 你介意幫我指向正確的方位嗎？ (A) **很高興我能幫到這個忙。** (B) 地理概念很難背。 (C) 天啊！你好奇怪。

答案：(A)

 解析

這題可能是給對方一個明確的方向，也可能是先表達出願意幫忙等等，故答案要選**選項A**。

聽力原文與中譯	
26. When will the employee payment be transferred? (A) **Why ask me? Ask our accountant.** (B) The company cannot pay the salary this month. (C) I'm considering taking the transfer in the company.	26. 員工的薪資會於何時轉帳？ (A) **為什麼問我呢？問我們的會計人員。** (B) 公司無法支付這個月的薪資。 (C) 我正考慮在公司內調換部門。

答案：(A)

解析

這題有可能提供給對方一個答案，也可能是出於不知道答案或疑惑對方怎麼會問自己，不是詢問真的知道答案的人，也要注意其他干擾選項，故答案為**選項A**。

聽力原文與中譯

27. Please get the aquarium manager on line. (A) The manager doesn't have a good temper. (B) I went to the aquarium and had a blast. (C) **I'll get right on it.**	27. 請讓水族館的經理接電話。 (A) 經理脾氣不好。 (B) 我去了水族館且玩得很盡興。 (C) **我馬上去辦。**

答案：(C)

這題是個指示，很明顯答案為**選項C**。

聽力原文與中譯

28. Why did Cindy get promoted as the head of the department? (A) The CEO is leaning on our department even more. (B) I cherish every opportunity for getting promoted. (C) **She bribed the CFO.**	28. 為什麼辛蒂升職成部門的主管呢？ (A) 執行長更仰賴我們部門了。 (B) 我珍惜每個升遷的機會。 (C) **她賄賂財務長。**

答案：(C)

這題要選原因，答案很明顯是**選項C**，儘管有些負面。

聽力原文與中譯

29. How long can I use this Easy Card? (A) You can get it in the convenience store. (B) It can deposit lots of money (C) **As long as you please**	29. 我使用悠遊卡的期限有多長呢？ (A) 你可以在便利商店裡購得。 (B) 它能夠存許多錢。 (C) **只要你高興。**

答案：(C)

解析

這題也是沒有提供明確答案，而是另一種的回答，故答案為**選項C**。

聽力原文與中譯	
30. Personal shoppers rely heavily on commissions. (A) They are getting exploited by the company. (B) The coat is high on the customer's list. (C) **Then they have to bring it.**	30. 個人購物者很大程度地仰賴佣金。 (A) 他們正受到公司的剝削。 (B) 大衣是顧客想購得的商品清單上。 (C) **那麼他們就要使出渾身解數。**

答案：(C)

解析

這題要選接續主題表達的語句，故答案要選**選項C**。

聽力原文與中譯	
31. Shouldn't diamond rings and gold necklaces be stashed in the safe? (A) The safe remains locked, so don't worry. (B) **Unfortunately, it's broken.** (C) The jewelry shop deemed our expensive items quite valuable.	31. 鑽石戒指和金項鍊不是該儲藏在保險箱裡頭嗎？ (A) 保險箱仍鎖著，所以不要擔心。 (B) **不幸的是，它損壞了。** (C) 珠寶店認為我們得昂貴物品相當有價值。

答案：(B)

解析

這題是詢問原因，答案要選一個解釋，故答案為**選項B**。

 **PART 3**

聽力原文和對話

Questions 32-34 refer to the following conversation

Rachel: hello...this is Rachel Collins...I'm a student majoring in biology...I'd like to apply for the stay in Best National Park for three months...

Jack: why...and for what purpose?

Rachel: for a research purpose...I do need to write a report about bison, wolves, and brown bears...please don't turn me down

Jack: ...the thing is the deadline is yesterday...and we don't validate students' research project...

Rachel: ..but I'm with two professors...they will be with me during the whole summer...

Jack: ..why don't you tell your professors and let them do the phone call...the sooner the better...and I'm not sure my supervisor is going to permit the paperwork after the deadline...

Rachel: ...you've gotta help me out here...

Jack: ...since there are no research teams applying this year...perhaps you can pull it off...

Rachel: ...thanks...that's all I need to hear...

問題32-34，請參考以下對話內容

瑞秋：嗨...這是瑞秋・柯林斯...我是主修生物學的學生...我想要申請待在倍斯特國家公園三週...

傑克：為什麼...是以甚麼性質的目的呢？

瑞秋：是研究的性質...我確實需要撰寫關於北美野牛、狼群和棕熊的報告...請別拒絕我...。

傑克：...昨日就是截止日期了...而且我們不承認學生研究的正當性...。

瑞秋：但是我會跟兩個教授同行...在這整個夏天的期間我的兩位教授都會陪同我...

傑克：為什麼你不告訴你的教授且讓他們致電...越快越好...而且我也不確定我的主管在截止日期後會批准這份文件...。

瑞秋：你一定要幫幫我...

傑克：...既然今年沒有研究團隊申請...或許你可能成功...

瑞秋：...謝謝...這就是我所需要聽到的...

試題中譯與解析	
32. Which of the following is not the intended animals for the student's research? (A) bison. (B) **foxes.** (C) wolves. (D) brown bears.	32. 下列哪項動物並非學生意圖研究的對象呢？ (A) 北美野牛。 (B) **狐狸。** (C) 狼。 (D) 棕熊。
33. What can be predicted about the outcome of the application? (A) with the help of the employee there, she has nothing to worry about. (B) **she still has a shot.** (C) if other research teams are willing to make room for her, her application will be accepted. (D) she will put it off by talking to the employee's supervision directly.	33. 關於申請的結果可能預測出什麼呢？ (A) 有了員工的幫助，她沒有什麼好擔心的。 (B) **她仍有申請成功的機會。** (C) 如果其他研究團隊願意將位子讓出的話，她的申請就會通過。 (D) 藉由直接與員工的頂頭上司洽談，她的申請將會通過。
34. Why does the woman say, "you've gotta help me out here"? (A) because she really needs help. (B) because saying that usually works. (C) **to plead the employee to see if there is still a chance.** (D) to sway the decision.	34. 為何女子提到「you've gotta help me out here」？ (A) 因為她真的需要幫助。 (B) 因為説那些話通常有用。 (C) **向該員工懇求看是否仍有機會。** (D) 動搖決定。

答案：32. B 33. B 34. C

解析

- **第32題**，學生有提到了研究的三種生物bison, wolves, and brown bears，很明顯答案是**選項B**。
- **第33題**，這題的話要看到對話後段的部分，其實負責的員工跟女子聊天的最後有提到或許還有機會，所以答案為**選項B**。其他選項也有誘答和干擾的成分在也要小心。
- **第34題**，女子講這句話時其實有點懇求的成分在，且希望能有一絲希望。其他選項雖有部分提到但並不是主因，例如選項A的真的需要幫助，女子是需要幫助，但講這句話更是出於拜託對方等等的，而選項D的sway也不全然是主因，雖然該員工有可能因此動容而看有什麼能幫忙的部分，但女子並無法sway對方最後決定。

聽力原文和對話

Questions 35-37 refer to the following conversation

Jason: triple latte...you must be really tiresome...

Cindy: ...what can I say it keeps me awake...

Jason: are you also on that roster...?

Cindy: no...everyone...but me...I guess they will fly for long-haul for the following months...but I will fly for domestic locations though...it's not that I didn't do well for the in-flight training...there are still plenty of things for us to learn...since we are new here...what about you...?

Jason: I'm going to Africa on Friday...

Cindy: oh...that sure is a long flight...and I almost forgot that you are a pilot...that's an enormous pressure.

Jason: flying to some long-haul destinations is...exhausting...you have to be attentive...

Cindy: cool...I guess we will have to meet serendipitously

Jason: perhaps...probably

問題35-37，請參考以下對話內容

傑森：三倍濃縮拿鐵...你是真的相當累

辛蒂：...我能說什麼呢...它讓我醒著...

傑森：你也在值勤名單上嗎...？

辛蒂：不...每個人都是...但我除外...我想在接下來數個月，他們都會飛長途...但我會飛國內地點...這並不是我在機內訓練中沒有表現好... 既然我們都是新來的...仍然還有很多事情是我們要學習的...你呢？

傑森：我週五要前往非洲

辛蒂：喔...那真的是長途飛行...而且我幾乎忘記你是駕駛員了...那有很龐大的壓力在...

傑森：...飛往有些長途的目的地是...令人感到筋疲力盡的...你必須要專注...。

辛蒂：好酷...我想我們就只能憑緣分遇見了...

傑森：或許...可能吧

試題中譯與解析

35. Why does the man say, "are you also on that roster..."? (A) because he wants the woman to be on the same flight. (B) because he wants the woman to be responsible. (C) **just a casual talk for people who are in the same industry.** (D) because the woman doesn't seem to like a long haul material.	35. 為何男子提及「are you also on that roster...」？ (A) 因為他想要女子在同個班機上。 (B) 因為他想要女子對此負責任。 (C) **只是在同個產業工作者相遇時的閒話家常。** (D) 因為該女子似乎不像是能飛長途班機的料。
36. What is the man's profession? (A) an operator. (B) **a captain.** (C) a flight attendant. (D) a ground crew.	36. 男子的職業為何？ (A) 操作員。 (B) **機長。** (C) 空服員。 (D) 地勤人員。

37. Why does the woman say, "I guess we will have to meet serendipitously"?
(A) to show that their meeting is a serendipitous encounter.
(B) to end the unpleasant conversation.
(C) to demonstrate they are meant to be together.
(D) **to leave the imagination for both parties.**

37. 為何女子提及「I guess we will have to meet serendipitously」?
(A) 顯示他們的碰面是個奇遇。
(B) 結束不愉快的對談。
(C) 顯示出他們命中注定要在一起。
(D) **讓雙方都留下想像空間。**

答案：35. C 36. B 37. D

解析

- **第35題**，僅是詢問的話語，非常像是兩個在相同領域工作的人之間的閒話家常。
- **第36題**，對話中有提到男子是pilot，選項中替換成了captain，故答案為**選項B**。
- **第37題**，其他幾個選項均不太正確，其實講這句話有點是預留些空間給彼此，而且確實是不知道下次會於何時再遇見對方，故**選項D**是最合適的。而選項中出現跟試題相似或相同的字，該選項幾乎是錯誤或誘答的選項，例如選項A。

聽力原文和對話

Questions 38-40 refer to the following conversation

Cindy: I'm still trying to fit in here...however...I do love some of the drinks in the canteen...though...it's still odd to drink pearl milk tea in the Dubai version

Candy: that's so hard to believe...how many dishes in your meal...you need to dial down for a bit...there is no photoshop in real life...and this morning you barely fitted into the uniform. There is a reason why airline companies prefer females over males...women are lighter...that means...less gasoline consumed...stop eating...the company is not happy about staff being overweight...

Cindy: perhaps trying that spicy dish later...

Candy: I'm still feeling the pressure of flying long-haul and being away from home...

Cindy: relax...try this...it goes really well with mango juice..

Candy: thanks...though...I don't wanna puke in the economy class while serving water to the customer...

問題38-40，請參考以下對話內容

辛蒂：我仍試著要適應這裡的環境...可是...儘管如此...我卻喜愛著販賣部有些飲品...喝著杜拜版本的珍珠奶茶仍是怪怪的。

糖糖：真的令人有點難以相信...你餐點有幾道菜餚呀...你有點需要節制下了...在現實生活中沒有photoshop這軟體的...而且今天一早你幾乎快穿不下制服了。航空公司傾向聘用女性大於聘請男性是有原因的...女性體重較輕...這意謂著要消耗的汽油更少...別再吃了... 對於職員體重過重，公司是會感到不太高興的...

辛蒂：或許等等試試看那道辣的菜餚好了。

糖糖：我正因為要飛長途感到有壓力而且離家遠...。

辛蒂：放鬆點...試這個看看...這跟芒果汁好搭喔...。

糖糖：謝謝囉...儘管如此...我不想要在經濟艙服侍客人水的時候吐了

試題中譯與解析

38. Why does the woman say, "there is no photoshop in real life"? (A) because she is not good at photoshop. (B) because she wants to perfect the skill of photoshop. (C) **to remind her friend software things can't fix things in the real world.** (D) because she uses too many photo-editing software.	38. 為何女子提到「there is no photoshop in real life」？ (A) 因為她不擅長photoshop的軟體。 (B) 因為她想要完善photoshop的技巧。 (C) **提醒她朋友軟體這種東西沒辦法修復現實中的變化。** (D) 因為她使用了太多的修圖軟體了。

39. Which of the following vocabulary is the synonym of overweight? (A) obedient. (B) opaque. (C) greasy. (D) **obese.**	39. 下列哪個字彙是「overweight」的同義字呢？ (A) 順從的。 (B) 半透明的。 (C) 油膩的。 (D) **肥胖的。**
40. Where most likely is the conversation taking place? (A) **at the restaurant.** (B) at the office. (C) at the boarding gate. (D) on the airplane.	40. 這段對話最有可能發生在何處？ (A) **在餐廳。** (B) 在辦公室。 (C) 在登機口。 (D) 在飛機上。

答案：38. C 39. D 40. A

 解析

- 第**38**題，這句話其實是個比喻，現實生活中確實沒辦法像是虛擬世界那樣有修圖軟體可以改，女子也是要提醒對方要注意些呀，只是用比較生動的比喻，所以最合適的選項是**選項C**。
- 第**39**題，這題是選同義字，所以答案很明顯是**選項D**。
- 第**40**題，這題是詢問地點，而其實最有可能的地點是在餐廳，雖然兩個人均是空服員，但是一開始就有提到兩個人是在販賣部，還有坐下來點餐和用餐的部分，所以別選成在飛機上或登機口了，所以最合適的選項是**選項A**。

聽力原文和對話

Questions 41-43 refer to the following conversation

Principal: your son looks lovely. How old is he?

Mom: he is four.

Principal: he seems shy and introvert...though

Mom: once he is familiar with the surroundings...you will know how chatty and outgoing he is.

Dad: will there be any tests for him?

Principal: actually, there is...our interviewer will ask him a few questions and of course he has to answer that himself in the room...all the while you get to see your kid through a transparent glass wall...

Dad: sounds great...I do hope it's not something too hard...though...he is only four...

Principal: just don't worry about it...and please fill out the questionnaire for me...and I will ask my assistant to take him to the room.

Mom: ...sure

問題41-43，請參考以下對話內容

校長：你兒子看起來很可愛。他幾歲了呢？

媽媽：他四歲。

校長：他似乎害羞且內向...的説。

媽媽：一旦他熟悉環境...你就知道他有多多話且有多外向。

爸爸：他會有任何的考試嗎？

校長：實際上，有的...我們的面試官會詢問他幾個問題而當然他必須要在房間裡頭回答...而與此同時你們可以透過透明的玻璃牆看到你的小孩...。

爸爸：聽起來不錯...我希望這不會太難...儘管他才四歲...。

校長：就別擔心囉...而且請替我填上這份問卷...然後我請我的助理將他帶至面試間。

媽媽：...當然。

試題中譯與解析

41. What are the speakers talking about?	41. 説話者所談論的是什麼？
(A) interview the applicant and his family.	(A) 面試申請者和他的家庭。
(B) **a brief talk of getting to know the applicant.**	(B) **逐步認識申請者的簡介。**
(C) explanation for the son's personality.	(C) 解釋他兒子的個性。
(D) a transparent glass wall.	(D) 透明的玻璃牆。

42. What is the father worried about? (A) the tuition fee is expensive. (B) the son has to do the test individually. (C) **the test being too difficult.** (D) the test taking too long.	42. 對話中的父親所擔心的是什麼？ (A) 學費是昂貴的。 (B) 兒子必須獨自完成考試。 (C) **考試過難。** (D) 考試時間過久。
43. What is required for the parents to do? (A) help their son cheat. (B) calm their son. (C) go to the test room with him. (D) **fill in the needed information.**	43. 父母必須要做什麼呢？ (A) 幫助他兒子作弊。 (B) 安撫他兒子。 (C) 跟他兒子一起去考試場所。 (D) **填所需資訊的表格。**

答案：41. B 42. C 43. D

解析

- **第41題**，其實這個對話是校長和家長間的閒聊跟大概認識一下彼此，還沒到面試的階段，最適合的答案為**選項B**，其他選項都不太適合或只是對話中的細節點。
- **第42題**，男子的父親有提到擔心的點是怕考試會過難，hard和difficult為同義字，這個同義轉換相信對考生來說不難。
- **第43題**，這題的話需要掌握更進階的理解，對話中有要求該父母要填問卷，填問卷換成了選項D的敘述，故答案為**選項D**。

聽力原文和對話

Questions 44-46 refer to the following conversation

Assistant: I guess I will leave you here...and on the table there are drinks and desserts for you...sit straight...and don't be afraid of talking...

Interviewer: hi...my name is Cindy...how does the chocolate taste like?

Kid: Peter..

Interviewer: bitter?...how about the drink? Can you describe a little bit about it?

Kid: sweet

Interviewer:...and?

Kid:...tasty...

Interviewer: great...hey look...I have two clips about bears to show you...it's in my smartphone...wait a second...

Interviewer: ..don't you think they look lovely...?

Kid: yes...

Interviewer: ...what's the creature that they are holding right now...

Kid: crabs...

Interviewer: ...excellent...now I want you to read this short paragraph for me...

Kid:...ok...

Interviwer: it's kind of on and off...but ok...I guess we have to take a short break...

問題44-46，請參考以下對話內容

助理：我想我就將你放在這了...而在桌上有替你準備了飲料和甜點...坐直了...且不要懼怕交談...。

面試官：嗨...我的名字是辛蒂...這個巧克力嚐起來如何呢？

小孩：彼得...。

面試官：苦的？...那關於這個飲料呢？你可以描述一下嗎...？

小孩：甜的。

面試官：...然後呢？

面試官：可口的...。

小孩：很棒...嗨...瞧...我有兩則熊的視頻要展示給你看...在我的智慧型手機裡頭...。

面試官：你不覺得牠們看起來可愛嗎？

小孩：是啊！...。

面試官：他們現在手上正握著什麼呢？

小孩：螃蟹...。

面試官：好極了...現在我想要你閱讀這個短段落給我聽...。

小孩：好的...。

面試官：這有點斷斷續續的...但是好的...我想我們必須要短暫的休息一下...。

試題中譯與解析

44. Which of the following is the device that interviewer uses? (A) a TV. **(B) a cellphone.** (C) a camera. (D) a telephone.	44. 下列哪個裝置是面試官所使用的呢? (A) 電視。 **(B) 手機。** (C) 照相機。 (D) 電話。
45. Which of the following is creatures that are grasped in the video? (A) lobsters. **(B) crabs.** (C) bear cubs. (D) bears.	45. 在視頻中,下列哪個生物被抓住? (A) 龍蝦。 **(B) 螃蟹。** (C) 熊幼獸。 (D) 熊。
46. What is the task given that requires brainstorming? (A) answer questions after viewing the clip. (B) read the paragraph. (C) view the clip. **(D) describe the drink.**	46. 哪一項所給予的任務需要集思廣益呢? (A) 在觀看視頻後回答問題。 (B) 閱讀文章段落。 (C) 觀看視頻。 **(D) 描述飲品。**

答案:44. B 45. B 46. D

解析

- **第44題**,面試中,面試官有使用手機讓小孩觀看視頻,所以smartphone 對應到cellphone,故答案為**選項B**。
- **第45題**,視頻中有提到熊和螃蟹,但要注意的點是,題目問的是grasped,被熊抓住的是螃蟹,所以答案要選螃蟹,**選項B**。
- **第46題**,試題中提到了集思廣益的部分,其實就是需要思考的部分,所以可以看四個選項中那個部分是需要思考的,其實描述飲品的部分,通常資優的幼兒園要求的是一大段的描述不像對話中僅是一個單字表示感受,且要展現出組織文句等的表達力很明顯答案為**選項D**。像是B的話其實是照著唸一段文章,這部分不需要花額外心思去想就能達到。

Questions 47-49 refer to the following conversation

Bulletin board/African trip	
titles	O/X
All story editors	O
All photographers	X
All software programmers	X
Executives	O
All accountants	X
New recruits	X

Cindy: I can't believe that we are doing this? Visiting the National Park for two whole weeks...I'm so excited...

Mark: me too...after weeks of late-nights in the office...we deserve a break...

John: but that's not the purpose that we are there though...we have to emulate the movement of every African animals and use those to make our visuals more convincing to audiences...

Cindy: ...still...we can view the beautiful scenery and breathe some new air...it's gonna be great for the result of our film...

Mark: what should we bring?...perhaps filming something for later use...in case we cannot capture a certain movement at the moment...

Cindy: ...I'm going to check my passport to see if it needs to be renewed...just in case...

John: ...don't be so thrilled...not yet...only eight people in our department will be chosen for the African trip...

Cindy: ...you are such a killjoy

問題47-49，請參考以下對話內容

佈告欄／非洲之旅	
標題	O/X
所有故事編輯	O
所有攝影師	X
所有軟體工程師	X
業務主管	O
所有會計人員	X
新招募人員	X

辛蒂：我不敢相信我們即將要從事這件事？參訪國家公園整整兩週...我感到很興奮...。

馬克：我也是...在辦公室裡幾週的晚上加班...我們值得這個休息。

約翰：但是那不是我們到這裡來的目的囉...我們必須要模仿每個非洲動物的動作而且用那些動作使得我們的視覺效果更加令觀眾信服...。

辛蒂：...我們仍會瀏覽美麗的風景和呼吸一些新空氣...這對於我們的電影來説會是很棒的結果。

馬克：我們應該要攜帶什麼呢？...或許拍攝一些東西在稍後能用上的...以防我們無法在某個當下捕捉到特定的動作...。

辛蒂：...我正要檢查我的護照，看是否需要更新...以防萬一...。

約翰：...別太興奮了...還沒呢...我們部門之中僅有八個人能被選中這次的非洲之旅...。

辛蒂：...你真的很掃興...。

試題中譯與解析

47. Where most likely is the conversation taking place? (A) at the travel agency. (B) at the National Park. (C) at a theater. **(D) at an animation studio.**	47. 對話最有可能發生在何處呢？ (A) 在旅行社。 (B) 在國家公園。 (C) 在戲院。 **(D) 在動畫工作室。**

48. What is the main purpose of this trip? (A) the benefit of the company. (B) **to make their work more believable.** (C) to relax after ongoing exhausted work. (D) to breathe some new air.	48. 什麼是此次旅行的主要目的呢？ (A) 公司的福利。 (B) **使他們的工作令人感到信服。** (C) 在持續累人的工作後的放鬆。 (D) 呼吸些新鮮空氣。
49. Look at the graph. Who will be going to this trip? (A) programmers. (B) accountants. (C) rookies. (D) **editors.**	49. 請參考圖表。誰將前往此次的旅行呢？ (A) 工程師。 (B) 會計師。 (C) 菜鳥。 (D) **編輯。**

答案：47. D 48. B 49. D

解析

- **第47題**，這題需要注意到細節點，一開始提到要去國家公園參訪，但對話中的人物不在那頭，還沒啟程。也不可能是在旅行社或是戲院。另外根據約翰講到的部分等等可以推斷，他們最可能是在動畫工作室工作，故答案為**選項D**。
- **第48題**，這題是詢問主旨，也可以定位到約翰講話的部分we have to emulate the movement of every African animals and use those to make our visuals **more convincing to audiences**...，這部分對應到選項B的部分，故答案為**選項B**。
- **第49題**，圖表題的部分可以很清楚看到editors是O所以會去這次的旅行，故答案為**選項D**。而選項C的rookies其實就是new recruits的同義轉換。

聽力原文和對話

Questions 50-52 refer to the following conversation

Boss: after some deliberation, we have come to a consensus that software programmers and photographers will be going to the African trip...a fortnight trip...

Cindy: I'm a story editor...so I'm always on the list...this announcement clearly has nothing to do with me...

Mark: deep down...I have this odd feeling that it's not going to be that easy...

Boss: ...during this trip...all editors need to focus...the date of released film is prior to our original date...which will be four months earlier...so there is going to be a really tight deadline...

Mark: ...I knew it...they are not going to spend the money that easy...

Cindy: ...how hard can it be...relax...I already have the concept in mind...this trip is going to be great...traveling...while thinking of something great for the storylines....

問題50-52，請參考以下對話內容

老闆：在經過一些深思熟慮後，我們已經達成了共識，就是軟體計劃師和攝影師也會參與非洲之旅...為期14天的旅程...。

辛蒂：我是故事編輯...所以我總會在名單上頭...這個宣告全然跟我毫無關係...。

馬克：在心底...我有種很怪的感覺是，此趟行程不會這樣的簡單...。

老闆：...在這次的旅行期間...所有的編輯都需要專注...電影上映的日期比我們原先預定的日期更早了...也就是提前了4個月的時程...所以截止日期會是更緊密的...。

馬克：...我就知道...他們不會那麼隨易花這筆錢...。

辛蒂：...能有多難呢？...放鬆些...在心底我已經有了一些概念了...這次的旅程一定會很棒...旅行...而順道構想些棒的題材當作故事情節...。

試題中譯與解析	
50. How long does the entire trip take? (A) 10 days. (B) **14 days.** (C) A week. (D) 4 days.	50. 整個旅程花費多長的時間呢？ (A) 10 天。 (B) **14 天。** (C) 一週。 (D) 4 天。

51. Why does the man say, "there is going to be a really tight deadline"? (A) because the budget is too short to shoot for a long time. (B) because the story editors speed up to meet the deadline. (C) **because the time will be four months shorter.** (D) because the film company changes the date.	51. 為什麼男子提到「there is going to be a really tight deadline」？ (A) 因為預算太少而無法拍攝太久。 (B) 因為故事編輯們加快速度趕截止日期。 (C) **因為時間會比預期的少四個月。** (D) 因為電影公司更改了日期。
52. Who will not be going to this trip? (A) story editors. (B) **the boss.** (C) programmers. (D) photographers.	52. 誰將不會參加此次的旅行呢？ (A) 故事編輯。 (B) **老闆。** (C) 工程師。 (D) 攝影師。

答案：50. B 51. C 52. B

解析

- 第50題，這題要掌握的是**fortnight**這個字，代表的是兩週，即14天，故答案為**選項B**。
- 第51題，這題可以定位到老闆講話的部分，所以很明顯答案是**選項C**。
- 第52題，這題的話要用刪去法，在一開始有講到有兩個職位，原先設定是不同行的，而後來卻更改成同行，還有一點是女子説的story editors的部分，所以只剩選項B了，答案要選**選項B**。

聽力原文和對話

Questions 53-55 refer to the following conversation

Cindy: ...Serengeti is huge and breathtaking...and the truck we are taking isn't so bad...is that a cheetah on the road...that's so close...

Mark: ...I heard we are going to take a small plane in the afternoon...and then walk in the nearby village to see if we can get to know the local surroundings.

Cindy: ...sounds great...it's really sweltering hot over here...I wish I could have the coconut water...right now..

Mark: ...it's dazzling...after...staring at zebras for a long time...no wonder the stripes have the effects of disturbing the flies...

Cindy: ...yeah...elementary school biology...and where are ostriches...looking at those lions makes me sleepy...

Mark: ...I saw some meerkats...perhaps a few meerkats stealing something from a pride of lions could work in a scene...kids love meerkats...

Cindy: ...it's raining...I guess we will be back to the camp and wait till the weather is better...

問題53-55，請參考以下對話內容

辛蒂：...賽倫蓋地巨大且令人屏息...而且我們要乘坐的卡車並不差...在路上的那頭是獵豹嗎？...真的靠的好近...。

馬克：我聽說我們下午即將搭乘小型飛機...而且之後會走進鄰近的村莊裡頭，去看我們是否能更進一步地了解當地環境。

辛蒂：...聽起來很棒...這裡真的相當的悶熱...但願我能有杯椰子水...馬上有。

馬克：...這令人感到暈眩...在凝視班馬一長段時間後...難怪條紋能有干擾蒼蠅的效果...。

辛蒂：...是呀...小學的生物學課...而且鴕鳥去哪了呢？...看著那些獅子讓我昏昏欲睡...。

馬克：我看見一些貓鼬...或許幾隻貓鼬從獅群中竊取東西適用於一個場景中...小孩喜愛貓鼬...。

辛蒂：...下雨了...我想我們要回到營帳那了並等到天氣變好了...。

試題中譯與解析

| 53. Which of the following is not what speakers do during the trip?
(A) walking long distance.
(B) **animal riding.**
(C) taking the vehicle.
(D) having an air travel. | 53. 下列哪項不是說話者在旅行期間會從事的項目？
(A) 長途跋涉。
(B) **動物騎乘。**
(C) 搭交通工具。
(D) 空中旅遊。 |

54. What is the function of the Zebra stripes? (A) to make the flies sleepy. (B) **to distract the flies.** (C) to attract more flies. (D) to kill some flies.	54. 什麼是斑馬條紋的功用？ (A) 讓蒼蠅昏昏欲睡。 (B) **使蒼蠅分心。** (C) 吸引更多的蒼蠅。 (D) 殺死一些蒼蠅。
55. Which of the following animal is not seen in the conversation? (A) meerkats. (B) zebras. (C) lions. (D) **ostriches.**	55. 下列哪項動物並沒有在對話中出現呢？ (A) 蒙哥。 (B) 斑馬。 (C) 獅子。 (D) **鴕鳥。**

答案：53. B 54. B 55. D

解析

- **第53題**，這題是詢問相關細節點，其實並沒有談到選項B，故答案為**選項B**。
- **第54題**，這題是詢問功能，答案很明顯是**選項B**，其中distract = disturb。
- **第55題**，這題也不難，刪掉為看到的動物，其實有提到沒看到鴕鳥，故答案為**選項D**。

聽力原文和對話

Questions 56-58 refer to the following conversation

Employee: ...Best Aquarium...how can I help you?

Cindy: ...I'm the job applicant...I have sent my resume and the cover letter to your HR department last Thursday...but I haven't got any reply since...

Employee: ...normally,...there are too many applicants...and the screening process is long...unfortunately...there are only a few employees in our HR department...I'm sure you can understand that...it's not that they don't want to reply to the message...

Cindy: ...I am sorry about that...I'm just too eager to know the result...to see if I get to have a chance to attend the interview...

Employee: ...I heard that they are going to make the announcement next month...which is in December...

Cindy: ...that's wonderful...I can wait...I'm currently working part-time at Starbucks...

Employee: ...that's great...and good luck with everything...now I have to get back to work...

問題56-58，請參考以下對話內容

員工：...倍斯特水族館...我能夠幫你什麼呢？

辛蒂：...我是工作申請者...我已經寄了我的履歷和cover letter到你們的人事部門...但是我並未收到你們任何的回覆...。

員工：...通常...有太多的申請者了...而且篩選的過程很長...不幸的是目前我們人事部門僅有幾位員工...相信你可以了解這點的...並不是他們不想要回覆訊息...。

辛蒂：...對此我感到很抱歉...我太渴望想要得知結果了...看看我是否能夠有機會能夠參加面試...。

員工：...我聽說他們會於下個月公告...也就是12月的時候...。

辛蒂：...那太棒了...我可以等...我現在正在星巴克從事兼職的工作...。

員工：...太棒了...祝一切順利...現在我要弄手邊的工作了...。

試題中譯與解析

| 56. Why does the woman make the phone call?
(A) to make a complaint.
(B) to talk to the HR personnel.
(C) to confirm the date of the interview.
(D) **to inquire a few things about the application.** | 56. 為何女子會打這通電話？
(A) 為了抱怨。
(B) 為了跟人事專員談話。
(C) 確認面試的日期。
(D) **詢問關於申請的幾件事情。** |
| 57. When will the applicant know the outcome?
(A) October.
(B) November.
(C) **December.**
(D) January. | 57. 何時申請者會知道結果？
(A) 10月。
(B) 11月。
(C) **12月。**
(D) 1月。 |

58. Where is the place that the caller currently working at?	58. 來電者現在正在哪裡服務呢？
(A) at another Aquarium.	(A) 在另一間水族館。
(B) at the HR Department.	(B) 在人事部門。
(C) **at the coffee shop.**	(C) **在咖啡店。**
(D) at the restaurant.	(D) 在餐廳。

答案：56. D 57. C 58. C

解析

- **第56題**，這題也不難，有幾個選項為干擾選項，最後可以得知選項為**選項D**。
- **第57題**，這題也是，很明顯有提到是在12月會知道結果，故答案為**選項C**。
- **第58題**，這題要理解的部分有女子提到的在星巴克工作，所以可以得知要選咖啡店，故答案為**選項C**。

聽力原文和對話

Questions 59-61 refer to the following conversation

Best Aquarium	
descriptions	time
renovation	**July** 10 2021 – **Sep** 10 2021
exhibition	**Sep** 15 2021 – **Sep** 25 2021
Science Project Contest	**Sep** 27 2021 – **Sep** 30 2021
Wedding/governor Kim	**Oct** 20 2021

Employee: ...Best Aquarium...how can I help you?

Cindy: ...I'm the PR of ABC Drug Store...probably you've heard about our company...I'd like to book the entire Aquarium for the wedding venue...

Employee: ...normally...we don't lease our venue for that kind of purpose...

Cindy: ...can I talk to your manager or the head of the department... Mary Wang

Employee: ...definitely...I can direct the call for you...please wait for a few seconds...

Mary: ...Best Aquarium...this is Mary Wang speaking...

Cindy: ...I'm Cindy...from ABC Drug Store...remember...

Mary: ...it's been a long time...

Cindy: ...my boss would like to book the Aquarium for the wedding purpose...

Mary: ...wow...that sounds like a grand wedding...but the main building is under renovation so when is the wedding to be exact...

Cindy: ...April 8 2022...don't tell me that it's too late...don't let me down

問題59-61，請參考以下對話內容

倍斯特水族館	
描述	時間
裝修	**July** 10 2021 – **Sep** 10 2021
展覽	**Sep** 15 2021 – **Sep** 25 2021
科學計畫比賽	**Sep** 27 2021 – **Sep** 30 2021
婚宴/州長金	**Oct** 20 2021

員工：...倍斯特水族館...我能夠幫你什麼呢？

辛蒂：...我是ABC藥品店的公關人員...可能您有聽過關於我們公司...我想要訂整間水族館當作婚禮的場地...。

員工：...通常我們不租借場地用於那樣的目的...。

辛蒂：...我可以跟你們的經理或部門主管談談嗎？...瑪莉・王。

員工：...當然可以...我可以幫您轉接電話...請等幾秒鐘...。

瑪莉：...倍斯特水族館...這是瑪莉・王...。

辛蒂：...我是辛蒂... ABC藥品店的...記得了嗎...。

瑪莉：...真的好久了...。

辛蒂：...我的老闆想要訂水族館作為婚宴的性質...。

瑪莉：哇！...聽起來像是盛大的婚宴...但是主要大樓正在裝修...所以確切的婚宴日期是什麼時候呢？

辛蒂：...2022年4月8日...別跟我說這太晚喔...別讓我失望了。

59. Why does the woman make the phone call? (A) to purchase the Aquarium. (B) **to book the Aquarium.** (C) to lease the Aquarium. (D) to confirm the date of the wedding.	59.為什麼女子要打這通電話？ (A) 購買水族館。 (B) **租訂水族館。** (C) 租借水族館。 (D) 確認婚宴的日期。
60. Look at the graph. When could be the date that announces the champion of the Science Project Contest? (A) July 10 2021. (B) **Sep 30 2021.** (C) Sep 27 2021. (D) Oct 20 2021.	60.請參考圖表。何時可能會是宣布科學計畫冠軍的日期？ (A) July 10 2021。 (B) **Sep 30 2021。** (C) Sep 27 2021。 (D) Oct 20 2021。
61. Look at the graph. When will the Aquarium finish its renovation? (A) July 10 2021. (B) **Sep 10 2021.** (C) Oct 20 2021. (D) Sep 30 2021.	61.請參考圖表。何時水族館會完成裝修？ (A) July 10 2021。 (B) **Sep 10 2021。** (C) Oct 20 2021。 (D) Sep 30 2021。

答案：59. B 60. B 61. B

解析

- **第59題**，這題很清楚可以聽出女子打電話的意圖，故答案為**選項B**。
- **第60題**，這題可以對應回圖表，可以在Science Project Contest欄中找到時間，然後有一段時程，表示比賽是這段時間內舉行，而題目是問得知冠軍結果，所以最有可能的時間是最後一天宣布，故要選**選項B**。
- **第61題**，這題是詢問完成裝修的日期，所以最有可能的時間是**選項B**。

聽力原文和對話

Questions 62-64 refer to the following conversation

Cindy: ...I can't believe this...I have the lowest salary in our department...how come?

Mark: where did you learn this?

Cindy: I went to the sixth floor to ask one of the accountants for advice...then I accidentally saw a list of the salary in our department...

Mark: ...and you weren't supposed to see that...it's confidential

Cindy: ...I'm glad that I did...now I won't be such a fool and put so much effort into the work...but why? We are all recent graduates from universities...and I even have a better degree than some of my co-workers...

Mark: ...but...it's kind of your fault...you agreed to the salary in the first place and perhaps some of them demanded a higher salary...

Cindy: ...it really is a hard lesson...I was too desperate to land a job...and too happy to know that I get hired...

Mark: ...don't tell me that you're gonna quit the job...

問題62-64，請參考以下對話內容

辛蒂：我不敢置信...我是我們部門裡面薪資最低的...怎麼會這樣呢？

馬克：你從哪裡得知的呢？

辛蒂：我到公司六樓欲詢問其中一個會計師建議...然後我意外地看到一張我們部門的薪資列表...。

馬克：...而你本來就不該看到那個...這是機密。

辛蒂：...我很高興我看到了...現在我不會在當個如此笨的傻瓜了，在工作上付出那麼多的心力...但是為什麼呢？我們都是近期從大學畢業的畢業生...而且我還有比起我有些同事有著更好的學歷...。

馬克：...但是...這有點是你自己本身的錯...你起初同意了薪資而且或許你們之中有些人要求要有更高的薪資待遇...。

辛蒂：真的上了一個艱難的一課...我過於迫切要找到一份工作...而太過於高興得知我獲得錄取了...。

馬克：別告訴我你要辭職了...。

62. Which of the following is the closest in meaning to "confidential"? (A) confided. (B) confident. (C) revealed. (D) **concealed.**	62.下列哪一個選項近似於「confidential」？ (A) 吐露的。 (B) 自信的。 (C) 揭露的。 (D) **藏匿的。**
63. What is the problem? (A) the woman is forced to quit. (B) **the woman knows her colleagues' payments.** (C) the woman doesn't want to go back to school. (D) the woman finds the accountant untrustworthy.	63.發生什麼問題？ (A) 女子被迫辭職。 (B) **女子得知她同事的薪資。** (C) 女子不想要回學校。 (D) 女子覺得會計師不值得信賴。
64. Why does the woman say, "it really is a hard lesson"? (A) because it is difficult. (B) because now she knows. (C) because she wants the lesson to be easy. (D) **because the realization of the whole thing makes her understand that.**	64.為何女子提到「it really is a hard lesson」？ (A) 因為這是困難的。 (B) 因為現在她懂了。 (C) 因為她想要人生的課是簡單的。 (D) **因為了解整件事情後讓她懂了這些。**

答案：62. D 63. B 64. D

解析

- **第62題**，這題是詢問同義字，所以答案要選**選項D**。confidential在閱讀和聽力中都是常見的字彙，可以記起來。
- **第63題**，這題是問問題出在哪呢，主要就是女子得知了其他同事的薪資進而感到不滿，故答案為**選項B**。

- **第64題**，這題可能要理解一下，會講這句話的主因是，突然間對事情有了體悟，進而有很大的感觸，可以想見她的心情，所以釐清後就可以看選項，**選項D**是最適合的選項。

聽力原文和對話

Questions 65-67 refer to the following conversation

Nurse: ...here you go...this is your father's surgical consent form...make sure you read through all...

Cindy: thanks...I'll take a look...

Nurse: ...it needs to be signed right away...the surgery is urgent...

Cindy: ...ok...I will breeze through the first few pages...

Nurse: ...since your father is diagnosed with brain tumor...and bleeding in the blood vessels can really jeopardize his life...

Cindy: ...again thanks you are considerate...

Nurse: this column is about his illness in five years...and since this is his first time here...we don't quite know his previous conditions...

Cindy: he did have an operation in the stomach last year and a car accident that injured some parts of his left kidney...

Nurse: ok...and is he allergic to certain drugs or something...

Cindy: you beat me on this one...perhaps I will contact my mom to see if she knows...wait a second...

問題65-67，請參考以下對話內容

護士：...拿去吧！...這是你父親的手術同意表格...要確認你都看過喔...。

辛蒂：謝謝...我會看的...。

護士：...這需要即刻就簽好的...手術是緊急的。

辛蒂：...好的...我會飛快看過前幾頁的。

護士：...既然你父親被診斷出腦瘤...而血管處有流血會對他生命造成危害...。

辛蒂：...再次謝謝妳這麼體貼...。

護士：這欄是關於他這五年的疾病...還有既然這是他第一次到本院...我們不太知道他先前的狀況...。

辛蒂：他去年胃部有做過手術，然後一起車禍傷及了他一部份的左腎...。

護士：好的...他有對於特定藥物或什麼有過敏反應嗎？

辛蒂：這個你就考倒我了...或許我聯繫我母親看她知不知道...等我一下...。

65. Where most likely is the conversation taking place? (A) at a dental clinic. (B) **outside the ER room.** (C) at a stem cell center. (D) on a blood donation car.	65. 對話最有可能發生在何處？ (A) 在牙醫診所。 (B) **在急診室外頭。** (C) 在幹細胞中心。 (D) 在捐血車上。
66. Which of the following organ is not mentioned in the conversation? (A) brain. (B) stomach. (C) kidney. (D) **gall.**	66. 下列哪個器官在對話中沒有提及？ (A) 腦。 (B) 胃。 (C) 腎。 (D) **膽。**
67. Why does the woman say, "I will breeze through the first few pages"? (A) because she doesn't want to read it. (B) because the document is too lengthy. (C) **because the surgery is critical.** (D) because the nurse will roll her eyes at her.	67. 為何女子提及「I will breeze through the first few pages」？ (A) 因為她不想要閱讀它。 (B) 因為文件過於冗長。 (C) **因為手術是緊急的。** (D) 因為護士向她白眼。

答案：65. B 66. D 67. C

解析

- **第65題**，這題是詢問地方，不過很明顯是護士和病患家屬在談論病情和手術同意書的部分，最有可能的地方是在急診室外頭或辦公桌附近，故答案為**選項B**。
- **第66題**，這題要多注意幾個細節點，對話中沒有提到的部分是膽的部分，其他該病患都有受傷過且在對話中談及，故答案為**選項D**。
- **第67題**，女子會講這句話的原因是，手術很緊急，所以她才想要跳過一些頁面，故答案為**選項C**。其他選項都不太適合。

聽力原文和對話

Questions 68-70 refer to the following conversation

Cindy: I'd like to book four tickets...two adults and two teenagers...

Employee: I'm afraid that we no longer provide that kind of service

Cindy: what do you mean?...are you saying that we can't book tickets through cellphone...

Employee:..I'm sorry about that...it's our new policy

Cindy: it's too crowded over here at the entrance...I demand four tickets...right away...

Employee: ...I admire your enthusiasm...I just can't give you the ticket...

Cindy: ...you know what...I'd like to talk to your manager right away...

Employee: ...calm down...see the main page on our website?...you can directly book tickets by the following link and use your social security number (9 digits) and a series of number generated by the computer....then you can pay the price of the ticket by using your credit card...after the procedure is done...you will get what you need...

問題68-70，請參考以下對話內容

辛蒂：我想要訂購四張票...兩張成年票和兩張青少年票...。

員工：恐怕我們不再提供那樣性質的服務了。

辛蒂：你指的是什麼呢？...你是說我們無法透過手機訂票嗎？

員工：對此...我感到抱歉...這是我們的新政策。

辛蒂：入口處這裡太壅擠了...我要求要有四張票...馬上。

員工：...我欽佩你的熱忱...我就是沒辦法給你票...。

辛蒂：你知道嗎...我想要跟你的經理談談...馬上。

員工：...冷靜一下...看到我們網站主頁了嗎？...你能夠直接由下列的連結進行訂票服務，且使用社會安全碼（9碼），和一系列由電腦所產生的號碼...然後你可以藉由使用你的信用卡來付票的費用...在程序完成之後...你就會拿到你所需要的...。

68. Why does the woman make the phone call? (A) to provide the service. (B) **to buy tickets.** (C) to have a fight with the worker. (D) to have a chat with the manager.	68. 為何女子會打這通電話？ (A) 提供服務。 (B) **購票。** (C) 與工作人員爭吵。 (D) 與經理談話。
69. Why does the employee say, "I admire your enthusiasm"? (A) to compliment the customer. (B) to make a heart-felt comment. (C) to show her admiration. (D) **to sugarcoat and not irritate the customer.**	69. 為何員工提及「I admire your enthusiasm」？ (A) 稱讚顧客。 (B) 講述發自內心的評論。 (C) 顯示出她的欽佩。 (D) **使表達悅耳且不惹怒客戶。**
70. What information does the employee provide the woman with? (A) 9 digits social security number. (B) a set of computer password. (C) the use of credit card. (D) **how to use on-line service to book tickets.**	70. 員工將提供女子什麼樣的資訊？ (A) 9位數的社會安全碼。 (B) 一組電腦號碼。 (C) 使用信用卡。 (D) **如何使用線上服務去購票。**

答案：68. B 69. D 70. D

解析

- **第68題**，這題很明顯女子打電話是要買票，所以答案為**選項B**。
- **第69題**，這題可以理解一下，其實面對來電者的無理，員工其實一直保持正向應對，並且不希望觸怒到旅客，所以不太可能講不得體的話，所以進而講了這句話，以熱情帶過這部分，類似盛情難卻之類的，這樣一來就能發現答案很明顯是**選項D**。
- **第70題**，這題也不難，其實員工提供的方式是讓女子知道可以由線上服務買票並由信用卡付費，故答案為**選項D**。選項C是干擾選項，他沒有教導顧客使用信用卡的部分，要小心。

PART 4

聽力原文與中譯

Questions 71-73 refer to the following advertisement

After weeks of working out...Still worry that you are not gonna be physically fit...and those muscles just aren't what you want them to be looked like...then don't hesitate to try our new products...high protein bars...these bars contain the nutrition you need...your muscles can be instantly built...in a few weeks...our R&D has come up with four different kinds of flavor...strawberry, chocolate, green milk tea...and coffee...and of course excessive exercise is needed after consuming these bars...also...below is the link for the further discounts...you are getting a 20% discount if you buy more than four bars...and don't forget to follow us...you might get a free one...

問題71-73請參閱下列廣告

在幾週的健身後...仍是擔心你體格不精實嗎？...而且那些肌肉就是不會照你所想要長成的方式走嗎？...那麼別猶豫嘗試下我們的新產品...高蛋白棒...這些棒包含了你所需要的營養素...在幾週內...你的肌肉可以即刻建造好...我們的研發部門已經想出四種不同的口味...草莓、巧克力、綠奶茶...和咖啡口味的...而當然攝食這些高蛋白棒後，過量的運動是必須的...而...關於進一步的折扣...以下是我們的連結...你將得到八折的優惠，如果你買超過四個高蛋白棒...而別忘了追蹤我們喔...你可能可以獲得一根免費的。

試題中譯與解析

71. What is being advertised? (A) the coach's muscle. (B) strawberry. (C) **muscle-building bars.** (D) protein.	71.廣告在宣傳什麼？ (A) 教練的肌肉。 (B) 草莓。 (C) **肌肉建構棒。** (D) 蛋白。
72. How can listeners receive a price reduction? (A) follow the Instagram. (B) **buy to a certain number.** (C) talk to the gym coach. (D) upload the pic to Instagram.	72.聽者們如何才能享有折扣？ (A) 追蹤Instagram。 (B) **購買到特定的數量。** (C) 與健身教練談話。 (D) 上傳相片到Instagram。

73. Which of the following flavors is not mentioned in the advertisement?	73. 在廣告中並沒有提到下列哪個口味呢？
(A) coffee.	(A) 咖啡。
(B) chocolate.	(B) 巧克力。
(C) **green tea.**	(C) **綠茶。**
(D) strawberry.	(D) 草莓。

答案：71. C 72. B 73. C

解析

- 第**71**題，這題詢問的是「廣告的項目」，由廣告敘述中可以得知是高蛋白棒，只是選項中有進行改寫，其實高蛋白就是增進肌肉快速建造，所以改寫成muscle-building，故這題答案要選**選項C**。也要注意別誤選到protein等不完整的項目。

- 第**72**題，這題也要很小心，容易誤選，因為有提到說追蹤的話有可能會獲得免費的蛋白棒，但是題目是詢問折扣的部分，要達成折扣的話則是要購買超過四個，所以答案為**選項B**。

- 第**73**題，這題的話可以對應到四個口味，但是要注意細節，其中一個口味是green milk tea而不是選項C的green tea故要選**選項C**。

聽力原文與中譯

Questions 74-76 refer to the following video

This is youtuber...Jason Thornes...one of the villagers is asking me to take a larger raft with them so that it's safer...and I get to do the cooking on the raft...surprising...according the producer of the show I have to cook...what do I have the kimchi is prepared beforehand...and there is a small stove, made of precious stone...and there is a flagstone...so the villager is heating the flagstone and we can roast beef ribs as Korean cuisines...I'm using the stove cooking Chinese chicken soup...and there is still some more space on the flagstone...so I'm putting the prepared duck confit...a famous French dish...smells great...this is incredible...my first time cooking on the tremendous raft...

問題74-76請參閱下列視頻

這是記者...傑森・索恩...其中一位村民正要求我跟他們一起搭乘較大的竹筏，這樣的話會較為安全...而我可以在竹筏上煮菜...令人吃驚的是...根據節目製作人，我必須要煮菜...我有的是韓式泡菜，是預先準備好的...而這裡有小型的爐子，是由珍貴的石頭所製成的...這裡還有石板...所以村民正在石板上加熱，我們能在上頭烤牛肋排當作韓式菜餚...我正使用爐子燉煮中式雞湯...石板上...仍然還有一些空間...所以我正將準備好的油封鴨...有名的法式菜餚...聞起來很棒...這令人難置信...我首次在巨大竹筏上的廚藝初體驗...。

試題中譯與解析	
74. Where is the video most likely taking place? (A) on a lager ship. (B) on a canoe. (C) **on a small boat.** (D) at the river.	74. 這個視頻最可能發生在何處？ (A) 在較大型的船上。 (B) 在獨木舟上。 (C) **在小型的船上。** (D) 在河邊。
75. Which of the following country's dish is not mentioned? (A) China. (B) **Germany.** (C) Korea. (D) France.	75. 在視頻中，下列哪個國家的菜餚沒有提及？ (A) 中國。 (B) **德國。** (C) 韓國。 (D) 法國。
76. What is mentioned about the flagstone? (A) it's a valuable as the gold. (B) it's used to slice kimchi. (C) **it can be used to bake food.** (D) it has the same quality as the precious stone.	76. 關於石板何者正確？ (A) 跟金子一樣具有價值。 (B) 它用於切泡菜。 (C) **它能用於烘焙食物。** (D) 它與珍貴的石頭有同等的價值。

答案：74. C 75. B 76. C

解析

- **第74題**，視頻中提到的是a larger raft其實就是a small boat，故答案要選**選項C**。

177

- **第75題**，這題的話也是要注意細節點，並利用刪去法，所以可以得知並未提到德國料理的部分，故要選**選項B**。
- **第76題**，關flagstone的部分，可以找到它的用途是用於烤，所以可以很輕易對應到**選項C**，也要注意其他干擾選項的部分。

聽力原文與中譯

Questions 77-79 refer to the following video

Best Kitchen Channel	
Dish	**points**
fried fish	25
barbecued crocodile meat	55
fruit salads	20
beef	45

This is youtuber...Jason Thornes...my previous video has millions of hits ...halleluya...so...originally we are going to introduce you some plants and trees...but now I have to do another cooking...which is fine...I don't want to be too modest...because I still have plenty of dishes to show...the inhabitants have captured fish ready...so I'm gonna fry them...and the crocodile meat...it's cleaned...but are we sure about we would like to do that...ok...marinate the sauce and barbecue...and we have some fruits...so we get to make fruit salads...and I'm taking out the red wine...it's Pinot Noir...it goes well with the beef...how does that sound...leave any message and don't forget to follow...us...Best Kitchen Channel

問題77-79請參閱下列視頻

倍斯特廚房頻道	
菜餚	分數
炸魚	25分
烤鱷魚肉	55分
水果沙拉	20分
牛肉	45分

這是記者...傑森 ・索恩...我先前的視頻有數百萬的點擊率...哈雷路亞...所以...起初我們要向您介紹一些植物和樹木...但是我現在必須要做另一款的菜餚...也可以接受就是了...我不想要太謙虛...因為我仍有許多的菜餚要展示...居民們有準備好，捕獲好的魚...所以我要炸牠們...以及鱷魚肉...這是已經洗淨的...但是我們有確認好我們想要這樣做了嗎...好的...將鱷魚肉醃製好醬汁，然後烤肉...而我們有些水果...所以我們可以製作些水果沙拉...然後我要拿出紅酒...這是黑皮諾...跟牛肉很搭...這樣聽起來如何呢？...留下任何訊息且別忘了追蹤我們喔...倍斯特廚房頻道

試題中譯與解析	
77. Who most likely is the speaker addressing? (A) students. (B) chefs. (C) **audiences.** (D) youtubers.	77. 說話者最可能在對誰説話？ (A) 學生。 (B) 廚師。 (C) **觀眾。** (D) youtubers。
78. Look at the graph. Which finished dish earns the highest point? (A) fish. (B) beef. (C) vegetables. (D) **meat that we seldom consume.**	78. 請參考圖表。哪道完成的菜餚會獲得最高的分數呢？ (A) 魚。 (B) 牛肉。 (C) 蔬菜。 (D) **我們很少會食用到的肉。**
79. What is mentioned about red wine? (A) it's from local inhabitants. (B) **it's a great blend with meat.** (C) it goes well with fruits. (D) it will be the gift for followers.	79. 關於紅酒的敘述，何者正確？ (A) 它是從當地居民那來的。 (B) **它跟肉是很棒的搭配。** (C) 它與水果很搭。 (D) 它將會是追蹤者的獎品
答案：77. C 78. D 79. B	

- **第77題**，這題的話很明顯視頻是給觀眾看的，故要選**選項C**。
- **第78題**，這題的話要對應到圖表，選分數最高的項目barbecued crocodile meat，而鱷魚肉其實是我們較少食用到或不曾時用到的稀有料理，試題也改寫成選項D的敘述，故答案為**選項D**。
- **第79題**，這題是詢問關於紅酒的部分，要掌握基礎的同義轉換it goes well with換成**it's a great blend**...故答案為**選項B**。

聽力原文與中譯

Questions 80-82 refer to the following video

Fashion & Design	
item	**Fees for the youtuber**
contact lenses	US 5 dollars
beach shorts	US 6 dollars
speedos	US 10 dollars
sunglass	US 8 dollars

This is youtuber...Jason Thornes...morning...I'm practicing wearing contact lenses without looking in the mirror...and I obvious cannot rely on the reflection of the river...I love this brand...enough oxygen and you get to wear it for longer hours...our videos are an instant hit...but obviously...that's not enough for those TV executives...that's why...I'm going to take off my shirts...we're on the land...It's sweltering hot...and I'm only wearing my beach shorts...what do you think?...I'm afraid that I can't wear a speedo...or more revealing...there might be some teenagers watching...and the latest sunglass...a bit too fashionable in here...kind of unfitting here...but I'm gonna wear the chic glass and cook for lunch...does that make me look like a celebrity...?

問題80-82請參閱下列視頻

時尚與設計	
項目	Youtuber能獲取的費用
隱形眼鏡	5 美元
海灘短褲	6美元
三角褲	10美元
太陽眼鏡	8美元

這是記者…傑森・索恩…早安…我正在練習不看著鏡子戴隱形眼鏡…而我顯然不能仰賴河裡的反射…我喜愛這個品牌…足夠的含氧而且你可以長時間攜帶…我們的視頻是立刻爆紅…但是顯然…這對於那些電視高層們不太夠…這就是為什麼我要脫掉上衣了…我們在陸地上了…悶熱異常…我僅穿著我的海灘褲…你們覺得呢？…恐怕我無法只穿三角褲…或更裸露的…可能有青少族群在觀看視頻…而這是最新款的太陽眼鏡…在這顯得太時髦了些…有點不太合宜…但是我還是要戴著這副時髦的眼鏡然後煮中餐…這樣有讓我看起來像是名人嗎…？

試題中譯與解析

80. Where most likely is the speaker? (A) at the gym. (B) in the kitchen. (C) on the beach. (D) **at the stream.**	80.說話者最有可能身在何處？ (A) 在體育館。 (B) 在廚房。 (C) 在海灘上。 (D) **在溪邊。**
81. Look at the graph. Which is the most profitable for the youtuber? (A) contact lenses. (B) beach shorts. (C) sunglass. (D) **speedos.**	81.請參考圖表。下列哪個項目對youtuber獲利最高呢？ (A) 隱形眼鏡。 (B) 海灘短褲。 (C) 太陽眼鏡。 (D) **三角褲。**

| 82. Which of the following is mentioned but not showcased in the video?
(A) sunglass.
(B) contact lenses.
(C) beach shorts.
(D) **speedos.** | 82. 下列哪個說話者所提到的項目在視頻中並未展示出？
(A) 太陽眼鏡。
(B) 隱形眼鏡。
(C) 海灘短褲。
(D) **三角褲。** |

答案：80. D 81. D 82. D

解析

- **第80題**，這題用刪除法，可以由and I obvious cannot rely on the reflection of the river，得知是在溪邊，river替換成stream了，故答案是**選項D**。
- **第81題**，the most profitable可以對應到圖表中價格最高的部分，故要選**選項D**。
- **第82題**，這題要對回.I'm afraid that I can't bear **speedo**...or more revealing...there might be some teenagers watching，故可以得知這是有提及的項目沒有展示出的部分，故答案為**選項D**。

聽力原文與中譯

Questions 83-85 refer to the following news report

Government's emergent aid/by helicopters	
time	Food and beverages
9:00 a.m.	Beef and pork
11:00 a.m.	Egg and butter
12:00 a.m.	milk
1 p.m.	Instant noodles

This is news anchor Bella James...good morning...the huge blizzard really takes its toll on the local residents and several schools announced earlier that schools suspended the classes, saying it's within the standard given by the Education Bureau...while pupils are happy that there is plenty of snow out there...and they don't have to go to school...local residents aren't happy about it...several roads are entirely blocked in the area...and some towns don't have enough supplies and food...if the weather continues......other than edibles...gas and electricity are gonna be short...let's take a look at the footage provided by some inhabitants...cars are buried under the snow...and it's now a regular scene in the area...

問題83-85請參閱下列新聞報導

政府的緊急救援／藉由直升機	
時間	食物和飲料
9:00 a.m.	牛肉和豬肉
11:00 a.m.	蛋和奶油
12:00 a.m.	牛奶
1 p.m.	速食麵

這是新聞主播貝拉‧詹姆士...早安...巨大的暴風雪真的造成了當地居民的傷亡,而幾間學校於稍早之前宣布了消息,學校停課,述説著這已經達到了教育局所給予的停課標準了...而孩童們對於外頭兒有許多雪感到快樂萬分...而且他們不用上學...當地居民卻快樂不起來...地區中的幾個道路受到阻擋...而有些小鎮沒有足夠的補給品和食物...如果天氣持續的話...除了可食品外...瓦斯和電力也會因此短缺...讓我們看下由一些居民所提供的視頻...車子埋在雪下方...而且在地區中,這成了常態了。

83. Who most likely are happy about the snowstorm? (A) local residents. (B) **students.** (C) school principals. (D) officials at the Educational Bureau.	83. 對於暴風雪的到來，誰最可能感到快樂？ (A) 當地居民。 (B) **學生們。** (C) 學校校長們。 (D) 在教育局的官員們。
84. Look at the graph. What will be provided to inhabitants at noon? (A) beef. (B) egg. (C) instant noodles. (D) **milk.**	84. 請參考圖表。在正午時將會提供給居民什麼？ (A) 牛肉。 (B) 蛋。 (C) 速食麵。 (D) **牛奶。**
85. Which of the following is not seen as a problem during the huge snow storm? (A) electricity. (B) cars. (C) **water.** (D) food.	85. 在暴風雪期間，下列何者不會被視為是問題？ (A) 電力。 (B) 車。 (C) **水。** (D) 食物。

答案：83. B 84. D 85. C

解析

- **第83題**，試題中的snowstorm對應到blizzard，接續聽，可以發現感到開心的是學生pupils，故答案要選**選項B**。
- **第84題**，由noon對應到圖表中的12:00 a.m.，可以馬上找到milk，故答案為**選項D**。
- **第85題**，在聽力敘述中有提到gas和electricity，還有supplies和food，另外受影響的還有汽車，所以這題答案很明顯是**選項C**，水的供給沒有受到影響。

聽力原文與中譯

Questions 86-88 refer to the following advertisement

I'm the PR of the Best Antique Store...this is our grand opening.... welcome...decorations of our entrance is made from green crystal...quite striking...it's actually from the shipwrecks and it's believed to be made hundreds of years ago...and we are also selling pearls that are harvested by one of the largest clams under the sea...I am wearing the pearl necklace right now...so if you are wedding planner...there are so many precious things you can find here...and if you are tarot lovers...and fortune tellers...you surely will love our purple crystal...there seems to be some magic...and as for the red crystal...it's not quite fortuitous but it is believed to bring you great wealth...and we are running out of the yellow crystal...

問題86-88請參閱下列

我是倍斯特古董店的公關人員這是我們盛大的新開幕...歡迎...我們入口的裝飾是由綠水晶所製成...相當耀眼...它實際上是由船骸而來而且據說是數百萬年前所製...而我們也販售了珍珠，在海水中其中一個大型的蛤蠣所收穫而來的...我現在所戴的珍珠項鍊就是了...所以如果你是婚宴策畫者....你可以在這裡找到許多珍貴的東西...如果你是塔羅牌愛好者...和算命師的話，你一定會喜愛我們的紫水晶的...這似乎有些魔力存在著...而至於紅水晶的話...它不是那麼吉利但是據說能替你帶來很多財富...然後我們正缺乏黃色水晶...。

試題中譯與解析

86. Which of the following item is retrieved from an underwater creature? (A) green crystal. (B) purple crystal. (C) **pearls.** (D) red crystal.	86. 下列哪個項目是由水底生物所取出的？ (A) 綠水晶。 (B) 紫水晶。 (C) **珍珠。** (D) 紅水晶。

87. According to the advertisement, which will attract fortune-seekers? (A) **red crystal.** (B) pearls. (C) purple crystal. (D) green crystal.	87. 根據廣告所述，哪個會吸引追求財富者？ (A) 紅水晶。 (B) 珍珠。 (C) 紫水晶。 (D) 綠水晶。
88. Which of the following item is currently out of stock? (A) red crystal. (B) green crystal. (C) purple crystal. (D) **yellow crystal.**	88. 下列哪個項目目前沒有庫存呢？ (A) 紅水晶。 (B) 綠水晶。 (C) 紫水晶。 (D) **黃水晶。**

答案：86. C 87. A 88. D

解析

- 第86題，這題要注意的是underwater，所以有可能是green crystal和pearls，但是還有creatures，所以顯而易見的是pearls，由clams所harvest的，故答案為**選項C**。
- 第87題，這題要等到四種水晶的敘述都結束後，而試題中的fortune-seeker對應到**bring you great wealth**，所以答案為**選項A**，紅水晶。
- 第88題，試題中的is currently out of stock對應到聽力原文中的are running out of，故答案為黃水晶，故答案為**選項D**。

聽力原文與中譯

Questions 89-91 refer to the following advertisement
Although we are an organic farm...we are known for our chicken soup and other products...that's quite odd you might think...we have hundreds of mushrooms...that can be a great foundation for the sweetness and freshness of the soup...also...the ABC Airline which books lots of fruits and vegetables from us...and passengers love those...ifyou are traveling long-distance...it's essential to take enough nutrients...the modern disease of a sudden death is not a joke...saving money for cheaper prices of vegetables and fruits won't do you any

good...and we're offering discounts for those who are truly in need...finally we will be having a cooking demonstration of the chicken soup...if you are intrigued...visits us the date before Thanksgiving...you'll get a basket of free mushrooms

問題89-91請參閱下列廣告

儘管我們是間有機農場...我們以我們的雞湯和其他產品而聞名...你可能會想，這相當的怪異...我們有數百樣的蘑菇...這能夠成為湯頭甜度和新鮮度的基礎湯底...而且...ABC航空公司也從我們這裡訂購了許多的水果和蔬菜...而乘客喜愛那些...如果你正在長途旅行...攝取足夠的營養是必要的...猝死這個現代化疾病不是開玩笑的...省錢以購買較便宜價格的蔬菜和水果對你來說不會有任何益處...然後我們提供那些真的需要者折扣...最後，我們即將會有雞湯的烹飪展示活動...如果你感到有興趣的話...在感恩節前一天來拜訪我們...，你將會獲得一籃免費的蘑菇。

試題中譯與解析	
89. What kind of product is being advertised? (A) fruits and vegetables. (B) vitamin tablets. (C) **chicken soups.** (D) diverse mushrooms.	89.廣告的是什麼項目？ (A) 水果和蔬菜。 (B) 維生素錠。 (C) **雞湯。** (D) 各式的蘑菇。
90. What will happen on the date prior to a major holiday? (A) **a cooking demonstration.** (B) a free meal for the homeless. (C) cheaper prices of fruits. (D) quality chickens.	90.在主要假期的前一天會發生什麼事情？ (A) **烹飪展示。** (B) 無家可歸的人的免費一餐。 (C) 較便宜價格的水果。 (D) 具品質的雞。
91. What will be provided to visitors? (A) discounts. (B) a cooking demonstration. (C) a basket. (D) **free mushrooms.**	91.將會提供給觀光客什麼？ (A) 折扣。 (B) 烹飪展示。 (C) 一個籃子。 (D) **免費的蘑菇。**
答案：89. C 90. A 91. D	

解析

- **第89題**，這題也是廣告類，主打的廣告是chicken soup，別被干擾選項影響到了，所以答案為**選項C**。
- **第90題**，這題的話要注意到a major holiday=萬聖節，所以很明顯答案會是**選項A**。
- **第91題**，這題會贈送給拜訪者的是免費的蘑菇，所以要選**選項D**。別誤選成籃子。

聽力原文與中譯

Questions 92-94 refer to the following news report

Indignation is not a word that I would normally use...but yeah...tearing eyes of several elephants in the circus do make wildlife biologists wrathful...according to an earlier report...those do sound like a cry for help, and yet the performance in the Best Circus remains....hundreds of tourists are waiting outside for the performance...some are adults with children...most with their latest smartphones...can't wait to upload the performance on IG...and possibly photograph click-baited pics...however...the performance took a surprising turn...when one of the young elephants ran out the fences...and it became an odd show without the performer...how ironic...and hours later the elephant was found dead on the city's street...possibly killed by electrical guns...how cruel...

問題92-94請參閱下列新聞報導

憤怒不是一個我常會用到的字...但是是的...馬戲團裡頭幾頭大象的淚眼讓野生生物學家們感到憤怒...根據稍早前的報導...那些看起來像是求救的呼喊，然而倍斯特馬戲團的表演仍舊進行著...數以百計的觀光客們正在外頭等著表演...有些是陪同小孩一同前來的大人們...大多數攜帶著最新款的智慧型手機...等不要在ig上頭上傳表演的照片...而且可能是拍攝誘導式點擊的照片...然而...表演出現了驚奇的大轉彎...當其中一頭年輕象逃出圍籬...而這變成是一場奇怪的表演，沒有表演者...多麼諷刺呀！...且幾小時之後，那頭大象被發現死在市區街道上...可能是死於電擊槍...多麼殘酷呀！...。

試題中譯與解析

92. What is the main topic of the news report? (A) tourists happily view the performance with their kids. (B) tourists applaud the authenticity of the show and upload enticing pics. **(C) a call for proper treatment of animals in the circus.** (D) a call for capturing an escaped young elephant instantly.	92. 此篇新聞報導的主題是什麼？ (A) 觀光客們很快樂地與孩子們一同觀看表演。 (B) 觀光客們喝采表演的真實性且上傳吸引人的照片 an。 **(C) 呼籲對於馬戲團內動物的適當對待。** (D) 呼籲立即捕捉已經逃走的年輕象。
93. What gadget is mentioned to record the show? (A) high-end cameras. (B) telephones. **(C) cell phones.** (D) filming devices in the circus.	93. 哪個提到的器具用於錄製這個表演？ (A) 高端相機。 (B) 電話。 **(C) 手機。** (D) 在馬戲團的拍攝裝置。
94. What most likely will occur hours after the show? (A) tourists cheering for the performance. (B) tourists uploading those click-baited photos. **(C) tourists finding an animal corpse outside the circus.** (D) tourists practicing using electrical guns.	94. 在表演的幾個小時後，最可能發生什麼事情？ (A) 觀光客們替表演歡呼。 (B) 觀光客們上傳那些誘導按讚的圖片。 **(C) 觀光客們在馬戲團外頭發現動物屍體。** (D) 觀光客們練習使用電子槍。

答案：92. C 93. C 94. C

- 第**92**題，這題是詢問新聞的主旨，其他選項有的僅是細節部分，其實主要的重點在喚起大家對於馬戲團動物虐待等的意識，所以最適合的選項是**選項C**，對於馬戲團動物能有妥善對待的呼籲。
- 第**93**題，這題中gadget指的是cell phones所以要選**選項C**。
- 第**94**題，試題中的will occur hours after the show對應到對話中的hours later the elephant was found dead on the city's street，所以最有可能的是**選項C**，在馬戲團外發現動物屍體（大象屍體）。

聽力原文與中譯

Questions 95-97 refer to the following news report

The Police Report	
Predicted Time	**Description**
8:42 a.m.	abnormality of the dashboard
8:45 a.m.	the plane losing control
8:46 a.m.	trying to remain at a certain height
8:47 a.m.	descended
8:48 a.m.	exploded

Is it just me or...that plane is really close...a local inhabitant told us that he witnessed the plane lost its control and managed to maintain at a certain altitude...this contradicts the rumor that it was caused by a natural disaster...but the cause could be birds...which accidentally dragged into the engine of the plane...Best Airline did have a bad reputation that the pilot fell asleep during the flight across the Pacific...the plane eventually crashed onto the island...and none of the passengers survived...now the police are looking for more evidence about the plane that landed unsuccessfully...and hopefully it was not a human error...the further search can find a miracle...

問題95-97請參閱下列新聞報導

The Police Report	
Predicted Time	**Description**
8:42 a.m.	儀錶板的異常
8:45 a.m.	飛機失去控制
8:46 a.m.	試圖維持在特定的高度
8:47 a.m.	登陸
8:48 a.m.	爆炸

是我的問題亦或是...那架飛機真的靠近...一位當地居民告訴我們說他目睹到飛機失去控制且設法要維持在一定的高度...這與傳言説是由天災所引起的相矛盾...但是起因可能是鳥類...意外地拖曳進飛機引擎中...倍斯特航空公司確實有壞名聲，駕駛員在飛機橫跨太平洋時睡著了...飛機最終墜毀於小島上...而無任何的乘客生還...現在警方正找尋更多關於飛機無法成功降落的證據...然後希望起因不是由人為所引起的失誤...而進一步的搜尋能夠發現奇蹟...。

試題中譯與解析	
95. What is the main topic of the news report? (A) a natural disaster. (B) **a plane crash.** (C) an anecdote told by a local villager. (D) the importance of the company's reputation.	95. 這則新聞報導的主題是什麼？ (A) 天災。 (B) **飛機墜機。** (C) 由當地居民講述的軼事。 (D) 公司聲譽的重要性。
96. Look at the graph. When did the plane land uncontrollably? (A) 8:45 a.m. (B) 8:42 a.m. (C) 8:48 a.m. (D) **8:47 a.m.**	96. 請參考圖表。飛機於何時失控性地登陸？ (A) 上午8:45。 (B) 上午8:42。 (C) 上午8:48。 (D) **上午8:47。**

97. What could be the cause of the plane crash?	97. 什麼可能是飛機失事的主因？
(A) a human error.	(A) 人為失誤。
(B) **fowls.**	(B) **禽鳥。**
(C) a natural disaster.	(C) 天災。
(D) an inexperienced pilot.	(D) 經驗不足的機長。

答案：95. B 96. D 97. B

解析

- **第95題**，這題雖然有提到天災等，但僅是部分內容，主要還是在說墜機和飛機失事的部分，所以要**選B**。
- **第96題**，這題先看到試題中的land uncontrollably對應到對話末的 **landed unsuccessfully**，也對應到圖表中的descended，所以答案要選**選項D**。（而整起事件也是有順序的）
- **第97題**，這題詢問引起墜機的主因，對話中提到的因素很多，要很仔細聽，有的是干擾選項，最主要的部分是記者說的but the cause could be birds，所以birds可以對應到**fowls**，故答案要選**選項B**。

聽力原文與中譯

Questions 98-100 refer to the following live show

Best Interior Design Company has been awarded the Best Design in ten years award...and it is currently looking for two designers...so what's the requirement...that's what most people are eager to know...I'm gonna ask that for you...here is the HR manager of the Best Design...so what are you looking for?

Manager: what we are looking for is the quality of a person...you don't necessarily have to bring the portfolio...although it is actually a plus...and I've got to tell you...most of the new hires are inexperienced ones...but with the potential to do what's best for the company...and normally we interview people at least four times to determine the finalist...

問題98-100請參閱下列現場節目

倍斯特設計公司已經獲得了十年來最佳設計的獎項了…然後現在正招募兩位設計師…所以需要的條件是什麼呢？…這是大多數的人迫切想要知道的…我來替你們問…倍斯特設計的人事經理就在這兒…所以你們要找尋怎麼樣的人呢？

經理：我們所要找尋的是一個人的特質…你不一定要攜帶著作品集…儘管那確實是個加分項目…而我必須要告訴你…大多數的新聘人員都是毫無經驗的…但是卻有著對公司發展而言最好的潛質…而通常我們面試面試者至少四次來決定最終的候選人…。

試題中譯與解析	
98. Who most likely is the speaker addressing? (A) **jobseekers.** (B) professors. (C) finalists. (D) experienced designers.	98. 說話者最可能在對誰說話？ (A) **求職者。** (B) 教授。 (C) 最終候選人。 (D) 有經驗的設計師。
99. Who could be the potential new hire? (A) experienced candidates with diverse portfolios. (B) **inexperienced interviewees with the great personality and potential.** (C) experienced candidates who have gone through three interviews. (D) inexperienced interviewees without great portfolios.	99. 那類性的新雇員有可能被錄取？ (A) 有各式不同作品集的有經驗候選人。 (B) **有著良好個性和潛質的無經驗面試者。** (C) 已經參加過三輪面試的有經驗的候選人。 (D) 攜帶優秀作品集但無經驗的面試者。

100.According to the manager, what will happen after going through four rounds of interviews?	100.根據經理所言，在經歷4回合的面試後，可能會？
(A) getting hired.	(A) 獲得雇用。
(B) getting promoted.	(B) 獲得升遷。
(C) getting rejected.	(C) 被拒絕。
(D) **getting considered.**	(D) **可能考慮錄用。**

答案：98. A 99. B 100. D

解析

- **第98題**，這題是發生在現場錄影，邀請面試官來談話，所以主要的對象是觀眾，客群最可能是想進這間公司的眾多求職者，所以要選**選項A**。
- **第99題**，這題要注意選項的用字和一些細節跟干擾選項，對話中有提到公司大多錄用的人是毫無經驗但具潛質的，而且公司重的是個人的特質，最有可能的是**選項B**。
- **第100題**，這題也要很小心，對話中有提到經過四輪面試會是finalist，但是finalist並不代表錄取了，所以要選**選項D**，**getting considered**。

Note

- 【花店話題】要注意許多細節性資訊和推測能力，並搭配「刪去法」，這樣就能迅速攻略這方面的出題。

- 【婚宴話題】包含基礎的數字題，只要夠專注有聽到訊息都能答對。另外要注意的是運用圖表題訊息和聽力訊息來判斷電話是打給誰的部分。

- 【新聞話題】要注意也要看完圖表題的其他訊息後再答題，別剛聽到就馬上畫卡，很容易誤選。

模擬試題（三）

In the Listening Test, you must demonstrate your ability to understand spoken English. This section is divided into four parts and will take approximately 45 minutes to complete. There are four parts, and directions are given for each part. Do not mark the answers in your test book. Use the answer sheet that is provided separately.

▶ **PART 1**

Directions: For each question, you will listen to four short statements about a picture in your test book. These statements will not be printed and will only be spoken one time. Select the statement that best describes what is happening in the picture and mark the corresponding letter (A), (B), (C), (D) on the answer sheet.

Example   Sample Answer
                                                A ● C D

Statement (B), "**Some people are wearing backpacks**", is the best description of the picture. So you should select answer (B) and mark it on your answer sheet.

1.

(A)　(B)　(C)　(D)

2.

(A)　(B)　(C)　(D)

3.

(A) (B) (C) (D)

4.

(A) (B) (C) (D)

5.

(A)　(B)　(C)　(D)

6.

(A)　(B)　(C)　(D)

Directions: For each question, you will listen to a statement or a question followed by three possible responses spoken in English. They will not be printed and will only be spoken one time. Select the best response and mark the corresponding letter (A), (B), or (C) on your answer sheet.

7. Mark your answer on your answer sheet.
8. Mark your answer on your answer sheet.
9. Mark your answer on your answer sheet.
10. Mark your answer on your answer sheet.
11. Mark your answer on your answer sheet.
12. Mark your answer on your answer sheet.
13. Mark your answer on your answer sheet.
14. Mark your answer on your answer sheet.
15. Mark your answer on your answer sheet.
16. Mark your answer on your answer sheet.
17. Mark your answer on your answer sheet.
18. Mark your answer on your answer sheet.
19. Mark your answer on your answer sheet.
20. Mark your answer on your answer sheet.
21. Mark your answer on your answer sheet.
22. Mark your answer on your answer sheet.
23. Mark your answer on your answer sheet.
24. Mark your answer on your answer sheet.
25. Mark your answer on your answer sheet.
26. Mark your answer on your answer sheet.

27. Mark your answer on your answer sheet.

28. Mark your answer on your answer sheet.

29. Mark your answer on your answer sheet.

30. Mark your answer on your answer sheet.

31. Mark your answer on your answer sheet.

▶ **PART 3**   MP3 011

Directions: In this part, you will listen to several conversations between two or more speakers. These conversations will not be printed and will only be spoken one time. For each conversation, you will be asked to answer three questions. Select the best response and mark the corresponding letter (A), (B), (C), (D) on the answer sheet.

32. **Where most likely is the conversation taking place?**
(A) in a restaurant
(B) at a wine cellar
(C) in the kitchen
(D) on the airplane

33. **What does the man recommend?**
(A) take the complaint to the customer
(B) tell customers the truth
(C) do as instructed
(D) give customers more expensive wine

34. **Why does the man say, "definitely not using what's holding on your hands"?**
(A) to extinguish the fire
(B) to remind the woman
(C) to control the situation
(D) to cultivate the relationship

35. What industry do the speakers most likely work in?
(A) fire-fighting
(B) airline
(C) police
(D) safety training

36. What is the problem?
(A) the smoke is too heavy.
(B) using both hands to clear up the fog is not enough.
(C) the woman fails to do the task
(D) the woman shouldn't use the mask

37. Why does the woman say, "don't you think you are overreacting..."?
(A) she knows in advance that the examiner is going to overreact.
(B) she doesn't want the examiner to act like this way.
(C) she is pointing out the problem of the examiner.
(D) she is being dramatic about how the examiner said about her.

38. What is the problem?
(A) the shipment of the flowers will be postponed.
(B) the artificial setting for the flower is malfunctioned.
(C) the shop owner can't come to the shop because of the blizzard.
(D) the customer demands the flower right away.

39. Which of the following flowers are not currently available in the flower shop?
(A) begonias
(B) lavenders
(C) carnations
(D) lilies

40.What industry does the female speaker most likely work in?
   (A) flower
   (B) wedding
   (C) shipment
   (D) design

41.How did these flowers get shipped during the storm?
   (A) cut corners
   (B) by a jet plane
   (C) by two major transportations
   (D) through relations

42.What could be the truck driver's plan on Valentine's Day?
   (A) ask the woman out on a date
   (B) get the double fee for the shipment
   (C) buy the flower at a discount
   (D) inform the woman about a shoplifter

43.Under what circumstance, will the woman get a day off?
   (A) have a huge customer for lilies
   (B) a date from an admirer
   (C) all merchandise is out of stock
   (D) flowers miraculously arrive at the shop during the storm

 44.Why does the woman say, "that makes you on top of the list"?
   (A) because they are hired
   (B) because she likes the guys a lot and quite suitable for the requirement
   (C) because she has the authority to move them up
   (D) because passion is the key

45.How did the man learn about the recruitment?
   (A) pamphlets and the website
   (B) the school

(C) bulletin board
(D) news report

46. Where most likely is the conversation taking place?
   (A) in the campus
   (B) in the interview room
   (C) at the travel agency
   (D) at a process plant

47. Why does the man say, "I'm counting the time"?
   (A) he really wants to be on time.
   (B) he cannot wait for this to be over.
   (C) he knows perfectly well about the concept of time management
   (D) he has a feeling that counting the time makes time pass quicker.

48. What are the speakers mainly discussing?
   (A) the dishes in the lunchbox
   (B) the wearisome look they are getting per day
   (C) the treatment and the job content
   (D) the holiday after the work

49. Where most likely is the conversation taking place?
   (A) in a restaurant
   (B) outside the supervisor's office
   (C) in the kitchen
   (D) at the factory

50. What is the request of the men?
   (A) rewrite the contract
   (B) renegotiate the contract
   (C) demand a better offer
   (D) free from the bond of the agreement

51.Why does the boss say "we are out of workforce"?
(A) because he wants the guys to know about his predicament
(B) to let the guys know that short-staffed problems are temporary
(C) to let the guys know that the current situation makes him hard to concede
(D) because it's not an off-season

52.Which of the following is not what makes the two guys displeased?
(A) what's written on the brochure
(B) what's being said during the interview
(C) what's written on websites
(D) what's being said about the barbecue

53.What is the highest price that the woman can offer?
(A) US 70,000
(B) US 100,000
(C) US 90,000
(D) US 200,000

54.According to the manager, what is the regular price for the wedding?
(A) US 70,000
(B) US 90,000
(C) US 100,000
(D) US 200,000

55.Why does the woman say, "fritter away the money"?
(A) she wants to profuse the money
(B) she thinks it's good for the economy and the flow of cash
(C) she thinks money can solve all problems
(D) she is mentioning that as the lifestyle of the rich

56.Why does the man come to the company?
    (A) he wants to see the castle
    (B) he is on behalf of the governor Clarke
    (C) he is the representative here for a mission
    (D) he needs hot cappuccino

57.Why does the man say, "now I have to do the heavy lifting"?
    (A) he hates the heavy workload but still has to do it.
    (B) he considers himself unlucky
    (C) he doesn't want to be a representative
    (D) he is making a complaint that he has to do his coworker's daunting job while she is on vacation

58.What is not mentioned about the third building?
    (A) it contains a castle.
    (B) it has an underground tunnel.
    (C) there lives a real prince.
    (D) there is a buffet in there.

Contact/ABC Drug Store	
PR/Cindy	555-666-600 #100
Sales/Jason	555-666-601 #115
Manager	555-666-602 #115
CFO	555-666-603 #125
Boss	555-666-604 #115

59.Look at the graph, which of the following phone number did the woman dial?
    (A) 555-666-601 #115
    (B) 555-666-602 #115
    (C) 555-666-603 #125
    (D) 555-666-604 #115

60. Why does the man say, "my mission is done here"?
    (A) he thinks the boss has made up his mind.
    (B) he is relieved that they don't have to discuss any detail.
    (C) he knows perfectly well that his boss won't have a second thought.
    (D) now he can enjoy desserts and cookies without worrying about it.

61. What does the woman say about the contract?
    (A) it's easily read
    (B) it contains all information
    (C) it will be put in a folder
    (D) it could change his boss's mind

62. Where most likely are the speakers?
    (A) at the owner's house
    (B) at the owner's coffee shop
    (C) at the realtor's lunch meeting room
    (D) at the potential buyers' conference room

63. What is mentioned about landowner's nephew?
    (A) he hates the design of the balcony
    (B) he committed suicide
    (C) he doesn't like the haunted house
    (D) he already discloses the information to potential buyers

64. What does the woman suggest the owner do?
    (A) run away from the haunted house as fast as he can
    (B) hide the information
    (C) increase the values of the house
    (D) think of other ways to convince buyers

65.Which of the following creatures cannot be found near the lake?
(A) chickens
(B) ducks
(C) swans
(D) dogs

66.Why does the woman say, "Ring any bell"?
(A) she wants to make sure the owner hears the ring of the bell
(B) she wants the owner to have excellent memory
(C) the association might evoke the owner to think about something
(D) the landscape only reminds the lady to think about something

67.Why does the woman say, "can jog your memory"?
(A) because the owner has amnesia.
(B) because one's memory can be lost after a trauma
(C) because these photos might stimulate the owner to recall the image
(D) because the owner has to jog so that he can remember something

68.What does the man say about the form?
(A) it needs to be signed.
(B) the procedure is not mandatory.
(C) the item number on the form is vaguely seen.
(D) visitors do necessarily have to read it to sign.

69.What most likely is the man's occupation?
(A) a helicopter driver
(B) a lawyer
(C) the rescuer
(D) a park ranger

70. Where most likely is the conversation taking place?
    (A) in the village
    (B) in the mountain
    (C) at the entrance of the National Park
    (D) at the hiking trail

▶ **PART 4** 🎧 MP3 012

    Directions: In this part, you will listen to several talks by one or two speakers. These talks will not be printed and will only be spoken one time. for each talk, you will be asked to answer three questions. Select the best response and mark the corresponding letter (A), (B), (C), (D) on your answer sheet.

 71. Why does the man say, "a bit overshadowed by"?
    (A) because he exaggerates the claim
    (B) because he wants the flagstone as a gift from villagers
    (C) because he thinks the flagstone actually prevails the company's expensive products
    (D) because now he cannot cook faster

72. Why does the man want the camera to have a close-up?
    (A) to make villagers jealous
    (B) to impress the producer of the show
    (C) to give photographers a genuine feel
    (D) to highlight and promote the product

73. What distinguishes the food processor with villagers' knife?
    (A) its engine
    (B) its efficiency
    (C) its price
    (D) its weight

74.What is being advertised?
(A) the Chinese woks
(B) the dough with scallions
(C) fried water spinach
(D) the ladle

75.What aspect of the pan does the speaker applaud?
(A) the origin
(B) the light weight
(C) the heating part
(D) the shipment

76.Who most likely is the speaker addressing?
(A) housewives
(B) villagers
(C) executives of the kitchen wares
(D) the producer

77.What can be inferred about the merger?
(A) successful
(B) fruitful
(C) futile
(D) mysterious

78.Which of the following is closet in meaning to disintegrate?
(A) intact
(B) mystify
(C) consolidate
(D) dismiss

79.Why does the spokesperson say, "adds salt to injury"?
(A) To salvage the public image of the company
(B) to provide proof of the transferred money
(C) to refute the information from earlier news report

(D) to show that it makes the situation even worse

---

80. **According to the news report, what is the CEO getting accused of?**
(A) forgery
(B) murder
(C) insider trading
(D) corruption

---

81. **According to the news report, what can be found on a large ship?**
(A) money
(B) illegal documents
(C) cruise
(D) corpse

---

82. **Where is the news report given?**
(A) Egypt
(B) Europe
(C) America
(D) Asia

---

83. **Which of the following item is not instantly-lit in the fire accident?**
(A) inflammable items
(B) furniture
(C) plastics
(D) clothes

---

84. **What is mentioned about the firefighters?**
(A) they are able to tackle the explosion
(B) they are forced to leave the house
(C) they demand more help
(D) they don't have the authority to use helicopters

85. **Which of the following was ravaged by the forest fire?**
    (A) beasts
    (B) helicopters
    (C) firefighters
    (D) local inhabitants

86. **What is unique about the Best Jewelry at the exhibition?**
    (A) its comparatively low price
    (B) its durability
    (C) its design
    (D) its debut

 87. **Why does the speaker mention "don't worry that if you have a spouse that is not a local here"?**
    (A) to enhance the authenticity of the jewelry
    (B) to demonstrate the credibility of the company
    (C) to clear the doubts
    (D) to make sure everyone will get the ticket

88. **Which of the following will not be showcased in the approaching exhibition?**
    (A) silver
    (B) gold
    (C) pearls
    (D) blue-like gems

Rescue	
animals	**fees**
Barnacle geese	US 20
Camels	US 290
Horses	US 250
Wolves	US 240
Note: barnacle geese will be not used as vehicles	

89.Why does the local villager mention barnacle geese?
(A) to applaud the sanctity of the cliff
(B) to downplay the negative feelings of the news report
(C) to entertain news reporters
(D) to satirize the foolish behavior

90.What could be the means of transportation to carry the survivors?
(A) automobiles
(B) ladders
(C) airplanes
(D) creatures

91.Look at the graph. Which of the following animal transportation will cost the least money?
(A) barnacle geese
(B) horses
(C) wolves
(D) camels

92.Who most likely are the listeners?
(A) trainers who are about to start the session
(B) customers sitting on the row of evacuation seats
(C) guests sitting on the economy seats
(D) flight attendants at the training school

93.What is the purpose of mentioning the swap list?
(A) to entertain the students
(B) to make students sleepy
(C) to make students vigilant
(D) to meet the demand of the students

94.What is the topic of the talk?
(A) how to avoid smell the heavy jet fuel
(B) how to use the swap list

(C) how to stay awake
(D) continuation of the training lessons

95. What is the requirement of this assignment?
    (A) 500 words
    (B) it depends
    (C) no longer than 1000 words
    (D) 2000 words

96. Where most likely is the talk given?
    (A) in a classroom
    (B) at the gallery
    (C) at the museum
    (D) at the swimming pool

97. Why does the speaker find the last painting odd?
    (A) it was painted by a famous painter
    (B) it has worms on the woodpecker
    (C) because the shape of the apple
    (D) because how the leg is perceived

Descriptions	Time
DWI/citizens	8:39 A.M.
DWI/mayor	9:45 A.M.
Train derailed	10:20 A.M.
Restaurant fire	11:35 A.M.
Note: DWI = driving while intoxicated	

98. According to the speaker, what will the donation money be used for?
    (A) the film companies
    (B) the prize
    (C) the ceremony

(D) academic achievement

99.According to the talk, who will not be attending the event?
   (A) the CEO
   (B) the mayor
   (C) the senator
   (D) the governor

100.Look at the graph. When did the mayor get involved in a car accident?
   (A) 8:39 A.M.
   (B) 9:45 A.M.
   (C) 10:20 A.M.
   (D) 11:35 A.M.

第三回
模擬試題解析

 PART *1*

聽力原文與中譯	
1. (A) **Several traditional rural houses are adjacent to the temple.** (B) Fruits are being sold at the gate of the temple. (C) Several monks are fixing these pillars. (D) Some people are talking to the monk in the temple.	1. (A) **有幾間傳統鄉村建築比鄰寺廟。** (B) 水果在寺廟的入口處販售。 (C) 幾個和尚正在修復這些柱子。 (D) 有些人在寺廟中跟和尚談話。

答案：(A)

這題可以看到是在寺廟的高處拍攝的圖片，俯瞰而下可以看到有些傳統式的建築在寺廟旁，故答案要選**選項A**。

聽力原文與中譯	
2. (A) Artificial light is used in the library. (B) **The bookshelves are specifically designed.** (C) Booklovers are sitting next to the shelves. (D) The view is photographed on the first floor.	2. (A) 圖書館裡使用人工燈光。 (B) **書櫃是特別設計的。** (C) 書的愛好者正坐在書櫃旁。 (D) 影像是在一樓拍攝的。

答案：(B)

 解析

這題有些難，但是還是可以看出在樓層中有超過一層以上的書架放置許多書籍，這些書架很明顯跟尋常書架不同，是需要特別設計，故答案要選**選項B**。

聽力原文與中譯	
3. (A) The tree in sight is shorter than those cars. (B) The bus is twice the size of these cars. (C) Cars are waiting in line for passengers. (D) **There are several tall buildings in sight.**	3. (A) 視野所及的樹比那些車高。 (B) 公車是這些車子的兩倍大。 (C) 車子正大排長龍地等待乘客。 (D) **視野所及有幾棟高樓。**

答案：(D)

解析

這題有幾個選項都出現的比較級的部分，但釐清後可以看到圖片中有幾棟高樓，這符合選項D的描述，故**答案為D**。

聽力原文與中譯	
4. (A) A narrator is eager to explain the concept of art works. (B) Only a few people are able to get closer to the painting. (C) **Lots of filaments are used to partially cover the painting.** (D) Empty coconut shells are used as decorations on the ground.	4. (A) 解說員熱切的解釋藝術品的概念。 (B) 僅有幾個人能夠靠近這幅畫。 (C) **許多線用於遮蓋住部分的畫。** (D) 地面上使用了空的椰子殼當作裝飾。

答案：(C)

解析

這題有些難，但是可以看到的是在牆上的畫前，有線之類的東西，懸掛式的蓋住部分圖片，故答案為**選項C**。

聽力原文與中譯	
5. (A) **Three skyscrapers have been erected here.** (B) Nothing can be found atop these skyscrapers. (C) A crowd of people are gathering on the street. (D) Other buildings are as high as these skyscrapers.	5. (A) **三座摩天大樓佇立於此。** (B) 在這些摩天大樓上沒有東西。 (C) 擁擠個人群聚集在街頭。 (D) 其他建築物跟這些摩天大樓一樣高。

答案：(A)

解析

這題很明顯地可以看到有三個摩天高樓佇立在圖片裡頭，故答案要選**選項A**。

聽力原文與中譯	
6. (A) There is no shadow because of the sun. (B) No trees can be seen in the view. (C) No seashells can be seen on the sand. (D) **Tremendous English alphabet props are randomly scattered on the sand.**	6. (A) 因為太陽的關係所以沒有陰影。 (B) 視野所及看不到樹。 (C) 在沙上看不到貝殼。 (D) **大型的英文字道具隨意散佈在沙發上。**

答案：(D)

解析

這題可以看到有大型的英文字母散佈在沙灘上且擺放的不規則，故答案要選**選項D**。

PART 2

聽力原文與中譯

7. Aren't you supposed to be in the bride's room? (A) Oh...it turns out the restaurant won't be serving fish. (B) **The bride needs some fresh air.** (C) She went the grapes of wrath on me	7. 你不是應該要待在新娘的房間嗎？ (A) 噢！...最終發現餐廳不會上魚這道菜。 (B) **新娘需要一些新鮮的空氣。** (C) 她對我上演了憤怒的葡萄。

答案：(B)

解析

這題也是要選沒有待在房間的原因，較合理的是選項B，故答案為**選項C**，另外關於表達憤怒或生氣的用法，除了angry or be mad at等等，更生動的有選項中的went the grapes of wrath和go ballistic等等，考生也可以一併記起來，在生活中也可以使用。

聽力原文與中譯

8. Why don't you join us to the ranch? (A) The ranch has the worst wine in town. (B) I usually find cowboys there romantic. (C) **To be honest, I don't want to be intruded.**	8. 為什麼你不跟我們一起參加農場行呢？ (A) 農場裡頭有著小鎮最糟糕的酒。 (B) 我通常覺得那裡的牛仔羅曼蒂克。 (C) **說實話，我不想要打擾到你們。**

答案：(C)

解析

這題也是要解釋原因，另一類的表達會像選項C這樣，怕打擾到人，故答案為**選項C**。

9. Is the garage sale going to be on this week? (A) **Maybe next July.** (B) it's cheaper. (C) The number of items is miscellaneous.	9. 車庫銷售是於這個星期開始嗎？ (A) **可能是下個七月。** (B) 它比較便宜。 (C) 項目的數量是琳瑯滿目的。

答案：(A)

這題有可能是明確的回答，也有可能是聽者根本不知道答案或被考倒了之類的，也有可能是表達可能是某個時間點，故答案為**選項B**。

10. Where do you prefer to meet up? At the carousal or the bumping car. (A) I'm writing a letter recommending the upgrade of the bumping car. (B) The carousal is outdated for us. (C) **I think it depends.**	10. 你偏好在哪裡碰面呢？在旋轉木馬那裡還是在碰碰車呢？ (A) 我正要寫封信，建議升級碰碰車。 (B) 對我們來說，旋轉木馬過時了。 (C) **我想這要視情況而定。**

答案：(C)

這題也是二選一但是答案為第三個選項，或其他表達，故答案為**選項C**。

11. Unfortunately, the second interview is collided with my wedding date. (A) Wow...lucky you (B) **I don't know what to say and I feel bad.** (C) It cannot be and I am a genius.	11. 不幸的是，第二次的面試跟我的婚禮撞期。 (A) 哇！...你真幸運 (B) **我不知道該說什麼，我覺得糟。** (C) 不可能的，而且我是個天才。

答案：(B)

解析

這題有可能是解釋，也可能是不知道如何反應了，故答案為**選項B**。

聽力原文與中譯	
12. Is tunnel 990 temporarily closed because of the drunk driving incident? (A) It's the safest in the country. (B) **No, that's a rumor.** (C) Unless there is a mudslide	12. 隧道990暫時封閉是因為酒駕事件的發生嗎？ (A) 這是國內最安全的地方。 (B) **不是的，那只是謠傳。** (C) 除非有土石流發生。

答案：(B)

解析

這題是詢問原因，答案有可能是肯定，也可能是反駁這件事，故答案為**選項B**。

聽力原文與中譯	
13. Why are you displeased with the groom? (A) The wedding venue is not great. (B) **He had a criminal record.** (C) No offense, but the groom's mom is here.	13. 為什麼你對於新郎感到不滿呢？ (A) 婚禮的場地不是很棒。 (B) **他曾有犯罪紀錄。** (C) 沒有冒犯的意思，但是新郎的媽媽也在這兒。

答案：(B)

解析

這題是要選解釋的原因，答案要選**選項B**。

14. I can't think of anything good for the campaign. (A) Thinking requires time. (B) The campaign is not going very well, isn't it? (C) **Then you will be fired.**	14. 我想不出任何比這個更佳的競選活動。 (A) 思考需要時間的。 (B) 競選活動進行的不是很順利，是不是呢？ (C) **那麼你會被開除。**

答案：(C)

這題有可能答案是沒達成的話要承擔的後果會是如何，故答案要選**選項C**。

15. How much does it cost for a wedding like that? (A) The wedding dress looks prefect for you. (B) We certainly need more red envelopes. (C) **After haggling, it's cheaper than you think.**	15. 像這樣的婚禮要花費多少錢呢？ (A) 婚宴禮服看起來很適合你。 (B) 我們確實需要更多的紅包。 (C) **在議價後，比你想個更便宜。**

答案：(C)

這題也沒有直接提供一個答案，而是提供一個較隱晦的回答，故答案為**選項C**。

16. Do you want to take a walk? (A) **Not after we've tried the dessert.** (B) Sure, my father is coming. (C) You know what...Jane's walking monitor is malfunctioned.	16. 你想要散步走走嗎？ (A) **除非在我們品嚐過甜點後** (B) 當然，我的父親正要來訪了。 (C) 你知道嗎...珍的行走監測器故障了呢！

答案：(A)

 解析

這題也沒有直接答好，而是以除非怎樣來回答，故答案要選**選項A**。

聽力原文與中譯	
17. Where did you bury the body? (A) The police are going to be here any time soon. (B) I hate to bring this up, but I'm guilty. (C) **an esteemed animal shelter house.**	17. 你在哪兒埋葬屍體呢？ (A) 警方馬上就會來這兒了。 (B) 我不想提起這個，但是我是有罪的。 (C) **一間受尊敬的動物庇護之家。**

答案：(C)

 解析

這題要選擇一個地點，答案很明顯是**選項C**。

聽力原文與中譯	
18. What lipsticks are you wearing? (A) I love the pink paint on the wall. (B) My daughter is not old enough to wear one. (C) **Can't you tell, you are right beside me.**	18. 你所擦的唇膏是什麼顏色的呢？ (A) 我喜愛牆面漆成粉紅色的。 (B) 我的女兒還沒有大到能擦口紅。 (C) **你分辨不出來嗎，你就在我身旁唉！**

答案：(C)

 解析

這題也沒有明確提到顏色，而是反問，故答案為**選項C**。

聽力原文與中譯	
19. Have you considered changing a boyfriend? (A) My boyfriend is taking me to the night market. (B) My dad doesn't allow me to date a guy. (C) **If a better one shows up, then yes.**	19. 你有考慮過換個男友嗎？ (A) 我的男朋友正要帶我去夜市。 (B) 我父親不允許我跟那個男子約會。 (C) **如果有更好的對象出現的話，那麼答案是「是的」。**

答案：(C)

 解析

這題也是沒有提供是或否的答案，而是表明如果....的話...，故答案為**選項C**。

聽力原文與中譯	
20. Which of our customers don't have to pay subscription fees? (A) We cannot help but raise the cost. (B) I want you to be supportive about subscription fees. (C) **Those viewing not longer than 20 hours.**	20. 我們的哪位顧客不需要支付訂購費用呢？ (A) 我們不得不提高費用。 (B) 我想要你對於訂購費用部分的支持。 (C) **那些瀏覽不長於20小時的顧客。**

答案：(C)

 解析

這題要選符合不收費的條件，故答案要選**選項C**。

聽力原文與中譯	
21. Where do you need me to sign? (A) Using Easy Card is faster. (B) **Column B only.** (C) I'm practicing my handwriting.	21. 需要我在哪裡簽名呢？ (A) 使用悠遊卡更快速。 (B) **僅有B欄位需要簽名。** (C) 我正在練習我的手寫簽名。

答案：(B)

解析

這題有明確講述簽名的欄位，故答案要選**選項B**。

聽力原文與中譯	
22. Do you need someone to pick you up after the walk? (A) **I think I will take the camel ride back to the hotel.** (B) The desert is worth visiting. (C) The taxi here charges too much.	22. 在走段路後，你需要有人來接你嗎？ (A) **我想，我會騎乘駱駝回到酒店裡。** (B) 這個沙漠真的值得參觀。 (C) 這裡的計程車索費過於高昂。

答案：(A)

解析

在這題也沒有直接表達是或否，而是提供自己的另一個選擇，故答案為**選項A**。

聽力原文與中譯	
23. The ostrich owner demands more fees. (A) **Don't give him...just run...** (B) He is not under medication. (C) My credit card is not working.	23. 鴕鳥的主人要求更多的費用。 (A) **別給他...快點跑就是了...。** (B) 他只是處於沒吃藥的情況之下。 (C) 我的信用卡無法使用了。

答案：(A)

解析

這題有點滑稽，答案要選比較創意性的，故答案要選**選項A**。

24. As far as Saturday's nights are concerned, consider that permanent work nights.
(A) **Luckily, the effect date of my resignation is today.**
(B) Saturday is not considered a holiday here.
(C) The boss will be here all the time.

24. 至於週六夜晚的話，把它視為是永久的工作之夜！
(A) **幸運的是，我的離職生效日是今天。**
(B) 在這裡，週六並不被視為是假期。
(C) 老闆無時無刻都會在這裡。

答案：(A)

 解析

這題的回答算是一個對抗式的回應上司指令，答案要選**選項A**。

25. Would you like some tea to go with the cake?
(A) **That would be nice, thanks.**
(B) This cake tastes delicious.
(C) Tea is not usually my favorite.

25. 你想要一些茶來搭蛋糕嗎？
(A) **那會很棒的，謝謝啊！**
(B) 這個蛋糕嚐起來美味。
(C) 茶不太是我喜愛的飲品。

答案：(A)

 解析

這題的答案也很直接，故答案要選**選項A**。

26. Have you been to the new night market yet?
(A) Old-fashioned guys are not suited to go there.
(B) Of course, we have gone to the market.
(C) **Sure, the beef noodle tastes delicious.**

26. 你曾到過新的夜市嗎？
(A) 舊觀念的男子並不適合去那裡。
(B) 當然，我們已經去過那個市場了。
(C) **當然，那裡的牛肉麵嚐起來美味。**

答案：(C)

 解析

這題的答案直接回到有到過該處且表明原因，故答案要選**選項C**。

聽力原文與中譯

27. Will The Ghost be recruiting more sailors this year? (A) Normally, I don't take no for an answer. (B) They hired 50 more guys last year. (C) **I think you'd better check that information from the captain.**	27. 今年，幽靈號會雇用更多的水手嗎？ (A) 通常，我不接受拒絕。 (B) 他們去年雇用了超過50位男子。 (C) **我想你最好向船長確認一下訊息。**

答案：(C)

 解析

這題沒有提供一個明確的答案，而是要對方確認訊息，故答案為**選項C**。

聽力原文與中譯

28. How much does taking this kind of bamboo raft cost? (A) There's a small jungle that houses lots of bamboo. (B) You can make a raft yourself. (C) **depends on the going rate**	28. 搭乘像這樣的竹筏要花費多少錢呢？ (A) 這裡有個小型的叢林，儲藏許多竹子。 (B) 你可以自己製作竹筏。 (C) **要視行情價而定。**

答案：(C)

 解析

這題也沒有提供一個明確的金額，而是表達要視情況而定，故答案為**選項C**。

聽力原文與中譯	
29. When can I get to consult with the fortune-teller? (A) I bet it's popular because lots of people are waiting. (B) **did you make a reservation?** (C) You should work hard and not relying on those things.	29. 我甚麼時候可以請教算命師呢？ (A) 我敢打賭這很蔚為風潮，因為許多人都等著。 (B) **你有預約嗎？** (C) 你應該要努力工作而且不要仰賴那些事情。

答案：(B)

這題也沒有提供答案，而是反問對方，故答案要選**選項B**。

聽力原文與中譯	
30. This is the second time I'm making the wedding vow. (A) Two is my favorite number. (B) **two is better than none.** (C) Wow...the church is so magnificent.	30. 這是第二次我宣示婚宴誓言。 (A) 2號是我最喜愛的號碼。 (B) **兩次總比一次都沒有過要好。** (C) 哇！...教堂是如此華麗。

答案：(B)

這題是接續該句的表達，且有些出其不意，故答案為**選項B**。

聽力原文與中譯	
31. Who is in charge of assembling those ingredients? (A) **The job was assigned to a villager.** (B) From Christmas to Chinese New Year. (C) Those ingredients are not cheap.	31. 誰負責裝配那些材料呢？ (A) **那個工作被分配給一位村民。** (B) 從聖誕節到中國新年。 (C) 那些材料並不便宜。

答案：(A)

這題也沒有明確表達是誰，但是有講述這個工作分配給其他人了，故答案為**選項A**。

PART 3

聽力原文和對話

Questions 32-34 refer to the following conversation

Cindy: great...now I have to tell lies...and imagine how many lies I have to spin while I'm in the economy class cabin...

Jason: what do you mean...lies?

Cindy: yep...L-I-E-S...lies...whenever a customer asks me something...I have to calm he or she by saying something that is just not true...

Jason: it's just a white lie...

Cindy: ...just...we are having engine troubles...and all I can say is that's not a big deal...it can be easily fixed...don't worry about it...more wine...white or red...I knew you prefer red...red wine right away...

Jason: I'm afraid that's part of our job...

Cindy: OMG...FIRE...in the cockpit...what am I supposed to do?

Jason: putting out the fire...quick...but definitely not using what's holding on your hands...

Cindy: yep...it will only make things worse.

問題32-34，請參考以下對話內容

辛蒂：好棒喔...現在我必須要說謊...試想我要編織多少的謊話，當我在經濟艙時...

傑森：對於「謊言」...你所指的是什麼呢？

辛蒂：是啊...L-I-E-S...謊言...每當有客人問我一些事情時...我必須要安撫他或她，然後要說些不是那麼真實的事情。

傑森：這只是善意的謊言...。

辛蒂：...只是...我們有引擎問題...而我所能說的是沒什麼大不了的...這很輕易就能修復...別擔心...需要更多酒嗎？白酒或紅酒...我知道你偏好紅酒...紅酒馬上到...

傑森：恐怕這就是我們工作的一部分...。

辛蒂：我的天啊！...火...在駕駛艙...我該怎麼辦？

傑森：快點...將火撲滅...但是千萬別使用你手上正拿著的東西...。

辛蒂：是呀...這只會讓事情更糟了。

試題中譯與解析	
32. Where most likely is the conversation taking place? (A) in a restaurant. (B) at a wine cellar. (C) in the kitchen. (D) **on the airplane.**	32. 對話最有可能發生在何處? (A) 在餐廳。 (B) 在酒窖。 (C) 在廚房。 (D) **在飛機上。**
33. What does the man recommend? (A) take the complaint to the customer. (B) tell customers the truth. (C) **do as instructed.** (D) give customers more expensive wine.	33. 男子建議什麼? (A) 向顧客抱怨。 (B) 告訴顧客實情。 (C) **遵照指示做。** (D) 給予顧客更多的紅酒。
34. Why does the man say, "definitely not using what's holding on your hands"? (A) to extinguish the fire. (B) **to remind the woman.** (C) to control the situation. (D) to cultivate the relationship.	34. 為何男子提到「definitely not using what's holding on your hands」? (A) 撲滅火源。 (B) **提醒女子。** (C) 控制情況。 (D) 培養關係。

答案:32. D 33. C 34. B

解析

- **第32題**,從對話中最一開始的在economy class cabin等訊息跟後來的在cockpit,均可以推斷對話發生的地點會是在飛機上,故要選**選項D**。
- **第33題**,男子建議的是I'm afraid that's part of our job,其實並沒有煽動或影響另名空服員,而這也是在向女空服員說道就照做吧或這是公司規定,所以要選**選項C** do as instructed。
- **第34題**,男子會說這句的原因是出於提醒,比較是幽默式的提醒對方,因為得知女空服員手上拿的是紅酒,故要選**選項B**。

Questions 35-37 refer to the following conversation

Examiner: enter the cabin...

Cindy: OK...wow...for real...lots of smoke...that's not good

Examiner: so how are you going to respond...?

Cindy: (coughing)...wow the fire is too big...I'm kneeing down...I need some fresh air...

Examiner: 20 seconds...and still cannot do anything about it...

Cindy: what?...am I getting a bad review?...

Examiner: didn't you learn anything at the training school...?

Cindy: ...see...I'm already doing something...using both hands to clear up the fog...

Examiner: ...that's all you can do?...I guess I am going to comment...a contestant who can't seem to understand the task and probably need more time...next one

Cindy: wait a second...I just figured something out...I'm putting my clinical mask...and I lean towards the passenger seat, telling passengers...evacuate...quick...quick...

Examiner: ...game over...loose cannon...next one...

Cindy: don't you think you are overreacting...?

問題35-37，請參考以下對話內容

檢測官：進飛機客艙...

辛蒂：好的...哇！...來真的...煙霧好大...這不太好。

檢測官：所以，你要如何反應...呢？

辛蒂：（咳嗽）... 哇！這火太大了...我要蹲下了...我需要一些新鮮空氣...。

檢測官：20秒了...而卻完全沒轍...

辛蒂：什麼？...我拿到負面的評論了嗎？...

檢測官：你在訓練學校的時候沒有學到任何相關的東西嗎？...

辛蒂：...瞧...我已經正在做了...使用我的雙手揮散大霧...

檢測官：...這就是你所能做的嗎？...我想我要評論...一個受評者似乎不了解這項任務而且可能需要更多時間...下一位。

辛蒂：等一下...我正好想到了要怎麼做了...我戴上我的醫護面具...然後我倚身靠向乘坐椅，告訴乘客...撤離...快點...快點

檢測官：...遊戲結束了...鬆螺絲...下一位...

辛蒂：你不覺得你有點反應過度了嗎...？

試題中譯與解析

35. What industry do the speakers most likely work in? (A) fire-fighting. (B) **airline.** (C) police. (D) safety training.	35. 説話者最有可能在哪個行業工作？ (A) 消防。 (B) **航空業。** (C) 警局。 (D) 安全訓練。
36. What is the problem? (A) the smoke is too heavy. (B) using both hands to clear up the fog is not enough. (C) **the woman fails to do the task.** (D) the woman shouldn't use the mask.	36. 發生什麼問題？ (A) 煙霧太濃厚了。 (B) 使用雙手除掉霧不太足夠。 (C) **女子執行任務失敗。** (D) 女子不應該使用面罩。
37. Why does the woman say, "don't you think you are overreacting..."? (A) she knows in advance that the examiner is going to overreact. (B) she doesn't want the examiner to act like this way. (C) she is pointing out the problem of the examiner. (D) **she is being dramatic about how the examiner said about her.**	37. 為何女子提到「don't you think you are overreacting...」？ (A) 她事先知道檢測官將會反應過度。 (B) 她不想要檢測官以這樣的方式表現。 (C) 她正指出檢測官的問題。 (D) **她只是對於檢測官講述她的評論而表現的戲劇化。**

答案：35. B 36. C 37. D

解析

- **第35題**，這題是詢問説話者所從事的產業，從對話中的enter the cabin等可以推斷説話者是航空業，很可能是測驗官在訓練中心中考空服員，故要選擇**選項B**。
- **第36題**，而主要的問題是女子無法完成任務，故要選擇**選項C**。

- **第37題**，經過對話內容後可以看出女子比較隨意、搞笑的一面，最後沒有反省自己，還反問這句真的只有dramatic可以形容了，這題最適合的選項是**選項D**。

Questions 38-40 refer to the following conversation

Cindy: I was told by the shop owner that there is going to be a blizzard...so flowers won't be arrived until next Tuesday...

Jake: ...but it's Valentine's Day...and if you guys don't have any flowers to sell...what are you going to do...?

Cindy: ...thank god...we do have lavenders and carnations ready...in-house cultivation...in an artificial setting where temperatures are controlled...

Jake: ...what about roses...I need pink roses...a few dozens and other flowers...

Cindy: are they used for the wedding centerpiece? What about begonias? Let me show you those...strikingly beautiful...

Jake: ...wow...looks great...how much?

Cindy: ...since you are a regular...there's gonna be a discount...you know it...and what else do you need?

Jake: ...lilies...the petals will be used in the wedding main gate...

Cindy: ...I don't think that would be a problem...

問題38-40，請參考以下對話內容

辛蒂：我聽花店的老闆說即將要有一場大雪...所以花朵直到下週二後才會抵達。

傑克：...但是這是情人節...而且如果你們沒有花朵可以銷售，你們要怎麼辦呢？

辛蒂：...謝天謝地...我們確實備有薰衣草和康乃馨...室內耕種...在溫度受控制的人工環境裡頭。

傑克：...那麼關於玫瑰花呢？...我需要粉紅色的玫瑰花...幾打還有其他的花朵...。

辛蒂：它們是用於婚禮餐桌上的中心擺飾品嗎？那麼秋海棠呢？讓我向你展示那些...美麗耀眼...。

傑克：...哇！...看起來很棒...多少錢呢？

辛蒂：...既然你是常客...會給你折扣...你知道的...你還有需要什麼嗎？

傑克：...百合...花瓣會用於婚禮的主要通道...。
辛蒂：...我不認為這會有什麼問題。

試題中譯與解析

38. What is the problem?	38. 發生什麼問題？
(A) **the shipment of the flowers will be postponed.**	(A) **花朵的運送將會延期。**
(B) the artificial setting for the flower is malfunctioned.	(B) 替花朵所做的人工環境故障了。
(C) the shop owner can't come to the shop because of the blizzard.	(C) 花店雇主因為暴風雪而不能來花店。
(D) the customer demands the flower right away.	(D) 顧客要求立即拿到花朵。
39. Which of the following flowers are not currently available in the flower shop?	39. 下列哪種花現在在花店中沒有存貨呢？
(A) begonias.	(A) 秋海棠。
(B) lavenders.	(B) 薰衣草。
(C) carnations.	(C) 康乃馨。
(D) **lilies.**	(D) **百合。**
40. What industry does the female speaker most likely work in?	40. 女性説話者最有可能從事什麼行業呢？
(A) **flower.**	(A) **花朵。**
(B) wedding.	(B) 婚宴。
(C) shipment.	(C) 運輸。
(D) design.	(D) 設計。

答案：38. A 39. D 40. A

解析

- **第38題**，主要問題是因為有暴風雪所以花無法如期送到，所以要選**選項A**，延期。

- **第39題**，這題要注意到好幾個細節點，we do have lavenders and carnations ready和What about begonias? Let me show you those，僅能確定的是花店目前有的花有ABC三項，故答案為**選項D**。
- **第40題**，這題很明顯，女子工作的產業是花業，故要選**選項A**。

聽力原文和對話

Questions 41-43 refer to the following conversation

Cindy: ...wait a second...the truck arrived...a total life saver...

Jake: ...ok...I'm gonna wait here...

Cindy: ...I thought the weather is bad enough that flowers won't be arrived until next week...

Jason: yep...snowstorms...but those flowers are shipped through air travel and then are delivered by the vehicle...

Cindy: ...where do you need me to sign?...the same place as usual...

Jason: ...the same column...totally an unrelated topic...I guess you won't be available during the Valentine's Day..

Cindy: ...are you kidding...our busiest time..

Jason: ...ok...I get it...

Cindy: ...unless all flowers are sold out before the festival...and normally that's not gonna happen...and you have to excuse me...I have a huge customer waiting inside...

Jake: ...wow early shipment...now you are relieved...

Cindy: ...yeah...and see several boxes right over there...enough lilies for your wedding...

問題41-43，請參考以下對話內容

辛蒂：...等一下...卡車抵達了...全然是個救星...。

傑克：...好...我想在這等著...。

辛蒂：...我認為天氣遭到花朵要到下週才能抵達了...。

傑森：是的...暴風雪...但是那些花朵是透過空運，然後以陸上交通工具運送至此...。

辛蒂：...你需要我簽在哪頭呢？...一樣是在之前同樣的地方...。

傑森：...相同的欄位...全然不相干的話題...我想你在情人節期間就不會有空了...。

辛蒂：...你在開玩笑嗎？...我們最忙的時候...。

傑森：好...我知道了。

辛蒂：...除非所有的花朵都在節慶前賣光吧...通常這種事情是不可能發生的...然後請見諒一下...我有個超大個客戶在裡面等著...。

傑克：哇！提早的運貨...現在你如釋重負了...。

辛蒂：...是呀...還有你看那裡那幾箱...足夠你婚禮要使用的百合花了。

試題中譯與解析

41. How did these flowers get shipped during the storm? (A) cut corners. (B) by a jet plane. (C) **by two major transportations.** (D) through relations.	41. 在風暴期間，這些花朵是如何運送的呢？ (A) 抄捷徑。 (B) 藉由噴射機。 (C) **藉由兩種主要的交通工具。** (D) 透過關係。
42. What could be the truck driver's plan on Valentine's Day? (A) **ask the woman out on a date.** (B) get the double fee for the shipment. (C) buy the flower at a discount. (D) inform the woman about a shoplifter.	42. 在情人節時，卡車司機最可能的計劃是什麼呢？ (A) **約女子約會。** (B) 獲取兩倍的運送費用。 (C) 以折扣價格購買花朵。 (D) 告知女子關於扒手的事。
43. Under what circumstance, will the woman get a day off? (A) have a huge customer for lilies. (B) a date from an admirer. (C) **all merchandise is out of stock.** (D) flowers miraculously arrive at the shop during the storm.	43. 在什麼情況下，女子將有可能獲得一天假？ (A) 有個訂購百合的巨大客戶。 (B) 有愛慕者的約會。 (C) **所有商品都沒有存貨。** (D) 在風暴期間，花朵都奇蹟似地抵達店裡頭了。

答案：41. C 42. A 43. C

解析

- **第41題**，這題可以對應到but these flowers are shipped through air travel and then are delivered by the vehicle，所以是由空運和陸運的方式，也就是答案選項表達的兩種主要交通運送方式，故答案為**選項C**。

- **第42題**，這題是考推測的部分，最有可能的是要約女子出去，所以答案為**選項A**。
- **第43題**，這題要把the woman get a day off和對話中的unless all flowers are sold out before the festival...and normally that's not gonna happen聯想起來，所以女子要在該天放假的話，等同花店的花均要銷售一空，所以要選**選項C**，all merchandise is out of stock。

聽力原文和對話

Questions 44-46 refer to the following conversation

Interviewer: what we are looking for is muscularly-built guys who can move the frozen fish in a quick manner...

Jason: I think my buddy and I fit right in...we are junior students and would love to make some money during the vacation and I read the description from job hunt and pamphlets that there will be plenty of free time after the first few weeks of fish shipment...that's wonderful...

Interviewer: ...the heavy work takes about four or five weeks top and the rest of the time is yours...so you get to enjoy yourself during the whole trip...

Jason: ...how many vacancies are left?

Interviewer: ...two..actually...and I just love your enthusiasm...that makes you on the top of the list...

Jason: ...thanks...but when will we know the result...

Interviewer: ...normally...we don't do this....but I am telling you...you two are hired...

Jason: ...I'm so thrilled...

問題44-46，請參考以下對話內容

面試官：我們要找尋的是體格健壯的男生，能夠快速地搬動冷凍的魚...。

傑森：我想我夥伴和我超級適合的...我們兩個是大三的學生，且想要在假期期間賺取一些錢，然後我從獵人頭和小冊子那裡讀到關於這份工作，在前幾週的魚運輸後會有許多的自由時間...那樣是很棒的...。

面試官：...那樣沉重的工作大概最多只會花費4到5週而已，然後其餘的時間是你自己的...所以你在整個假期期間你也能夠自我享受的...。

傑森：...還會有多少的空缺呢？

面試官：實際上還有...兩個...然後我真的很喜愛你們的熱忱...這讓你們兩個列於清單前端了...。

傑森：...謝謝...但是我們什麼時候能夠得知結果呢...？

面試官：...通常...我們不這樣做的...但是我現在告訴你們...你們兩個都錄取了...

傑森：...我感到很興奮...。

試題中譯與解析

44. Why does the woman say, "that makes you on top of the list"? (A) because they are hired. (B) **because she likes the guys a lot and quite suitable for the requirement.** (C) because she has the authority to move them up. (D) because passion is the key.	44.為何女子提到「that makes you on top of the list」？ (A) 因為他們被雇用了。 (B) **因為她很喜歡男子而且覺得他們相當符合需求。** (C) 因為她有權能把他們移到前頭。 (D) 因為熱情是關鍵。
45. How did the man learn about the recruitment? (A) **pamphlets and the website.** (B) the school. (C) bulletin board. (D) news report.	45.男子是如何得知招募的？ (A) **手冊和網站。** (B) 學校。 (C) 公佈欄。 (D) 新聞報導。
46. Where most likely is the conversation taking place? (A) in the campus. (B) **in the interview room.** (C) at the travel agency. (D) at a process plant.	46.對話最有可能發生在何處？ (A) 在校園裡頭。 (B) **在面試間。** (C) 在旅行社。 (D) 在加工廠。

答案：44. B 45. A 46. B

解析

- **第44題**，這題要注意的是**makes you on top of the list**不代表錄取了，僅代表面試官對他們印象極好、很可能錄用或對方條件很接近公司想要的，故答案要選擇**選項B**。

- **第45題**，這題很明顯是由手冊和網站上看到的，所以要選**選項A**。
- **第46題**，對話最有可能的是發生在面試房間，故答案為**選項B**。

Questions 47-49 refer to the following conversation

Jason: it's kind of awful...living in such a filthy place...and the heavy workload...

Mike: I'm counting the time...they told us that there is going to be a few weeks that we don't have to work...right?

Jason: ...yeah...that's what they said...but I'm hoping that it's true...

Mike: ...what do you mean?

Jason: ...by the way they are treating us and other workers...I am starting to doubt about the whole deal...and we signed the contract for two months...

Mike: ...I'm so not in a mood to talk about this...I'm too exhausted...

Jason: ...it's about noon...let's go get the lunchbox...

Mike: ...today's lunchbox better be good; otherwise, I'm going to make a complaint to the supervisor here...

Jason: ...I feel so bad for dragging you into this...

問題47-49，請參考以下對話內容

傑森：有點糟糕...居住在這樣骯髒的地方...還有沉重的工作負擔在...。

麥克：我在數時間了...他們告訴我會有幾週是我們不用工作的時候...對吧？

傑森：...是的...這是他們當初說的...但是我現在只希望這是真的...。

麥克：...你指的是什麼呢？

傑森：...藉由他們對待我們和其他工人們...我開始懷疑著整個交易...而我們簽了兩個月的合約...。

麥克：我真的沒心情去談這些了...我真的筋疲力盡了...。

傑森：...快到中午了...我們去拿午餐盒吧...。

麥克：...今天的午餐盒最好給我很棒，否則的話，我要向這裡的上司抱怨了...。

傑森：...把你捲進這份工作裡讓我感到很抱歉...。

試題中譯與解析

47. Why does the man say, "I'm counting the time"? (A) he really wants to be on time. (B) **he cannot wait for this to be over.** (C) he knows perfectly well about the concept of time management. (D) he has a feeling that counting the time makes time pass quicker.	47. 為何男子提及「I'm counting the time」？ (A) 他真的想要準時。 (B) **他等不及要這件事情快點結束。** (C) 他深知時間管理的概念。 (D) 他有種感覺就是數時間讓時間過得更快些。
48. What are the speakers mainly discussing? (A) the dishes in the lunchbox. (B) the wearisome look they are getting per day. (C) **the treatment and the job content.** (D) the holiday after the work.	48. 說話者們主要在討論什麼？ (A) 午餐盒內的佳餚。 (B) 他們每日日益疲倦的面容。 (C) **對待和工作內容。** (D) 工作後的假期。
49. Where most likely is the conversation taking place? (A) in a restaurant. (B) outside the supervisor's office. (C) in the kitchen. (D) **at the factory.**	49. 這段對話最有可能發生在何處？ (A) 在餐廳。 (B) 在管理者的辦公室外頭。 (C) 在廚房。 (D) **在工廠。**

答案：47. B 48. C 49. D

解析

- **第47題**，男子會講這句話的主因是，他在算日子了，代表日子不好過，他只想要快點結束這件事，故答案為**選項B**。

- **第48題**，有幾個選項均是對話中提到的細節點，不過最主要的原因是**選項 C**，關於工作內容的不滿和對待員工的方式。
- **第49題**，對話最有可能發生的地點在工廠，而對話到一半剛好快正午，他們要取拿午餐盒，所以答案要選**選項D**。

聽力原文和對話

Questions 50-52 refer to the following conversation

Jason: ...I can't stand it any longer...and we smell like dead fish...can't believe we were dumb enough to believe what's written on the brochure and what's on websites...and the HR personnel is such a liar...they are treating us like an idiot...baiting...naïvely young college students...let's go talk to the boss...

Jason: ...we'd like to release the contract...and go back to our country...

Boss: that's impossible...I need you guys here...and you agreed to be here...plus we are out of workforce here...can't you see that?...and those salmons only come in this season...if it was an off-season...I'd say yes...but now...no...and I'm begging you to stay...tonight I'm hosting a barbecue party for you guys...please stay...

Jason: fine...the party better be good...

問題50-52，請參考以下對話內容

傑森：...我無法再忍受了...而且我們聞起來像是死魚一般...無法相信我們笨到足以相信在手冊上所寫和網站上的部分...而人事專員是如此的騙子...他們把我們當成了白痴了...誘導...天真爛漫的年輕大學學生們...我們去跟老闆說吧...。

傑森：...我們想要從合約中釋放出來...然後回到我們的國家...。

老闆：這是不可能的...我需要你們在這兒...而且你們當初同意到這兒...再說，我們這裡極缺人力...你們看不到嗎？...而且那些鮭魚只有在這個季節上來...如果是淡季的話，那麼我就會答應...但是現在的話...不...而現在我乞求你們待著...今晚我會辦個烤肉派對...請待著吧...。

傑森：好吧...那個派對最好給我很棒...。

試題中譯與解析	
50. What is the request of the men? (A) rewrite the contract. (B) renegotiate the contract. (C) demand a better offer. (D) **free from the bond of the agreement.**	50. 男子的要求是什麼？ (A) 重寫合約。 (B) 重新協商合約。 (C) 要求更佳的待遇。 (D) **從合約中的束縛中解脫。**
51. Why does the boss say "we are out of workforce"? (A) because he wants the guys to know about his predicament. (B) to let the guys know that short-staffed problems are temporary. (C) **to let the guys know that the current situation makes him hard to concede.** (D) because it's not an off-season.	51. 為何老闆提到「we are out of workforce」？ (A) 因為他想要男子們了解他的困境。 (B) 讓男子們知道人力短缺的問題是暫時的。 (C) **讓男子們知道現在的情況讓他更難讓步。** (D) 因為這不是淡季。
52. Which of the following is not what makes the two guys displeased? (A) what's written on the brochure. (B) what's being said during the interview. (C) what's written on websites. (D) **what's being said about the barbecue.**	52. 下列哪一項不是兩位男子所不滿的部分？ (A) 所寫在手冊上的內容。 (B) 在面試中所提到的部分。 (C) 在網站中所撰寫的部分。 (D) **所提及的烤肉的部分。**
答案：50. D 51. C 52. D	

- **第50題**，男子所提出的要求是we'd like to release the contract，這部分對應到了**free from the bond of the agreement**，所以答案為**選項D**。
- **第51題**，老闆講這句話的原因可能要思考下，有幾個選項講的是事實，但不太是老闆講這句話的原因，老闆講這句話的原因其實代表了不太可能讓步，因為就沒有足夠人力了，還能讓員工解約嗎？這樣一來人手更為不足了，所以才講這句話，讓他們知難而退，故答案為**選項C**。
- **第52題**，對話中有提到幾項讓兩位男子不快的原因，但D選項很明顯不是原因，故答案為**選項D**。

聽力原文和對話

Questions 53-55 refer to the following conversation

Mary: ...you are an early bird...

Cindy: ...I guess I am...so is that a yes...

Mary: ...I don't think that would be a problem...

Cindy: ...so what's the going rate...? US 70,000?

Mary: ...you know how many celebrities want to have a wedding in our aquarium...

Cindy: ...is that within the range...I can't possibly go higher than US 100,000

Mary: ...normally...it's US 90,000 ...but still it depends...

Cindy: ...what do you mean...?

Mary: ...on how luxurious that wedding is...the senator Lincoln's wedding cost US 200,000 dollars...

Cindy: ...no way...

Mary: ...an excellent wedding band is gonna cost you extra....

Cindy: ...I guess rich people have to find a way to fritter away the money...

Mary: ...there are still too many details that need to discuss...I just can't tell you how much a wedding is...

問題53-55，請參考以下對話內容

瑪莉：...你是個早鳥唉！...。

辛蒂：...我想我是吧...所以答案是可以囉...。

瑪莉：...我不覺得會有什麼問題...。

辛蒂：...所以價格上會是多少呢？七萬美元嗎？

瑪莉：...你知道有多少名人想要在我們水族館辦婚禮...。

辛蒂：...我提的價格在範圍之內嗎？...我無法給高於10萬美元喔。

瑪莉：...通常...價格在9萬美元...但仍然要視情況而定...。

辛蒂：...你的意思是...？

瑪莉：...要視婚宴的豪華程度而定囉...林肯議員的婚宴就花了20萬美元囉...。

辛蒂：不是吧...。

瑪莉：...一個卓越的婚宴樂隊又會花上額外的錢...。

辛蒂：我猜想有錢人必須要找個將錢揮霍掉的方式...。

瑪莉：...還有很多細節是需要討論的部分...我無法告訴你一場婚宴要花費多少囉。

試題中譯與解析	
53. What is the highest price that the woman can offer? (A) US 70,000. **(B) US 100,000.** (C) US 90,000. (D) US 200,000.	53. 對話中女子所能提供的最高金額為多少呢？ (A) 70,000 美元。 **(B) 100,000 美元。** (C) 90,000 美元。 (D) 200,000 美元。
54. According to the manager, what is the regular price for the wedding? (A) US 70,000. **(B) US 90,000.** (C) US 100,000. (D) US 200,000.	54. 根據經理所述，婚宴的常規價格為多少呢？ (A) 70,000 美元。 **(B) 90,000 美元。** (C) 100,000 美元。 (D) 200,000 美元。

模擬試題（一）

模擬試題（二）

模擬試題（三）

模擬試題（四）

模擬試題（五）

| 55. Why does the woman say, "fritter away the money"?
 (A) she wants to profuse the money.
 (B) she thinks it's good for the economy and the flow of cash.
 (C) she thinks money can solve all problems.
 (D) **she is mentioning that as the lifestyle of the rich.** | 55. 為何女子提及「fritter away the money」？
 (A) 她想要揮霍這筆錢。
 (B) 她認為這對於經濟和現金流來說是件好事。
 (C) 她認為金錢可以解決所有的問題。
 (D) **她提及這是富人的生活型態。** |

答案：53. B 54. B 55. D

 解析

- **第53題**，這題要對應到I can't possibly go higher than US 100,000，故答案為**選項B**。
- **第54題**，這題要對應到normally...it's US 90,000 dollars，故答案為**選項B**。
- **第55題**，主要是因為富人的生活方式才提到這點的，所以答案為**選項D**。

聽力原文和對話

Questions 56-58 refer to the following conversation

Jason: ...I'm representing ABC Drug Store for the wedding venue...
Employee: ...please...wait here...and do you need a cup of coffee...?
Jason: ...hot..cappuccino thanks
Employee: ...I will be here right away...
Mary: ...hey...I heard that Cindy is on vacation...
Jason: ...lucky for her...now I have to do the heavy lifting...
Mary: ...(chuckling)...let me show you hundreds of slides in the conference room
Jason: ...sure...
Mary: ...this one was governor Clark's wedding...romantic and luxurious...
Jason: ...I didn't know your aquarium has a castle...

Mary: ...it's somewhere near our third building...after the bride and groom walking down the tunnel in the basement...there is a huge cafeteria...an all-you-can-eat buffet...in the castle...it's like prince and princess eating in the castle...

Jason: ...I'm sure my boss is gonna love this one...but I can't make the decision for him though...

問題56-58，請參考以下對話內容

傑森：... 我是代表ABC藥品店來看婚宴的場地...。

員工：請...在這稍等...還有你需要一杯咖啡嗎...。

傑森：...熱的...卡布奇諾...謝謝。

員工：我馬上就回來...。

瑪莉：...嗨...我聽說辛蒂正在放大假...。

傑森：...她走運囉...我現在要做沉重的工作...。

瑪莉：...（呵呵）...讓我在會議室向你展示數百張簡報圖。

傑森：...當然...。

瑪莉：...這是州長克拉克的婚禮...浪漫且豪華...。

傑森：...我不知道你們水族館有個城堡呢...？

瑪莉：...這位於接近我們第三棟建築物...在新娘和新郎走入地下室的隧道中時...有間大型的自助餐廳...吃到飽自助餐...在城堡裡頭...就像是王子和公主在城堡裡頭用餐一樣...。

傑森：...我確信我們老闆一定會很喜愛這個的...但是我不能替他做決定就是了...。

試題中譯與解析

| 56. Why does the man come to the company?
(A) he wants to see the castle.
(B) he is on behalf of the governor Clarke.
(C) **he is the representative here for a mission.**
(D) he needs hot cappuccino. | 56. 為什男子來公司拜訪呢？
(A) 他想要觀看城堡。
(B) 他代表州長克拉克。
(C) **他身為代表來這是有任務的。**
(D) 他需要熱卡布奇諾。 |

57. Why does the man say, "now I have to do the heavy lifting"? (A) he hates the heavy workload but still has to do it. (B) he considers himself unlucky. (C) he doesn't want to be a representative. (D) **he is making a complaint that he has to do his coworker's daunting job while she is on vacation.**	57. 為何男子提及「now I have to do the heavy lifting」？ (A) 他討厭繁重的工作負擔，但是仍舊必須做。 (B) 他認為自己並不幸運。 (C) 他不想要成為代表。 (D) **他正抱怨著，他必須要從事他同事令人感到畏懼的工作，而她卻在度假。**
58. What is not mentioned about the third building? (A) it contains a castle. (B) it has an underground tunnel. (C) **there lives a real prince.** (D) there is a buffet in there.	58. 關於第三大樓，沒有提到的部分是？ (A) 它包含城堡。 (B) 它有著地下隧道。 (C) **裡頭住著一位王子。** (D) 裡頭有自助餐。

答案：56. C 57. D 58. C

解析

- 第56題，選項有改寫過，不過卻是男子來公司的主因，故要選擇**選項C**。
- 第57題，男子講這句話意思是重擔卻落在他頭上，而同事卻去渡假，講這句話的主要原因是有點小抱怨或覺得不該是他責任範圍的事情但他卻要來扛，這題選**選項C**最為適切。
- 第58題，對話中有提到城堡、新郎新娘就像王子公主般，但是沒有提到真實的王子住在該城堡裡頭，故要選**選項C**。

聽力原文和對話

Questions 59-61 refer to the following conversation

Contact/ABC Drug Store	
PR/Cindy	555-666-600 #100
Sales/Jason	555-666-601 #115
Manager	555-666-602 #115
CFO	555-666-603 #125
Boss	555-666-604 #115

Mary: ...you are probably tired...and we still have 500 slides to go through...why don't you drink some coffee...and I will be right back...

Jason: ...ok...thanks

Employee: ...here are some desserts for you...

Jason: ...how kind of you...thanks...

Employee: ...I have been dreaming a wedding like this...but it's just too extravagant...and I should really get back to work

Jason: ...(yawning...)...thank god I have taken some notes...

Mary: ...don't worry about it...I was just on the phone with your boss...and he seems to like the thirteen slide...the concept is very simple...and luckily...we don't have to go through what's left...

Jason: ...my mission is done here...

Mary: ...I have drafted a contract...in the folder...and some information...in case your boss has a second thought...

Jason: ...wonderful...really nice meeting you today...and thanks for the cookies and coffee...

問題59-61，請參考以下對話內容

聯絡／ABC 藥品店	
公關人員／辛蒂	555-666-600 #100
銷售／傑森	555-666-601 #115
經理	555-666-602 #115
財務長	555-666-603 #125
老闆	555-666-604 #115

瑪莉：…你可能累了…然後我們仍有500張簡報要看…你為什麼不先喝些咖啡…我馬上就回來…。

傑森：…好的…謝謝。

員工：…這裡有些甜點給你…。

傑森：你真好…謝謝…。

員工：…我一直都夢想著有像這樣的婚禮…但是這真的太奢華了…而且我真的該回去工作了。

傑森：…（打哈欠）…謝天謝地…我已經先做了筆記了…。

瑪莉：…別擔心…我剛與你們老闆通過電話…而他似乎喜歡第13張簡報…這個概念非常簡單…幸運的是…我們不用再觀看接下來剩下的部分了。

傑森：…我的任務到此已經完成了…。

瑪莉：…我已經草擬了一份合約…在資料夾裡頭…以及一些資訊…以防你的老闆有其他的想法…。

傑森：…太棒了…今天見到您真的很榮幸…而且要謝謝招待的餅乾和咖啡了…。

試題中譯與解析

59. Look at the graph, which of the following phone number did the woman dial? (A) 555-666-601 #115 (B) 555-666-602 #115 (C) 555-666-603 #125 (D) **555-666-604 #115**	59. 請參考圖表，下列哪個電話號碼是對話中女子所撥的號碼？ (A) 555-666-601 #115 (B) 555-666-602 #115 (C) 555-666-603 #125 (D) **555-666-604 #115**

60. Why does the man say, "my mission is done here"? (A) he thinks the boss has made up his mind. **(B) he is relieved that they don't have to discuss any detail.** (C) he knows perfectly well that his boss won't have a second thought. (D) now he can enjoy desserts and cookies without worrying about it.	60. 為何男子提及「my mission is done here」？ (A) 他認為老闆已經下了決定了。 **(B) 他對於他們不用在談論任何細節感到如釋重負。** (C) 他早就全然了解到他的老闆不會有第二種念頭存在。 (D) 現在他可以享用甜點和餅乾而不用擔憂了。
61. What does the woman say about the contract? (A) it's easily read. (B) it contains all information. **(C) it will be put in a folder.** (D) it could change his boss's mind.	61. 關於合約的部分，女子提到什麼呢？ (A) 合約易讀。 (B) 合約包含了所有資訊。 **(C) 合約會被放在資料夾裡頭。** (D) 合約可能可以改變他老闆的心。

答案：59. D 60. B 61. C

解析

- **第59題**，這題的話要注意別看錯，要細心些，重點放在最後三碼和分機號碼。然後要對應到女子說的don't worry about it...I was just on the phone with your boss，所以可以推測出跟女子講電話的對象是老闆，故要選**選項D**。
- **第60題**，男子會講這句話的主因是，沒他的事情了，因為老闆決定好要什麼了，故男子突然感到擔子一鬆、如釋重負，而且不用在看一堆簡報等等的，故答案要選**選項B**。
- **第61題**，這題的話女子有提到合約以及合約會放在folder內，故答案為**選項C**，其餘的選項均為干擾選項。

Questions 62-64 refer to the following conversation

Mark: hey...over here...

Cindy: ...I saw you...it's not easy to find...I mean the location...

Mark: ...that's the main reason that we'd like to sell it...are there any ways to make this happen...as fast as you can...

Cindy: ...I'm sure I can find a way...I'm the best realtor in town...remember...and that's the reason why you contacted me...

Mark: it's pretty hot over here... let's head in side and have some coffee...

Cindy: ...then after that...I need you to show me around...that way I get to find what's attractive to potential buyers...and is there anything you'd like to tell me...?

Mark: ...a few months ago...my nephew killed himself on the balcony...

Cindy: ...that makes this place a haunted house...

Mark: ...should I disclose the information...the values of the house are gonna get affected...

Cindy: ...then we just have to come up with something creative and perfect the technique of paraphrasing...

問題62-64，請參考以下對話內容

馬克：嘿！...在這裡...。

辛蒂：...我看到你了...這裡真的不太好找...我指的是位置...。

馬克：...這就是我們想要銷售的主要原因...有什麼方式可以讓這成真嗎...越快越好...。

辛蒂：...我確信我可以找到方法...我是鎮上最棒的房地產經紀人...記得嗎...而這是你聯繫我的原因...。

馬克：這裡相當的熱...讓我們進去裡頭並且喝些咖啡吧...。

辛蒂：...那麼之後呢...我需要你帶我到處看下...這樣的話我就可以找到吸引潛在買家的吸引點了...而且還有什麼是你想要告訴我的嗎...。

馬克：...幾個月前...我外甥在陽台自殺了...。

辛蒂：...這讓這裡變成了鬼屋了...。

馬克：...我應該要揭露這個資訊嗎...房子的價值就會受到影響了...。

辛蒂：那麼我們就要想些創意的回答而且完善釋義的技巧...。

試題中譯與解析	
62. Where most likely are the speakers? (A) **at the owner's house.** (B) at the owner's coffee shop. (C) at the realtor's lunch meeting room. (D) at the potential buyers' conference room.	62. 説話者們最可能身處何處？ (A) **在屋主的房子內。** (B) 在屋主的咖啡店內。 (C) 在房仲人員的午餐會議室內。 (D) 在潛在買家的會議室內。
63. What is mentioned about landowner's nephew? (A) he hates the design of the balcony. (B) **he committed suicide.** (C) he doesn't like the haunted house. (D) he already discloses the information to potential buyers.	63. 關於地主的姪子何者為非？ (A) 他討厭陽台的設計。 (B) **他自殺了。** (C) 他不喜歡鬼屋。 (D) 他已經揭露訊息給潛在買家。
64. What does the woman suggest the owner do? (A) run away from the haunted house as fast as he can. (B) hide the information. (C) increase the values of the house. (D) **think of other ways to convince buyers.**	64. 對話中的女子建議屋主做什麼？ (A) 他要盡快地逃離鬼屋。 (B) 藏匿資訊。 (C) 增加房屋的價值。 (D) **思考其他的方式來說服買家。**
答案：62. A 63. B 64. D	

解析

- **第62題**，從女子說的I saw you...it's not easy to find...I mean the location...和男子說的let's head in side and have some coffee等等可以得知發生的地點是在房東家，故要選**選項A**。
- **第63題**，這題要的話對應到my nephew killed himself on the balcony，killed himself就是**commit suicide**故答案為**選項B**。
- **第64題**，這題的話要對應到just have to come up with something creative其實就是選項中**think of other ways**的意思，兩者為同義轉換，故要選**選項D**。

聽力原文和對話

Questions 65-67 refer to the following conversation

Cindy: ...it's a nice view over here...and there's a **translucent** lake nearby...

Mark: ...that's something...

Cindy: ...I guess we have to upgrade our photograph skills...putting several pics of the lakes...and highlight this part...I'm sure some twentysomethings who are still living in a romantic bubble and can't afford the price of the house in the city would consider buying it...

Mark: ...do you see the swans over there? And several ducks?

Cindy: ...really cute...but no chickens?

Mark: ...no...but you can raise some if you want

Cindy: ...that actually reminds me of something? Ring any bell?

Mark: ...what?

Cindy: ...The King's Lake...in Germany...perhaps a few pictures of the Lake can jog your memory...I'm gonna modify the title of your house on the website and upload more pictures...

Mark: ...thanks...

問題65-67，請參考以下對話內容

辛蒂：...這裡的景色很美...而且這裡有半透明的湖泊在旁...。

馬克：...這就是特色了...。

辛蒂：...我想我們必須要升級我們的拍照技巧...放置幾張湖泊的相片...然後強調這個部分...我相信有些20幾歲仍活在浪漫泡泡裡頭的人，且無法負擔的起城市房價的人，就會考慮購買它了...。

馬克：你有看到那裡有天鵝在那裡嗎？還有幾隻鴨子？

辛蒂：...相當可愛...但是沒有雞？

馬克：沒有，但是如果你想要的話你可以飼養。

辛蒂：...那真的讓我想到了一些東西？想起什麼了嗎？

馬克：...什麼？

辛蒂：...在德國的國王湖...或許幾張湖泊的照片能刷新你的記憶...我想要重新修改網站上你房子的標題以及上傳更多照片...。

馬克：...謝謝...。

試題中譯與解析	
65. Which of the following creatures cannot be found near the lake? (A) chickens. (B) ducks. (C) swans. **(D) dogs.**	65. 下列哪項生物在靠近湖泊的地方不會發現到？ (A) 雞。 (B) 鴨。 (C) 鵝。 **(D) 狗。**
66. Why does the woman say, "Ring any bell"? (A) she wants to make sure the owner hears the ring of the bell. (B) she wants the owner to have excellent memory. **(C) the association might evoke the owner to think about something.** (D) the landscape only reminds the lady to think about something.	66. 為何女子提到「Ring any bell」？ (A) 她想要確保屋主聽到鈴響。 (B) 她想要屋主有卓越的記憶力。 **(C) 聯想可能喚起屋主想到某些事情。** (D) 景色僅讓女士想起一些事。

67. Why does the woman say, "can jog your memory"? (A) because the owner has amnesia. (B) because one's memory can be lost after a trauma. (C) **because these photos might stimulate the owner to recall the image.** (D) because the owner has to jog so that he can remember something.	67. 為何女子提到can jog your memory」？ (A) 因為屋主有健忘症。 (B) 因為在創傷過後，一個人的記憶力可能會喪失。 (C) **因為這些相片可能激起屋主回想到某些畫面。** (D) 因為屋主必須要慢跑，這樣他才能記起一些事情。

答案：65. D 66. C 67. C

解析

- 第**65**題，這題的話沒有提到的是狗，故要選**選項D**，也要注意的是chickens，男子有提到no...but you can raise some if you want，所以chickens還是可能出現在該地區的或有人有眷養。
- 第**66**題，這題要思考下，不過這些映入眼簾的畫面確實讓女子想到了國王湖，所以才會説這句話，因為她預期房東可能是不是也會因為這些畫面想到這些事情等等，所以最適合的答案是**選項C**。
- 第**67**題，這題也是，在解釋後講出了這句話，意思是湖的照片可能讓房東想起一些畫面等等，所以説這句話的原因是**選項C**。

聽力原文和對話

Questions 68-70 refer to the following conversation

Cindy: we'd better get going...it's a long trail

Park ranger: before you go, I'd like you two sign the form...it's required though...you should read through from item number 1 to 50.

Cindy: ...just sign the document and give it to him...

Park ranger: you didn't even read it...it's very important...if anything does happen...there won't be a helicopter or the plane for the rescue...some rocky roads are dangerous...and narrow...

Cindy: why do we need those vehicles...you are making it look like a horror film...

John: perhaps we should read it first...my reading speed is incredibly fast...

Park ranger: ...and I'm going to pick a guide for you...preferably a stronger one..

Cindy: ...is it necessary? I'm with my husband...

Park ranger: ..you surely do...our guide is trained and experienced...

問題68-70，請參考以下對話內容

辛蒂：我們最好快點啟程了...這是長的步道。

公園管理員：你走之前，我想要你簽這兩份表格...這是必須要簽署的...你應該要讀完項目數字1到50。

辛蒂：...快簽了文件，然後交給他。

公園管理員：你根本完全沒有讀...這是很重要的...如果任何的事情發生了...不會有直升機或飛機來救援...有些崎嶇的道路是危險...且狹窄的...。

辛蒂：為什麼我們需要那些交通工具呢？...你把它描述的像是在拍恐怖片了...。

約翰：或許我們應該要先讀完它...我的閱讀速度相當快的...。

公園管理員：...而且我正要替你選一位嚮導...偏好一位較強壯的...。

辛蒂：...這有必要嗎？我跟我先生一起同行唉...。

公園管理員：...你確實有必要...我們的嚮導是訓練有素且有經驗的...。

試題中譯與解析

68. What does the man say about the form? (A) **it needs to be signed.** (B) the procedure is not mandatory. (C) the item number on the form is vaguely seen. (D) visitors do necessarily have to read it to sign.	68. 關於表格的部分男子提到了什麼？ (A) **表格需要有簽名。** (B) 程序不是強制性的。 (C) 表格上的項目號碼幾乎是看不清楚的。 (D) 訪客不需要閱讀就能在上頭簽名。

69. What most likely is the man's occupation? (A) a helicopter driver (B) a lawyer (C) the rescuer (D) **a park ranger**	69. 對話中的男子的職業最有可能是什麼？ (A) 直升機駕駛 (B) 律師 (C) 救援者 (D) **公園管理者**
70. Where most likely is the conversation taking place? (A) in the village (B) in the mountain (C) **at the entrance of the National Park** (D) at the hiking trail	70. 對話最有可能發生在何處？ (A) 在村莊裡 (B) 在山裡頭 (C) **在國家公園的入口處** (D) 在健行小徑

答案：68. A 69. D 70. C

 解析

- **第68題**，關於form的部分，其實理解後不難選，排除掉一些干擾選項後，其實**答案是A**。
- **第69題**，由對話中的描述，包含在表格上簽名到最後的安排嚮導陪同，男子最有可能的職業是公園管理員，故答案為**選項D**。
- **第70題**，這題是詢問地點，最有可能的地方是國家公園的入口處，故答案為**選項C**。

 PART 4

聽力原文與中譯

Questions 71-73 refer to the following video

This is...Jason Thornes...welcome to wildlife Kitchen...apparently, I have competition...so one of the inhabitants is going to use traditional kitchen wares...and I have the delivered cooking utensils...let's take a look...grill pan...it's new but it seems a bit overshadowed by the villager's flagstone...I've gas so that makes me quicker to finish a table for ten...I also have a whisk and a food processor...that makes me more efficient...they are still using knife to chop the large slice of beef...I'm gonna put the beef into the food processor...it's done in a few seconds...great...oh dear...the producer brings me with a new refrigerator...is it necessary? I've got to say that the whisk is amazing...the camera should really take a close-up...though villagers are experienced chefs using rolling pins....my dough is almost done and I'm gonna scatter some scallions...

問題71-73請參閱下列視頻

這是記者...傑森・索恩...歡迎來到野生生物廚房...顯然我已經有了競爭對手了...所以其中一位居民要用傳統的廚具...而我有送至的烹飪廚具...我們來看下吧...方形平底烤鍋...這是新的但是這跟村民的石板相比似乎有點相形見絀...我有瓦斯所以讓我能更快完成一桌十人份的料理...我還有攪拌器和食物處理器...所以這樣讓我看起來更有效率...他們還在用刀子在切大片的牛肉...我要將牛肉放置到食物處理器中...這在幾秒內就完成了...很棒...噢！我的天啊...製作人幫我帶了新型冰箱...這真的有必要嗎？我不得不說這個攪拌器令人感到吃驚...這台相機應該要拍下近距離的...儘管村民們是有經驗的廚師使用著麵棍...我的麵團已經好了，然後我要撒些青蔥了...。

71. Why does the man say, "a bit overshadowed by"? (A) because he exaggerates the claim. (B) because he wants the flagstone as a gift from villagers. (C) **because he thinks the flagstone actually prevails the company's expensive products.** (D) because now he cannot cook faster.	71. 為何男子提到「a bit overshadowed by」？ (A) 因為他誇大的宣傳效果。 (B) 因為他想要從村民那獲取石板當作禮物。 (C) **因為他認為石板實際上勝過公司價格昂貴的產品。** (D) 因為他現在無法烹飪的更快速。
72. Why does the man want the camera to have a close-up? (A) to make villagers jealous. (B) to impress the producer of the show. (C) to give photographers a genuine feel. (D) **to highlight and promote the product.**	72. 為何男子想要攝相機近距離拍攝呢？ (A) 讓村民們感到忌妒。 (B) 打動節目的製作人。 (C) 給攝影師真實的感受。 (D) **強調並推薦產品。**
73. What distinguishes the food processor with villagers' knife? (A) its engine. (B) **its efficiency.** (C) its price. (D) its weight.	73. 食物處理器和村民刀子的區隔處在於？ (A) 引擎。 (B) **效率。** (C) 價格。 (D) 體重。

答案：71. C 72. D 73. B

解析

- **第71題**，這題的話，其實男子對於送來的廚具感到振奮也覺得應該會勝過這種不起眼地方的用具，但是看到村民的flagstone卻不免感到相形見絀，才講了這句話（覺得可能用石板烤或煮更勝用廚具或更有風味），所以最可能的答案為**選項C**，廚具的鋒芒被蓋過了。

- **第72題**，男子在講這句話時，是特地要攝影師打了特寫，其實有故意要觀眾看到這個產品，有推銷和廣告的效果在，故答案為**選項D**。（視頻中的廚具均是置入性行銷的產品）
- **第73題**，這題是比較兩樣產品的優缺，the food processor確實在效率上勝過村民的刀子，故答案為**選項B**。

聽力原文與中譯

Questions 74-76 refer to the following video

This is ...Jason Thornes...welcome to wildlife Kitchen...the competition is still on...I'm gonna fry the dough with scallions...hmmm smells good...and the egg...totally forget to mention that I have one of the expensive Chinese woks delivered today...I'm gonna fry water spinach with beef and onions...it can be instantly heated...that makes it highly recommended...would like to have one myself...the villager is now making a traditional soup and stir it with a large ladle...I've got to say that lumber-made ladle is good...I should probably sneak back out there and steal it...kidding...where is my ladle?...it's got to be here somewhere...it's metal made...kind of ok...what...the producer just told me the price of the ladle...a price that I can barely afford...

問題74-76請參閱下列視頻

這是記者...傑森・索恩...歡迎來到野生生物廚房...競爭仍存在著...我正要煎裹有蔥的麵團...嗯嗯聞起來蠻好的...還有蛋...全然忘記提到我有很昂貴的中式炒菜鍋今天送到了...我要先炒空心菜和牛肉跟洋蔥...這鍋能夠即刻受熱...如此一來讓其值得高度推薦...自己都想要有一個這樣的鍋子了...村民正製作傳統的湯以大型的長柄勺攪動...我必須要說的是那個木材製的勺子蠻好...我可能應該要偷偷跑到那裡去然後偷走...勺子...開玩笑的...我的長柄勺在哪呢...一定在某處...這是金屬製的勺子...還可以啦...什麼...製作人剛告知我這個勺子的價格...幾乎是我勉強能付的起的價格呀...。

74. What is being advertised? (A) **the Chinese woks** (B) the dough with scallions (C) fried water spinach (D) the ladle	74. 廣告所宣傳的是什麼？ (A) **中國鐵鑄鍋。** (B) 裹著蔥的麵糰。 (C) 炒空心菜。 (D) 勺子。
75. What aspect of the pan does the speaker applaud? (A) the origin (B) the light weight (C) **the heating part** (D) the shipment	75. 鍋子的哪個部份是說話者說讚譽的呢？ (A) 起源。 (B) 輕盈的體積。 (C) **加熱的部份。** (D) 運送。
76. Who most likely is the speaker addressing? (A) **housewives** (B) villagers (C) executives of the kitchen wares (D) the producer	76. 說話者最可能在對誰說話？ (A) **家庭主婦。** (B) 村民們。 (C) 廚具的主管。 (D) 製作人。

答案：74. A 75. C 76. A

解析

- **第74題**，打廣告的項目很明顯是Chinese woks故答案要選**選項A**。
- **第75題**，這題可以對應到對話中的it can be instantly heated，故答案很明顯是**選項C**，加熱的部分。
- **第76題**，這個視頻最有可能的談話對象有很多，不過最有可能的收視觀眾會是家庭主婦，所以有煮菜和相關廚具的主打。

聽力原文與中譯

Questions 77-79 refer to the following news report

After a few discussions and further attempts to merger with the largest car company, the result is not fruitful...the company actually has more problems than they are to the eyes of the audiences...the issue remains...if none of the investors is willing to finance...then the company disintegrates and employees are jobless.......hold on we have a breaking news...the spokesperson is making an announcement...

Spokesperson: It's sad to say that our CFO of the company transferred the money that is gonna use to pay the employees and some of it actually came from earlier investors...this actually adds salt to injury...and unfortunately...the CFO is in another country now...

問題77-79請參閱下列新聞報導

在幾次的討論和嘗試性的與最大型的車廠合併後，結果是無效的...公司實際上比起觀眾們所著眼的部分，有更多的問題存在著...議題仍舊...如果沒有投資客願意資助的話...那麼公司就會瓦解而且員工會失業...等等...我們有新聞快訊...發言人有公告要發佈...

發言人：令人感到悲傷的是，我們公司的財務長將用於支付員工薪資和有些實際上來自於投資客的金錢轉移了...實際上這讓問題更為雪上加霜...而不幸的是...財務長現在正位於其他國家...。

試題中譯與解析

77. What can be inferred about the merger? (A) successful. (B) fruitful. (C) **futile.** (D) mysterious.	77. 關於併購可以推測出什麼呢？ (A) 成功的。 (B) 富有成效的。 (C) **無效的。** (D) 神秘的。
78. Which of the following is closet in meaning to disintegrate? (A) intact. (B) mystify. (C) consolidate. (D) **dismiss.**	78. 下列哪個選項近似於「disintegrate」？ (A) 完整的。 (B) 使困惑。 (C) 鞏固。 (D) **解散。**

79. Why does the spokesperson say, "adds salt to injury"?
(A) To salvage the public image of the company.
(B) to provide proof of the transferred money.
(C) to refute the information from earlier news report.
(D) **to show that it makes the situation even worse.**

79. 為何發言人提及「adds salt to injury」？
(A) 拯救公司的大眾形象。
(B) 提供移轉金錢的證據。
(C) 駁斥稍早之前新聞報導的資訊。
(D) **顯示這會讓情況更糟。**

答案：77. C 78. D 79. D

解析

- **第77題**，試題中提到的merger是not fruitful，所以可以對應到選項的futile，故要選**選項C**。
- **第78題**，這題是詢問同義字的部分，所以其實答案是**選項D**。
- **第79題**，發言人會說這句話的原因是這讓情況更糟了，因為後來注入的資金又遭到財務長的挪用等，故答案要選**選項D**。

聽力原文與中譯

Questions 80-82 refer to the following news report

Normally, this kind of news only lasts for a week...but it seems that things are going to be more dramatic than we can imagine...in the morning news, the CEO of the company is being put into the custody for insider trading...and the CFO of the company was found dead on a cruise...according to the police report...there wasn't defense wound of any sort...which makes this incident more creepier...is he getting framed and murdered? Is this a conspiracy? Perhaps he didn't take the money and flee the country? there are still many suspicious points that we can only wait for the police to find out...and this is Cindy Chen at London...

問題71-73請參閱下列新聞報導

通常，像這樣的新聞只會維持一週...但是奇怪的是，這似乎比我們想像中的更為戲劇化...在晨間新聞中，公司的執行長因為涉及內線交易而被拘留...而公司的財務長被發現死於航遊客輪上...根據警方的報告...現場沒有任何的防衛性傷害...這使得事件變得更為毛骨悚然...他是被誣陷且謀殺的嗎？這會是個陰謀嗎？或許他不該將錢帶走且逃離國家？而還有許多可疑的疑點，我們只能等待警方找出真相...這是辛蒂・陳在倫敦的報導。

試題中譯與解析	
80. According to the news report, what is the CEO getting accused of? (A) forgery. (B) murder. (C) **insider trading.** (D) corruption.	80. 根據新聞報導，執行長被控告什麼罪名？ (A) 偽造文書。 (B) 謀殺。 (C) **內線交易。** (D) 貪汙。
81. According to the news report, what can be found on a large ship? (A) money. (B) illegal documents. (C) cruise. (D) **corpse.**	81. 根據新聞報導，在較大型的船上頭可以發現什麼？ (A) 金錢。 (B) 違法文件。 (C) 航遊。 (D) **屍體。**
82. Where is the news report given? (A) Egypt. (B) **Europe.** (C) America. (D) Asia.	82. 新聞是在何處播報的呢？ (A) 埃及。 (B) **歐洲。** (C) 美國。 (D) 亞洲。

答案：80. C 81. D 82. B

解析

- **第80題**，這題要注意細節的部分，還有是詢問關於CEO的部分，故要選**選項C**。

- **第81題**，這題的話試題中的a large ship要對應到cruise，這樣一來就很容易選了，所以可以得知在船上發現的是財務長的屍首，故答案要選**選項D**。
- **第82題**，這題的話最後結尾記者有說道自己所在何處，記者身處的地方是英國，英國包含在歐洲的範疇，故要選擇**選項B**，即歐洲。

聽力原文與中譯

Questions 83-85 refer to the following recording

There is an explosion in the huge warehouse...but it is deducted that this is a result of the mega forest fire...those items in the storehouse are inflammable, paper, wood furniture, and clothes...and the forest fire somehow spurs the growth of fire...we are asking for more assistance...the helicopters are spreading water to halt the increasingly rampant fire...whereas some of the rescue teams use both the chemical powder and water to make the fire smaller...nearby local residents are forcing to leave their houses...and luckily no one was injured...finally here comes massive rainfall...really like a miracle...but unfortunately some forest animals died...

問題83-85請參閱下列錄製訊息

在這大型的倉庫發生的爆炸...但是可以推論這是大型森林火災的結果...那些項目在倉庫中是易燃的，紙、木製傢俱和衣服...而森林火災有點促成了火勢的成長...我們要求更多的支援...直升機正灑水來暫緩日益蔓延的火勢...而有些救援團隊同時使用了化學粉末和水讓火勢變得更小...鄰近的當地居民被迫要離開他們的房子...而幸運的是，沒有人受傷...最終來了豪大雨...真的像是奇蹟一般...但是不幸的是，有些森林動物死亡了...。

試題中譯與解析

83. Which of the following item is not instantly-lit in the fire accident? (A) inflammable items. (B) furniture. (C) **plastics.** (D) clothes.	83. 下列哪個項目在火災意外中不是易燃品？ (A) 易燃的品項。 (B) 傢俱。 (C) **塑膠。** (D) 服飾。

84. What is mentioned about the firefighters? (A) they are able to tackle the explosion. (B) they are forced to leave the house. (C) **they demand more help.** (D) they don't have the authority to use helicopters.	84. 關於消防隊員的部分何者正確？ (A) 他們能夠處理爆炸事件。 (B) 他們被迫離開居住的房子。 (C) **他們要求更多的幫助。** (D) 他們沒有權力使用直升機。
85. Which of the following was ravaged by the forest fire? (A) **beasts.** (B) helicopters. (C) firefighters. (D) local inhabitants.	85. 下列哪一項受到森林大火的肆虐？ (A) **野獸。** (B) 直升機。 (C) 消防隊員們。 (D) 當地居民。

答案：83. C 84. C 85. A

解析

- **第83題**，試題是詢問not instantly-lit，故可以排除掉inflammable的所有項目，選項出題也沒有照著列，還是可以先排除掉大範疇的inflammable items, furniture, clothes，故答案為**選項C**。
- **第84題**，視頻中沒有提到消防隊員能應付爆炸的部分等等，最主要的部分是他們需要幫助，這對應到聽力原文中的we are asking for more assistance以及選項C的內容，故答案為**選項C**。
- **第85題**，這題的話要看到最後unfortunately some forest animals died，animals等同於**beasts**故答案要選**選項A**，也要注意前面聽到的物品或項目就是了。

Questions 86-88 refer to the following advertisement

Best Jewelry is having an exhibition in the coming Fall...the tickets are harder to get than usual...because international celebrities will be attending the event...all tickets are sold out in a day...which makes the hosting company profitable...there are four types of jewelry that will be exhibited...diamonds, gold, sapphires, and pearls....and they have never been exhibited...of course there are interpreters on the scene...all of them are actually multi-lingual, can converse several languages at the same time...don't worry that if you have a spouse that is not a local here...and you are probably wondering whether the resold tickets on other websites is authentic...it's not false...you might get the profit of selling them to others...grab the chance...

問題86-88請參閱下列廣告

倍斯特珠寶在即將來臨的秋天要舉辦展覽....門票比起以往更是一票難求...因為國際名人都會參加這個活動...所有的門票都在一天內銷售一空了...這也讓主辦公司獲利...一共有四個類型的珠寶即將要展示出...鑽石、黃金、藍寶石和珍珠...它們都未曾被展示過。當然，現場會有口譯員在...實際上，他們所有人都懂數國的語言，能夠同時以幾種語言進行交談...別擔心如果你的配偶不是當地人...而且你可能也會想，在其他網站上重新銷售的票是真實的...不是仿冒的...你可能可以藉由銷售票給其他人而獲利...抓住機會吧...。

試題中譯與解析	
86. What is unique about the Best Jewelry at the exhibition? (A) its comparatively low price. (B) its durability. (C) its design. (D) **its debut.**	86. 在展覽會場中，倍斯特珠寶的獨特處為何？ (A) 價格相對低廉。 (B) 耐用性。 (C) 設計。 (D) **首映。**

模擬試題（一）

模擬試題（二）

模擬試題（三）

模擬試題（四）

模擬試題（五）

87. Why does the speaker mention "don't worry that if you have a spouse that is not a local here"? (A) to enhance the authenticity of the jewelry. (B) to demonstrate the credibility of the company. (C) **to clear the doubts.** (D) to make sure everyone will get the ticket.	87. 為何說話者提到「don't worry that if you have a spouse that is not a local here」？ (A) 提高珠寶的真實性。 (B) 彰顯公司的信用度。 (C) **清除疑慮。** (D) 確保每個人都會拿到票。
88. Which of the following will not be showcased in the approaching exhibition? (A) **silver.** (B) gold. (C) pearls. (D) blue-like gems.	88. 下列哪一項不會於接下來的展覽會中展示出？ (A) **銀飾。** (B) 金子。 (C) 珍珠。 (D) 藍色般的寶石。

答案：86. D 87. C 88. A

 解析

- **第86題**，這題要小心些，因為沒有一開始就提到這部分，而是到了中段才提到they have never been exhibited...這其實是要說明展示會會是珠寶首次亮相，故要選**選項D**。
- **第87題**，說話者會講這句話是因為展示會其實有設想到這點，所以有準備口譯員，故可以不用擔心這部分，但題目中沒有提到這點，而是用較隱晦的方式表達，其實也是澄清一下疑慮，這樣購票人就不會因為一些考量而不購買了，故答案要選**選項C**。
- **第88題**，這題是詢問不會展示的部分，其實沒有提到silver故答案要選**選項A**，另外要注意的是藍寶石sapphires換成了blue-like gems。

Questions 89-91 refer to the following news report

Rescue	
animals	fees
Barnacle geese	US 20
Camels	US 290
Horses	US 250
Wolves	US 240
Note: barnacle geese will be not used as vehicles	

This is news anchor Bella James...good morning...first...let's take a look at what happened at the resort yesterday...as you can see the cliff is at least 2,000 feet...and youtubers went to the extreme...trying to climb down and filmed the video...but slipped...according to the residents two people got injured and four died in the accident...a local villager told us that they are no barnacle geese...and mimicking the behavior of these creatures to get more hits just is not worthy of it...and the rescue team which arrived at the scene found it hard to rescue...cars are unable to drive on the steep road...so only animal-transportation is more likely...and it's really cold out there...losing body temperatures can be detrimental according to our health experts...and stretchers and ladders will also be using to rescue them.

問題89-91請參閱下列新聞報導

救援	
動物	費用
黑雁	20 美元
駱駝	290 美元
馬匹	250 美元
狼	240 美元
註：黑雁不會用於交通工具	

這是新聞主播貝拉‧詹姆士...早安...首先...讓我們來看下在昨天度假勝地所發生的事情...你可以看到峭壁至少有2000尺...而youtubers走極端路線...試圖要爬下來拍攝些視頻...但是滑跤了...根據當地居民...兩人受傷而有四個人死於這起事件之中...有位當地居民告訴我們他們並不是黑雁...而且模仿這些生物的行為以換取更多的點擊...關於這點是不值得的...而剛抵達的搜救團隊發現搜救是有多麼困難...車子無法駛向陡峭的道路上頭...所以僅有動物交通工具是較有可能的...而這裡真的相當冷...失去體溫的話真的會有危害，根據我們的健康專家所述...而擔架和梯子將會用於救援他們。

試題中譯與解析

89. Why does the local villager mention barnacle geese? (A) to applaud the sanctity of the cliff. (B) to downplay the negative feelings of the news report. (C) to entertain news reporters. (D) **to satirize the foolish behavior.**	89.為什麼當地居民會提到黑雁？ (A) 盛讚峭壁的神聖性。 (B) 輕描淡寫新聞報導的負面感受。 (C) 娛樂新聞記者們。 (D) **諷刺愚蠢的行為。**
90. What could be the means of transportation to carry the survivors? (A) automobiles. (B) ladders. (C) airplanes. (D) **creatures.**	90.什麼可能會用於搭載生還者的交通工具？ (A) 汽車。 (B) 梯子。 (C) 飛機。 (D) **生物。**
91. Look at the graph. Which of the following animal transportation will cost the least money? (A) barnacle geese. (B) horses. (C) **wolves.** (D) camels.	91.請參考圖表。下列哪一個動物運輸將花費最少的金錢？ (A) 黑雁。 (B) 馬。 (C) **狼。** (D) 駱駝。

答案：89. D 90. D 91. C

- **第89題**，這題要意會一下，而當地村民會講到黑雁的部分主要是嘲諷這樣行為其實是愚蠢的，故答案要選**選項D**。
- **第90題**，要對應到cars are unable to drive on the steep road...so only animal-transportation is more likely，故可以刪除掉非動物的運送方式，也要注意animals換成了creatures，故答案為**選項D**。
- **第91題**，這題是詢問花費最少的，但是別太快選表格中對應到最少的金額，在表格下方的note有提到黑雁不會用於交通運送，僅用於救援，所以雖然黑雁是金額最低的，但仍要排除掉，故答案要選擇**選項C**。

聽力原文與中譯

Questions 92-94 refer to the following video

I'm your trainer...Jason Lin......this is the back of the Boeing 747...you certainly can smell the heavy jet fuel...right?...let's head inside to the economy seats...last time we talked about the manners and request each of you to practice the serving part...and this week...we are practicing the evacuation parts...this is especially important because it involves the safety of both passengers and members of the flight attendants...I saw some of you back there are feeling sleepy...being at training school can be boring sometime...I get it...but lighten up...there are a bunch of fun things ahead of you after the training...for example...you get to use the swap list to exchange the flight you don't want as long as someone is willing to make a change...I used to do that very often...

問題92-94請參閱下列視頻

我是你們的訓練師...傑森・林...這是波音747後部...你確實可以聞到濃厚的噴射機燃料...對吧？...讓我們到經濟艙裡頭...上次，我們談論到儀態和要求你們練習了關於服務的部分...而這週...我們會練習撤離的部分...這是特別重要的，因為這牽涉到乘客和機組成員的安全...我看到你們有幾個在後方有瞌睡蟲敲門了...在訓練學校有時候可能是很無趣的...我懂的...但是打起精神吧...例如，你能夠用交換名單來更換掉你不想要飛的行程，只要有人願意跟你交換...我之前就常幹這種事...。

試題中譯與解析	
92. Who most likely are the listeners? (A) trainers who are about to start the session. (B) customers sitting on the row of evacuation seats. (C) guests sitting on the economy seats. (D) **flight attendants at the training school.**	92. 聽眾最有可能是誰？ (A) 正要開始上課的訓練師們。 (B) 坐在逃生排位的乘客們。 (C) 坐在經濟艙的客戶們。 (D) **在訓練學校的空服員們。**
93. What is the purpose of mentioning the swap list? (A) **to entertain the students.** (B) to make students sleepy. (C) to make students vigilant. (D) to meet the demand of the students.	93. 提及交換清單的目的是什麼？ (A) **娛樂學生們。** (B) 讓學生們感到昏昏欲睡。 (C) 讓學生們有警覺性。 (D) 達到學生們的需求。
94. What is the topic of the talk? (A) how to avoid smell the heavy jet fuel. (B) how to use the swap list. (C) how to stay awake. (D) **continuation of the training lessons.**	94. 這個談話的主題是什麼？ (A) 如何避免聞到噴射機的燃料味道。 (B) 如何使用交換清單。 (C) 如何保持清醒。 (D) **接續的訓練課程。**

答案：92. D 93. A 94. D

解析

- **第92題**，根據聽力原文的敘述，最有可能的是空服員在訓練學校上課的內容，故答案為**選項D**。
- **第93題**，教練會提到是因為想要娛樂學生或希望他們能打起精神，所以才講些無關或較能引起他們興趣的事情，故答案要選**選項A**。
- **第94題**，這篇談話的主題是接續上次訓練課程的內容，故答案為**選項D**。

聽力原文與中譯

Questions 95-97 refer to the following talk

We have been to four galleries and you all have demonstrated your ability to draw...now it's time that we do the analysis of the following paintings...four to be exact...feel free to comment on them...although one of the paintings could be my work...ha...but it's ok and hand in five hundred words for each...painting...the first one is a two-headed worm crawling out the apple...it's amazingly crafted...next...a horrifying scene...only a closer look can know what's going on...the third one....is a woodpecker and its back is filled with worms...that allures other birds...and the last...a muscular guy swimming in the lake...but at some angles...the leg seems amputated...how bizarre...

問題95-97請參閱下列談話

我們去過了四間藝廊，而你們都顯示了你們的繪畫技巧了...現在是時候，我們要替接下來的繪畫作評析了...實際上確實有四個...可以隨意評論它們...儘管其中有幅繪畫可能是我所繪製的...哈...但是這是ok的，還有要提交每幅繪圖各500字的報告...第一幅是從蘋果中爬出的兩頭蟲...下一幅...是一個恐怖的場景...只有近看後才能知道發生了什麼事情...第三幅...是啄木鳥而其背後佈滿了蟲子...這吸引了其他鳥類...最後一張是...一位肌肉健壯的男子在湖中游泳...但是在某些角度...腿像是截肢般...多麼奇特呀！...。

試題中譯與解析

95. What is the requirement of this assignment? (A) 500 words. (B) it depends. (C) no longer than 1000 words. (D) **2000 words.**	95. 這項作業的需求是什麼？ (A) 500字。 (B) 視情況而定。 (C) 1000 字以內。 (D) **2000字。**
96. Where most likely is the talk given? (A) **in a classroom.** (B) at the gallery. (C) at the museum. (D) at the swimming pool.	96. 此篇談話最有可能發生在何處？ (A) **在課堂中。** (B) 在藝廊。 (C) 在博物館。 (D) 在泳池裡。

97. Why does the speaker find the last painting odd?	97. 為什麼說話者覺得最後一幅畫古怪？
(A) it was painted by a famous painter.	(A) 由知名畫家所繪製。
(B) it has worms on the woodpecker.	(B) 有蟲在啄木鳥上頭。
(C) because the shape of the apple.	(C) 因為蘋果的形狀。
(D) **because how the leg is perceived.**	(D) **因為觀看腿的方式。**

答案：95. D 96. A 97. D

- **第95題**，這題也要小心，教授有提到要交每篇500字的分析報告，然後有四項藝術品，所以別誤選了500字的選項，500*4=2000，故答案為**選項D**。
- **第96題**，這題是詢問地點，最有可能的地方是教室內，故答案為**選項A**。
- **第97題**，最後要注意的是最後一幅畫，講者為什麼會覺得怪呢，其實主要原因是腳的觀看角度，這對應到選項D，故答案為**選項D**。

聽力原文與中譯

Questions 98-100 refer to the following talk

Descriptions	Time
DWI/citizens	8:39 A.M.
DWI/mayor	9:45 A.M.
Train derailed	10:20 A.M.
Restaurant fire	11:35 A.M.
Note: DWI = driving while intoxicated	

Hi...I'm the host Jeremy...this event is for father-son...and all donations will go right to our charity and use as the scholarship for either single fathers and those kids who are parentless...first is the ceremony...the governor is awarding the prize to the CEO of our charity...feel free to take pictures...then we are moving on the speech given by the senator...welcome...third...we are having tea time with several homeless kids and the meal is prepared by one of the famous chefs...and also the assistant of the mayor...but the mayor is not coming due to a drunk-driving accident...fourth...we're going to take the hot air balloon...those kids are so thrilled...and is totally sponsored by one of the largest Film companies...

問題98-100請參閱下列談話

描述	時間
DWI/市民	上午8:39
DWI/市長	上午9:45
火車出軌	上午10:20
餐廳失火	上午11:35
註: DWI = driving while intoxicated	

嗨...我是主持人傑瑞米...這個活動是替「父-子」而辦的...而且所有的捐贈都會直接到我們的慈善會，並且充當成單親父親的孩子或那些無父母的小孩的獎學金...首先這是儀式...州長會頒贈獎品給我們慈善會的執行長...可以隨意拍照...然後我們會接續進行由議長的致詞...歡迎...第三，我們會有與無家可歸的孩子一同的茶時光，然後餐點是由其中一位名廚所準備...而且同時也是市長的助理...但市長無法到場，由於一場酒駕意外...第四...我們會搭乘熱氣球...那些小孩都會感到無比興奮...而且全數由其中一個大型的電影公司所資助...。

試題中譯與解析

98. According to the speaker, what will the donation money be used for? (A) the film companies. (B) the prize. (C) the ceremony. (D) **academic achievement.**	98. 根據說話者，捐贈的錢會用於什麼用途？ (A) 電影公司。 (B) 獎品。 (C) 儀式。 (D) **學術成就。**

99. According to the talk, who will not be attending the event? (A) the CEO. (B) **the mayor.** (C) the senator. (D) the governor.	99. 根據此篇談話，誰不會參加這場活動？ (A) 執行長。 (B) **市長。** (C) 議員。 (D) 州長。
100. Look at the graph. When did the mayor get involved in a car accident? (A) 8:39 A.M. (B) **9:45 A.M.** (C) 10:20 A.M. (D) 11:35 A.M.	100. 請參考圖表。何時市長牽涉到一場車禍事件裡頭呢？ (A) 上午8點39分。 (B) **上午9點45分。** (C) 上午10點20分。 (D) 上午11點35分。

答案：98. D 99. B 100. B

解析

- **第98題**，這題可以先看到聽力原文中的all donations will go right to our charity and used as the scholarship，所以是scholarship，scholarship對應到academic achievement故答案要選**選項D**。
- **第99題**，根據談話內容，不會參加的是市長，因為酒駕意外的關係，故答案為**選項B**。
- **第100題**，這題要對應到圖表的內容，很明顯可以對應到**選項B**。

- 【地勤話題】收錄了另一類型的檢測考點，包含將聽到的訊息轉換成「形容詞」的同義轉換，考生需要較好的反應能力。
- 【海產貿易公司話題】包含數道試題是要「理解慣用語」才能選對的試題，考生可以多揣摩這類的出題，提升靈活應答能力。
- 【天氣報導話題】要注意所提供的資訊和整合訊息的能力，訊息整合後就能馬上理解颱風路徑。

模擬試題（四）

▶ **Listening Test 4**　🎧 MP3 013

In the Listening Test, you must demonstrate your ability to understand spoken English. This section is divided into four parts and will take approximately 45 minutes to complete. There are four parts, and directions are given for each part. Do not mark the answers in your test book. Use the answer sheet that is provided separately.

▶ **PART 1**

Directions: For each question, you will listen to four short statements about a picture in your test book. These statements will not be printed and will only be spoken one time. Select the statement that best describes what is happening in the picture and mark the corresponding letter (A), (B), (C), (D) on the answer sheet.

Example   Sample Answer

A ● C D

Statement (B), "**Some people are wearing backpacks**", is the best description of the picture. So you should select answer (B) and mark it on your answer sheet.

1.

(A)　(B)　(C)　(D)

2.

(A)　(B)　(C)　(D)

3.

(A)　(B)　(C)　(D)

4.

(A)　(B)　(C)　(D)

5.

(A) (B) (C) (D)

6.

(A) (B) (C) (D)

Directions: For each question, you will listen to a statement or a question followed by three possible responses spoken in English. They will not be printed and will only be spoken one time. Select the best response and mark the corresponding letter (A), (B), or (C) on your answer sheet.

7. Mark your answer on your answer sheet.
8. Mark your answer on your answer sheet.
9. Mark your answer on your answer sheet.
10. Mark your answer on your answer sheet.
11. Mark your answer on your answer sheet.
12. Mark your answer on your answer sheet.
13. Mark your answer on your answer sheet.
14. Mark your answer on your answer sheet.
15. Mark your answer on your answer sheet.
16. Mark your answer on your answer sheet.
17. Mark your answer on your answer sheet.
18. Mark your answer on your answer sheet.
19. Mark your answer on your answer sheet.
20. Mark your answer on your answer sheet.
21. Mark your answer on your answer sheet.
22. Mark your answer on your answer sheet.
23. Mark your answer on your answer sheet.
24. Mark your answer on your answer sheet.
25. Mark your answer on your answer sheet.
26. Mark your answer on your answer sheet.

27.　Mark your answer on your answer sheet.
28.　Mark your answer on your answer sheet.
29.　Mark your answer on your answer sheet.
30.　Mark your answer on your answer sheet.
31.　Mark your answer on your answer sheet.

▶ **PART 3**　 MP3 015

　　Directions: In this part, you will listen to several conversations between two or more speakers. These conversations will not be printed and will only be spoken one time. For each conversation, you will be asked to answer three questions. Select the best response and mark the corresponding letter (A), (B), (C), (D) on the answer sheet.

32.Why does the man say, "I will get right on it"?
　　(A) he finds something that isn't right
　　(B) he doesn't want to offend the boss
　　(C) he will memorize all standard procedures
　　(D) he wants to have the right chemistry with the boss

33.What does "go easy on you" mean?
　　(A) be harsh with someone
　　(B) be more tolerant with someone
　　(C) give someone an easy task
　　(D) an expression that the flight attendant will normally get

34.What is the female employee's problem?
　　(A) She forgot to take copious notes
　　(B) She is being too anxious
　　(C) she should've made up excuses
　　(D) she should ask other colleagues for assistance

35. Why does the woman say, "I can only take her for a small dose"?
   (A) she finds the executive unbearable
   (B) she can only take a small dose of the drug
   (C) this job makes her small
   (D) this job is too handful for a rookie

36. Where do these speakers most likely work?
   (A) at the restaurant
   (B) at the hotel
   (C) at the wine cellar
   (D) on the airplane

37. What is the female employee asked to do?
   (A) be upfront
   (B) talk something behind the leader's back
   (C) get more red wine
   (D) be clear about the task given

38. What is the problem?
   (A) there were only a few planes
   (B) the flight is cancelled
   (C) the plane is impaired
   (D) the staff is a know-it-all

39. Which of the following is not the result of the incident?
   (A) the delay of the plane
   (B) the damage of the plane
   (C) the plane that needs repairment
   (D) the need of upgrading the SOPs

40. What could not be the penalty of the incident?
   (A) a lawsuit
   (B) monetary compensation

(C) jobless
(D) health risk

41. Who most likely are being investigated?
(A) pilots
(B) fly attendants
(C) ground crews
(D) plane technicians

42. What can be inferred about the weather that day?
(A) cloudy
(B) windy
(C) misty
(D) sunny

43. Where could they be, after the arrest?
(A) at the police station
(B) in the jail
(C) at the airport
(D) in a courtroom

44. According to the conversation, who stole the wedding cake?
(A) the bride
(B) the groom
(C) the groom's father
(D) the attendee

45. Which of the following could be the next target of the raccoon?
(A) the wedding cake
(B) red envelopes
(C) the ice sculpture
(D) wedding balloons

46. Where could the wedding take place?
(A) on the boat

(B) on the beach
(C) at a five-star restaurant
(D) on the skyscraper

47. **What solution does the woman come up with?**
    (A) take down the raccoon herself
    (B) get the narcotics
    (C) get in the car because it's safer in there
    (D) ask the groom for help

48. **What can be inferred about the groom?**
    (A) is senseless at the moment
    (B) is answering the reporter's questions
    (C) is getting his wife back
    (D) is trying to get the sedatives himself

49. **What does the sleeping beauty refer to?**
    (A) the actual sleeping beauty in the fairy tale
    (B) the bride who is sleeping on the canoe
    (C) the criminal raccoon
    (D) the doll on the boat

Location guide	description
First floor	Storage room
Second floor	Dining area
Third floor	Dining area
Fourth floor	Office room
Fifth floor	Cooking and preparation
Sixth floor	Viewing deck

50. Why does the hotel man mention short staffed?
    (A) he wants customers to reflect the situation to the senior leaders
    (B) he wants customers to understand and be empathetic
    (C) he demands the situation of understaffed improved
    (D) he wants to win the Employee Month Award

51. What could not be the food that the restaurant currently serves?
    (A) Some Chinese dishes
    (B) French cuisines
    (C) Spanish noodles and meat
    (D) Thai seafood salad

52. Look at the graph. What is located on the sixth floor?
    (A) observatory
    (B) imported fish
    (C) ingredients and kitchen wares
    (D) dining area

53. Why does the man say, "I will be needing a doggie bag"?
    (A) he is with a dog
    (B) he might be having a vomit soon
    (C) he is allergic with the lobster
    (D) he wants to wrap the leftovers

54. How much does the dessert cost?
    (A) It depends
    (B) It's free
    (C) It will be deducted from their company credit card
    (D) It's added benefit if you are using a premium credit card

55. Which of the following item is not in the doggie bag?
   (A) the lobsters with the bread
   (B) steamed crabs
   (C) an ice cream castle
   (D) fired squid

Activity	
Description	**time**
1. Celebration for capturing the largest tuna	9 a.m.
2. Seminar for marine biologists	10 a.m.
3. Cruise for amateur fishermen	11 a.m
4. Cooking demonstration	1 p.m.

56. What type of business is this company?
   (A) a processing plant
   (B) aquaculture
   (C) fishery industry
   (D) a wholesaler for various types of fish

57. Which of the following is not the assignment given to the new recruit?
   (A) classify squids
   (B) understand each part of the squid
   (C) finish at least a hundred squid
   (D) coach other inexperienced fishermen

58. Look at the graph. What type of event is taking place at 1 p.m.?
   (A) celebration for capturing the largest tuna
   (B) seminar for marine biologists
   (C) cruise for amateur fishermen
   (D) cooking demonstration

item	remuneration
7-day Dubai trip	US 250
5-day Russia trip	US 200
14-day West Europe	US 750
14-day South Europe	US 850

59. Why is the customer calling?
   (A) she wants to cancel the trip because it's humane
   (B) she thinks she has been fooled by the company
   (C) she has doubts about the camel riding service
   (D) she doesn't want the camel in the picture

 60. Why does the customer say, "that thought does cross my mind"?
   (A) she wants to be totally honest with the sales rep
   (B) she finds that thought disturbing
   (C) the idea of the camel riding makes her doubt about this trip
   (D) she wants to keep her fingers crossed that those camels are properly taken care of

 61. Look at the graph. If the customer is cancelling the trip, what monetary reward will the sales rep lose?
   (A) US 250
   (B) US 200
   (C) US 750
   (D) US 850

62. What concern does the man mention?
   (A) the watch is a second-hand
   (B) the watch is a knock-off
   (C) the watch does not have the waterproof function
   (D) the watch is a real one

63.What must the man do?
(A) get the watch examined by a great master
(B) demand the store to reimburse him
(C) call the police
(D) inform his best friend about the watch

64.What problem has the woman identified?
(A) the counterfeit watch cannot detect water pressure
(B) the fake watch is a false alarm
(C) underwater conditions will be misjudged
(D) the man's best friend will be furious

65.Why is the man calling?
(A) to cancel the order of the long bench
(B) to inquire about the furniture that was mistakenly sent
(C) to make a purchase
(D) to give his bank account

66.What furniture is incorrectly delivered to the man's house?
(A) a short bench
(B) a bed
(C) item 65
(D) item 120

67.What is the solution offered by the woman?
(A) the man should go to the bank himself
(B) she will send the delivery guy to get the furniture
(C) she wants the man to transfer the money
(D) she demands further charges

68.Where most likely is the conversation taking place?
(A) at a bank
(B) at the police station
(C) at the headquarter
(D) at the computer lab

69. Why does the woman say, "I'm no computer prodigy"?
    (A) she really wants to be humble in front of her colleague
    (B) she hasn't passed the advanced computer test
    (C) she is not proficient enough to maintain the operation of the system
    (D) she wants to be a computer genius to take down hackers

 70. Why does the man say "our computer system is encountering a bit of a snag"?
    (A) he wants the lady to come tomorrow
    (B) he tries to explain and makes a clarification about the delay
    (C) he wants the lady to know he has no obligation to do that
    (D) he wants to snag the transaction because it's illegal

▶ **PART 4** 🎧 MP3 016

Directions: In this part, you will listen to several talks by one or two speakers. These talks will not be printed and will only be spoken one time. for each talk, you will be asked to answer three questions. Select the best response and mark the corresponding letter (A), (B), (C), (D) on your answer sheet.

71. What does disembark mean?
    (A) board
    (B) transfer
    (C) strand
    (D) get off

72. Which of the following is True?
    (A) the court ruled something that damage the fame of the company
    (B) the teenager is unwilling to sue
    (C) the spokesperson picked up the phone and then hung up
    (D) the flight attendant takes a few days off

73.What most likely will happen next?
(A) The flight attendant will respond on behalf of the company
(B) The company will respond information to the press
(C) The court will send the document to the company
(D) The teenager will drop the charge

74.Which of the following creatures are not used as attractions?
(A) dolphins
(B) lions
(C) koalas
(D) octopuses

75.Who calls for the proper treatment of circus animals?
(A) the reporter
(B) the government
(C) the biologist
(D) the trainer

76.What creatures cannot endure the Circus anymore?
(A) meerkats
(B) koalas
(C) whales
(D) tigers

77.Whose decisions will determine the winner?
(A) villagers
(B) the previous winner
(C) the sponsor
(D) guest judges

78.What prize is the speaker is expected of?
(A) US 8,000 dollars
(B) a fantastic dish
(C) a mobile phone
(D) the entire kitchen wares

79. Why does the man say, that's a new definition of winning?
(A) he wants everyone to win at all costs
(B) he wants to pioneer that in the show
(C) he thinks for everyone that's worth thinking
(D) he thinks the winning prize is not worth it

 80. Why does the man say, "it's not robbed"?
(A) to show that it's fairly evaluated
(B) to show the producer manipulates the outcome
(C) to demonstrate the importance of the whisk in the contest
(D) to let those subscribers keep following him

81. Who eventually gets the cash?
(A) Jason
(B) producers
(C) guest judges
(D) villagers

82. Which of the following is not what Jason learned from villagers?
(A) make a fire
(B) capture a carnivore
(C) set the tent
(D) doing the dish on a traditional instrument

83. Who committed forgery?
(A) the police
(B) CFO
(C) CEOs of other companies
(D) auditors

84. What does the lawyer recommend?
(A) hide the evidence
(B) make a deal with D.A.
(C) flee the country
(D) hand in the money

85. Where is the news report taking place?
(A) outside the court
(B) at the Best Automobile
(C) at the bank
(D) at the law firm

86. What can be inferred about the criminal?
(A) convicted
(B) detained
(C) released
(D) absconded

87. Which of the following is True?
(A) the felon has never been to California
(B) the felon is a senior accountant
(C) the criminal is good at disguising
(D) the criminal's gender is identified

88. Where is the news report most likely taking place?
(A) at the felon's cherished shop
(B) at the Best Automobile
(C) at the California
(D) at the supermarket

89. Where most likely are the listeners?
(A) at an annual auction
(B) at the precious metal exhibition
(C) at the jewelry processing plant
(D) at the interpreter training center

90. Which of the following could be about to be served?
(A) mini-burgers
(B) chicken-wings
(C) candy apple
(D) wine

91. What field does the speaker work in?
   (A) jewelry design
   (B) cuisine catering
   (C) music industry
   (D) journalism

92. What can be inferred about the weather before the typhoon?
   (A) cloudy and with different types of clouds
   (B) clear
   (C) windy
   (D) rainy

93. According to the weather man, where did the typhoon gather the most strength?
   (A) at Korea
   (B) at Japan
   (C) at Guam
   (D) at the Philippines

94. If the prediction of the typhoon goes as the international news, where will the typhoon first strike?
   (A) Guam
   (B) The Philippines
   (C) Yilan
   (D) Japan

95. What is the main topic of the talk?
   (A) How to get free tickets
   (B) How to get higher scores in Earth Science
   (C) A brief introduction of the park's favorite site
   (D) A brief introduction of the National Science Museum

96.Where can tourists get the free tickets?
(A) at The National Science Museum
(B) at the campus
(C) at the Facebook headquarter
(D) at the coffee shop

97.What will suffer if there is an algae bloom?
(A) sediments
(B) living organisms
(C) the land
(D) minerals and nutrients

98.According to the castle owner, which of the following color is not suited for the photoshoot at the castle?
(A) white
(B) black
(C) gray
(D) yellow

99.Where does this talk most likely taking place?
(A) the wedding venue
(B) an ancient castle
(C) a film studio
(D) the speaker's house

100.Who can be the potential candidate allowed to use the castle?
(A) a student responsible for the festival party
(B) a professor wanting to know the history of the castle
(C) a tourist who is an avid castle lover
(D) a movie director

第四回
模擬試題解析

 PART 1

聽力原文與中譯	
1. (A) **Bags of flour remain motionless on the rack.** (B) The chef is opening a bag of flour. (C) The store manager is moving bags of flour to the other rack. (D) Factory workers are unloading bags of flour.	1. (A) **數袋麵粉靜置在架上。** (B) 廚師正打開一袋麵粉。 (C) 店經理正把幾袋麵粉放置到其他架上。 (D) 工廠工人正將數袋麵粉卸下。

答案：(A)

這題可以看到圖片中間有類似麵粉類的物品堆疊放置在架上，剛好符合了選項A的描述，故答案要選**選項A**。

聽力原文與中譯	
2. (A) Some people are consuming their desserts. (B) Some people are talking to the waitress. (C) Some people are reading the menus. (D) **The dessert and the coffee have been served on the table.**	2. (A) 有些人正在食用他們的甜點。 (B) 有些人正在跟女服務生談話。 (C) 有些人正在看菜單。 (D) **甜點跟咖啡已送至餐桌上。**

答案：(D)

 解析

這題可以看到映如眼簾的是在風景區的餐桌上放置了餐點和飲料，最有可能符合的敘述就是選項D，故答案為**選項D**。

聽力原文與中譯	
3. (A) A guy is bargaining to the vendor on the sandy beach. (B) **A few coconut trees can be seen from here.** (C) A girl is drinking fruit juice and enjoys the sun. (D) There are several waste baskets on the sandy beach.	3. (A) 一個男子在沙灘上跟攤販討價還價。 (B) **從這兒可以看見幾棵椰子樹。** (C) 一位女子正在飲用水果汁且享受陽光。 (D) 沙灘上有幾個垃圾桶。

答案：(B)

 解析

這題可以看到遠處有幾株高大的椰子樹佇立在這，故答案要選**選項B**。

聽力原文與中譯	
4. (A) **There are escalators in the building.** (B) The security is blocking people's way. (C) The circle of the building is not oval-like. (D) People are waiting for the instructions to get to other stories.	4. (A) **建築物中有電扶梯。** (B) 保全正阻擋人進入。 (C) 這棟建築不是像橢圓形的。 (D) 人們正等待指示以進入其他樓層。

答案：(A)

解析

這題有些難，仔細看後可以看到樓層下方有兩排的電扶梯提供給人們上樓，故答案要選**選項A**。

聽力原文與中譯	
5. (A) **More than half of the seats are empty.** (B) The newcomer cannot find any more seats. (C) The tables are filled with drinks. (D) There are some souvenirs on these seats.	5. (A) **超過一半以上的座位是空的。** (B) 新來的人找不到其他椅子。 (C) 桌子上放滿了飲料。 (D) 有些紀念品放在椅子上頭。

答案：(A)

 解析

這題可以看到兩種座椅，一種是靠近餐區的，另一種是類似提供給乘客座的座椅，但是共同點是椅子上幾乎沒有人，故答案為**選項A**。

聽力原文與中譯	
6. (A) A pet dog is left on one of the long benches. (B) Vendors are persuading people into buying drinks. (C) **There are some coconut trees mingled with observatory tables.** (D) All canopies are oval-like.	6. (A) 寵物狗被遺留在其中一個長凳上。 (B) 攤販們正說服人們購買飲料。 (C) **有些椰子樹夾雜在觀測台的桌子上。** (D) 所有的屋頂都是像橢圓狀的。

答案：(C)

 解析

這題要多注意一些，但是可以清楚看到的是椰子樹夾雜在這些風景區所架設的餐桌中，故答案要選**選項C**。

PART 2

聽力原文與中譯	
7. How often do you go to the museum? (A) **Twice a year.** (B) Since August. (C) Two-hour drive from my home.	7. 你多久去一次博物館呢? (A) **一年兩次。** (B) 自從八月。 (C) 從我家要兩小時車程。

答案：(A)

這題是詢問頻率，答案很明顯是**選項A**。

聽力原文與中譯	
8. How soon can we get the food? (A) **I'm afraid that your order has been cancelled.** (B) I don't mind frozen seafood. (C) Wait a second, where is our chef?	8. 我們最快可以何時拿到食物? (A) **恐怕你的訂單已經取消了。** (B) 我不介意冷凍的海鮮。 (C) 等一下，我們的廚師去哪兒了呢?

答案：(A)

這題沒有明確提供一個時間點，而是使用另一類的表達，答案要選**選項A**。

聽力原文與中譯	
9. The flight to Paris has been cancelled. (A) Call my Paris agent. (B) Purchasing tickets on-line is cheaper. (C) **I guess we'll just have to take the next one.**	9. 前往巴黎的航班已經取消了。 (A) 打電話給我的巴黎代理人 (B) 線上訂購機票更便宜。 (C) **我猜想，我們也只能搭乘下一班了。**

答案：(C)

這題要接續本來句子的敘述回答，故最合理的答案為**選項C**。

聽力原文與中譯	
10. What is the charge? (A) You can't charge over 2 dollars. (B) **murder.** (C) you can't leave the crime scene like that.	10. 指控的項目是什麼呢？ (A) 你不能索求超過2元的費用。 (B) **謀殺。** (C) 你不能像這樣離開犯罪現場。
答案：(B)	

這題很明確提供一個答案，要注意干擾選項也出現charge的音，故答案要選**選項B**。

聽力原文與中譯	
11. Are you feeling a little chilly? (A) The wind is not that gusty. (B) **Somewhat. I need to get the coat.** (C) It's under room temperatures.	11. 你有感到有些冷嗎？ (A) 這風並沒有那麼強烈。 (B) **有點吧。我需要拿件大衣。** (C) 這在室溫之下。
答案：(B)	

這題有直接的表明加上解釋的部分，答案要選**選項B**。

聽力原文與中譯	
12. Would you like to hold the bag for a moment? (A) I just love the manufacturers. (B) **Of Course. I love LV products.** (C) You should buy a new one.	12. 你想要拿這個包包一下下嗎？ (A) 我就是喜愛這製造商。 (B) **當然。我喜愛LV產品。** (C) 你應該要買件新的。
答案：(B)	

模擬試題（一）
模擬試題（二）
模擬試題（三）
模擬試題（四）
模擬試題（五）

解析

這題也有直接的表明部分，答案為**選項B**。

聽力原文與中譯	
13. Is Dr. Mark going to drop the charges? (A) I didn't see that coming. (B) **Yes, in a few minutes.** (C) No, the judge is not here.	13. 馬克醫生會撤銷控訴嗎？ (A) 我沒預期那樣的事情發生。 (B) **是的，在幾分鐘之內。** (C) 沒有，法官並不在這兒。

答案：(B)

 解析

這題也有直接表明是或否並加上其他敘述，故答案為**選項B**。

聽力原文與中譯	
14. What do you think of this dress? (A) The clothing company has to rethink about the whole thing. (B) **expensive.** (C) we're relying more on the feedback from customers.	14. 你覺得這件服裝怎樣？ (A) 服飾公司已經重新思考了整件事情了。 (B) **昂貴的。** (C) 我們正仰賴從顧客哪裡得到的更多的回饋。

答案：(B)

解析

這題的答案要選形容的部分，**選項B**即為形容詞，故為正確答案。

聽力原文與中譯

15. I was wondering if you can donate the money to the charity. (A) Yes, my blood is pure. (B) **Normally, I would say yes, but my wallet got stolen.** (C) The rumor about the charity is bad.	15. 我正思考著，如果你能夠捐贈金錢給慈善機構的話。 (A) 是的，我的血液是純的。 (B) **正常情況下，我會說好的，但是我的皮包才剛被偷。** (C) 關於慈善機構的傳聞是不好的。

答案：(B)

這題答案沒這麼明顯，思考後**選項B**最適合。

聽力原文與中譯

16. Can I talk to you manager? (A) I'll have to talk to the CEO about it. (B) You seem chatty. (C) **If it's about the complaint about me, then no.**	16. 我可以跟你的經理談談嗎？ (A) 我會跟執行長談下這部分的。 (B) 你似乎長舌。 (C) **如果是關於我的抱怨的話，那麼答案是「否」。**

答案：(C)

這題也是沒有明確表達，而是使用「如果」，故答案為**選項C**。

聽力原文與中譯

17. We need advanced movements of animals to attract viewers. (A) The animal doctor will be here in a minute. (B) **I'll have all trainers know that.** (C) Viewers are uploading sophisticated movements of our circus animals.	17. 我們需要動物們進階的動作來吸引瀏覽的人。 (A) 動物醫生馬上就會過來了。 (B) **我會讓所有的訓練師知道這個的。** (C) 瀏覽者正上傳我們馬戲團中動物索表演的複雜的動作。

答案：(B)

這題也是接續表達描述句，**選項B**最適合。

18. Aren't there other customers waiting to be served? (A) I don't like customers waiting. (B) **I think they just left.** (C) Customers are giving us a bad review.	18. 沒有其他的顧客是等待需要服務的嗎？ (A) 我不喜歡顧客等待。 (B) **我認為他們剛離開了。** (C) 顧客正給我們壞評論。

答案：(B)

這題也沒有明確表達有或沒有，而是另一類的表達，答案為**選項B**。

19. Aren't there other animal riders in the waiting area? (A) **Not one that I can think of.** (B) It's too inhumane. (C) I'm a big fan of animals.	19. 沒有其他的動物騎乘者在等候區嗎？ (A) **沒有一個是我可以想的起來的。** (B) 這太不人道了。 (C) 我是個動物迷。

答案：(A)

這題也是提供另一類的表達，答案為**選項A**。

聽力原文與中譯

20. Hasn't the Circus upgraded the equipment? (A) I'll have to talk to the CEO about it. (B) The advanced equipment is something we can afford. (C) **The executives are working on the details and purchases.**	20. 馬戲團怎麼還沒有升級設備呢？ (A) 我必須要跟執行長談談這個。 (B) 進階設備是我們所能負擔的起的東西。 (C) **主管正在進行細節和購買上。**

答案：(C)

 解析

這題要選解釋原因的句子，故答案為**選項C**。

聽力原文與中譯

21. The Boston lobster soup seems rotten. (A) The chef still doesn't know the nuisance. (B) It can go with the rotten tomatoes. (C) **Can't agree more. I'm giving them a bad review.**	21. 波士頓龍蝦湯似乎有腐爛味。 (A) 廚師仍不知道這麻煩事。 (B) 它味道跟爛番茄搭。 (C) **不能同意你更多了。我正給予他們負面評論。**

答案：(C)

 解析

這題也是提供了另一類的表達加上一段描述，故答案為**選項C**。

聽力原文與中譯	
22. When will you be back at the hotel? (A) The hotel waitress wants me to be back. (B) **after painting the whale on the cruise.** (C) The review about the hotel is true.	22. 你何時會回到旅館裡頭呢？ (A) 旅館服務生想要我回來。 (B) **在航遊上繪畫鯨魚後。** (C) 關於旅館的評論是正確的。

答案：(B)

 解析

這題要選一個時間點，選項B表明在一段時間後，故答案為**選項B**。

聽力原文與中譯	
23. Why aren't animals getting punished in the Circus? (A) **Because not long ago, a customer sued.** (B) Punishing animals is so inhumane. (C) The circus should be closed for a day.	23. 為什麼馬戲團裡的動物沒有受到懲罰了？ (A) **因為不久之前，一位顧客控告。** (B) 懲罰動物是如此地不人道。 (C) 馬戲團應該要關閉一天。

答案：(A)

 解析

這題要選解釋原因的句子，句子有因為所以很明顯答案為**選項A**。

聽力原文與中譯

24. How long can the food sustain our trip to the Amazon rainforest? (A) **According to the expert, 7 days.** (B) I prepare the most diverse food. (C) We can eat the animals there.	24. 食物能夠支撐我們去亞馬遜雨林的旅遊多久呢？ (A) **根據專家的說法，七日。** (B) 我準備最多樣的食物。 (C) 我們可以吃那裡的動物。

答案：(A)

 解析

這題也有明確的時間點，故答案為**選項A**。

聽力原文與中譯

25. Which Circus are you currently working at? (A) I don't think the salary is that good. (B) **The Best Circus.** (C) The Circus doesn't recruit me.	25. 你現在正在哪個馬戲團裡工作？ (A) 我不認為薪水有多好。 (B) **倍斯特馬戲團。** (C) 馬戲團沒有雇用我。

答案：(B)

 解析

這題選項B有提供一個明確的馬戲團名，故答案為**選項B**。

聽力原文與中譯

26. Excuse me. Is this boat rented? (A) It's quite expensive. (B) Please don't take this the wrong way. (C) **By an Indian prince.**	26. 不好意思。這艘船租出去了嗎？ (A) 這艘船相當昂貴。 (B) 請不要誤解這個說法。 (C) **由一位印度的王子租走了。**

答案：(C)

這題很明顯使用了BY+名詞的表達，表示由誰租走了，故答案為**選項C**。

聽力原文與中譯	
27. Where can we get the largest clam? (A) My biology teacher doesn't know the answer. (B) Why don't you raise one? (C) **Under the Pacific.**	27. 我們可以從哪裡購得最大的蚌？ (A) 我的生物學教師不知道這個答案。 (B) 你自己怎麼不養個呢？ (C) **在太平洋下方。**

答案：(C)

這題選項C有提供一個地點，故答案為**選項C**。

聽力原文與中譯	
28. How do you get to the remote island? (A) I have to google the route. (B) **by a water motorcycle.** (C) I'm clever ok, so I won't get lost.	28. 你如何到達遙遠的島嶼呢？ (A) 我需要google路線。 (B) **藉由騎乘水上摩托車。** (C) 我很聰明的，好嗎，所以我不會迷路的。

答案：(B)

這題要回答方式，答案為**選項B**。

聽力原文與中譯	
29. When are you planning to dive? (A) **when crabs and lobsters are looking for food** (B) if diving earns more money (C) Planning is not the best policy.	29. 你什麼時候計畫要開始潛水呢？ (A) **當螃蟹和龍蝦開始找尋食物的時候。** (B) 如果潛水賺取更多錢。 (C) 計劃不是最佳的政策。

答案：(A)

 解析

這題是詢問時間，選項A有表示時間點的「當...」，故答案為**選項A**。

聽力原文與中譯	
30. Would you prefer to dine at the night market? (A) I love the lighting in the restaurant. (B) **If that costs less money.** (C) The night market is usually crowded.	30. 你偏好在夜市用餐嗎？ (A) 我喜愛餐廳的燈光。 (B) **如果那樣會花費較少的錢的話。** (C) 夜市通常是壅擠的。

答案：(B)

 解析

這題也是使用如果，答案要選**選項B**。

聽力原文與中譯	
31. What is the favorite food for the raccoons? (A) But they are vegetarians. (B) **cotton candy perhaps.** (C) wow...they look equally the same.	31. 浣熊最喜愛的食物是什麼？ (A) 但是他們是素食主義者。 (B) **或許棉花糖。** (C) 哇！...他們看起來都是一樣的。

答案：(B)

 解析

這題選項B有提供一個答案，故答案為**選項B**。

PART 3

聽力原文和對話

Questions 32-34 refer to the following conversation

Cindy: ..oh...Jason...you are really an angel for doing this...I cannot do this without you...

Jason: ...it's nothing...but I think you'd better memorize all standard procedures...

Tina: why are you helping her? aren't you supposed to prepare meals for passengers.

Jason: ...right...I will get right on it...I'm so sorry...

Cindy: sorry...it's clearly my fault...don't blame him...though

Tina: ....people making excuses don't have the floor to stand up for someone...and...I don't want to hear any more excuses...didn't you learn these during the training?

Cindy: I did...and I took copious notes into it...but for some reason, my nervousness gets the best of me...and I just forgot for no reason...I promise it won't happen again...

Tina: ...again?...if you acted like a flight attendant...perhaps I would go easy on you...

問題32-34，請參考以下對話內容

辛蒂：噢！...傑森...你真的是個好人做這事...沒有你我真的無法完成這個...。

傑森：這沒有什麼...但是我認為妳最好記下所有標準的程序...。

緹娜：為什麼你要幫她呢？你不是該替乘客準備餐點嗎？

傑森：...對...我馬上去辦...我真的感到抱歉...。

辛蒂：抱歉...這確實是我的錯...別責怪他囉...。

緹娜：找藉口的人沒有替別人辯護的發言權...而且...我不想要聽到任何更多的藉口...你不是在訓練期間學過這些嗎？

辛蒂：我當時確實有...而且我抄下了豐碩的筆記...但是因為有些原因，我的緊張壓倒我了...而且不知道什麼原因我就是忘了...我向你承諾不會再發生了...。

緹娜：...再發生？...如果你的舉止表現得像是空服員...或許我會對你客氣些...。

試題中譯與解析

32. Why does the man say, "I will get right on it"? (A) he finds something that isn't right. (B) **he doesn't want to offend the boss.** (C) he will memorize all standard procedures. (D) he wants to have the right chemistry with the boss.	32. 為何男子提到「I will get right on it」？ (A) 他察覺有些地方不太對勁。 (B) **他不想要惹怒老闆。** (C) 他將背誦好所有程序。 (D) 他想要跟老闆間有著對的火花。
33. What does "go easy on you" mean? (A) be harsh with someone. (B) **be more tolerant with someone.** (C) give someone an easy task. (D) an expression that the flight attendant will normally get.	33. 「go easy on you」指的是什麼？ (A) 對某人嚴苛。 (B) **對某人更寬容。** (C) 給予某人更輕鬆的任務。 (D) 空服員常會接收到的表情。
34. What is the female employee's problem? (A) She forgot to take copious notes. (B) **She is being too anxious.** (C) she should've made up excuses. (D) she should ask other colleagues for assistance.	34. 女性員工的問題是什麼？ (A) 她忘記抄滿筆記了。 (B) **她太過於焦慮。** (C) 她早該想好藉口了。 (D) 她應該要向其他同事尋求幫助。

答案：32. B 33. B 34. B

解析

- **第32題**，這句的意思是「馬上去辦、立即去做」，其實也是男子不想要惹怒到已經怒火中燒的上司，如果再回其他理由可能一起被罵之類的，講這句話還能馬上離開戰火區，所以這題要選擇**選項B**最為適當。

- 第**33**題，這句話在聽力結尾，其實是蠻不客氣的講法，其實這個俗諺意思是對某人更為寬容或更為容忍些，答案要選擇**選項B**，對話中上司當然不可能對她客氣些，所以用了假設語氣XD。
- 第**34**題，該女子，即女空服員的問題是她過於緊張，所以很多東西都忘掉了等等而造成缺失，故答案要選**選項B**。

聽力原文和對話

Questions 35-37 refer to the following conversation

Cindy: ...I can only take her for a small dose...for god's sake...

Jason: ...yep...you really need to be careful though...is this your first flight as an operating crew member...?

Cindy: ...yes and too bad that my very first time isn't going very well...and she is just too fastidious...and can't seem to endure...any mistakes...

Jason: ...I think we should probably talk about this during the layover of the plane in Korea.

Cindy: ......thanks...I'm going to get more red wine...

Tina: ...to the cockpit...

Tina: If you have any issue with me...I'd like you to talk to me face-to-face...

Cindy: ...Ok

Tina: ...I don't want someone talking something behind my back...are we clear?

Cindy: ...sure...

Tina: ..now get back to work...

問題35-37，請參考以下對話內容

辛蒂：天哪...我只能容忍她很小部分...。

傑森：...是的...你真的需要更小心...這是你身為執勤機組成員的首次飛航嗎？

辛蒂：...是的而且真不巧，我的第一次進行的不是很順利...而且她真的太過於挑剔了...而且似乎無法容忍...任何的錯誤...。

傑森：...我認為我們可能應該等班機在韓國短暫停留時再談這些。

辛蒂：...謝謝...我正要去拿更多紅酒...。

緹娜：到機艙...。

緹娜：如果你對我有任何意見的話...我希望你面對面跟我講...。

辛蒂：...好的。

緹娜：我不想要有些人在我背後説我什麼...清楚了嗎？

辛蒂：當然...。

緹娜：現在回去工作...。

試題中譯與解析	
35. Why does the woman say, "I can only take her for a small dose"? (A) **she finds the executive unbearable.** (B) she can only take a small dose of the drug. (C) this job makes her small. (D) this job is too handful for a rookie.	35. 為何女子提及「I can only take her for a small dose」？ (A) **她發覺主管令人難以忍受。** (B) 她對於藥品僅能忍受一小部分。 (C) 這份工作讓她感到自己渺小。 (D) 這份工作對於菜鳥來説負擔太大了。
36. Where do these speakers most likely work? (A) at the restaurant. (B) at the hotel. (C) at the wine cellar. (D) **on the airplane.**	36. 這些對話中的説話者們最有可能在哪裡工作？ (A) 在餐廳。 (B) 在旅館。 (C) 在酒窖。 (D) **在飛機上。**
37. What is the female employee asked to do? (A) **be upfront.** (B) talk something behind the leader's back. (C) get more red wine. (D) be clear about the task given.	37. 女性員工被要求做什麼？ (A) **直率的。** (B) 在領導人背後説壞話。 (C) 拿取更多的紅酒。 (D) 清楚所交付的任務。
答案：35. A 36. D 37. A	

解析

• **第35題**，女子會説這句話的原因是，她也不太能忍受主管，僅能容忍的幅度極小，故答案要選擇**選項A**。

- **第36題**，從這幾個說話者聊天，提到to the cockpit等可以推斷他們是在飛機上喔，故答案要選擇**選項D**，別因為出現了紅酒等訊息就選了像是餐廳這樣的地點。
- **第37題**，女子在跟男同事閒聊時被上司聽到了對談，這使得她被叫到機艙，可以對應到If you have any issue with me...I'd you talk to me face-to-face...，這對應到A選項的be upfront故答案要選擇**選項A**。

聽力原文和對話

Questions 38-40 refer to the following conversation

Mark: what's going on here? I told you we have to follow the standard SOPs.

Jason: I thought there were only a few planes...and I curtailed

Mark: ...the left wing of the CX 1500 is damaged and it caused another flight delay...

Jason: what should we do now?

Mark: since you think that you are a know-it-all...you take care of that...

Jason: are they going to sue us?

Mark: us?...

Jason: you are the supervisor and the senior leader of the ground crew...

Mark: it's going to be on the breaking news...and the cost of fixing the plane is not cheap...

Jason: what will the company do? Are they going to fire us?

Mark: probably...and our payment is not going to cover the repairment.

問題38-40，請參考以下對話內容

馬克：發生了什麼事了嗎？我告訴過你我們必須要照著標準的程序。

傑森：我以為這裡僅有幾架飛機在...所以我縮短了程序。

馬克：... CX 1500飛機的左翼受損了而且這會造成另一個航班延誤...。

傑森：我們應該要怎麼做呢？

馬克：既然你認為你什麼都懂，你來處理它...。

傑森：他們會告我們嗎？

馬克：我們？...。

傑森：你是上司而且是地勤的資深領導人...。
馬克：這將會出現在新聞快訊了...而且修護飛機的代價是不便宜的...。
傑森：公司會怎麼處理呢？他們會解雇我們嗎？
馬克：可能會...而且我們的薪資是無法負擔起維修的費用的。

試題中譯與解析	
38. What is the problem? (A) there were only a few planes. (B) the flight is cancelled. (C) **the plane is impaired.** (D) the staff is a know-it-all.	38. 發生了什麼問題？ (A) 只有幾架飛機。 (B) 航班取消了。 (C) **飛機受到損害。** (D) 員工無所不知。
39. Which of the following is not the result of the incident? (A) the delay of the plane. (B) the damage of the plane. (C) the plane that needs repairment. (D) **the need of upgrading the SOPs.**	39. 下列何者不是這起事件的結果？ (A) 飛機的延遲。 (B) 飛機的損害。 (C) 飛機需要修護。 (D) **升級SOP的需要性。**
40. What could not be the penalty of the incident? (A) a lawsuit. (B) monetary compensation. (C) jobless. (D) **health risk.**	40. 什麼不可能會是這起事件的懲罰？ (A) 法律訴訟。 (B) 金錢補償。 (C) 失業的。 (D) **健康風險。**

答案：38. C 39. D 40. D

解析

- **第38題**，對話中有提到the left wing of the CX 1500 is damaged，故可以得知對應到的是the plane is impaired，故答案要選擇**選項C**才正確。
- **第39題**，其實最主要原因是沒有照程序走，而這題問的是事件的結果，但沒有提到的部分是升級SOPs，故答案要選擇**選項D**。
- **第40題**，對話中有提到幾項可能的懲罰，但沒有提到health risk，故答案要選擇**選項D**。

Questions 41-43 refer to the following conversation

Officer: I'm the officer investigating the incident of the plane...I heard there was a fire a few moments after the plane's left wing had been damaged...who were responsible for this..?

Jason: ...I was assigned the task that day for the plane and many other things...I'm afraid that it was entirely due to the negligence...on our part

Officer: ...so you are admitting the fact that you didn't comply with the standard procedures...because if you had followed...the plane wouldn't have hit the building...who's your superior?

Jason: ...Mark...

Officer: yes luckily...I'm sure the monetary compensation is going to be huge...forensic experts are still examining the evidence at the scene...

Mark: ...hey...officer...I'm his supervisor...no one was injured that day...and there was a dense fog that day

officer 2 : put your hands behind your back...you two are under arrest for the offense against public safety...

問題41-43，請參考以下對話內容

警官：我是來調查這起飛機事件的警官...我聽説在飛機左機翼受損後，有發生火災...誰是負責此事件的...？

傑森：...那天我受派這項飛機任務和許多事情...這起事件恐怕全然是我們這邊所引起的疏忽所造成的...。

警官：...所以你承認了，你們並未照著標準程序...因為如果你有遵循的話...飛機就不會撞擊到大樓了...誰是你的上司呢？

傑森：...馬克...。

警官：是的...幸運的是...我很確定金錢的賠償是巨額的...刑事鑑定的專家正檢視著現場的證據...。

馬克：...嗨...警官...我是他的上司...那天沒有人受傷...而且當天有起了很濃的霧...。

警官2 ：將你的手放到背後...你們兩個都因為危及公眾安全危險的罪名被捕了...。

試題中譯與解析

41. Who most likely are being investigated? (A) pilots. (B) fly attendants. (C) **ground crews.** (D) plane technicians.	41. 誰最有可能會被調查？ (A) 機師。 (B) 空服員。 (C) **地勤人員。** (D) 飛機機械維修師。
42. What can be inferred about the weather that day? (A) cloudy. (B) windy. (C) **misty.** (D) sunny.	42. 可以推測出當天的天氣是什麼？ (A) 多雲的。 (B) 風大的。 (C) **起霧的。** (D) 陽光充足的。
43. Where could they be, after the arrest? (A) **at the police station.** (B) in the jail. (C) at the airport. (D) in a courtroom.	43. 在被逮捕後，他們有可能會在哪裡？ (A) **在警局。** (B) 在牢房。 (C) 在機場。 (D) 在法庭內。

答案：41. C 42. C 43. A

解析

- **第41題**，題目是詢問最有可能被調查的對象，很明顯是地勤人員，故答案要選擇**選項C**。
- **第42題**，這題要注意的是當天天候狀態，這部分要到後面馬克提到的 there were a dense fog that day，所以可以得知當天起霧，而選項關於天氣的描述都是形容詞，起霧代表是misty，故答案要選擇**選項C**。
- **第43題**，問到被逮捕後，這部分要用推測的，所以最有可能的地方是在警局，故答案為**選項A**。

Questions 44-46 refer to the following conversation

Jason: ...we're gathered here for Ben and Mary's matrimony...you may kiss the bride...

Mary: lots of reporters are taking the pictures and filming...but you're not gonna believe this...

Mark: ...what is it?

Mary: I guess my two-year smartphone just recorded...a raccoon...whose name I cannot verify...stole the wedding cake...and red envelopes...it's like he is saying...I object...

Mark: ...that's ludicrous...isn't he...Ben's father...?

Mary: ...that makes it even weirder...

Cindy: someone...stops him...or I will...

Mary: ...OMG...he bumped into the ice sculpture...and remains unharmed...

Cindy: ...security...escort him out of the venue...before he breaks any wedding balloons...

Mark: ...I love this wedding...it's getting funnier...

Mary: ...he is eating the crab on this sandy beach...and refuses to go...

問題44-46，請參考以下對話內容

傑森：...我們今天聚首在此慶祝班和瑪莉的婚禮...你可以親吻新娘了...。

瑪莉：許多記者都到場拍照和攝影...但是你不會相信這個的...。

馬克：...什麼呢？

瑪莉：我想我滿兩週年的智慧型手機正好錄到...一隻浣熊...我無法確認牠的名字...偷了婚宴蛋糕...和紅包，就像是述說著...「我反對」...。

馬克：...這太荒謬了...牠不是...班的爸爸嗎...？

瑪莉：...這讓事件變得更怪異了...。

辛蒂：...來人啊...快阻止牠...不然我會的...。

瑪莉：...我的天啊...牠撞上了冰雕...而且維持毫髮無傷...。

辛蒂：...保安人員...護送牠出場...在牠破壞掉任何婚宴氣球之前...。

馬克：...我喜愛這場婚宴...變得更有趣啦...。

瑪莉：...牠正在沙灘上吃著螃蟹...而且拒絕離開...。

試題中譯與解析	
44. According to the conversation, who stole the wedding cake? (A) the bride. (B) the groom. (C) **the groom's father.** (D) the attendee.	44. 根據對話所述，誰偷了婚禮的蛋糕？ (A) 新娘。 (B) 新郎。 (C) **新郎的父親。** (D) 參加者。
45. Which of the following could be the next target of the raccoon? (A) the wedding cake. (B) red envelopes. (C) the ice sculpture. (D) **wedding balloons.**	45. 下列何者可能會是浣熊的下個目標？ (A) 婚宴蛋糕。 (B) 紅色信封袋。 (C) 冰雕。 (D) **婚宴氣球。**
46. Where could the wedding take place? (A) on the boat. (B) **on the beach.** (C) at a five-star restaurant. (D) on the skyscraper.	46. 哪裡可能會是婚宴發生的地點？ (A) 在船上。 (B) **在海灘上。** (C) 在五星級餐廳。 (D) 在摩天大樓。

答案：44. C 45. D 46. B

解析

- **第44題**，這題要綜合兩個訊息一個是we're gathered here for Ben and Mary's matrimony，以及isn't he...Ben's father...?，雖然對話中可以得知這是動物婚禮，但選項中沒有提到浣熊，而Ben's father即是the groom's father故答案為**選項C**。

- **第45題**，這題可以使用刪除法，也可以看到女子說的security...escort him out of the venue...before he breaks any wedding balloons...，所以可以得知浣熊下個目標會是婚宴氣球，故答案為**選項D**。

- **第46題**，這題是詢問婚宴的地點，從最後的敘述he is eating the crab on this sandy beach...，最有可能的婚宴地點是在海邊，故答案為**選項B**。

Questions 47-49 refer to the following conversation

Cindy: ...can you help out here...

Mary: ...but I'm a guest...fine...what should I do?

Cindy: ...getting the narcotics for me...it's in the box on my car...here is the key...

Mary: ...ok...I'll be right back...

Reporter: it's the hour three of the wedding...it seems that the groom has been knocked out unconsciously...and I have got to tell you it was not a fair fight....he is trying to take away the bride...where is he...right now...Ben's father and the bride are on the boat...are they trying to kayak back to the hiding place...OMG...the sedatives were aimed at the criminal raccoon...but unexpectedly shot on the Mary...I guess...he is taking the sleeping beauty away....period...

Mark: ...that's the worst wedding that I have ever attended...

問題47-49，請參考以下對話內容

辛蒂：...你可以幫下忙嗎？...

瑪莉：...但是我是客人唉...好吧...我該怎麼做呢？

辛蒂：...替我拿麻醉劑...在我車上的箱子裡頭...這是鑰匙...。

瑪莉：...好的...我會馬上回來的...。

記者：這是婚宴進行的第三小時了...似乎新郎被擊暈且沒了意識...而我必須要跟你們說這不是場公平的決鬥...牠正將新娘帶走了...牠在哪兒...現在...他們在船上...牠們是要划向隱匿的地方嗎？...我的天啊...鎮定劑對準了罪犯浣熊...但是出乎意料之外的是其射向了瑪莉...我想...牠正要將睡美人帶走...句號...。

馬克：...這真的是我參加過最糟的婚宴了...。

試題中譯與解析	
47. What solution does the woman come up with? (A) take down the raccoon herself. (B) **get the narcotics.** (C) get in the car because it's safer in there. (D) ask the groom for help.	47. 女子所想出的解決之道是什麼？ (A) 她自己親自擊倒浣熊。 (B) **拿取麻醉劑。** (C) 進車內，因為那裡比較安全。 (D) 向新郎求救。
48. What can be inferred about the groom? (A) **is senseless at the moment.** (B) is answering the reporter's questions. (C) is getting his wife back. (D) is trying to get the sedatives himself.	48. 從對話中可以推測出新郎的什麼？ (A) **在當下不省人事的。** (B) 正在回應新聞記者的問題。 (C) 正試圖搶回新娘。 (D) 正試著奪取鎮定劑。
49. What does the sleeping beauty refer to? (A) the actual sleeping beauty in the fairy tale. (B) **the bride who is sleeping on the canoe.** (C) the criminal raccoon. (D) the doll on the boat.	49. 對話中的睡美人指的是什麼？ (A) 童話故事中真實的睡美人。 (B) **獨木舟上睡著的新娘。** (C) 浣熊罪犯。 (D) 船上的洋娃娃。

答案：47. B 48. A 49. B

解析

- **第47題**，問題是詢問女子所想到的辦法，而很明顯答案是**選項B**。她要求另一名女子去拿鎮定劑。
- **第48題**，關於新郎的部分，可以對應到it seems that the groom has been knocked out unconsciously，所以可以對應到選項A的is senseless at the moment，故答案為**選項A**。
- **第49題**，睡美人指的是新娘，因為她在逃亡中被誤射到鎮定劑而昏睡，睡美人影射的是她，故答案為**選項B**。

Questions 50-52 refer to the following conversation

Location guide	description
First floor	Storage room
Second floor	Dining area
Third floor	Dining area
Fourth floor	Office room
Fifth floor	Cooking and preparation
Sixth floor	Viewing deck

Cindy: ...normally...I only dine here....when the company is having a recruit...quite expensive though...I guess we're making some money from the restaurant...and it is making a tremendous amount from seafood-lovers...would you like some Chinese food?

Jason: ...yep...great...I will see what's on the menu...

Mark: hey...what brings you here...you and the new rookie...I assume...

Cindy: ...we'd like to have a table by the window....preferably on the third floor...

Mark: ...no problem...and I am going to bring red wine as usual...

Jason: ...this place is exquisite...it's like a French restaurant...

Mark: ...sorry it takes long...come with me...we're short staffed...even at a senior position...I still can't relax...this is our latest menu...we've added Spanish cuisines and Thai dishes...

問題50-52，請參考以下對話內容

地方嚮導	描述
第一層樓	儲藏室
第二層樓	用餐區
第三層樓	用餐區
第四層樓	辦公室
第五層樓	烹飪和準備
第六層樓	觀景台

辛蒂：…通常我只有當公司有招聘新人時會在這用餐…價格相當貴的說…我想我們正從餐廳那賺一些些錢…而它卻從愛好海產的人身上大賺了一筆…你要點些中國菜嗎？

傑森：…是的…蠻棒的…我會看菜單上有什麼的…。

馬克：嘿…什麼風把你吹來這兒…你和你的新菜鳥…我猜想…。

辛蒂：…我想要靠窗的餐桌…偏好在三樓的…。

馬克：…沒問題…而我正如往常一樣要帶紅酒…。

傑森：…這個地方好別緻呀…這像是間法國餐廳…。

馬克：…抱歉讓你們久等了…跟我來吧…我們人手短缺…甚至是身處資深職位…我仍然無法放鬆下…這是我們新的菜單…我加進了西班牙菜餚和泰國料理…。

試題中譯與解析

50. Why does the hotel man mention short staffed?
(A) he wants customers to reflect the situation to the senior leaders.
(B) **he wants customers to understand and be empathetic.**
(C) he demands the situation of understaffed improved.
(D) he wants to win the Employee Month Award.

50. 為什麼旅館的男子提及人力短缺？
(A) 他想要顧客將情況反映給資深領導人。
(B) **他想要顧客了解情況並且對此有同理心。**
(C) 他要求人手不足的情況能有所改善。
(D) 他想要贏得每月員工獎。

51. What could not be the food that the restaurant currently serves? (A) Some Chinese dishes. (B) **French cuisines.** (C) Spanish noodles and meat. (D) Thai seafood salad.	51.哪樣不可能是現在餐廳所上的菜？ (A) 一些中國佳餚。 (B) **法國佳餚。** (C) 西班牙麵與肉。 (D) 泰式海鮮沙拉。
52. Look at the graph. What is located on the sixth floor? (A) **observatory.** (B) imported fish. (C) ingredients and kitchen wares. (D) dining area.	52.請參考圖表。什麼位於六樓？ (A) **觀測台。** (B) 進口魚貨。 (C) 原料和廚具。 (D) 用餐區。

答案：50. B 51. B 52. A

解析

- **第50題**，這要對應到對話結尾的部分，其實提到這部份的原因是他希望顧客能有同理心且能了解這情況，所以即使他的職位高也還是要做這些基層的事情，也因為人手短缺，送餐等也不可能多快等等。
- **第51題**，這題要小心些，可以用刪除法，一開始女子詢問你要點些中國菜嗎，其實代表店內有中國菜，所以可以排除中國菜，然後在對話結尾處，店員有提到新加入的菜，包含西班牙和泰國料理，所以答案為法式菜餚，雖然對話中男子也有說到這像是間法國餐廳，不過這是干擾選項，只是描述外觀，不能由此推斷出餐廳內有這樣的料理，故答案為**選項B**。
- **第52題**，試題是詢問六樓有什麼呢，可以對應到圖表上的六樓，所以是 view deck，再由view deck回選項找找到同義字**observatory**，故答案為**選項A**。

聽力原文和對話

Questions 53-55 refer to the following conversation

Jason: time flies...it's already 3:30 in the afternoon...

Cindy: don't worry...the boss gave us the afternoon off...and I need to go to the lady's room...

Jason: ...OK...

Jason: ...I think I will be needing a doggie bag...too many courses....and it would be such a waste...

Jason: ...you can wrap up this for me...the lobsters with the bread...steamed crabs

Waiter: no problem...what else do you need...

Jason: ...fried squid also...this tastes really good...

Jason: ...what's this...we didn't order this

Waiter: ...the dessert...it's on the house...

Jason: ...an exquisite ice cream castle and a cake...I'm gonna take a picture...

Cindy: ...wow a castle...you eat it...I'm feeling a bit too cold.

Waiter: ...how are you gonna pay?

Cindy: ...credit card...

問題53-55，請參考以下對話內容

傑森：時光飛逝...現在已經是下午3點30分了...。

辛蒂：別擔心...老闆給我們半天的下午假...然後我需要去下女生化妝室...。

傑森：...好的...。

傑森：...我認為我會需要剩菜打包袋...太多道菜了...而且這樣很浪費...。

傑森：...你可以替我打包這個...龍蝦裹麵包...蒸螃蟹。

服務生：沒問題...還有需要什麼嗎？

傑森：...還有炸魷魚...品嚐起來滋味相當好...。

傑森：...這是什麼呢？...我們沒點這個...。

服務生：...甜點...這是餐廳免費贈送的...。

傑森：...精緻的冰淇淋城堡和蛋糕...我想要拍張照片...。

辛蒂：...哇！城堡...你吃吧...我感到有點冷。

服務生：...您要如何付費呢？

辛蒂：...信用卡...。

試題中譯與解析

53. Why does the man say, "I will be needing a doggie bag"? (A) he is with a dog. (B) he might be having a vomit soon. (C) he is allergic with the lobster. **(D) he wants to wrap the leftovers.**	53. 為何男子提及"I will be needing a doggie bag"？ (A) 他跟狗狗在一起。 (B) 他可能快要吐了。 (C) 他對龍蝦過敏。 **(D) 他想要打包剩菜。**

329

54. How much does the dessert cost? (A) It depends. (B) **It's free.** (C) It will be deducted from their company credit card. (D) It's added benefit if you are using a premium credit card.	54. 甜點花費多少錢呢？ (A) 視情況而定。 (B) **這是免費的。** (C) 將會由他們公司裡的信用卡扣除消費金額。 (D) 這是額外附加的，如果你正使用高級信用卡。
55. Which of the following item is not in the doggie bag? (A) the lobsters with the bread. (B) steamed crabs. (C) **an ice cream castle.** (D) fired squid.	55. 下列哪項沒有包含在打包袋中？ (A) 龍蝦裹麵包。 (B) 清蒸螃蟹。 (C) **冰淇淋城堡。** (D) 炸魷魚。

答案：53. D 54. B 55. C

解析

- **第53題**，男子提到的原因是，食物還剩很多，而食物均高檔，他希望能夠外帶，也有陸續提到想要外帶的項目，故答案為**選項D**。

- **第54題**，這題是詢問甜點的價格，但是在對話中沒有提到食物的價格，也沒有圖表顯示數據，不過可以從服務生口中得知甜點是**on the house**，代表這是餐廳免費贈送的，所以甜點是不需要花到一毛錢的，要選**選項B** it's free。

- **第55題**，這題是詢問項目，可以扣除男子提到的部分，該三項是一會打包的部分，而對話中無法判別甜點有沒有打包，但既然該三項食品一定會打包代表僅剩甜點的部分，故答案要選**選項C**。

聽力原文和對話

Questions 56-58 refer to the following conversation

Activity	
Description	time
1. Celebration for capturing the largest tuna	9 a.m.
2. Seminar for marine biologists	10 a.m.
3. Cruise for amateur fishermen	11 a.m
4. Cooking demonstration	1 p.m.

Boss: how's the progress...of our new recruit?

Cindy: he has learnt plenty...and I'm driving him to the processing plant...from there he will learn more...

Boss: sounds great...

Cindy: ..morning Jason..

Jason: ...good morning...

Cindy: ..you will be going to one of the processing plants...and you will learn more knowledge about squids...

Jason: ...ok...today...I'm dressing more casually...kind of fitting.

Cindy: ...I'm gonna leave you here and pick you up by noon...if you have questions...just ask...them...they are experienced fishermen...

Fisherman: ...your first assignment...sorting out the fresh ones and know each part of the squid...trunk...fin...head...and you have to remove the ink sac...classifying at least a hundred before noon...I guess that won't be too hard...

Jason: ...ok...I'll get right on it...

問題56-58，請參考以下對話內容

活動	
描述	時間
1. 慶祝捕獲體積最大的鮪魚	上午9點
2. 海洋生物學家們的研討會	上午10點
3. 業餘漁夫們的航遊	上午11點
4. 烹飪示範	下午1點

老闆：進度如何呢...我們那位新來的雇員？

辛蒂：他學習了很多...我今天要開車載他去加工廠...在那裡他會學習到更多...。

老闆：聽起來很棒...。

辛蒂：早安傑森...。

傑森：...早安...。

辛蒂：你今天要去其中一個加工廠...你會學到更多關於魷魚的知識...

傑森：...好的...今天...我穿著的更隨意點...有點合拍。

辛蒂：我會把你留在那裡，然後在中午的時候去接你...如果你有問題的話...儘管詢問他們...他們都是有經驗的漁夫...。

漁夫：...你的第一個任務是...篩選出最新鮮的以及知道每個魷魚的部位...軀幹...鰭...頭部...以及你要移除掉墨水囊...在中午前至少要分類好一百隻魷魚...我想我並不是那麼嚴格...。

傑森：好的...我馬上去辦...。

試題中譯與解析

56. What type of business is this company? (A) a processing plant. (B) aquaculture. (C) fishery industry. (D) **a wholesaler for various types of fish.**	56. 公司是什麼類型的商業性質？ (A) 加工處理廠。 (B) 水產養殖。 (C) 漁業。 (D) **銷售不同類型魚類的批發商。**

| 57. Which of the following is not the assignment given to the new recruit?
(A) classify squids.
(B) understand each part of the squid.
(C) finish at least a hundred squid.
(D) **coach other inexperienced fishermen.** | 57. 下列哪一項不是給予新聘雇員的任務呢？
(A) 將魷魚分類。
(B) 了解魷魚的每個部位。
(C) 完成至少一百隻魷魚。
(D) **指導其他不專業的漁夫。** |
| 58. Look at the graph. What type of event is taking place at 1 p.m.?
(A) celebration for capturing the largest tuna.
(B) seminar for marine biologists.
(C) cruise for amateur fishermen.
(D) **cooking demonstration.** | 58. 請參閱圖表。什麼類型的活動會於下午一點舉行？
(A) 慶祝捕獲的大型鮪魚。
(B) 海洋生物學家們的研討會。
(C) 業餘漁夫們的航遊。
(D) **烹飪展示。** |

答案：56. D 57. D 58. D

解析

- **第56題**，選項中有好幾個干擾選項，不過最有可能的是該公司是批發商，批發漁貨，故答案為**選項D**。
- **第57題**，這要對應到對話結尾的項目，沒有要他coach其他漁民的部分，故答案為**選項D**。
- **第58題**，這題可以對應到圖表下午一點，答案很明顯為**選項D**。

聽力原文和對話

Questions 59-61 refer to the following conversation

item	remuneration
7-day Dubai trip	US 250
5-day Russia trip	US 200
14-day West Europe	US 750
14-day South Europe	US 850

Cindy: ...Best Travel...how can I help you?

Customer: great to know that your company is also offering a camel riding service in a Dubai trip...but on second thought...it's kind of inhumane...I wondered how they are gonna treat those creatures...

Cindy: ...then perhaps...you shouldn't go...are you considering cancelling the trip?

Customer: ...that thought does cross my mind....perhaps I will just take a few pictures with the animal...and decide not to go for camel ride...

Cindy: ...it's entirely up to you

Customer: ...you have been really helpful...you are so kind...

Cindy: ...I know this is not the right place to vent...I'm feeling low today...

Customer: ...are you OK?...I'm not cancelling...so don't worry about it ok...take care...

問題59-61，請參考以下對話內容

項目	報酬
7日 杜拜之旅	250 美元
5日 俄羅斯之旅	200 美元
14日 西歐之旅	750 美元
14日 南歐之旅	850 美元

辛蒂：...倍斯特旅遊...我能幫你什麼嗎？

顧客：很高興得知你們公司在杜拜旅遊時也提供一項駱駝騎乘服務...但是經過再思考後...這有點太不人道了...我在想他們會怎樣對待那些生物呢...。

辛蒂：...那麼或許...你不該前往...你正考慮要取消這項旅程嗎？

顧客：...這個想法真的在我心中浮現過...或許我就拍攝幾張跟動物的合照...然後決定不騎乘牠們...。

辛蒂：...這就要看你自己本身了...。

顧客：...你真的幫助很大...你太好了...。

辛蒂：...我知道這不是宣洩情緒的地方...但是我今天真的感到很低潮...。

顧客：...你還好嗎？...我沒有打算取消行程...所以別擔心了好嗎...照顧好自己。

試題中譯與解析	
59. Why is the customer calling? (A) she wants to cancel the trip because it's humane. (B) she thinks she has been fooled by the company. **(C) she has doubts about the camel riding service.** (D) she doesn't want the camel in the picture.	59. 為何顧客打電話到公司呢？ (A) 她想要取消旅程，因為這不人道。 (B) 她認為她被公司騙了。 **(C) 她對於駱駝騎乘的部分感到疑惑。** (D) 她不想要照片中有駱駝。
60. Why does the customer say, "that thought does cross my mind"? (A) she wants to be totally honest with the sales rep. (B) she finds that thought disturbing. **(C) the idea of the camel riding makes her doubt about this trip.** (D) she wants to keep her fingers crossed that those camels are properly taken care of.	60. 為何顧客提及 "that thought does cross my mind"？ (A) 她想要對銷售業務完全坦承。 (B) 她發現那個想法干擾人心。 **(C) 駱駝騎乘的想法讓她對於這次的旅遊感到疑惑。** (D) 她想要駱駝如願地受到完善的照顧。
61. Look at the graph. If the customer is cancelling the trip, what monetary reward will the sales rep lose? **(A) US 250.** (B) US 200. (C) US 750. (D) US 850.	61. 請參考表格。如果顧客取消此次旅程，銷售業務會損失多少呢？ **(A) 250 美元。** (B) 200 美元。 (C) 750 美元。 (D) 850 美元。
答案：59. C 60. C 61. A	

- **第59題**，對話前面有提到打電話的女子其實是對於騎乘駱駝感到有疑慮，故答案為**選項C**。
- **第60題**，顧客腦海中有浮現出該想法，而講這句話的原因是因為騎乘駱駝讓她對於這次旅行產生質疑，故答案為**選項C**，其他選項都有部分切中，但不是她講這句話的原因。
- **第61題**，這題的話monetary reward對應到圖表中的**remuneration**，所以在杜拜的地方找到對應的金額是250美元，故答案為**選項A**。

聽力原文和對話

Questions 62-64 refer to the following conversation

Cindy: oh my god...that's a knock-off...

Jason: how do you know?

Cindy: I've been in Best Watch for twenty years...of course I can tell it's a counterfeit...

Jason: ...what should I do? I already sent it to a good friend of mine...and he is probably now diving in New Zealand...hope that he does not wear the fake one...

Cindy: good news is that the waterproof function of the fake watch is the same as that of the authentic one...

Jason: ...thanks...that's a relief...

Cindy: ...but there is bad news....

Jason: ...what...the...shoot...

Cindy: ...if you go down further than twenty feet...it will go malfunctioned...that means you can't tell the real water pressure...

Jason: ...he will definitely go ballistic if he finds out...

問題62-64，請參考以下對話內容

辛蒂：我的天啊！...那是仿冒品...。

傑森：你如何得知的呢？

辛蒂：我已經在倍斯特手錶待了20年了...當然我能分辨出這是不是仿冒品...。

傑森：...我該怎麼做呢？我已經送了一支錶給我一位好友了...而他可能現在正在紐西蘭潛水...希望他不要戴到贗品...。

辛蒂：好消息是仿冒的手錶的防水功能和真品的防水功能是一樣的...。

傑森：...謝謝...真令人鬆了一口氣...。

辛蒂：...但是也有壞消息...。

傑森：...什麼呢...快說吧...。

辛蒂：...如果你下水超過20尺...手錶會發生故障...這意味著你無法分辨真實的水壓...。

傑森：如果他發現的話，他一定會大發雷霆...。

試題中譯與解析	
62. What concern does the man mention? (A) the watch is a second-hand. **(B) the watch is a knock-off.** (C) the watch does not have the waterproof function. (D) the watch is a real one.	62. 男子所提到的擔憂是什麼呢？ (A) 手錶是二手品。 **(B) 那隻手錶是仿冒品。** (C) 那隻手錶沒有防水的功能。 (D) 那隻手錶是真品。
63. What must the man do? (A) get the watch examined by a great master. (B) demand the store to reimburse him. (C) call the police. **(D) inform his best friend about the watch.**	63. 男子必須做什麼？ (A) 去拿由大師檢查過的手錶。 (B) 要求店家補償他。 (C) 打電話給警方。 **(D) 告知他最好的朋友關於手錶的事情。**
64. What problem has the woman identified? (A) the counterfeit watch cannot detect water pressure. (B) the fake watch is a false alarm. **(C) underwater conditions will be misjudged.** (D) the man's best friend will be furious.	64. 女子察覺出什麼問題呢？ (A) 手錶贗品無法檢測出水壓。 (B) 手錶仿冒品是虛驚一場。 **(C) 水下的情況被誤判了。** (D) 男子的最好的朋友將會感到憤怒。

答案：62. B 63. D 64. C

解析

- 第62題，男子所提到的部分是手錶是仿冒的，而這也是他所擔心的部分，故答案為**選項B**。
- 第63題，這題是問男子必須做什麼呢，其實最主要的就是要通知他最好朋友關於手錶的事情，故答案為**選項D**。
- 第64題，女子所辨識到的問題有幾個，其中一項是關於手錶的防水功能，另一個是用於檢測水壓的部分，if you go down further than twenty feet...it will go malfunctioned...that means you can't tell the real water pressure...，試題選項中並未提及水壓或故障，但是卻以濃縮式的表達出該句句意，改寫成較隱晦的答案**underwater conditions will be misjudged**，故答案要選擇**選項C**。

聽力原文和對話

Questions 65-67 refer to the following conversation

Cindy: ... Best furniture...how can I help you...?

Mark: ...I didn't order the furniture that you sent me...

Cindy: ...let me check on the computer...what is your social security number?

Mark: ...555-777-999

Cindy: ...and the date of your purchase...?

Mark: ...2025 June 8

Cindy: ...ok...let's verify....you did order item number 5, 65, 90, and 120...is that correct...?

Mark: ...yes...wait a second...I forgot that I didn't cancel item 120 in the shopping chart...it's a long bench...is it?

Cindy: ...yes...

Mark: ...what should I do now?

Cindy: ...let me think...our shipping guy happens to be in your area...is it ok that he goes over now and retrieves the bench...

Mark: ...sure...but how about the money...?

Cindy: ...give me your bank account...and I'm going to transfer the money to you...

問題65-67，請參考以下對話內容

辛蒂：...倍斯特像俱...我該怎樣幫助你呢？

馬克：...我沒有訂購貴公司所寄的像俱...。

辛蒂：...讓我在電腦上檢查一下...你的社會安全碼是多少呢？

馬克：...555-777-999。

辛蒂：...你的訂購日期是幾號呢？

馬克：...2025年6月8日。

辛蒂：...好的...讓我們來確認下...你曾經訂購項目5, 65, 90和120...項目正確嗎...？

馬克：...是的...等一下...我忘記了我在購物車中，沒有取消項目120...是長板凳...對吧？

辛蒂：...是的...。

馬克：我現在應該要怎麼做呢？

辛蒂：...讓我想下...我們的運送員碰巧在你住的地區...如果他現在過去那裡並且取回板凳的話，這樣ok嗎...？

馬克：...當然...但是那麼錢呢...？

辛蒂：...給我你的銀行帳號...我會將錢轉給你的...。

試題中譯與解析	
65. Why is the man calling? (A) to cancel the order of the long bench. (B) **to inquire about the furniture that was mistakenly sent.** (C) to make a purchase. (D) to give his bank account.	65. 為什麼男子打此通電話？ (A) 取消長板凳的訂單。 (B) **詢問關於誤送的傢俱。** (C) 下單訂購。 (D) 交付他銀行帳戶。
66. What furniture is incorrectly delivered to the man's house? (A) a short bench. (B) a bed. (C) item 65. (D) **item 120.**	66. 什麼傢俱誤送到男子家呢？ (A) 一張短的板凳。 (B) 一張床。 (C) 項目65號。 (D) **項目120號。**

67. What is the solution offered by the woman? (A) the man should go to the bank himself. (B) **she will send the delivery guy to get the furniture.** (C) she wants the man to transfer the money. (D) she demands further charges.	67. 對話中女子所提供的解決方法是什麼？ (A) 男子應該要自行跑銀行一趟。 (B) **她會派運送員去取傢俱。** (C) 她想要男子將金錢轉帳。 (D) 她索求更進一步的費用。

答案：65. B 66. D 67. B

解析

- 第65題，男子打電話的原因是詢問誤送的家俱，故答案要選**選項B**。
- 第66題，誤送的家俱在對話中有提到，所以要選item 120，故答案為**選項D**。
- 第67題，由女子所提供的辦法，也可以由對話中輕易找到，她會派人去取，故答案要選**選項B**。

聽力原文和對話

Questions 68-70 refer to the following conversation

Cindy: there is an irregular activity happening in the computer...I'm gonna shut it down for a while...

Jason: that's odd...it's gonna affect several transactions...

Cindy: that's why I'm doing the right thing...shutting it down...

Jason: hope it's not some hackers...breaking into the system...

Cindy: ...I hope not...I'm no computer prodigy...I cannot deal with hackers...and if there is a safety concern...I'm calling the headquarters and the police...

Customer: ...I wanna to transfer the money...and this is the transferring form and the money...

Jason: ...may I see your ID...don't mean to trouble you...but if the transferring money exceeds to that amount...it's our obligation to see the ID...

Customer: ...here is my ID...thanks...

Jason: ...but you have to wait for a few seconds because our computer system is encountering a bit of a snag...

問題68-70，請參考以下對話內容

辛蒂：在電腦中...有著不尋常的活動...我要先將電腦關閉一陣子...。

傑森：那樣好奇怪...這會影響幾筆交易...。

辛蒂：這就是為什麼我要做對的事情...將電腦關閉...。

傑森：希望此舉不是一些駭客...入侵系統...。

辛蒂：我希望不是...我不是電腦天才...我沒辦法處理駭客問題...而且如果有安全性的疑慮的話...我會致電給總部並且報警...。

顧客：...我想要將錢轉帳...這是轉帳清單和金錢...。

傑森：...我可以看下你的ID嗎...沒有意圖要麻煩到你...但是如果轉移金錢超過某個金額時...我們是有義務要看下ID的...。

顧客：...這是我的ID...謝謝。

傑森：...但是你必須要等幾秒鐘，因為電腦正遭遇到一點障礙...。

試題中譯與解析

68. Where most likely is the conversation taking place? (A) **at a bank.** (B) at the police station. (C) at the headquarter. (D) at the computer lab.	68.此對話最有可能發生在何處？ (A) **在銀行。** (B) 在警局。 (C) 在總部。 (D) 在電腦實驗室。
69. Why does the woman say, "I'm no computer prodigy"? (A) she really wants to be humble in front of her colleague. (B) she hasn't passed the advanced computer test. (C) **she is not proficient enough to maintain the operation of the system.** (D) she wants to be a computer genius to take down hackers.	69.為何女子提及「I'm no computer prodigy」？ (A) 她真的想要在她同事面前保持謙遜。 (B) 她並未考過電腦高級考試。 (C) **她的電腦能力並未精通到足以維持電腦系統的運作。** (D) 她想要成為電腦天才以擊倒電腦駭客們。

| 70. Why does the man say "our computer system is encountering a bit of a snag"?
(A) he wants the lady to come tomorrow.
(B) **he tries to explain and makes a clarification about the delay.**
(C) he wants the lady to know he has no obligation to do that.
(D) he wants to snag the transaction because it's illegal. | 70. 為何男子提及「our computer system is encountering a bit of a snag」？
(A) 他想要女士明天再來。
(B) **他試圖解釋且澄清關於延遲的事情。**
(C) 他要該女士了解，他並沒有義務要做那些事情。
(D) 他想要阻撓交易，因為其是違法的。 |

答案：68. A 69. C 70. B

解析

- **第68題**，對話中有提到交易和關閉系統等等的，所以答案要選擇銀行，答案為**選項A**。
- **第69題**，女子講這句話的原因是，她並不是電腦天才，所以她也無能去維護這件事，如果銀行系統真的被入侵的話，故答案要選擇**選項C**。
- **第70題**，男子說這句話的原因是，他試圖要說明會有些許延誤的原因，故答案要選**選項B**。

Part 4

聽力原文與中譯

Questions 71-73 refer to the following news report

The beautiful flight attendant of the Best Airline was accused of overly using the power...and an innocent teenager was forced to disembark...because of the passenger safety...and if this takes to court...it surely can damage the reputation of the company...and the PR spokesperson refused to take the call by any news reporters...there must be something going on in the office...and this morning...the company explained to us there is a terrible misunderstanding...and the flight attendant is taking the leave of absence for a few days...so they will respond related messages when the flight attendant returns...

問題71-73請參閱下列新聞報導

這位倍斯特航空的美麗空服員被控於過度使用她的權力...而一位無辜的青少年被迫下機...因為乘客的安全性...而如果這起事件開庭的話...這一定會對公司的聲譽造成損害...而公關發言人拒絕接任何新聞記者的來電...辦公室裡頭一定有什麼事情發生了...而在今日早晨...公司向我們解釋這是個糟糕的誤會...而空服員目前請了幾天假...所以他們會等到空服員回來上班後在一併作回應...。

試題中譯與解析

71. What does disembark mean? (A) board. (B) transfer. (C) strand. (D) **get off.**	71. Disembark指的是什麼？ (A) 登機。 (B) 轉機。 (C) 擱淺。 (D) **起飛。**
72. Which of the following is True? (A) the court ruled something that damage the fame of the company. (B) the teenager is unwilling to sue. (C) the spokesperson picked up the phone and then hung up. (D) **the flight attendant takes a few days off.**	72. 下列何者為真？ (A) 法庭宣判了一些損害公司名譽事情。 (B) 青少年不願提告。 (C) 公司發言人接起電話後掛斷。 (D) **空服員請了幾天假。**

73. What most likely will happen next?	73. 接下來最有可能發生什麼事情？
(A) The flight attendant will respond on behalf of the company.	(A) 空服員會代表公司回應。
(B) **The company will respond information to the press.**	(B) **公司將會於新聞記者會回應資訊。**
(C) The court will send the document to the company.	(C) 法庭會將文件送至公司。
(D) The teenager will drop the charge.	(D) 青少年將會撤銷控告。

答案：71. D 72. D 73. B

解析

- **第71題**，這題是很明顯答案是下機，故答案要選**選項D**。
- **第72題**，只有D選項是正確的敘述，空服員安排幾天休假，故答案要選**選項D**。
- **第73題**，這題是推測題，接下來最有可能發生的情況為空服員休假完畢，公司回應媒體相關訊息，故答案為**選項B**。

聽力原文與中譯

Questions 74-76 refer to the following news report

Despite these warnings...the craze for the show of Best Circus remains...as long as there is a need...the torture for animals exists...wrote by the biologist of the prestigious journal...and the Circus has lured more marine creatures, tigers, meerkats, and star koalas....although the koalas stay sluggishly...that totally makes me laugh...however, during the show on Wednesday...our live-camera captured something unusual...two tigers disobey the instruction given by the trainers...and the next is the bloody scenes...that one of the trainers got killed by the tigers...the footage is removed from the website...but it still sends a clear message that there is still a need for the protection of animals...and you just can imagine the wrath those tiger have accumulated...

問題74-76請參閱下列新聞報導

儘管這些警告...對於倍斯特馬戲團的狂熱仍舊持續著...只要有需求的話...虐待動物的行為就存在著...知名期刊的生物學家寫道...而馬戲團已經引誘了更多的海洋生物、老虎、蒙哥和明星無尾熊...儘管無尾熊維持著懶散狀...那讓我整個笑出來了呢！...然而，在週三表演秀期間...我們的現場攝影機捕捉到一些不尋常的畫面...兩隻老虎不服從由訓練師所給予的指示...而接下來的畫面是血腥的場景...有位訓練師被老虎殺死了...視頻在網站上被移除了...但是仍舊傳遞了清楚的訊息，也就是仍有保護動物的需要存在...而你就可以想像一下，那些老虎對於訓練師累積了多少的憤怒...。

試題中譯與解析	
74. Which of the following creatures are not used as attractions? (A) dolphins. (B) **lions.** (C) koalas. (D) octopuses.	74. Which of the following creatures are not used as attractions? (A) 海豚。 (B) **獅子。** (C) 無尾熊。 (D) 章魚。
75. Who calls for the proper treatment of circus animals? (A) the reporter. (B) the government. (C) **the biologist.** (D) the trainer.	75. Who calls for the proper treatment of circus animals? (A) 新聞播報員。 (B) 政府。 (C) **生物學家。** (D) 訓練師。
76. What creatures cannot endure the Circus anymore? (A) meerkats. (B) koalas. (C) whales. (D) **tigers.**	76. What creatures cannot endure the Circus anymore? (A) 蒙哥。 (B) 無尾熊。 (C) 鯨魚。 (D) **老虎。**

答案：74. B 75. C 76. D

- 第**74**題，其實沒有提到的部分是獅子，故答案為**選項B**。而要注意的是 **marine creatures**換成了章魚，但還是是用於吸引觀光客的點。
- 第**75**題，這題是詢問誰呼籲妥善對待，要選生物學家，故答案為**選項C**。
- 第**76**題，這題是詢問無法忍受的動物，很明顯是老虎，因為他們咬死了訓練師，故答案為**選項D**。

聽力原文與中譯

Questions 77-79 refer to the following video

This is ...Jason Thornes...welcome to wildlife Kitchen...it's almost noon...and I am really hungry...but I still have to wait for the guest judges to taste first...can't help but wonder what they would think about my food...ok...now these judges are here....great and they have no idea which dish is cooked by whom...the winner will get the entire kitchen wares...that's huge...around US 8,000 dollars and bonuses...I'm expecting the prize would be a smartphone or something...but ok...and apparently the villagers cannot afford to buy one...perhaps I should just have messed up and lost the champion...that's the least I can do...they can use the money and buy smartphones...things we have taken for granted...that's a new definition of winning...

問題77-79請參閱下列視頻

這是記者...傑森 ・索恩...歡迎來到野生生物廚房...幾乎要正午了...而我真的餓昏頭了...但是我仍要等著客座評審先品嚐...無法不去想他們會覺得我的食物如何呢？...好的...現在這些評審都到了...很棒而且他們都不知道料理是由誰所烹飪的...獲勝者將會得到整組的廚房廚具...那很棒...大約是8千美元和獎金...我期待獎品會是隻智慧型手機或什麼的...但是還可以...而顯然村民們無法負擔起智慧型手機...或許我本該搞砸且輸掉冠軍...這是最低限度中我所能做的了...他們可以使用金錢然後買智慧型手機...我們所視為理所當然的事物...這是獲勝的新的定義。

試題中譯與解析

77. Whose decisions will determine the winner? (A) villagers. (B) the previous winner. (C) the sponsor. (D) **guest judges.**	77. 誰的決定裁定勝利者是誰？ (A) 村民們。 (B) 先前的獲勝者。 (C) 贊助商。 (D) **客座評審。**
78. What prize is the speaker is expected of? (A) US 8,000 dollars. (B) a fantastic dish. (C) **a mobile phone.** (D) the entire kitchen wares.	78. 哪一項獎品是說話者所期盼的？ (A) 8000美元。 (B) 很棒的佳餚。 (C) **一隻手機。** (D) 整組廚具。
79. Why does the man say, that's a new definition of winning? (A) he wants everyone to win at all costs. (B) he wants to pioneer that in the show. (C) **he thinks for everyone that's worth thinking.** (D) he thinks the winning prize is not worth it.	79. 為何男子提及「that's a new definition of winning」？ (A) 他想要每個人不計一切代價地贏。 (B) 他想要在節目中成為先驅。 (C) **他認為對大家來說這是值得思考的。** (D) 他認為贏得獎項不值得。

答案：77. D 78. C 79. C

解析

- **第77題**，這題的話決定勝利者的是客座評審，故答案要選**選項D**。
- **第78題**，這題要避免跟真的獎品混淆，說話者期待的是一支手機，故答案為**選項C**。
- **第79題**，男子會說這句的原因是因為他認為許多人都只為了贏，但是贏卻能有不同的意義或定義，這部分也確實是值得思考的，故答案為**選項C**。

Questions 80-82 refer to the following video

This is ...Jason Thornes...welcome to Wildlife Kitchen...it's an odd feeling...but I have got to be totally honest with you...it's not robbed...but I am the winner of the cooking contest...and thanks to the amazing whisk and the great food processor...my steamed stuffed buns look perfect, but I'm handling the money to those villagers...that's probably the best thing to do...they have taught me how to build a fire, cook on the flagstone, catch a small crocodile, and erect the tent...it's truly a meaningful trip...and I am taking the pictures with them and later will upload to my IG...tell us what you would like to do with the winning money and don't forget to follow us...

問題80-82請參閱下列視頻

這是記者...傑森・索恩...歡迎來到野生生物廚房...有種奇怪的感覺...但是我必須要完全坦誠相告...這不是非法剝奪...但是我是烹飪競賽的贏家...而多虧了驚人的攪拌器以及很棒的食物處理器...我的包子看起來完美，但是我要將獎金給那些村民們...這可能會是最棒的事情了...他們已經教會我如何生火、在石板上煮東西、抓小型鱷魚和搭帳篷...這真的是個有意義之旅...告訴我們，是你的話你會怎麼使用這筆獎金呢...然後別忘了追蹤我們唷...

80. Why does the man say, "it's not robbed"? (A) **to show that it's fairly evaluated.** (B) to show the producer manipulates the outcome. (C) to demonstrate the importance of the whisk in the contest. (D) to let those subscribers keep following him.	80. 為何男子提及「it's not robbed」？ (A) **顯示這場比賽是經由公平的評估。** (B) 顯示製作人操控結果。 (C) 顯示在比賽中攪拌器的重要性。 (D) 讓那些訂閱者持續追蹤他。

81. Who eventually gets the cash? (A) Jason. (B) producers. (C) guest judges. (D) **villagers.**	81. 誰最終會獲得該筆金錢？ (A) 傑森。 (B) 製作人。 (C) 客座評審。 (D) **村民們。**
82. Which of the following is not what Jason learned from villagers? (A) **make a flagstone.** (B) capture a carnivore. (C) set the tent. (D) doing the dish on a traditional instrument.	82. 下列哪一項不是傑森從村民那裡學習到的？ (A) **製作石灰板。** (B) 捕獲肉食動物。 (C) 架設帳棚。 (D) 以傳統的工具製作菜餚。

答案：80. A 81. D 82. A

- **第80題**，男子講這句話的原因是要解釋比賽的公平性，故答案要選**選項A**。
- **第81題**，談話中Jason有提到最後獎金會給村民，所以答案要選**選項D**。
- **第82題**，要注意選項和談話中的同義轉換，答案為**選項A**，談話中沒有提到製作石灰板這部分。

聽力原文與中譯

Questions 83-85 refer to the following news report

After months of investigation, the police have found evidence linking to the conspiracy of the Best Automobile bankruptcy...several senior accountants are admitting in court that they forged the signatures of both the CFO and CEO...which is deemed impossible to CEOs of other businesses...and there are abnormal bank activities and transactions in those employees...the defense attorney wants them to take the plea in exchange for a lesser punishment...and the jury hasn't yet reached a verdict...so we are waiting outside the court...and next month a criminal court will determine whether or not they are responsible for the death of the CFO...

問題83-85請參閱下列新聞報導

在數個月的調查後，警方已經找到的證據跟倍斯特汽車破產的陰謀有關...幾個資深的會計人員在法庭中坦承他們偽造財務長和執行長的簽名...這對於其他行業的執行長來說這是不可能會發生的事...在那些員工們中，還有異常的銀行活動和交易...辯護律師要求他們要抗辯以換取較輕易的罪罰...而陪審團也尚未達成判決協議...所以我們正在法庭外面等候著...下個月刑事法庭就會決定他們是否跟財務長的死亡有相關的責任...。

試題中譯與解析	
83. Who committed forgery? (A) the police. (B) CFO. (C) CEOs of other companies. (D) **auditors.**	83. 誰犯下偽造文書罪？ (A) 警方。 (B) 財務長。 (C) 其他公司的執行長們。 (D) **審計員。**
84. What does the lawyer recommend? (A) hide the evidence. (B) **make a deal with D.A.** (C) flee the country. (D) hand in the money.	84. 律師建議了什麼？ (A) 藏匿證據。 (B) **與檢控官達成協議。** (C) 逃離國家。 (D) 交出金錢。
85. Where is the news report taking place? (A) **outside the court.** (B) at the Best Automobile. (C) at the bank. (D) at the law firm.	85. 新聞報導是在何處？ (A) **法庭外頭。** (B) 在倍斯特汽車公司。 (C) 在銀行。 (D) 在法律事務所。
答案：83. D 84. B 85. A	

解析

- **第83題**，這題的話偽造文書的是會計師，試題選項中換成了auditors故答案為**選項D**。
- **第84題**，這題是詢問律師建議的部分，談話中提到的是wants them to take the plea in exchange for a lesser punishment，試題選項中改寫成了**make a deal with D.A.**故答案要選**選項B**。
- **第85題**，記者有提到so we are waiting outside the court，故答案要選**選項A**。

聽力原文與中譯

Questions 86-88 refer to the following news report

Also the news about Best Automobile....and it turns out the those accountants were paid to do the dirty works...and the criminal is still at large...according to earlier reports, the last phone signal of the criminal is in California but it was a few months ago...yet the police still cannot verify the gender of the criminal...here is the footage of the criminal at the mall, but the criminal wore an eyeglass and was fully clothed...according to reliable sources...the criminal is jealous of the love affairs between the company CEO and CFO...which makes this murdering case more enigmatic...and this is Judy Lin at the department store...the criminal's favorite shop...

問題86-88請參閱下列新聞報導

也是關於倍斯特汽車的新聞...最終發現那些會計師是受支付去做這些骯髒活...而罪犯仍然在逃...根據稍早的報導，罪犯的最後手機訊號是在加州，但是這已經是幾個月之前的事了...而警方仍無法證實罪犯的性別...這是罪犯在購物中心的視頻，但是罪犯戴了太陽眼鏡而且被衣服包裹住...根據一個可靠的消息來源...罪犯可能出於忌妒公司執行長和公司財務長之間的戀愛情事...這使得這起謀殺案顯得更為撲朔迷離...這是朱蒂·林在百貨公司...罪犯最喜愛的店家...。

86. What can be inferred about the criminal? (A) convicted. (B) detained. (C) released. (D) **absconded.**	86. 關於罪犯可以推測出什麼？ (A) 判定有罪。 (B) 拘留。 (C) 釋放。 (D) **潛逃。**
87. Which of the following is True? (A) the felon has never been to California. (B) the felon is a senior accountant. (C) **the criminal is good at disguising.** (D) the criminal's gender is identified.	87. 下列何者為真？ (A) 罪犯未曾到過加州。 (B) 罪犯是資深會計師。 (C) **罪犯擅於偽裝。** (D) 罪犯的性別被辨識出了。
88. Where is the news report most likely taking place? (A) **at the felon's cherished shop.** (B) at the Best Automobile. (C) at the California. (D) at the supermarket.	88. 新聞報導最有可能發生在何處？ (A) **在罪犯最喜愛的店。** (B) 在倍斯特汽車廠。 (C) 在加州。 (D) 在超市。

答案：86. D 87. C 88. A

解析

- **第86題**，談話中有提到了the criminal is still at large，代表嫌犯還在逃，試題中改寫成了**absconded**，故答案要選**選項D**。
- **第87題**，從but the criminal wore an eyeglass and was fully clothed，可以推斷出嫌犯善於偽裝，故答案為**選項C**。其餘選項敘述均是錯誤的。
- **第88題**，記者有提到this is Judy Lin at the department store...the criminal's favorite shop...，所以答案要選**選項A**。

聽力原文與中譯

Questions 89-91 refer to the following news report

Six months have passed since we launched the news...time truly flies....and I'm the reporter ...and of course there are other reporters...let's see who is here also...those sitting near the giant glass wall...they are interpreters and...there are a few waiters walking around serving wine and mini-burgers...I'm loving the chicken wings...but they haven't been served yet...and there are plates of candy apple...I'm gonna taste that for you...finally lots of people waiting outside at the entrance....and where are the those celebrities...I see...they are in the auditorium...listening to music...and those curtains are about to be removed...wow...the dazzling jewelry...just too striking...

問題89-91請參閱下列新聞報導

自從我們新聞發佈到現在，已經過了六個月...時光真的飛逝...而我是新聞記者...而當然有其他的記者們...讓我們來看看誰也到這兒了...那些坐在靠近大型玻璃...他們是口譯員和...這裡有幾個服務生四處走動服務酒和微型漢堡...我喜愛雞翅...但是還未上菜...還有幾盤糖霜蘋果...我來替你嚐嚐...最後許多人都在入口處等候著...還有那些名人們...我懂了...他們在講堂裡...聽音樂...而那些簾子正要移除了...哇！眩人奪目的珠寶...真的太耀眼了...。

試題中譯與解析

89. Where most likely are the listeners? (A) at an annual auction. (B) **at the precious metal exhibition.** (C) at the jewelry processing plant. (D) at the interpreter training center.	89. 聽眾們最有可能在何處？ (A) 在年度銷售會。 (B) **在珍貴金屬的展示會。** (C) 在珠寶加工廠。 (D) 在口譯員的訓練中心。
90. Which of the following could be about to be served? (A) mini-burgers. (B) **chicken-wings.** (C) candy apple. (D) wine.	90. 下列哪樣料理正要上菜？ (A) 微型漢堡。 (B) **雞翅。** (C) 糖霜蘋果。 (D) 酒。

91. What field does the speaker work in?	91. 說話者最有可能在哪裡工作？
(A) jewelry design.	(A) 珠寶設計。
(B) cuisine catering.	(B) 佳餚外燴。
(C) music industry.	(C) 音樂產業。
(D) **journalism.**	(D) **新聞業。**

答案：89. B 90. B 91. D

 解析

- **第89題**，從聽力段落中可以得知是珠寶展，聽眾是在珠寶展示會，珠寶換成了precious metal故答案為**選項B**。
- **第90題**，其餘三個選項都端出了，僅有雞翅是還未上菜的，故答案為**選項B**。
- **第91題**，可以推斷出說話者是記者，記者是新聞產業，故答案要選**選項D**。

聽力原文與中譯

Questions 92-94 refer to the following weather report

This is news anchor Bella James...good afternoon...it's been quite tranquil...outside...the clear view and clouds and altocumuluses...don't seem to show up in the sky...but a typhoon is about to approach...and let our weather man tell you the weather in the following week...

Weather man:...thanks Bella...the typhoon tripled its size near Guam...and we are predicting three different routes...first...it's gonna land on the Philippines...and then moves towards the southern parts of the Taiwan...the second route is...it will first hit Yilan and make its landing...and move north towards Japan...the third prediction is that it will be the largest in history and set its foot on Japan...then sails towards Korea, prediction of other international news coincides with our second route...

問題92-94請參閱下列天氣預報

這是新聞主播貝拉・詹姆士...下午好...外頭...一直相當的寧靜...晴朗的景色...雲和高積雲在天空中似乎都看不見...但是颱風正接近中...讓我們的天氣員告訴你接下來一週的天氣狀況...。

天氣員：謝謝貝拉...颱風將會在靠近關島時以三倍的體積增大...而我們預測了三個不同的路徑...首先...它會在菲律賓登陸...而然後移至南台灣...第二個路徑是...它會先襲擊宜蘭並且在宜蘭登陸...之後北移至日本...第三個預測是，颱風會是史上最大的且在日本登陸...然後駛向韓國，其他的國際性新聞的預測與我們所預測的第二個路徑吻合...。

試題中譯與解析	
92. What can be inferred about the weather before the typhoon? (A) cloudy and with different types of clouds. (B) **clear.** (C) windy. (D) rainy.	92. 颱風來之前，可以推測出天氣是如何？ (A) 多雲且有各式不同的雲體。 (B) **晴朗的。** (C) 風大的。 (D) 下雨的。
93. According to the weather man, where did the typhoon gather the most strength? (A) at Korea. (B) at Japan. (C) **at Guam.** (D) at the Philippines.	93. 根據天氣播報員，颱風於何處獲取最大的威力？ (A) 在韓國。 (B) 在日本。 (C) **在關島。** (D) 在菲律賓。
94. If the prediction of the typhoon goes as the international news, where will the typhoon first strike? (A) Guam. (B) The Philippines. (C) **Yilan.** (D) Japan.	94. 如果颱風預測路徑跟國際性新聞吻合的話，那麼颱風會先襲擊哪裡？ (A) 關島。 (B) 菲律賓。 (C) **宜蘭。** (D) 日本。

答案：92. B 93. C 94. C

- 第**92**題，聽力段落中提到了晴朗無雲且有高積雲，所以要選**選項B**，clear。
- 第**93**題，天氣播報員提到...thanks Bella...the typhoon tripled its size near Guam...，故答案要選**選項C**。
- 第**94**題，這題是詢問颱風的預測路徑，如果預測跟國際預測路徑一樣的話，颱風首先會攻擊的哪裡，而在聽力結尾敘述出現prediction of other international news coincides with our second route...，所以找到第二路徑時颱風首先襲擊或登陸的地點是哪裡就是答案，所以可以得知答案為**選項C**。

聽力原文與中譯

Questions 95-97 refer to the following talk

This is Mark Wang......and I'm so pleased to introduce you the design near our park...it's vivid...and thousands of tourists take pictures with lively volcanoes and the model of the formation of the lake...but they often forget that uploading the photo to the Facebook will get free tickets of the National Science Museum...which are attainable at our coffee shop...I'm sure some of you learned those during high-school...first...the rainfall washes away several minerals and nutrients on land and those things are sedimented into the lake...which make the algae bloom...the oxygen is deprived from the algae which make the fish and other living organisms harder to live...eventually all species die and more sediments are washed into the lake making the lake smaller...eventually it has become the land...this is called the formation of the lake...

問題95-97請參閱下列談話

這是馬克‧王......我對於要向你們介紹我們公園的設計感到開心...這是生動的...數以千計的觀光客都會跟活現的火山和湖泊形成的模型拍照...，但是他們通常都忘記，上傳照片到臉書上能獲取國家科博館的免費門票，而門票在我們咖啡店可以拿到...我確信你們之中有些人在高中時學習過這個了...首先降雨從陸地上沖刷了一些礦物質和營養素，而那些物質沉積到湖泊裡頭...讓藻類繁盛...氧氣被藻類剝奪了，此舉讓魚和其他活生生的有機物更難生存了...最後所有物種死亡，而更多的沉積物沖刷到湖泊裡頭，讓湖泊更小了...最終成了陸地...這就是所謂的湖泊的形成...。

試題中譯與解析

95. What is the main topic of the talk? (A) How to get free tickets. (B) How to get higher scores in Earth Science. (C) **A brief introduction of the park's favorite site.** (D) A brief introduction of the National Science Museum.	95. 此篇談話的主題為何？ (A) 如何得到免費的門票。 (B) 如何在地球科學科目上獲得更高分數。 (C) **公園最受喜愛景點的簡介。** (D) 國家科博館的簡介。
96. Where can tourists get the free tickets? (A) at The National Science Museum. (B) at the campus. (C) at the Facebook headquarter. (D) **at the coffee shop.**	96. 觀光客於何處可以獲取免費的門票呢？ (A) 在國家科博館。 (B) 在校園裡。 (C) 在臉書總部。 (D) **在咖啡店。**
97. What will suffer if there is an algae bloom? (A) sediments. (B) **living organisms.** (C) the land. (D) minerals and nutrients.	97. 如果藻類繁盛的話，什麼會受到影響？ (A) 沉積物。 (B) **具生命的有機體。** (C) 陸地。 (D) 礦物質和營養物質。

答案：95. C 96. D 97. B

解析

- **第95題**，這題的話其實是公園最受喜愛地點的簡述，故答案為**選項C**。
- **第96題**，聽力段落中有提到which are attainable at our coffee shop，故答案要選**選項D**。
- **第97題**，這題仔細聽的話可以得知答案就是**選項B** living organisms，其會因為藻類的繁盛而影響。

Questions 98-100 refer to the following live show

We're lucky enough to invite the castle owner...and he is not here to talk about the castle...but about the wedding...welcome...James...

James: you probably wonder how many people are having a wedding photoshoot at our castle...I've got to tell you fewer than ten...so using fingers can count that...you can see what's on the slide...really enigmatic...right...there are some effects of the fog...make it even more illusional...I highly recommend white, black, gray wedding dress...but not purple and yellow...and we're not renting it for educational purposes or Halloween parties...or opening it for tourists...but we really can use it for films...horror films or thrillers...that someone is chasing after you...

問題98-100請參閱下列現場節目

我們很幸運能邀請城堡的擁有者...而他來此不是來談論城堡的...而是談關於婚宴...歡迎...詹姆士...。

詹姆士: 你可能會想有多少的婚宴在我們的城堡中拍照過...我必須要告訴你少於10個...所以用手指頭就能數的出來了...你可以看到簡報圖...真的神祕...對的...有些霧的效果...讓這看起來更錯覺的...我高度推薦白色、黑色、灰色婚宴服飾...但不是紫色和黃色...而我們不將場地租借用於教育目的或是萬聖節派對...或是開放給觀光客們...但是我們真的可以將其用於電影...恐怖片或驚悚片...那種有人在你後面追著你的...。

98. According to the castle owner, which of the following color is not suited for the photoshoot at the castle? (A) white. (B) black. (C) gray. (D) **yellow.**	98. 根據城堡主人,下列哪一個顏色不適合於城堡拍攝? (A) 白色。 (B) 黑色。 (C) 灰色。 (D) **黃色。**

99. Where does this talk most likely taking place? (A) the wedding venue. (B) an ancient castle. (C) **a film studio.** (D) the speaker's house.	99. 此篇談話最有可能發生在何處？ (A) 婚宴場地。 (B) 一棟古代城堡。 (C) **攝影棚。** (D) 說話者的家裡。
100.Who can be the potential candidate allowed to use the castle? (A) a student responsible for the festival party. (B) a professor wanting to know the history of the castle. (C) a tourist who is an avid castle lover. (D) **a movie director.**	100.誰可能是能允許使用城堡的潛在人選呢？ (A) 負責節慶派對的學生。 (B) 想要知道城堡歷史的教授。 (C) 極度愛好城堡的觀光客。 (D) **電影導演。**

答案：98. D 99. C 100. D

解析

- **第98題**，男子有提到幾個顏色適合，也有提到不適合的，可以直接用刪去法，故答案為**選項D**。
- **第99題**，地點的話最有可能的是在攝影棚，故答案為**選項C**。
- **第100題**，這題要看到結尾but we really can use it for films...horror films or thrillers，所以僅可能租借給電影公司，故答案要選跟電影公司相關的人或接洽談租城堡者，最有可能的是**選項D**。

- 【動物葬禮】包含更多圖表題訊息和聽力訊息的整合答題，兩個聽力訊息的整合以判定最終的日期。
- 【巧克力工廠】包含「較為進階」的計算，比起單純檢測是否聽到一個精確的數值，考生更需要將聽到的訊息再多一道計算的程序，最終計算出加薪後的金額。
- 【房屋仲介】也包含了較進階的計算，以及較高階「結合道地慣用語」的出題，考生需要具備一定的整合訊息能力和推測能力才能答好。

模擬試題（五）

▶ **Listening Test 5** 🎧 MP3 017

In the Listening Test, you must demonstrate your ability to understand spoken English. This section is divided into four parts and will take approximately 45 minutes to complete. There are four parts, and directions are given for each part. Do not mark the answers in your test book. Use the answer sheet that is provided separately.

▶ **PART 1**

Directions: For each question, you will listen to four short statements about a picture in your test book. These statements will not be printed and will only be spoken one time. Select the statement that best describes what is happening in the picture and mark the corresponding letter (A), (B), (C), (D) on the answer sheet.

Example   Sample Answer

                                                                A ● C D

Statement (B), "**Some people are wearing backpacks**", is the best description of the picture. So you should select answer (B) and mark it on your answer sheet.

1.

(A)　(B)　(C)　(D)

2.

(A)　(B)　(C)　(D)

3.

(A) (B) (C) (D)

4.

(A) (B) (C) (D)

5.

(A)　(B)　(C)　(D)

6.

(A)　(B)　(C)　(D)

▶ **PART 2** MP3 018

Directions: For each question, you will listen to a statement or a question followed by three possible responses spoken in English. They will not be printed and will only be spoken one time. Select the best response and mark the corresponding letter (A), (B), or (C) on your answer sheet.

7. Mark your answer on your answer sheet.
8. Mark your answer on your answer sheet.
9. Mark your answer on your answer sheet.
10. Mark your answer on your answer sheet.
11. Mark your answer on your answer sheet.
12. Mark your answer on your answer sheet.
13. Mark your answer on your answer sheet.
14. Mark your answer on your answer sheet.
15. Mark your answer on your answer sheet.
16. Mark your answer on your answer sheet.
17. Mark your answer on your answer sheet.
18. Mark your answer on your answer sheet.
19. Mark your answer on your answer sheet.
20. Mark your answer on your answer sheet.
21. Mark your answer on your answer sheet.
22. Mark your answer on your answer sheet.
23. Mark your answer on your answer sheet.
24. Mark your answer on your answer sheet.
25. Mark your answer on your answer sheet.
26. Mark your answer on your answer sheet.

27. Mark your answer on your answer sheet.

28. Mark your answer on your answer sheet.

29. Mark your answer on your answer sheet.

30. Mark your answer on your answer sheet.

31. Mark your answer on your answer sheet.

▶ **PART 3** 🎧 MP3 019

Directions: In this part, you will listen to several conversations between two or more speakers. These conversations will not be printed and will only be spoken one time. For each conversation, you will be asked to answer three questions. Select the best response and mark the corresponding letter (A), (B), (C), (D) on the answer sheet.

COUPON

40% discount for the Cinema

BEST PARK   **Expire:** 2025 June 1

---

32. Look at the graph. What service is the coupon valid for?
- (A) at the theater
- (B) at the hotel
- (C) at the gym
- (D) at the restaurant

---

33. Why is the woman depressed?
- (A) Because the food delivered is cooled
- (B) because his cooking lesson is cancelled

(C) because the romantic candle looks horrible
(D) because the rain is pouring

34. What will the man and the woman probably do next?
    (A) go to the gallery
    (B) take a rest in the pool
    (C) challenge the long slippery trail
    (D) take a cooking lesson

35. What are the speakers mainly discussing?
    (A) time management
    (B) a small crystal ball
    (C) various types of collections
    (D) a white elephant figurine

36. Why do the women go back to the office?
    (A) she forgets her electronic card
    (B) she wants to show her friend about something
    (C) she wants to give her friend a birthday gift
    (D) she wants to engrave a few words on the crystal ball

37. Who most likely is the woman?
    (A) the antique shop owner
    (B) a jewelry designer
    (C) a wedding planner
    (D) a zealous collector

Desolate Orchard

❶ North
❷ South
❸ East
❹ West

Note: West Orchard is currently disused

38. What does the woman inquire about?
　　(A) to confirm the date of the tiger funeral
　　(B) to verify the date of the monkey
　　(C) to check the computer system
　　(D) to give the feedback about the Orchard

39. What will happen on July 1?
　　(A) the funeral of the tiger
　　(B) the burial of the macaque
　　(C) the funeral of other animals
　　(D) the first day that the woman stays at the Shelter House

 40. Look at the graph. Where will the tiger be buried?
　　(A) at West Orchard
　　(B) at East Orchard
　　(C) at South Orchard
　　(D) at North Orchard

41. What is mentioned about the employee?
　　(A) she really wants to say something to her colleagues before she leaves
　　(B) she doesn't like the HR personnel
　　(C) she will be escorted by the security
　　(D) she erases all confidential information on the computer

42. Who will be responsible for handling the document?
　　(A) HR personnel
　　(B) Co-workers
　　(C) the manager
　　(D) the security

43. Which of the following is not what the employee will hand in?
　　(A) documents
　　(B) keys

(C) passport
(D) ID badge

44. What does "dig in" mean?
  (A) eat something creatively
  (B) eat something in direct proportion to his/her weight
  (C) work diligently
  (D) eat something voraciously

45. What does the manager tell listeners to do?
  (A) get his permissions before toss the coin in the machine
  (B) be a grown-up and he doesn't want micromanage the team
  (C) savor different types of chocolates
  (D) have the fantasy for chocolates

46. Why does the woman say, "my fantasy for the chocolate is gone"?
  (A) to emphasize the importance of retaining fantasy
  (B) to highlight that it's not a good time to fantasize at work
  (C) to make a point that she doesn't find it appealing
  (D) to devalue the quality of the company's chocolate

47. What does "tailor-made" mean?
  (A) creative
  (B) specifically-designed
  (C) meticulously-researched
  (D) thought-provoking

48. What does the woman suggest?
  (A) say what really pleases the manager
  (B) have the plan supported by lab researchers
  (C) have a trendy design appealing to younger generations
  (D) do something gallant and low-cost

49. Why does the man say, "it's best if I don't get involved"?
(A) because he is irresponsible
(B) because he does not want to get involved
(C) because the schedule is too tight
(D) because he wants employees to have the autonomy

 50. Why does the woman say, "it's so serendipitous"?
(A) because it's a deliberate pursuit
(B) because it's by chance
(C) because it comes from her hard work
(D) because she demands the promotion

 51. Why does the man say, "that means more responsibility shouldering on you"?
(A) because she only has to do her current job well
(B) because she can now be a shoulder to cry on
(C) because she will be given more tasks and share more responsibilities
(D) because she has to own her mistakes

52. Which of the following is not what will be like after the promotion?
(A) late night in the office
(B) more contact with lab workers
(C) being beforehand in the morning
(D) make chocolates of animal shape individually

53. What does "the upside" in "what the upside is" mean?
(A) the advantage
(B) the disadvantage
(C) the interest
(D) the secret

54.Which of the following is not the benefit of the promotion?
  (A) the increase in salary
  (B) individual parking space
  (C) private space in the office
  (D) an assistant

55.If the employee's previous salary is US 50,000 dollars, what payment will she get after the promotion?
  (A) US 50,000
  (B) US 60,000
  (C) US 70,000
  (D) US 80,000

56.What does "eyeing on the house" mean?
  (A) have to take a thorough look at the house
  (B) can't wait to see the house
  (C) have a less keen interest in the house
  (D) have a strong interest in the house

57.What is the purpose of saying "tomorrow I'm swamped with work"?
  (A) to show her work is more important than the house
  (B) to let the buyer know potential buyers will be the first to see the house
  (C) to emphasize she is a conscientious worker
  (D) to make the buyer more eager to take a look at the house

58.When will the buyer visit the house?
  (A) Friday
  (B) next Monday
  (C) Wednesday before noon
  (D) Thursday before noon

59.What is the purpose of saying "let's not jump right to that"?
(A) because cat got her tongue
(B) because the owner didn't tell her that part
(C) to emphasize she is a shrew negotiator
(D) to procrastinate the house price part and also have some time to show other parts that are fantastic

60.Which of the following is what the buyer finds pleasing to look at?
(A) domestic fowls
(B) squirrels
(C) amphibians
(D) snakes

61.Which of the following is what the buyer dreads?
(A) raccoons
(B) monkeys
(C) frogs
(D) domestic fowls

 62.Why does the woman say, "I guess someone has done her homework"?
(A) to clarify that it's a tragic
(B) to make a point that the buyer finishes writing an assignment
(C) to deflect the topic that the two are discussing
(D) To demonstrate that the buyer is prepared and harder to convince

 63.Why does the buyer say, "that's an extortion"?
(A) he thinks the price is fairly reasonable
(B) he thinks he is being taken advantage of
(C) he thinks the price is too unreasonable
(D) he cannot think of the tactics at the moment

64.What is the ultimate price for the house?
   (A) US 550,00
   (B) US 750,000
   (C) US 700,000
   (D) US 625,000

65.Which of the following is not used to enhance security?
   (A) rigorous SOPs
   (B) identity check
   (C) surveillance cameras
   (D) blood sample

66.What does the woman mean when she says "could be an inside job"?
   (A) she really wants to help out by entering inside the door
   (B) she has doubts about how the blood sample getting switched
   (C) she remains doubtful about the investigation
   (D) she treats everyone like a suspect

67.Who could be the female speaker?
   (A) a judge
   (B) a defense attorney
   (C) a lab researcher
   (D) the director

68.Why does the speaker say, "that makes things a whole lot easier"?
   (A) because there is a new opening drug store in town
   (B) because it doesn't need the prescription
   (C) because the traffic is not heavy
   (D) because the store has the best painkillers

69. Which of the following kinds of medicine is what the speaker used to take?
   (A) Chinese herbal ointment
   (B) tablets of aspirins
   (C) capsule-made painkillers
   (D) powder-made medicine

70. Which of the following will be applied to before the speaker heads to the drug store?
   (A) ointment
   (B) medicine powder
   (C) tablets
   (D) the painkiller

▶ **PART 4** MP3 020

Directions: In this part, you will listen to several talks by one or two speakers. These talks will not be printed and will only be spoken one time. for each talk, you will be asked to answer three questions. Select the best response and mark the corresponding letter (A), (B), (C), (D) on your answer sheet.

71. Which of the following is closet in meaning to "dissect"?
   (A) scrutinize
   (B) deliver
   (C) classify
   (D) describe

72. Which of the following is used to preserve the steam inside?
   (A) the sauce
   (B) a rug
   (C) the cooking method
   (D) the urn

73. What is the flavor of the ostrich egg?
    (A) bitter
    (B) sour
    (C) sweet
    (D) salty

74. Who is not the target audience?
    (A) truck drivers
    (B) hikers
    (C) taxi drivers
    (D) animal lovers

75. Why does the speaker say, "running out of blood serums"?
    (A) to warn the danger of getting bitten in the forest
    (B) to highlight the importance of the venoms
    (C) to call for the donation of the serums
    (D) to relieve the stress of the mountain climbers

76. What could be featured in the upcoming news?
    (A) the tunnel is fixed by construction workers
    (B) the firefighters are sending supplies to the mountain
    (C) villagers miraculously discover a new blood serum
    (D) people parading outside the department store

Best Restaurant

· 10 large **Boston Lobsters** for free
· A bottle of **Red Wine**

Expire Date: 2025/01/25

---

77. Where most likely is the talk taking place?
  (A) at the travel agency
  (B) at the restaurant
  (C) at the museum
  (D) at the theater

78. What is not mentioned in the talk?
  (A) visitors might find the lectures not interesting
  (B) souvenir-like chocolates are used as the winning prize
  (C) the difficulty of the carnivore dinosaurs is greater than that of the herbivore dinosaurs
  (D) jigsaw puzzles are only for kids

79. Look at the graph. Where can the coupon be used?
  (A) at the cafeteria
  (B) at the museum
  (C) at the recreational theme park
  (D) at the chocolate plant

80. What will be provided to the listeners?
  (A) beverages
  (B) dehydration
  (C) treasure
  (D) orange

81. Which of the following is what participants are asked to find?
  (A) colors
  (B) pebbles
  (C) a jewelry box
  (D) an Easter egg

82. Why does the speaker mention, you might find some unwanted companies?
  (A) to remind participants of an interference on the beach

(B) to educate participants the function of crabs in the ecosystem
(C) to warn participants about impending dangers
(D) to increase the difficulty of the treasure hunt

83.What is the purpose of the news report?
(A) to raise funds for animals
(B) to demand more animal interactions in the Circus
(C) to protest the increasingly high entrance fees
(D) to enhance the awareness for animal mistreatment

84.According to the news report, who are not persuaded by the statement?
(A) college students
(B) biologists
(C) trainers
(D) the government

85.Which of the following does not suffer inhumane treatment?
(A) camels
(B) elephants
(C) horses
(D) tigers

86.Why does the linguist plan to talk first?
(A) he wants to entice listeners
(B) he wants to astound people
(C) he wants to make a good impression
(D) he understands perfectly about human nature

87.What can be inferred about the bestseller?
(A) the author stashes numerous books in the storehouse
(B) the company does not hire sales reps
(C) it's not a thriller
(D) the use of the language is elegant

88.According to the linguist, who deserves the most contribution of the book?
(A) the author
(B) the publisher
(C) the editors
(D) the experts

89.What could be the factor that attracts people the most?
(A) the fee
(B) the coupon
(C) the extensive care provided by the doctor
(D) the after-treatment service

90.Which of the following is not the promise of the teeth whitening?
(A) withstand sour juices
(B) reduce the consumption of coffee
(C) resist the corrasion of the chocolate
(D) form the protection on the teeth's exterior

91.What is being advertised?
(A) a skin-care hospital
(B) a research center
(C) a dental clinic
(D) a fitness center

92.Which of the following can be used up during long whirling?
(A) gas
(B) electricity
(C) cookies
(D) fog

93. Which of the following is something flight attendants can control?
(A) lightning
(B) gusty wind
(C) snowstorm
(D) the attitude towards passengers

94. Which of the following is not the repercussion of bad weather?
(A) the plane delaying uncontrollably
(B) the plane obliterating unexpectedly
(C) the plane smashing accidentally
(D) the plane landing successfully

95. Who might be the speaker?
(A) Science Project participants
(B) an assistant responsible for various errands
(C) HR managers
(D) the superintendent

96. When could be the date of the wedding photoshoot?
(A) June 1
(B) during the renovation
(C) May 18
(D) six months before the interview

97. Which of the following is not the task given by the speaker?
(A) to phone the project participant
(B) to discuss details with HR managers
(C) to arrange another time for the interview
(D) to turn down the further reservation

98. What can be inferred about the current status of the employee?
(A) jobless
(B) employed

(C) fully prepared
(D) anonymous

 99.Why does the CFO say, "he has already made a job hop"?
    (A) to confirm the layoff news is true
    (B) to consolidate the company's faith in him
    (C) to demonstrate that he has other option
    (D) to show his work ethics

100.What does "on the chopping block" mean?
    (A) on the breaking news
    (B) on the board meeting
    (C) on a cutting board
    (D) on the list of downsizing

第五回 模擬試題解析

 PART 1

聽力原文與中譯	
1. (A) The flight attendant is getting impatient. (B) Houses are big even from such a distance. (C) The view is filmed by the passenger sitting on the aisle seat. (D) **A checker board farmland can be seen from above.**	1. (A) 空服員正失去耐心。 (B) 從這麼遠看房子仍是很大間。 (C) 景象是在坐走道旁的乘客所拍攝的。 (D) **從上頭可以看到棋盤式的農田。**

答案：(D)

這題可以看到的是，似於在飛機的靠窗口往下拍攝的畫面，看到的部分是類似棋盤格狀的農田，這符合選項D的描述，故答案要選**選項D**。

聽力原文與中譯	
2. (A) Cars are for the filming purposes. (B) **Railroads are bordering the residential buildings.** (C) There is only one street lamp on the street. (D) Tunnels are blocked for unknown reasons.	2. (A) 車子是用於拍攝目的。 (B) **鐵路比鄰住宅區的建築物。** (C) 街道上僅有一個街燈。 (D) 隧道因為不明原因被阻擋了。

答案： (B)

 解析

這題有些難度，在地面上可以看到兩排類似提供給火車行走的鐵路在地上，這些緊鄰一般居民的房子旁，故答案要選**選項B**。

聽力原文與中譯	
3. (A) Vehicles are heading in different directions. (B) Vehicles are occupying the entire street. (C) A parking cop awaits on the street corner. (D) **There is a shop on the corner.**	3. (A) 汽車以不同的方向行駛。 (B) 汽車正占據整條街。 (C) 開罰單的警察正等在街口。 (D) **在街角有間商店。**

答案： (D)

 解析

這題可以看到，在歐式風格的街道上，角落處有間店，故答案要選**選項D**。

聽力原文與中譯	
4. (A) Two roads diverged in the wood. (B) Pedestrians are walking their dogs on the street. (C) **The road is straight.** (D) Trees on both sides are leafless.	4. (A) 林中的兩條路分岔了。 (B) 行人們正在街道上遛狗。 (C) **路是筆直的。** (D) 兩旁的樹都沒有葉子。

答案： (C)

 解析

這題也有些難度，不過可以很清楚地看到，在兩排的林地中有條筆直的路，所以很明顯答案為**選項C**。

5.
(A) The pyramid building is not half surrounded by other buildings.
(B) People are staying in the pyramid building.
(C) Half of the people are sitting on the bench.
(D) **Water is splashing from the small pool.**

5.
(A) 金字塔建築物沒有被其他建築物半包圍住。
(B) 人們待在金字塔的建築物裡。
(C) 有一半的人正坐在板凳上。
(D) **水從小池子中灑出。**

答案：(D)

 解析

這題也有許多小陷阱的部分，可以清楚看到的是，在金字塔建築物旁有兩小道噴水湧出，故答案要選**選項D**。

6.
(A) The height of the traffic lights is higher than that of the house.
(B) Iron fences are higher than trees.
(C) **There are traffic lights in front of the house.**
(D) There is a no smoking sign on the street.

6.
(A) 紅綠燈的高度比房子的高度更高。
(B) 鐵欄比樹還高。
(C) **房子前面有紅綠燈。**
(D) 街道上有禁止吸菸的標示。

答案：(C)

 解析

這題可以看到在這棟房子前面有架設紅綠燈，故答案要選**選項C**。

PART 2

聽力原文與中譯	
7. Does your vote trump CEO? (A) The CEO won't visit our office very often. (B) I'm getting the vote this year. (C) **What makes you think that?**	7. 你的決定權勝過執行長嗎？ (A) 執行長不常拜訪我們辦公室。 (B) 我今年會得到票。 (C) **什麼事情讓你會這樣想呢？**

答案：(C)

 解析

這題也是沒有直接回答，而是反問對方，故答案要選**選項C**。

聽力原文與中譯	
8. Can you do me a favor? (A) That does not favor you. (B) **can't you tell? I'm busy.** (C) Actually, I do need your help.	8. 你可以幫我個忙嗎？ (A) 這並不會對你有利。 (B) **你察覺不出來嗎？，我相當的忙碌。** (C) 實際上，我確實需要你的幫助。

答案：(B)

 解析

這題也是反問對方並加上一句描述，故答案要選**選項B**。

聽力原文與中譯	
9. Don't you think those monkeys are actually enjoying in the hot spring? (A) I do want to join them. (B) **Yep, I'm filming their family time.** (C) Those monkeys are afraid of water.	9. 你不認為那些猴子實際上正在享受熱泉嗎？ (A) 我確實想要加入他們。 (B) **是的，我正在拍攝他們的家庭時光。** (C) 那些猴子怕水。

答案：(B)

解析

這題有明確的表達是的的描述，很明顯答案為**選項B**。

聽力原文與中譯	
10. Which forest produces the most delicious fruit? (A) I might need you to steal those seeds. (B) **The wet one.** (C) Perhaps in the jungle.	10. 哪個森林產出最多美味的水果呢？ (A) 我可能需要你偷取那些種子。 (B) **那個潮濕的。** (C) 或許在叢林裡頭。

答案：(B)

解析

這題也有指出是哪裡，故答案為**選項B**。

聽力原文與中譯	
11. Which monkey is demoted to a lower position? (A) I have to call out for help. (B) **One of the females which cheated.** (C) My elementary biology doesn't help.	11. 哪個猴子降級至較低的職位呢？ (A) 我必須要打電話向外呼救。 (B) **其中一位偷吃的雌性猴子。** (C) 我的基礎生物學沒有幫到忙。

答案：(B)

解析

這題也有明確指出是哪個，故答案為**選項B**。

聽力原文與中譯

12. How to open the stone-like fruit? (A) It obviously cannot be opened. (B) **By using tools** (C) Under most circumstances, it can't.	12. 如何打開石頭般硬的水果呢？ (A) 這顯然無法打開。 (B) **藉由使用工具。** (C) 在大多數的情況下，它無法被打開。

答案：(B)

 解析

這題也要選方式或方法，故答案為**選項B**。

聽力原文與中譯

13. How does the octopus escape the situation like that? (A) **The octopus obviously uses coloration.** (B) The situation is inescapable. (C) It's not intelligent enough.	13. 章魚如何能夠逃離像這樣的情況呢？ (A) **章魚顯然使用了顏色變換。** (B) 這情況是必無可避的。 (C) 牠不夠聰明。

答案：(A)

 解析

這題要選擇能解釋的句子，故答案為**選項A**。

聽力原文與中譯

14. Why does the impala jump into the river? (A) The river is too beautiful. (B) he is too inexperienced. (C) **to avoid predators.**	14. 為什麼黑斑羚跳進了溪裡？ (A) 這條溪流太美麗了。 (B) 牠太沒有經驗了。 (C) **為了躲避掠食者。**

答案：(C)

解析

這題要選擇原因或表目的的表達,故答案為**選項C**。

聽力原文與中譯	
15. Would the lion prefer the more agile prey? (A) No, he is aiming at the small one. (B) **It depends.** (C) He wants to be as agile as the prey.	15. 獅子會偏好較為敏捷的獵物嗎? (A) 沒有,牠正瞄準較小型的目標。 (B) **這要視情況而定。** (C) 牠想要像獵物般的靈活。

答案:(B)

解析

這題也是沒有明確給答案,而是表明視情況而定,故答案為**選項B**。

聽力原文與中譯	
16. It's sweltering hot in the desert, don't you think? (A) Are you going to be a weatherman? (B) **Perhaps we should wait until the sunset.** (C) Camels look great in the desert.	16. 沙漠裡頭是悶熱的,你不認為是這樣嗎? (A) 你將要成為天氣預報員嗎? (B) **或許我們應該要等到太陽下山。** (C) 在沙漠裡頭,駱駝看起來棒極了。

答案:(B)

解析

這題也要選接續解釋的部分,故答案為**選項B**。

聽力原文與中譯	
17. Aren't those tents getting erected by noon? (A) I'm trying to get my phone back. (B) Tents can do those things themselves. (C) **Yes, but I am losing patience.**	17.那些帳篷在正午時分不是都該立好嗎？ (A) 我正試著將我的手機拿回來。 (B) 帳篷可以自己完成那些事情。 (C) **是的，但是我正失去耐心了。**

答案：(C)

 解析

這題有明確的表明是或否的答案，故答案要選**選項C**。

聽力原文與中譯	
18. What made you decide to be an animal doctor? (A) A physician will earn more money. (B) See the pic over there, me and those animals. (C) **Being with animals makes me happy.**	18.什麼讓你決定要成為動物醫生呢？ (A) 內科醫生將賺取更多的錢。 (B) 看這裡的照片，我和那些動物們。 (C) **與動物在一塊讓我感到快樂。**

答案：(C)

 解析

這題要選原因，故答案為**選項C**。

聽力原文與中譯	
19. Are you still looking for an oasis? (A) I love taking pics near the oasis. (B) The oasis contains lots of things. (C) **I'm afraid the answer is yes.**	19.你仍在找尋綠洲嗎？ (A) 我喜愛在綠洲旁拍照。 (B) 綠洲包含了許多事情。 (C) **恐怕答案是「是的」。**

答案：(C)

解析

這題也有是的的明確表達，只是前面又加上了恐怕，故答案為**選項C**。

聽力原文與中譯	
20. What is the raccoon doing on my car? (A) I don't know I just want to raise one. (B) Wow...you didn't recognize him. (C) **Perhaps learning how to drive.**	20. 那隻浣熊在我車上幹嘛呢？ (A) 我不知道，我只是想要養一隻。 (B) 哇！...你沒有認出牠啊！ (C) **或許學習怎麼開車吧！**

答案：(C)

解析

這題的答案為比較創意式的回答，**選項C**剛好符合。

聽力原文與中譯	
21. Can we throw a diet soda while driving? (A) It contains less sugar. (B) I'm trying to convince the Coke company to hire me as a driver. (C) **Why not?**	21. 我們可以在開車時投擲低熱量汽水？ (A) 它包含較少的糖。 (B) 我試圖要說服可口可樂公司雇用我當司機。 (C) **為什麼不能呢？**

答案：(C)

解析

這題要選反問對方的回答，要小心其他陷阱，故答案為**選項C**。

聽力原文與中譯

22. Why does the koalas want water? (A) Water is essential to all creatures. (B) Are they moving to our zoo? (C) **You haven't heard...the forest fire.**	22. 為什麼無尾熊想要水呢？ (A) 水對於所有生物來說是重要的。 (B) 牠們要移到我們的動物園嗎？ (C) **你還沒聽說呀！...森林大火。**

答案：(C)

 解析

這題也是沒有提供明確的答案，而是另一類的表達最後才告知對方原因，故答案為**選項C**。

聽力原文與中譯

23. Who is in charge of delivering the meat to those lions? (A) The shipment always delays (B) **I don't know...I'm new here.** (C) I have to put the meat in the refrigerator.	23. 誰負責將肉食遞給那些獅子呢？ (A) 運送總是延遲。 (B) **我不知道...我是新來的。** (C) 我必須將肉品放置到冰箱。

答案：(B)

 解析

這題也沒有表明是誰，而是不確定或不知道，答案為**選項B**。

聽力原文與中譯

24. I cannot run those pics. (A) I can, too. (B) **Neither can I.** (C) I guess those photos are good.	24. 我無法看那些照片。 (A) 我也可以。 (B) **我也無法。** (C) 我猜想那些照片並不錯。

答案：(B)

解析

這題有很明確的我也無法的表達，所以答案為**選項B**。

聽力原文與中譯	
25. Did the animal doctor contact you? (A) Some animals are on the brink of extinction. (B) **No, why should he?** (C) Of course, I can assist the veterinarian.	25. 動物醫生沒有聯繫你嗎？ (A) 有些動物正面臨絕跡。 (B) **沒有，為什麼他要呢？** (C) 當然，我可以協助那位獸醫。

答案：(B)

解析

這題選項B有很直接的回答「沒有」，故答案為**選項B**。

聽力原文與中譯	
26. The machine is used to clean the poo of those elephants. (A) I used to clean the poo in the fence. (B) Remembers all their names are so hard. (C) **That makes you pretty redundant.**	26. 機器用於清理那些大象的糞便。 (A) 我過去曾清理圍籬內的糞便。 (B) 記得他們所有的名字太難了。 (C) **這讓你相當多餘。**

答案：(C)

解析

這題有些難，接續敘述後的推論要想到可能的回答，也意謂著有了機器了，機器能取代做這些事，就造成了人力上的多餘或不需要人力了，答案為**選項C**。

聽力原文與中譯	
27. Would you like to have a dinner with those pandas? (A) Pandas are too fragile for visiting. (B) **I am bringing them desserts, if that's ok.** (C) News reports about pandas aren't true.	27. 你想要與那些貓熊共進晚餐嗎？ (A) 貓熊太脆弱了，而不適於觀賞用。 (B) **我給牠們帶了甜點，如果這樣是可以的話。** (C) 關於貓熊的新聞報導不真實。

答案：(B)

這題也是接續的表達，思考下答案為**選項B**。

聽力原文與中譯	
28. Why do you want to quit the job? (A) The resignation letter is on my desk. (B) **The payment isn't as good as it used to.** (C) The new CEO seems nice.	28. 為什麼你想要辭掉這份工作呢？ (A) 辭職信在我的辦公桌上。 (B) **薪資並沒有像過去那樣好了。** (C) 新的執行長似乎人很好。

答案：(B)

這題選項B提供了直接的原因，故答案為**選項B**。

聽力原文與中譯	
29. What made you fire from the promising job? (A) The promise is broken. (B) The fire came out of nowhere. (C) **I dated an employee, which I shouldn't.**	29. 什麼讓你從這份前景看好的工作解僱了呢？ (A) 承諾破裂了。 (B) 不知道從哪裡來的大火。 (C) **我與其中一位員工約會，而我不該這麼做。**

答案：(C)

 解析

這題也有提供一個解釋，只是沒那麼直接，答案為**選項C**。

聽力原文與中譯	
30. Have you met our new member, the brown bear. (A) I bet he stole the honey in the warehouse. (B) **He looks so adorable.** (C) I can't believe you take him back.	30. 你見過我們的新成員棕熊了嗎？ (A) 我打賭牠偷了倉庫中的蜂蜜。 (B) **牠看起來好可愛。** (C) 我不敢相信你把牠帶回來了。

答案：(B)

 解析

這題是接續回答問題，答案要選**選項B**。

聽力原文與中譯	
31. Where did you find my diamond ring? (A) The ring looks glamorous and striking. (B) **in the treasure box of the brown bear.** (C) I do think you should put it in the safe.	31. 你在哪裡找到我的鑽石戒指呢？ (A) 這個戒指看起來富有魅力且耀眼。 (B) **在棕熊的寶藏盒裡頭。** (C) 我認為你該將戒指放到保險箱裡頭。

答案：(B)

 解析

這題也有一個明確的位置，故答案為**選項B**。

 **Part 3**

聽力原文和對話

Questions 32-34 refer to the following conversation

COUPON

40% discount for the Cinema

BEST PARK **Expire:** 2025 June

Park ranger: hey...I'm the park ranger...I'm bringing you guys hot meals and coupons for cinemas in our second building...it's really raining cats and dogs...hopefully tomorrow it's going to stop...

Cindy: ...our weekend is ruined...our entire focus for this trip is to visit this National Park...

Park ranger: ..really slippery out there in the long trails...but there are other options for you too...we do have a cooking lesson in the main building...or are you fantasized by making a romantic candle...and there are specimens of exotic insects in the gallery...if you are an insect-lover.

Mark: that's intriguing...what's that smell...

Park ranger: it's from our hot springs...it's a group pool...

Cindy: perhaps after finishing eating...we can go there and meditate

Park ranger: ...that's your choice...now you have to excuse me...I've got a few more rooms to go to...

Cindy: sure...

問題32-34，請參考以下對話內容

優惠卷

影城六折折扣

倍斯特公園 截止日期：2025年6月1日

公園管理員：嗨...我是公園管理員...我替你們帶了熱食和我們第二棟大樓的電影優惠卷...這裡真的傾盆大雨...希望明天這雨會停了...。

辛蒂：...我們這個周末毀了...我們這個旅行的整個焦點都在這個國家公園上了...。

公園管理員：...外頭的長步道真的滑溜...但是你們也有其他的選擇...我們在主要大樓有廚藝課程...或是你們對於浪漫蠟燭存有幻象...而且在藝廊，有外來引進的昆蟲標本...，如果你是昆蟲愛好者的話。

馬克：這真的令人感到有趣...這是什麼味道...。

公園管理員：這是我們的熱泉...這是團體池...。

辛蒂：或許在吃完東西後...我們可以去那然後沉思下。

公園管理員：...那就是你們的選擇了...現在請見諒...我還有幾個房間要去...。

辛蒂：當然...。

試題中譯與解析

32. Look at the graph. What service is the coupon valid for?	32. 請參考圖表。優惠卷可以用於什麼服務？
(A) **at the theater.**	(A) **在戲院。**
(B) at the hotel.	(B) 在旅館。
(C) at the gym.	(C) 在體育館。
(D) at the restaurant.	(D) 在餐廳。
33. Why is the woman depressed?	33. 為何女子感到沮喪？
(A) because the food delivered is cooled.	(A) 因為送來的食物冷掉了。
(B) because his cooking lesson is cancelled.	(B) 因為他的烹飪課被取消了。
(C) because the romantic candle looks horrible.	(C) 因為浪漫的蠟燭看起來可怕。
(D) **because the rain is pouring.**	(D) **因為雨正傾盆而下。**

396

34. What will the man and the woman probably do next? (A) go to the gallery. (B) **take a rest in the pool.** (C) challenge the long slippery trail. (D) take a cooking lesson.	34. 對話中的男子和女子接下來可能會做什麼？ (A) 去藝廊。 (B) **在池子裡休息。** (C) 挑戰長且滑溜的小徑。 (D) 修個烹飪課。

答案：32. A 33. D 34. B

解析

- **第32題**，對應到圖表中可以得知，這個優惠券適用於電影院，故答案要選**選項A**。
- **第33題**，女子感到depressed的原因是傾盆大雨所以毀掉了周末，故答案要選擇**選項D**。
- **第34題**，對話中女子要提到等下要去泡溫泉池，故答案要選**選項B**，選項又有經過改寫過。

聽力原文和對話

Questions 35-37 refer to the following conversation

Cindy: ...where did you get this?

Mary: that antique store down the sixtieth Avenue. And it's not cheap...

Cindy: ...I guess that will be a constant reminder of ...cherishing time...

Mary: ...yep...do not waste time for that's what life is made of...

Cindy: that's the kind of the figurine that I would like to put on my desk...

Mary: actually...I have a small crystal ball engraving those words

Cindy: can I see it...

Mary: if you love it so much...I can give that to you as a present...it's in the office building...come with me...let me get my electronic card...

Cindy: wow...there are plenty of figurines on your desk...white elephant...

Mary: would you like to hold it...this purple crystal has a certain power...though...it's retrieved from a necklace...

模擬試題（一）

模擬試題（二）

模擬試題（三）

模擬試題（四）

模擬試題（五）

辛蒂：...你從哪裡拿到這個的？

瑪莉：在第60大道底頭的古董店。而且這不便宜...。

辛蒂：...我想這是個不斷提醒著的...珍惜時光...。

瑪莉：...是的...別浪費時間，因為時間是生活的組成...。

辛蒂：像這樣類型的小雕飾品也會是我想要放在我辦公桌上的...。

瑪莉：事實上...我有一個小型的水晶球，有雕刻那些字在上頭。

辛蒂：我可以看下嗎？

瑪莉：如果你這麼喜愛的話...我可以給妳當作禮物...在辦公室裡頭...跟我來吧...讓我拿我的電子感應卡...。

辛蒂：哇！...在你的辦公桌上有許多小雕飾品...白色大象...。

瑪莉：你想要拿著嗎？...這紫色的水晶有特別的力量在...儘管這是從項鍊上取下的...

試題中譯與解析

35. What are the speakers mainly discussing? (A) time management. (B) a small crystal ball. (C) **various types of collections.** (D) a white elephant figurine.	35. 説話者主要在討論什麼？ (A) 時間管理。 (B) 小型的水晶球。 (C) **不同類型的收藏品。** (D) 白色大象的小雕像。
36. Why do the women go back to the office? (A) she forgets her electronic card. (B) **she wants to show her friend about something.** (C) she wants to give her friend a birthday gift. (D) she wants to engrave a few words on the crystal ball.	36. 為何女子要返回辦公室？ (A) 她忘了她的電子感應卡。 (B) **她想向她朋友展示一些東西。** (C) 她想給她朋友一件生日禮物。 (D) 她想在水晶球上刻幾個字。
37. Who most likely is the woman? (A) the antique shop owner. (B) a jewelry designer. (C) a wedding planner. (D) **a zealous collector.**	37. 女子最可能是誰？ (A) 古董店持有者。 (B) 珠寶設計師。 (C) 婚宴策劃者。 (D) **熱情的收藏家。**

答案：35. C 36. B 37. D

 解析

- **第35題**，這題有很多干擾選項，不過主要討論的項目是各式不同類型的收藏品，故答案為**選項C**。
- **第36題**，女子回到辦公室的主因是要拿東西給朋友看，故答案要選擇**選項B**。
- **第37題**，女子最有可能的是具狂熱的收藏家，故答案要選**選項D**。

聽力原文和對話

Questions 38-40 refer to the following conversation

Desolate Orchard
1. North
2. South
3. East
4. West

Note: West Orchard is currently disused

Linda: ...I was a volunteer last summer and...I'm calling to confirm the date...

Jason: ...what date?...oh...we are gonna bury the tiger on July 15 2022...

Linda: no offense...I was gonna ask about the monkey...

Jason: ...let me check my computer...it's got to be here...let's see...the funeral of the macaque is two weeks prior to that of the tiger...can't believe that we have the busiest schedule...and totally an unrelated topic...carnivores will be buried at Desolate Orchard...either South or West

Linda: ...so sorry to hear that...

Jason: ...is there anything that you'd like me to check it for you?

Linda: ...I was wondering is it ok for me to stay at the Shelter House for a few days...probably at the end of the June...

Jason: ...I don't think that would be a problem...remember to bring your sleeping bag...just in case...

Linda: ...thanks...

問題38-40，請參考以下對話內容

荒棄果園

❶ 北方
❷ 南方
❸ 東方
❹ 西方

註：西方果園目前停止使用

琳達：...我去年當過自願者而且...我打這通電話的目的是要確認日期...。
傑森：...什麼日期呢？...噢！...我們於2022年6月15日要埋葬老虎...。
琳達：沒有冒犯的意思...我要詢問的是關於猴子的事...。
傑森：...讓我查詢下我的電腦...應該在這的...讓我看看...獼猴的葬禮是在老虎埋葬日期的前兩週...不敢相信我們有這麼忙碌的時程...，而全然無關的話題，肉食動物會葬在荒廢果園...南方或西方果園其中一個地方。
琳達：...對於聽到這個感到很抱歉...。
傑森：...還有什麼事你想要我幫你確認的嗎？
琳達：...我在想，我是否能夠待在庇護之家幾天...可能會是六月底...。
傑森：...我不認為那會是個問題...記得攜帶你的睡袋...這僅是要以防萬一...。
琳達：謝謝...。

試題中譯與解析

38. What does the woman inquire about? (A) to confirm the date of the tiger funeral. (B) **to verify the date of the monkey.** (C) to check the computer system. (D) to give the feedback about the Orchard.	38. 女子詢問關於什麼？ (A) 確認老虎的葬禮日期。 (B) **確認猴子的葬禮日期。** (C) 檢查電腦系統。 (D) 給予關於果園的意見回饋。

39. What will happen on July 1? (A) the funeral of the tiger. (B) **the burial of the macaque.** (C) the funeral of other animals. (D) the first day that the woman stays at the Shelter House.	39. 7月1日將會發生什麼事情？ (A) 老虎的葬禮。 (B) **獼猴的葬禮。** (C) 其他動物的葬禮。 (D) 女子待在動物庇護之家的首日。
40. Look at the graph. Where will the tiger be buried? (A) at West Orchard. (B) at East Orchard. (C) **at South Orchard.** (D) at North Orchard.	40. 請參考圖表。老虎會葬在哪裡？ (A) 在果園西方。 (B) 在果園東方。 (C) **在果園南方。** (D) 在果園北方。

答案：38. B 39. B 40. C

解析

- **第38題**，這題也要注意其他干擾選項和誤選，其實是要確認猴子的葬禮，故答案要選**選項B**。
- **第39題**，試題是詢問7/1日，聽力段落中有提到明確日期是老虎的部分，為7/15，還有更後面有提到猴子是在老虎**前兩週**，故7/1為猴子的葬禮，故答案要選**選項B**。
- **第40題**，試題是詢問「老虎會葬在哪」，先對應到聽力段落處carnivores will be buried at Desolate Orchard...either South or West，老虎即是肉食性動物，所以可以推斷老虎會葬在南方或西方，在看到圖表處，西方果園現在是disused，故老虎最可能葬在南方果園，故答案要選**選項C**。

聽力原文和對話

Questions 41-43 refer to the following conversation
Manager: what's this...?
Cindy: ...my resignation...
Manager: ...what...you have been hard-working and diligent...?what's going on?
Cindy: ...this job is just not for me...I guess...that's it...
Manager: ok...then I will have HR personnel to process the paper work...and are you gonna say something to your co-workers

Cindy: ...I think I will pass...and about the paper...the sooner the better...thanks...

Manager: ...good luck with everything...

Cindy: This is...the files from the company...and several documents...that's kind of the standard procedure...my ID badge...and keys of several lockers

HR: ...here is the place that we need you to sign...your signature...

Cindy: ...no problem....

HR: ...I'll have the security to escort you to the main gate...

Cindy: ...wonderful...

問題41-43，請參考以下對話內容

經理：這是什麼呢？

辛蒂：我的辭職...。

經理：...什麼...你一直都很努力工作且勤奮...？發生了什麼事情了呢？

辛蒂：這份工作真的不適合我...我想...就這樣囉...。

經理：好的...那麼...我會叫人事專員處理一下文件...然後你要跟你的同事們說下再見嗎？

辛蒂：...我想我就跳過這部份了...而關於文件的部分...越快越好...謝謝...。

經理：...祝一切都順利...。

辛蒂：這是...公司的檔案...以及幾份文件...這有點是標準的程序...我的身分識別證...和幾個抽屜鎖的鑰匙。

人事專員：...這裡是你需要簽的地方...你的簽名...。

辛蒂：...沒問題...。

人事專員：...我會讓保全人員護送你到大門入口...。

辛蒂：...棒呆了...。

試題中譯與解析

41. What is mentioned about the employee? (A) she really wants to say something to her colleagues before she leaves. (B) she doesn't like the HR personnel. (C) **she will be escorted by the security.** (D) she erases all confidential information on the computer.	41. 關於員工的敘述，何者為非? (A) 在她離開前，她真的想向她同事說些什麼。 (B) 她不喜歡人事專員。 (C) **她會由保全護送。** (D) 她消除電腦上所有機密資訊。
42. Who will be responsible for handling the document? (A) **HR personnel.** (B) Co-workers. (C) the manager. (D) the security.	42. 誰將負責處理文件? (A) **人事專員。** (B) 同事。 (C) 經理。 (D) 保全。
43. Which of the following is not what the employee will hand in? (A) documents. (B) keys. (C) **passport.** (D) ID badge.	43. 下列何者並不是員工會繳交的? (A) 文件。 (B) 鑰匙。 (C) **護照。** (D) 身分識別證。

答案：41. C 42. A 43. C

解析

- **第41題**，關於員工的敘述何者為非，一一比對後僅有選項C是正確的，故答案為**選項C**。
- **第42題**，試題中的handling the document對應到I will have HR personnel to process the paper work，故答案為**選項A**。
- **第43題**，聽力中沒有出現護照這個訊息，故答案為**選項C**。

Questions 44-46 refer to the following conversation

Manager: ...ok...now dig in...

Employee: that many...?

Manager: ...is that a problem?....you guys are hired to taste chocolates...so open your mouth and have a big bite...

Employee: ...ok...I'm gonna get some drinks from the automatic machine...I'm so thirty...

Manager: ...you guys are grown-ups...why ask my permission?? Go....I will be right back in twenty minutes...and by that time I want to know how each new flavor tastes like...ok...great...

Employee: ...now whenever I go to the store...my fantasy for the chocolate is gone...

Employee: ...can't agree with you more...but I've got to say that this one does stand out from the rest...it's unconventional...

Employee : ...perhaps I should've tried that one first...

問題44-46，請參考以下對話內容

經理：...好的...現在大口品嚐...。

員工：...這樣多呀...?

經理：...這樣有什麼問題嗎？...你們是受聘要品嚐巧克力味道的...所以打開你的嘴巴並且大口吃下...。

員工：...好的...我想要從自動販賣機那裡投遞些飲料...我好渴...。

經理：...你們都是成年人了...為什麼需要我批准呢？去吧...我20分鐘後會回來這裡...然後到那時候，我想要知道每個口味嚐起來是怎樣...好的...很棒...。

員工 ：...現在不論我走到哪間店...我對巧克力的幻想全都沒了...。

員工 ：...不能同意你更多了...但是我必須要說，這個巧克力口味是鶴立雞群的...這不...。

員工 ：...或許非常規的我應該要先試試看這個...。

試題中譯與解析	
44. What does "dig in" mean? (A) eat something creatively. (B) eat something in direct proportion to his/her weight. (C) work diligently. (D) **eat something voraciously.**	44.「dig in」指的是什麼？ (A) 創意性地品嚐食物。 (B) 跟自己體重等比例的進食。 (C) 勤奮地工作。 (D) **狼吞虎嚥地吃東西。**
45. What does the manager tell listeners to do? (A) get his permissions before toss the coin in the machine. (B) be a grown-up and he doesn't want micromanage the team. (C) **savor different types of chocolates.** (D) have the fantasy for chocolates.	45. 經理告知聽者要做什麼？ (A) 販賣機投幣時要有他的許可。 (B) 像個成年人，且他不想要微管理團隊。 (C) **品嚐不同類型的巧克力。** (D) 對巧克力持有幻想。
46. Why does the woman say, "my fantasy for the chocolate is gone"? (A) to emphasize the importance of retaining fantasy. (B) to highlight that it's not a good time to fantasize at work. (C) **to make a point that she doesn't find it appealing.** (D) to devalue the quality of the company's chocolate.	46. 為什麼女子提到「my fantasy for the chocolate is gone」？ (A) 強調保有幻想的重要性。 (B) 強調在工作時幻想不是個好時機。 (C) **強調巧克力對於她已經沒有吸引力了。** (D) 貶低公司巧克力的品質。
答案：44. D 45. C 46. C	

模擬試題（一）

模擬試題（二）

模擬試題（三）

模擬試題（四）

模擬試題（五）

- **第44題**，dig in就是have a big bite就是選項中的eat something voraciously，故答案要選**選項D**。
- **第45題**，經理要求聽者品嚐各種口味的巧克力，所以答案很明顯是**選項C**。
- **第46題**，女子會講到這句話的原因是，她對巧克力已無幻想，也是因為這份工作品嚐太多巧克力的緣故，而講這句話只是個凸顯點，表示她不再覺得巧克力具吸引力了，故答案要選**選項C**。

聽力原文和對話

Questions 47-49 refer to the following conversation

Manager: ...I've seen the questionnaires you guys filled...it's ok...I won't judge...I want the honest opinion...to see if there's room for improvement...and I'm giving the feedback to the lab...are there any questions?

Employee: ...if there is none...he is gonna be so furious...(lower the voice)

Employee: ...sorry...I have one...

Manager: ...shoot...why wait...? I'm dying to know...

Employee: ...I do love the decorations for type A...and I was thinking something bolder...can it be made into a cartoon character or tailor-made and go with the modern sayings...some phrases that teenagers usually use...

Manager: ...excellent...I think you've made a point...and I wanna you to go the lab with me and explain the concept to those lab researchers...and it's best if I don't get involved...otherwise...it's like an order...made by the boss...

問題47-49，請參考以下對話內容

經理：...我已經看過你們填的問卷了...這是OK的...我不會評論...我想要最真實的意見...去看是否還有進步的空間呢...而且我會將回饋的建議交給實驗室...還有什麼問題嗎？

員工：...如果沒有問題的話...他又要很憤怒了...（降低聲音）

員工 ：...抱歉...我有一個問題...。

經理：...快說...為何等待...？我超想知道...。

員工 ：...我喜愛A類型的裝飾品...而且我曾思考著一些更大膽的想法...能夠製作成卡通的角色或是量身訂作以及搭配現代化俗諺的...有些諺語青少年常使用的...。

經理：...很出色...我認為你已經講到重點了...而我想要你跟我一起到實驗室去將這些概念解釋給實驗室的研究人員...而且最好的就是我沒有牽涉其中...否則...這會像是由老闆所發出的命令...。

試題中譯與解析

47. What does "tailor-made" mean? (A) creative. (B) **specifically-designed.** (C) meticulously-researched. (D) thought-provoking.	47.「tailor-made」指的是什麼？ (A) 創意的。 (B) **特別設計的。** (C) 小心翼翼研究的。 (D) 激發人思考的。
48. What does the woman suggest? (A) say what really pleases the manager. (B) have the plan supported by lab researchers. (C) **have a trendy design appealing to younger generations.** (D) do something gallant and low-cost.	48. 女子建議什麼？ (A) 說些真的讓經理感到滿意的話。 (B) 由實驗室研究人員支持的計畫。 (C) **有著吸引年輕世代的新潮設計。** (D) 做些大膽且低成本的事情。
49. Why does the man say, "it's best if I don't get involved"? (A) because he is irresponsible. (B) because he does not want to get involved. (C) because the schedule is too tight. (D) **because he wants employees to have the autonomy.**	49. 為什麼男子提到「it's best if I don't get involved」？ (A) 因為他不負責任。 (B) 因為他不想要牽涉其中。 (C) 因為時程太緊了。 (D) **因為他想要員工有其自主性。**

答案：47. B 48. C 49. D

模擬試題（一）

模擬試題（二）

模擬試題（三）

模擬試題（四）

模擬試題（五）

聽力原文和對話

Questions 50-52 refer to the following conversation

Manager: ...the chocolate that is adapted into the animal shape sold really well...I've got to say that Mary is a rising star...so I'm giving her a promotion....the head of the department... congratulations...

Employee: ...thanks...I'm honored...and I wanna say thanks to all colleagues in the department...

Manager: ...I'm gonna get the cake...you have to excuse me for a few seconds..

Employee: ...I can't believe...it's so serendipitous...

Employee: ...that means more responsibility shouldering on you...

Employee: ...I guess...that means I have to be an early bird in the morning... I can't leave early and the frequent visit to the lab...

Employee: ...don't worry about it...you are gonna do the job just fine....

Manager: ...the cake is ready...let's cut the cake..... congratulations...

Employee: ...thanks...

問題50-52，請參考以下對話內容

經理：…這巧克力改製成動物的形狀銷售的相當好…我必須要說的是瑪莉是顆看漲的星星…所以我要給她升遷…這個部門的首腦…恭喜…。

員工：…謝謝…我感到榮幸…而且我想要對所有部門的同事說謝謝…。

經理：…我去拿蛋糕…你們必須要見諒下，我要離開幾秒鐘…。

員工：…我不敢相信…這太奇緣了…。

員工：…這意謂著更多的責任加在你身上…。

員工：…我想…這意謂著，每天早晨我都要早到公司，我不會早走而且要更頻繁的往實驗室走…。

員工：…別擔心…做這份工作你沒問題的…。

經理：…蛋糕準備好了…我們來切蛋糕…恭喜…。

員工：…謝謝…。

試題中譯與解析

50. Why does the woman say, "it's so serendipitous"? (A) because it's a deliberate pursuit. (B) **because it's by chance.** (C) because it comes from her hard work. (D) because she demands the promotion.	50. 為什麼女子提到「it's so serendipitous」？ (A) 因為這是刻意追求的。 (B) **因為這是偶然發生的。** (C) 因為這是出自於她辛苦的努力。 (D) 因為她要求升遷。
51. Why does the man say, "that means more responsibility shouldering on you"? (A) because she only has to do her current job well. (B) because she can now be a shoulder to cry on. (C) **because she will be given more tasks and share more responsibilities.** (D) because she has to own her mistakes.	51. 為什麼男子提到「that means more responsibility shouldering on you」？ (A) 因為她僅需要把她現在的工作做好即可。 (B) 因為她現在是位可以傾訴的對象。 (C) **因為她將被賦予更多的任務和分擔更多的責任。** (D) 因為她必須要承擔自己的過錯。

52. Which of the following is not what will be like after the promotion? (A) late night in the office. (B) more contact with lab workers. (C) being beforehand in the morning. (D) **make chocolates of animal shape individually.**	52. 下列哪一項不是升遷後會有的情況？ (A) 在辦公室待到很晚。 (B) 與更多實驗室工人的聯繫。 (C) 在早上都早到辦公室。 (D) **獨立製作動物形狀的巧克力。**

答案：50. B 51. C 52. D

解析

- 第50題，其實女子會講這句話的原因是，真的太突然或太偶然了，像是從天而降般的幸運，故答案要選**選項B**。
- 第51題，經理說這句話的主因是，因為女子升遷了，也代表工作責任的加重等等，所以才講這句話，故答案為**選項C**。
- 第52題，聽力段落中有提到幾個升遷後的影響和變動，用刪去法後可以得到答案為**選項D**，而且並沒有提到女子必須要獨力完成這部分。

聽力原文和對話

Questions 53-55 refer to the following conversation

Employee: ...I'm feeling a bit confused...about the promotion

Manager: ...confused about what...tomorrow I'll have the HR personnel to give you a new card and a new ID badge...and you'll have your own office room

Employee: ...this just happens so fast...

Manager: ...it's a rare opportunity...just embrace it...

Employee: ...tell me what the upside is...other than the office room...

Manager: ...there's going to be a 40% bump in your salary...I can't say that in public...

Employee: ...seriously...?...wow...then I will take it...I'm thrilled...

Manager: ...and you will have your own parking space...

Employee: ...terrific...now I'm feeling it....I eat my own way up to the position I'm in...I need more wine

Manager: ...you surely are...

問題53-55，請參考以下對話內容

員工 ：...關於升遷的事情......我正感到困惑

經理：...困惑什麼呢...明天我會要人事專員給你新的卡片和新的ID識別證...而且你會有你自己的辦公室。

員工 ：...只是這一切發生的太快了...。

經理：...這是罕見的機會...就接受它吧...。

員工 ：...告訴我優點是什麼...除了辦公室房間...。

經理：...你的薪資會有40%的調漲...我無法在大庭廣眾下説...。

員工 ：...真的嗎...？...哇！...那麼我會接受它...我感到興奮...。

經理：...而且你會有你自己的停車空位...。

員工 ：...太棒了...現在我感受到了...我靠吃爬升到我現在的位置上...我需要更多的酒...。

經理：...你確實需要...。

試題中譯與解析	
53. What does "the upside" in "what the upside is" mean? (A) **the advantage.** (B) the disadvantage. (C) the interest. (D) the secret.	53. 在「what the upside is」中的「the upside」指的是什麼？ (A) **優點**。 (B) 缺點。 (C) 興趣。 (D) 秘密。
54. Which of the following is not the benefit of the promotion? (A) the increase in salary. (B) individual parking space. (C) private space in the office. (D) **an assistant.**	54. 下列哪一項不是升遷後的益處？ (A) 薪資的增加。 (B) 個人的停車位。 (C) 私人的辦公室空間。 (D) **助理**。
55. If the employee's previous salary is US 50,000 dollars, what payment will she get after the promotion? (A) US 50,000. (B) US 60,000. (C) **US 70,000.** (D) US 80,000.	55. 如果員工先前的薪資是5萬美元，她在升遷後的薪資會是多少呢？ (A) 50,000 美元。 (B) 60,000 美元。 (C) **70,000 美元**。 (D) 80,000 美元。

答案：53. A 54. D 55. C

解析

- **第53題**，upside指的就是advantage故答案為**選項A**。
- **第54題**，聽力段落中並未提到升遷後會安排助理給她，所以答案為**選項D**。
- **第55題**，這題的話要對應到there's going to be a 40% bump in your salary，故要將月薪五萬元**乘以140%**，故答案為月薪七萬元，會是她升遷後的薪資，所以答案為**選項C**。

聽力原文和對話

Questions 56-58 refer to the following conversation

Cindy: ...can't believe someone is calling me...wait me a second..

Cindy: ...yes...this is she...hmm...what? You would love to take a look of this house...that's fantastic...

Buyer: ...yep the sooner the better...I've been to The King's Lake several times...this would the ideal house for us...just tell us the day...any time

Cindy: ...but...there are also other buyers who are eyeing on the house...

Buyer: ...what?...can we see the house tomorrow?

Cindy: ...tomorrow I'm swamped with work...and the next few days I have agreed to several potential buyers...who have shown a keen interest in the house...

Buyer: ...can you do Friday...?

Cindy: ...Friday...I'm wide open....but the road 555 will be having a construction...

Cindy: ...I guess the quickest date...would be next Monday...if that's ok

Buyer: ...ok...see you on Monday...preferably before noon

Cindy: ...sure...see you then...

問題56-58，請參考以下對話內容

辛蒂：...不敢相信有人來電給我...等我一下...。

辛蒂：...是的...這就是她...恩恩。...什麼？你想要來看下房子...那太棒了...。

買家：...是的越快越好...我曾經去過國王湖幾次...這會是我們理想中的房子了...就跟我們説觀看的日期...任何時候。

辛蒂：...但是...也還有其他買家也看中這間房子...。

買家：可以明天看房嗎？

辛蒂：...明天我的工作排山倒海而來...而且接下來的幾天，我已經同意幾個潛在的買家...他們對房子已經表現出很敏銳的興趣在...。

買家：你星期五可以嗎...？

辛蒂：...星期五，我相當有空...但是道路555正在修建中...。

辛蒂：...我想最快的日期...可能是下週一...如果這是可以的話。

買家：...ok...星期一見囉...偏好中午之前。

辛蒂：...當然...到時見囉...。

試題中譯與解析

56. What does "eyeing on the house" mean? (A) have to take a thorough look at the house. (B) can't wait to see the house. (C) have a less keen interest in the house. (D) **have a strong interest in the house.**	56. 「eyeing on the house」指的是什麼呢？ (A) 必須仔細盤看房子。 (B) 等不及要看房子了。 (C) 對於房子沒那麼有興致。 (D) **對房子有極濃厚的興趣。**
57. What is the purpose of saying "tomorrow I'm swamped with work"? (A) to show her work is more important than the house. (B) to let the buyer know potential buyers will be the first to see the house. (C) to emphasize she is a conscientious worker . (D) **to make the buyer more eager to take a look at the house.**	57. 提到「tomorrow I'm swamped with work」的目的是什麼呢？ (A) 顯示她的工作比起房子更為重要。 (B) 讓買家知道潛在買家們將會首先觀看房子。 (C) 強調她是個認真的工作者。 (D) **讓買家更急迫的想要看房。**

| 58. When will the buyer visit the house?
(A) Friday.
(B) **next Monday.**
(C) Wednesday before noon.
(D) Thursday before noon. | 58. 買家會於何時看房？
(A) 星期五。
(B) **下週一。**
(C) 週三中午前。
(D) 週四中午前。 |

答案：56. D 57. D 58. B

解析

- 第56題，eyeing on the house代表是看中了，所以也就是選項中的have a strong interest故答案要選**選項D**。
- 第57題，説這句話的目的是，其實明明有時間，但是卻裝忙或表明很多人要來看房，提高房子價值或讓對方更想要觀看或得到這間房子，所以最可能的選項是**選項D**。
- 第58題，這題的話聽力段落有提到最後喬定的看房日期是下週一，且偏好是中午前，所以答案要選**選項B**，另外也要別被noon干擾到而選錯了。

聽力原文和對話

Questions 59-61 refer to the following conversation

Mark: ...I've got to say that you are pretty good at the realtor things?

Cindy: ...thanks...I think they will be here in any minutes...

Buyer: ...hi...this place looks terrific...how much does this place cost...?

Cindy: ...let's not jump right to that...this is the owner of the house...and we would like to take you to a short trail...and it heads to the lake...

Buyer: ...wonderful...I thought you are gonna show me the house first..

Cindy: ...this way...besides those domestic fowls...there are some squirrels on the trees

Buyer: ...quite soothing...these swans look beautiful...don't tell me that there are raccoons...they are too playful...

Cindy: ...no raccoons...but there will be some amphibians crawling on the floor..

Buyer: ...the air is quite fresh...and finally...the lake...gorgeous and sanitary...how does this place remain to be a fairy tale-like place...

Cindy: ...some magic perhaps...ha

問題59-61，請參考以下對話內容

馬克：...我必須要說的是，你真的相當擅長地產銷售的事情？

辛蒂：...謝謝...我想他們幾分鐘之內就到了...。

買家：...嗨...這個地方看起來很棒...這個地方要花費多少錢呢...？

辛蒂：...我們先別跳到那部分...這位是房屋的主人...而我們想要帶你先走下短的小徑...而且小徑是朝向湖泊...。

買家：...太棒了...我以為你們會先帶我去看房子...。

辛蒂：...這邊...除此那些家禽類生物之外...還有一些松鼠在樹上。

買家：...相當撫慰人心...這些天鵝看起來很美麗...別告訴我這裡有浣熊...他們太頑皮了...。

辛蒂：沒有浣熊...但是這裡有一些兩棲生物爬行在地面上...。

買家：這裡的空氣相當清新...而且最終...這湖泊...美麗且衛生...這樣的地方怎麼能夠維持的像是仙境一般...。

辛蒂：...可能是一些魔法吧...哈哈。

試題中譯與解析

59. What is the purpose of saying "let's not jump right to that"?
(A) because cat got her tongue.
(B) because the owner didn't tell her that part.
(C) to emphasize she is a shrew negotiator.
(D) **to procrastinate the house price part and also have some time to show other parts that are fantastic.**

59. 提到「let's not jump right to that」的目的是什麼？
(A) 因為她說不出話了。
(B) 因為屋主不想告訴她那部分的事情。
(C) 強調她是精銳的協商者。
(D) **拖延房價的部分並且有時間去顯示其他部分是很棒的。**

60. Which of the following is what the buyer finds pleasing to look at? (A) **domestic fowls.** (B) squirrels. (C) amphibians. (D) snakes.	60. 下列哪一項是買家覺得賞心悦目的？ (A) **家禽**。 (B) 松鼠。 (C) 兩棲類動物。 (D) 蛇。
61. Which of the following is what the buyer dreads? (A) **raccoons.** (B) monkeys. (C) frogs. (D) domestic fowls.	61. 下列哪一項不是買家所懼怕的？ (A) **浣熊**。 (B) 猴子。 (C) 青蛙。 (D) 家禽。

答案：59. D 60. A 61. A

解析

- 第59題，這句話也是，要對方先別談某個部分，其實有點在拖延或是想要讓對方看看周遭環境或其他對房子有利的所有因素後，最後才來談，有點像談薪水，都理解工作內容等等的在談會比較有利，所以這題要選**選項D**。

- 第60題，the buyer finds pleasing to look at可以對應到quite soothing...these swans look beautiful，故答案為**選項A**，swans = **domestic fowls**。

- 第61題，what the buyer dreads可以對應到don't tell me that there are raccoons...they are too playful，所以答案為**選項A**。

聽力原文和對話

Questions 62-64 refer to the following conversation

Mark: ...my heart sank...apparently our neighbor told the buyer about a person who committed suicide in the house...

Cindy: ...don't worry about it...

Buyer: ...Actually, I heard about the incident...regarding...

Cindy: ...I guess someone has done her homework...yep it's quite a tragic...but...I have got to tell you when he shot himself...he slipped...and fell outside the roof on the road...he didn't die in the house...

Buyer: ...let's get done to business...the price...of the house...

Cindy: ...It's US 750,000...but we have trimmed a little since there was...indeed an incident...so US 700,000...

Buyer: ...that's an extortion.... US 550,000 is more reasonable...

Cindy: ...the owner bought the house at a price much higher than that...and with a view like that we'd prefer to sell to the cinema company...which came to haggle with the price with us a few days ago...I guess the price should be 75,000 higher than what you said earlier is that ok?

Buyer: ...fine...let's sign the contract...

問題62-64，請參考以下對話內容

馬克：...我的心一沉...顯然我的鄰居告訴買家關於一個人在屋內自殺的事情...。

辛蒂：...別擔心吧...。

買家：實際上，我聽過這個事件...關於...。

辛蒂：我想有些人已經事前有做功課了...是的...這是相當悲劇性的...但是...我必須要跟妳說，當他將槍射向自己時...他滑了一跤...然後跌到屋頂後到道路上了...他並沒有死在屋內...。

買家：...讓我們回到正事吧...房屋的...價格...。

辛蒂：...75萬美元，但是我們已經減了些零頭...既然...確實...曾經有起事件發生...所以價格是70萬美元...。

買家：...這真的是勒索...55萬美元才是較為合理的價格...。

辛蒂：...房屋的主人當初在購買房子時的價格時遠高於這個的...而且以這樣的景色，我們情願銷售給電影公司...公司幾天前來討價還價...我想價格應該要比起原先你所提的價格再高75000美元，這樣可以嗎？

買家：好吧...讓我們簽了這合約吧...。

62. Why does the woman say, "I guess someone has done her homework"? (A) to clarify that it's a tragic. (B) to make a point that the buyer finishes writing an assignment. (C) to deflect the topic that the two are discussing. (D) **to demonstrate that the buyer is prepared and harder to convince.**	62. 為什麼女子提到「I guess someone has done her homework」？ (A) 澄清這是個悲劇。 (B) 強調買家完成撰寫功課。 (C) 轉移他們倆人間所討論的話題。 (D) **顯示買家有備而來而且更難被說服。**
63. Why does the buyer say, "that's an extortion"? (A) he thinks the price is fairly reasonable. (B) he thinks he is being taken advantage of. (C) **he thinks the price is too unreasonable.** (D) he cannot think of the tactics at the moment.	63. 為什麼說話者提到「that's an extortion」？ (A) 他認為價格相當合理。 (B) 他認為他被利用了。 (C) **他認為價格過於不合理。** (D) 在當下，他想不出任何策略。
64. What is the ultimate price for the house? (A) US 550,00. (B) US 750,000. (C) US 700,000. (D) **US 625,000.**	64. 最後房子的成交價是多少呢？ (A) 550,00 美元。 (B) 750,000 美元。 (C) 700,000 美元。 (D) **625,000美元。**

答案：62. D 63. C 64. D

解析

- **第62題**，買方居然得知了房子的某個消息，所以女子回應了這句話，有點輕描淡寫的帶過去，女子是不怕對方得知這個消息會影響到談判籌碼，不過這意謂著比起不知情的情況，買家已經有備而來，是更難說服的，故答案要選**選項D**。

- **第63題**，講這句話有點激動，代表這根本像是勒索，所以很大程度是他認為價格過於高或太過於不合理了，故答案要選**選項C**。

- **第64題**，中間有出現議價的部分，可以綜合下買家講的價格US 550,000 is more reasonable和最後女子提到的I guess the price should be 75,000 higher than what you said earlier is that ok?，故答案為**選項D**，550,000+75,000 = **625000元**。

聽力原文和對話

Questions 65-67 refer to the following conversation

Cindy: Court ruled that the blood sample is contaminated...so it can't be used as evidence...therefore, I am enacting more stringent SOPs and considering adopting higher security system...

Mark: What do you mean? You think someone stole the sample and swapped it...so that it can obstruct the justice...

Cindy: it's possible...and could be an inside job...so from now on entering that door requires at least three senior executives' fingerprints on the computer outside the door...and there are gonna be ten surveillance cameras erected in the room...

Mark: ..you totally treat everyone like a criminal...

Cindy: ...it's the company's reputation...and I'm going to hire private detectives to do background checks to see if employees are related to this...

問題65-67，請參考以下對話內容

辛蒂：法庭判定血液樣本受到汙染...所以這不能用於呈堂的證據...因此，我會制定更嚴格的SOP並且考慮採用較高階的安全防護系統...。

馬克：你指的是什麼呢？你認為有人竊取了樣本，然後掉包了...這樣一來就能干擾司法嗎？

辛蒂：這情形是可能發生的...且可能是有內鬼...所以從現在起進入那扇門需要至少三位資深主管的指紋在外頭的那台電腦上...而且房間內會裝置10台監視器在裡頭...。

馬克：...你整個把每個人都當成像是罪犯了...。

辛蒂：...這關乎到公司的名聲...而且我正要雇用私家偵探來做背景調查，看看是否公司員工跟這起事件有關聯...。

試題中譯與解析

65. Which of the following is not used to enhance security? (A) rigorous SOPs. (B) identity check. (C) surveillance cameras (D) **blood sample**	65. 下列哪一項不會用於提高安全防護？ (A) 嚴格的SOP。 (B) 身分確認。 (C) 監視器。 (D) **血液樣本。**
66. What does the woman mean when she says "could be an inside job"? (A) she really wants to help out by entering inside the door. (B) **she has doubts about how the blood sample getting switched.** (C) she remains doubtful about the investigation. (D) she treats everyone like a suspect.	66. 女性說話者提到「could be an inside job」是什麼意思？ (A) 她真的想要藉由進入內門來幫助整起事件。 (B) **她對於血液樣本被調換的事情感到疑惑。** (C) 她對於整起調查事件抱持存疑的態度。 (D) 她把每個人都當成嫌疑犯。
67. Who could be the female speaker? (A) a judge. (B) a defense attorney. (C) a lab researcher. (D) **the director .**	67. 誰可能會是女性說話者？ (A) 法官。 (B) 辯護律師。 (C) 實驗室的研究人員。 (D) **主管。**

答案：65. D 66. B 67. D

解析

- **第65題**，這題是詢問何者不是用於提升安全防護，很明顯答案是血液樣本，故答案要選**選項D**。
- **第66題**，其實僅是猜測因為血液樣本被換很可能是有內鬼，故答案最可能是**選項B**。
- **第67題**，這題的話別受到法院等的混淆，女子最有可能是研究中心的高階人員或老闆等，才有可能講出這些話和提升安全防護的手續，故答案要選**選項D**。

聽力原文和對話

Questions 68-70 refer to the following conversation

Linda: I guess I'm having a migraine...Do you still have that aspirin...double dose...?

Cindy: ...let me check....it's not in here...and it's not in my drawer... sorry...I'm running out of that pill...perhaps you should go to the pharmacy...Best pharmacy...

Linda: ...yeah...severe headache could kill me...I'm getting my coat and head to the new opening store...by the way do I need the prescription...?

Cindy: ...you're an adult...and drugs like aspirin don't require any prescription...

Linda: ...that makes things a whole lot easier...

Cindy: I used to take the painkillers...they're made of capsules...so no bitter taste...now aspirins are made of tablets

Linda: ...as long as it's not powder kind of medicine...fine with me...

Cindy: before you go...I do have Chinese herbal ointment...you can put some and rub around your forehead...it helps...

Linda: ...thanks...

問題68-70，請參考以下對話內容

琳達：我想我有些偏頭痛...你還有那個阿斯匹靈...雙倍劑量的...？

辛蒂：讓我看下...不在這兒...也不在我的抽屜裡...抱歉...我的藥用完了...或許你該去藥局一趟了...倍斯特藥局...。

琳達：...是的...嚴重的頭痛可能會要我的命..我去拿件外套，然後朝新開的店走去...順便一提的是我會需要處方嗎？

辛蒂：...你是成年人了...而且像是阿斯匹靈這樣的藥品不需要任何處方...。

琳達：...那樣的話，那麼事情就變得簡單多了。

辛蒂：...過去我曾使用止痛劑...由膠囊所組成的...所以沒有苦的味道...現在阿斯匹靈是由藥錠所組成的。

琳達：...只要不是粉末狀那樣的藥物...我都可以接受的...。

辛蒂：在你去之前...我確實有中國的草藥藥膏...你可以敷一些並且在你前額周圍擦拭...這有幫助...。

琳達：...謝謝...。

試題中譯與解析	
68. Why does the speaker say, "that makes things a whole lot easier"? (A) because there is a new opening drug store in town. (B) **because it doesn't need the prescription.** (C) because the traffic is not heavy. (D) because the store has the best painkillers.	68. 為什麼說話者說，「這就讓整件事情容易辦的多了」？ (A) 因為小鎮新開了一間藥局。 (B) **因為就不需要藥品處方了。** (C) 因為交通沒那麼壅擠。 (D) 因為店裡有最佳的止痛劑。
69. Which of the following kinds of medicine is what the speaker used to take? (A) Chinese herbal ointment. (B) tablets of aspirins. (C) **capsule-made painkillers.** (D) powder-made medicine.	69. 下列哪個種類的藥品是過去說話者所服用的？ (A) 中國的草藥藥膏。 (B) 阿斯匹靈藥錠。 (C) **膠囊所製成的止痛劑。** (D) 粉末製成的藥品。
70. Which of the following will be applied to before the speaker heads to the drug store? (A) **ointment.** (B) medicine powder. (C) tablets. (D) the painkiller.	70. 下列哪一項可於前往藥局前先行敷用？ (A) **藥膏。** (B) 醫療粉末。 (C) 藥錠。 (D) 止痛劑。

答案：68. B 69. C 70. A

- **第68題**，因為不用處方的話就代表事情更簡單了，僅要去藥局講述要購買的藥物名稱即可，所以答案要選**選項B**。
- **第69題**，這題可以定位到I used to take the painkillers...they're made of capsules，所以答案要選**選項C**。
- **第70題**，這題的話很明顯要選藥膏的部分，在前往藥局前友人有提議要他敷上中國草藥藥膏，故答案要選**選項A**。

模擬試題（一）

模擬試題（二）

模擬試題（三）

模擬試題（四）

模擬試題（五）

 **Part 4**

Questions 71-73 refer to the following video

We're here at the local Chinese night market...aspiring to introduce you an ostrich egg...it's really special...but normally people visit here for the goat...the roasted goat in a huge urn...the chef dissects it into different parts...really tasty...or you get to see a different...a huge underground cooking method...it's specially designed...and the guy prepares five or six goats...which are cleaned and marinated the sauce...and put them beneath the ground...and fire it...then use a large blanket to cover on top...the steam is kept inside...while explaining to you guys...my ostrich egg is ready...it's 350 RMB...but quite worth it...you gotta try sometimes...really sugary...but not sour

問題71-73請參閱下列視頻

我們現在在當地的中國夜市裡頭...熱切地向您介紹鴕鳥蛋...這真的相當的特別...但是,通常人們來這參訪都是為了山羊而來...在大型甕裡烤山羊...廚師將其解剖成不同的部分...真的可口...或是你可以看到不同的...一個大型的地底下的烹飪方式...這是特別設計的...而男子準備著五或六隻山羊...是洗淨且浸泡過醬汁的...然後將牠們放置到地底下...然後用火燒...然後使用一條大型的毯子覆蓋在其上頭...蒸氣會保留在裡頭...而向你們解釋時...我的鴕鳥蛋好了...這顆蛋花費350元人民幣...但是相當划算...你有時候真的該嚐...真的甜甜的..., 而不是酸的。

71. Which of the following is closet in meaning to "dissect"? (A) **scrutinize.** (B) deliver. (C) classify. (D) describe.	71. 下列哪一個字近似於「解剖」? (A) **仔細審視**。 (B) 遞送。 (C) 分類。 (D) 描述。

72. Which of the following is used to preserve the steam inside? (A) the sauce. (B) **a rug.** (C) the cooking method. (D) the urn.	72. 下列哪一項被用於保存內部的蒸汽？ (A) 醬汁。 (B) **地毯。** (C) 烹飪方式。 (D) 甕。
73. What is the flavor of the ostrich egg? (A) bitter. (B) sour. (C) **sweet.** (D) salty.	73. 鴕鳥蛋的風味是？ (A) 苦的。 (B) 酸的。 (C) **甜的。** (D) 鹹的。

答案：71. A 72. B 73. C

解析

- **第71題**，這題其實就是選同義字，故要選scrutinize，答案為**選項A**。
- **第72題**，這題可以定位到then use a large blanket to cover on top...the steam is kept inside，而blanket就是選項中的rug，故答案為**選項B**。
- **第73題**，這題可以定位到my ostrich egg is ready...it's 500 RMB...but quite worth it...you gotta try sometimes...really sugary...but not sour，sugary就是sweet，故答案要選**選項C**。

聽力原文和對話

Questions 74-76 refer to the following news report

This is news anchor Jason James...good morning...for car drivers...it's advisable that you take Road 555 instead of Road 556...because the tunnel is blocked for other purposes...and it's the rainy season... mudslides could happen a lot lately...for the mountain climbers...we suggest you to stay indoors...the hiking trails might be too slippery... and it's now summer the season when snakes are roaming...and they like wet weather...the green forests are their protection...you might get bitten before you realize it...on top of that...some venoms are running out of blood serums...so...just be careful though...coming up...we are gonna see the news of the Black Friday....

問題74-76請參閱下列新聞報導

這是新聞主播傑森·詹姆士…早安…對於汽車駕駛者…建議你們要行駛道路555而非道路556…隧道因為其他用途而封閉了…而且這是雨季…山崩在近期常常發生…對於登山客們…我們建議你待在室內裡…健行步道可能滑溜…而且現在是夏天…這個季節是蛇漫遊的時候…而且牠們喜歡潮溼的天氣…綠色森林是牠們的保護色…在你意識到之前，你可能被咬到了…除此之外…有些毒液是沒有血清的…所以…真的要非常小心囉…接下來是…我們要看下關於黑色星期五的新聞…。

試題中譯與解析	
74. Who is not the target audience? (A) truck drivers. (B) hikers. (C) taxi drivers. (D) **animal lovers.**	74. 誰不是目標觀眾？ (A) 卡車司機。 (B) 健行者。 (C) 計程車司機。 (D) **動物愛好者。**
75. Why does the speaker say, "running out of blood serums"? (A) **to warn the danger of getting bitten in the forest.** (B) to highlight the importance of the venoms. (C) to call for the donation of the serums. (D) to relieve the stress of the mountain climbers.	75. 為什麼說話者說「血清用光了」？ (A) **警告在森林中被咬到的危險。** (B) 強調毒液的重要性。 (C) 呼籲捐贈血清。 (D) 緩和登山客們的壓力。

76. What could be featured in the upcoming news? (A) the tunnel is fixed by construction workers. (B) the firefighters are sending supplies to the mountain. (C) villagers miraculously discover a new blood serum. (D) **people parading outside the department store.**	76.什麼可能是接下來新聞的特別報導？ (A) 隧道由建築工人修復了。 (B) 消防隊員正運送補給品到山上。 (C) 村民們奇蹟似地發現了新的血清。 (D) **人們在百貨公司外頭大排長龍。**

答案：74. D 75. A 76. D

 解析

- **第74題**，這題的話雖然聽眾有可能是各行各業的人，不過在新聞報導中還是有針對幾類型的對象來談論的，其中不包含動物愛好者，雖然當中有提到蛇，不過是提醒健行登山客，故答案要選**選項D**。
- **第75題**，説話者講這句話的原因主要是用於警告危險，因為缺乏血清的情況下被咬到的話就慘了，故答案為**選項A**。
- **第76題**，這題的話是考推測的部分，不過最後主播有講到we are gonna see the news of the Black Friday....，所以接下來一定是跟黑色購物節相關的內容，答案要選**選項D**。

聽力原文和對話

Questions 77-79 refer to the following talk

Best Restaurant

· 10 large **Boston Lobsters** for free
· A bottle of **Red Wine**

Expire   **Date:** 2025/01/25

I'm your guide today...I'm Jason by the way...you all know the theory of meteorites that made the dinosaurs disappear...and there were lots of reasons behind it...after the whole slide show in the morning and a few lectures in the hall...you guys might feel so bored...I'm gonna show you the skeletons of different dinosaurs...I'm separating them into two categories...herbivores and carnivores....and we're going to play the game...jigsaw puzzles...four people in a team...the finished puzzles will be electrified ...and glow when the sun sets....and the winning team will get ten sets of chocolates with different dinosaur shapes...5 coupons and you might want to start right away...and for those who are doing the meat-eating dinosaurs you will get an extra 30 minutes...and I'm done explaining that Tyrannosaurus rex is a carnivore.

問題71-73請參閱下列談話

倍斯特餐館

· 10隻免費的大型**波士頓龍蝦**
· 一罐**紅酒**

截止日期：2025年1月25日

今天我是你們的嚮導...順帶一提的是...我是傑森...你們都知道隕石理論讓恐龍消失了...而這背後其實有許多原因...在早晨整個簡報圖介紹後和廳堂中幾場演講後...你們可能覺得無趣了...我要向你們展示不同的恐龍骨骼...我要把你們分成兩個範疇...草食性動物和肉食性動物...而我們要玩個遊戲...拼圖遊戲...四個人為一組......當太陽下山時，完成的拼圖會蓄電...而且會發光...。而贏的隊伍會獲得不同的恐龍圖樣的巧克力10組...優惠卷...而你們可能想要馬上開始了...對於那些選擇食肉恐龍者，你們將有額外30分鐘的時間...，而且我不想要再解釋雷克斯暴龍是肉食性動物。

試題中譯與解析

77. Where most likely is the talk taking place? (A) at the travel agency. (B) at the restaurant. (C) **at the museum.** (D) at the theater.	77. 此段談話最有可能發生在什麼地方？ (A) 在旅行社。 (B) 在餐廳。 (C) **在博物館。** (D) 在戲院。
78. What is not mentioned in the talk? (A) visitors might find the lectures not interesting. (B) souvenir-like chocolates are used as the winning prize. (C) the difficulty of the carnivore dinosaurs is greater than that of the herbivore dinosaurs. (D) **jigsaw puzzles are only for kids.**	78. 談話中沒有提及哪部分呢？ (A) 參加者可能會覺得講座沒那麼有趣。 (B) 紀念品般的巧克力會當成勝利者的獎品。 (C) 肉食性恐龍的困難度比起草食性恐龍的困難度還高。 (D) **拼圖遊戲是僅有小孩可以參與的活動。**
79. Look at the graph. Where can the coupon be used? (A) **at the cafeteria.** (B) at the museum. (C) at the recreational theme park. (D) at the chocolate plant.	79. 請參照圖表。優惠卷可以在哪裡使用？ (A) **在自助餐廳。** (B) 在博物館。 (C) 在娛樂的主題樂園。 (D) 在巧克力工廠。

答案：77. C 78. D 79. A

解析

- **第77題**，這題的話要注意是詢問最可能發生的地點，地點是在博物館喔，別被優惠卷上的餐廳影響到而誤選了，故答案要選**選項C**。
- **第78題**，這題是詢問何者為非，文中並未提到僅有小孩能參加喔，故答案要選**選項D**。
- **第79題**，這題可以看到是倍斯特餐廳的優惠卷，所以可以對應到選項A的 cafeteria，故答案要選**選項A**。

Questions 80-82 refer to the following talk

Now we are on the gorgeous beach...and all participants will be receiving a bottle of orange juice...so that you won't dehydrate...and the treasure hunt begins...right now...it's like the Thanksgiving ...finding an Easter egg in the maze when you are at some of the famous museums or a jewelry box in the jungle...there are 20 different colors of pebbles...they can be anywhere...hidden under the rock or else...it's naturally formed...and quite valuable...the show's giving the winning team a hundred thousand dollars as a reward...I'm totally getting jealous for not being able to join you...and you might find some unwanted companies...such as crabs...but don't worry they are not your competition....focus...that's the key to winning...

問題80-82請參閱下列談話

現在我們在美麗的海灘上...而所有的參賽者會拿到一瓶柳橙汁...這樣一來就不會脫水了，而寶藏狩獵開始了...就是現在...這像是感恩節...當你在一些有名的博物館時，在迷宮中找尋復活蛋或在叢林中找珠寶盒......有20種不同顏色的小卵石...它們可能在任何地方...藏匿在岩石底下或是其他地方...這是天然形成的...相當有價值...這個節目會給予贏的隊伍1萬元的獎金當作獎賞...我都因為無法加入你們而開始感到忌妒了...而你可能會發覺一些不速之客...像是螃蟹...但是別擔心，他們不是你的競爭對手...專注...這是贏的關鍵...。

試題中譯與解析	
80. What will be provided to the listeners? (A) **beverages.** (B) dehydration. (C) treasure. (D) orange.	80. 將會提供給聽者什麼？ (A) **飲料。** (B) 脫水。 (C) 寶藏。 (D) 橙。
81. Which of the following is what participants are asked to find? (A) colors. (B) **pebbles.** (C) a jewelry box. (D) an Easter egg.	81. 下列哪一項是參加者被要求要找到的？ (A) 顏色。 (B) **小卵石。** (C) 珠寶盒。 (D) 復活節的蛋。

82. Why does the speaker mention, you might find some unwanted companies? (A) **to remind participants of an interference on the beach.** (B) to educate participants the function of crabs in the ecosystem. (C) to warn participants about impending dangers. (D) to increase the difficulty of the treasure hunt.	82.為什麼說話者提到，你可能會發覺到不速之客？ (A) **提醒參加者海灘上的干擾物。** (B) 教育參加者生態系統中螃蟹的功能。 (C) 警告參加者迫近的危險。 (D) 增加寶藏狩獵的困難度。

答案：80. A 81. B 82. A

- **第80題**，在一開始有提到orange juice故可以對應到選項A的beverages，故答案要選**選項A**。
- **第81題**，這題要小心誤選，參加者是要找尋pebbles，故答案要選**選項B**。
- **第82題**，說話者提到這部份是要提醒在海灘上尋找時，可能會有些生物或什麼的影響或干預到收尋，像是在pebbles旁的螃蟹之類的，故答案要選**選項A**。

聽力原文和對話

Questions 83-85 refer to the following news report

Also the news about the Circus...after the pleading by lots of college students...the Circus has decided to relinquish the torture for those animals...yet the question remains and the sugar-coating way of saying what we would like to hear doesn't seem to convince the environmental biologists...the government should really step in...and laws should be strictly enforced so that wild animals can free from the harm of humans...there are still many animals out there which suffer from the cruel treatment...camels, elephants for the recreational purposes...or horses used to fill the romantic fantasy of certain people...but they do not want to drag the carriage for a long day without getting any rest...

問題83-85請參閱下列新聞報導

也是關於馬戲團的新聞...在許多大學學生的懇求後...馬戲團已經決定要放棄刑求那些動物...然而問題仍舊存在著而包裹著糖衣的述說著我們想要聽到的方式，似乎無法令環境生物學家們信服...政府應該要涉入其中...而法令應該要嚴格執行，如此一來野生動物就能免於人類的傷害了...仍有許多動物遭受殘酷的對待...駱駝、大象用於娛樂用途...或是馬匹用於填補特定人的浪漫幻想...但是牠們不想要一整天中長時間拖曳車子...卻無法有任何的休息時間...。

試題中譯與解析

83. What is the purpose of the news report? (A) to raise funds for animals. (B) to demand more animal interactions in the Circus. (C) to protest the increasing high entrance fees. (D) **to enhance the awareness for animal mistreatment.**	83. 此段新聞報導的目的是什麼？ (A) 替動物募款。 (B) 要求在馬戲團裡有更多與動物間的互動。 (C) 抗議日益增加的高昂入場費。 (D) **提高動物虐待的保護意識。**
84. According to the news report, who are not persuaded by the statement? (A) college students. (B) **biologists.** (C) trainers. (D) the government.	84. 根據新聞報導，誰不會被新聞陳述說服？ (A) 大學學生。 (B) **生物學家們。** (C) 訓練師們。 (D) 政府。
85. Which of the following does not suffer inhumane treatment? (A) camels. (B) elephants. (C) horses. (D) **tigers.**	85. 下列哪種動物不用遭受人類的不人道對待呢？ (A) 駱駝。 (B) 大象。 (C) 馬。 (D) **老虎。**
答案：83. D 84. B 85. D	

解析

- **第83題**，這題是詢問談話的目的，而最主要的原因是要提升動物虐待的保護意識，故答案為**選項D**。
- **第84題**，這題是詢問未被説服的人員，答案是生物學家，故要**選項B**。
- **第85題**，這題的話可以利用刪去法，僅有老虎是在談話中沒有提到的動物，故答案為**選項D**。

聽力原文和對話

Questions 86-88 refer to the following talk

I'm the linguist who majored in biology back in the university...I'm so pleased to be invited to the party here...and I heard that all participants have to share the book they have read during the past few months...sort of like a casual...book review thing...and I will go first...so if the comment is not enticing...everyone is more tolerant...I'm going to comment on a thriller...a bestseller...a book without any marketing effort or anything that involves authors buying tons of books and then put those in the storehouse...that kind of thing...it's really fluent...but I do notice something...that's the arduous effort made by many prestigious editors...the use of the language is refined I guess but...it's not that scary...it's just bizarre...

問題86-88請參閱下列談話

我是位語言學家，在就讀大學期間主修生物學…很高興能夠受邀至派對這裡…而且我聽説所有的參加者都要分享過去幾個月期間他們所讀過的書…有點像是隨意的…書評事情一樣…而我要先發言…所以如果評語不是那麼吸引人的話…每個人都會比較能容忍…我要評論一個驚悚書籍…一本暢銷書…一本沒有任何行銷手法或任何牽涉到作者自己購買許多書，然後把那些放置到倉庫…那樣的行徑…它相當的流暢…但是我卻注意到一些事情…就是這是由許多享譽盛名的編輯努力潤飾而成的…我想它語言使用上是優美的但是…它不是那麼恐怖…這真的奇異透頂了…。

86. Why does the linguist plan to talk first? (A) he wants to entice listeners. (B) he wants to astound people. (C) he wants to make a good impression. (D) **he understands perfectly about human nature.**	86. 為什麼語言學家意欲先説呢？ (A) 他想吸引聽者的注意力。 (B) 他想震驚聽眾。 (C) 他想有好印象。 (D) **他相當了解人性。**
87. What can be inferred about the bestseller? (A) the author stashes numerous books in the storehouse. (B) the company does not hire sales reps. (C) it's not a thriller. (D) **the use of the language is elegant.**	87. 談話中可以推測出關於暢銷書的什麼？ (A) 作者在倉庫中儲藏的為數眾多的書籍。 (B) 公司不需要雇用銷售業務。 (C) 它不是驚悚的。 (D) **語言的使用是優雅的。**
88. According to the linguist, who deserves the most contribution of the book? (A) the author. (B) the publisher. (C) **the editors.** (D) the experts.	88. 根據語言學家，誰對書籍的貢獻最多呢？ (A) 作者。 (B) 出版商。 (C) **編輯們。** (D) 專家們。

答案：86. D 87. D 88. C

解析

- **第86題**，語言學家搶先第一個回答的原因其實就是因為他太了解人性了，而且通常第一個講得不好不會受到太多的批評，所以答案要選**選項D**。
- **第87題**，這題要注意細節點，然後可以對應到the use of the language is refined，所以答案為**選項D**。
- **第88題**，根據語言學家的話答案很明顯是editors，故答案為**選項C**。

聽力原文和對話

Questions 89-91 refer to the following advertisement

Teeth are important to us...we need a smile to charm people...and whitening teeth can give you that kind of confidence...We are known for teeth cleaning and teeth whitening...for the latter, it involves an injection that only costs you half than other Clinics...and there is going to be a blue light after the shot...so the teeth can have such an extensive care...after the treatment...the teeth can maintain a few weeks of freeing from the erosion of the sweet food, the corrasion of sour juices, coffee's coloring...and many other things...you will be having a few weeks without worries and worries breed more wrinkles...eat anything you like...you deserve it...and we do offer an after-treatment service...

問題89-91請參閱下列廣告

牙齒對於我們來説是重要的...我們需要微笑來吸引人們...而牙齒美白能給予你那樣的自信...我們以牙齒清潔和牙齒美白聞名...至於後者的話，它牽涉到了注射，且僅花費您於其他牙醫診所費用的一半...而在注射後會有藍光照射...所以牙齒可以有如此的完整照護...在治療後...牙齒能於接下來的幾週免於甜食的侵蝕、酸性果汁的腐蝕、咖啡所引起的變色...和許多其他的部分...你會於接下來的幾週沒有煩惱，煩惱會滋生更多的皺紋...吃任何你所喜愛的食物...你值得的...而我們確實提供了療程後的服務...。

試題中譯與解析

89. What could be the factor that attracts people the most? (A) **the fee.** (B) the coupon. (C) the extensive care provided by the doctor. (D) the after-treatment service.	89. 哪個因素最吸引消費者呢？ (A) **費用**。 (B) 優惠卷。 (C) 由醫生所提供的完整照護。 (D) 治療後服務。

90. Which of the following is not the promise of the teeth whitening? (A) withstand sour juices. (B) **reduce the consumption of coffee.** (C) resist the corrasion of the chocolate. (D) form the protection on the teeth's exterior.	90. 下列哪一項不是牙齒美白的承諾？ (A) 抵抗酸性果汁。 (B) **減少咖啡的攝取。** (C) 抵抗巧克力的侵蝕。 (D) 形成牙齒外層的保護。
91. What is being advertised? (A) a skin-care hospital. (B) a research center. (C) **a dental clinic.** (D) a fitness center.	91. 廣告的是什麼？ (A) 皮膚照護醫院。 (B) 一間研究中心。 (C) **一間牙醫診所。** (D) 一間健身中心。

答案：89. A 90. B 91. C

解析

- **第89題**，這題的話可以推想吸引人消費的最大誘因是費用，廣告中題到收費僅是其他家的一半，所以答案最可能是**選項A**。
- **第90題**，這題要注意細節點，廣告中也有提到咖啡，但是並未提到reduce the consumption of coffee故答案為**選項B**。
- **第91題**，廣告的項目其實很明顯是牙醫診所，故答案要選**選項C**。

聽力原文和對話

Questions 92-94 refer to the following news report

The wearisome look of the flight attendant contrasts sharply for the previous shining example of a college graduate who got the offer...Planes circling at thousands of feet tall aren't novel...according to the new rookie, the flight attendant...sounds like she is losing the patience...since the plane isn't going to land any time soon under this kind of weather...heavy fog can be troubling sometimes...and the jet fuel can eventually run out if the plane whirls on the skies for too long...in addition...there are other things that flight attendants can't control...lighting, hurricanes, summer storms, gusty wind, and blizzard...all these can make the plane delayed...canceled...or worse...crashed...and this is Mary at the airport...

問題92-94請參閱下列新聞報導

這位空服員的疲憊容貌和稍早前剛接獲錄取通知、光鮮代表的大學畢業生形成了強烈的反差...飛機盤旋在幾千公尺高空並不是什麼新奇的事情了...根據我們新的菜鳥，這位空服員聽起來像是她正失去了耐心一般...既然在這樣的天候情況下，飛機不會即刻就登陸...濃霧可能有時候是很惱人的...而噴射機燃料可能最終會耗盡，如果飛機在天空中盤旋過久的話...此外，...還有其他事情是空服員無法控制的...閃電、颶風、夏季風暴、強烈陣風和暴風雪...所有這些都會讓飛機延誤...取消...或是出現更糟的情況...墜毀...而這是瑪莉在機場的報導...。

試題中譯與解析	
92. Which of the following can be used up during long whirling? (A) **gas.** (B) electricity. (C) cookies. (D) fog.	92. 下列哪一項是飛機在空中長時間盤旋時會耗盡的部分？ (A) **汽油。** (B) 電力。 (C) 餅乾。 (D) 霧。
93. Which of the following is something flight attendants can control? (A) lightning. (B) gusty wind. (C) snowstorm. (D) **the attitude towards passengers.**	93. 下列哪一項是空服員所能掌控的部分？ (A) 閃電。 (B) 強勁的風。 (C) 暴風雪。 (D) **對乘客的態度。**
94. Which of the following is not the repercussion of bad weather? (A) the plane delaying uncontrollably. (B) the plane obliterating unexpectedly. (C) the plane smashing accidentally. (D) **the plane landing successfully.**	94. 下列哪一項不是壞天氣所造成的影響？ (A) 飛機受不可控因素而延遲。 (B) 飛機出其不意地消失。 (C) 飛機意外地墜毀。 (D) **飛機成功地登陸。**

答案：92. A 93. D 94. D

 解析

- **第92題**，這題可以定位到and the jet fuel can eventually run out if the plane whirls on the skies for too long，所以jet fuel等於gas，故答案要選**選項A**。
- **第93題**，空服員不可控制的就是天災的部分，能控制的僅剩下選項D，故答案為**選項D**。
- **第94題**，這題包含了動詞加副詞的眾多形式，但絕不可能是landing successfully，故答案為**選項D**。

聽力原文和對話

Questions 95-97 refer to the following talk

Best Planetarium is currently under renovation...for the wedding issue of the Journal...so it will be closed for a week...and I wanna you to contact all National Science Project participants to retrieve their works because only the winner's project will continue being showcased on the third building...and make sure to decline the booking from all private companies...the planetarium is fully booked in the following six months...also...reschedule the date for all interviewees to June 1, two weeks after the wedding issue is shot...and bring all resumes to my office...I'm going to take a quick look and go through with the HR managers to make sure we have the best hire...that's all for your afternoon's work...

問題95-97請參閱下列談話

倍斯特天文館現在正在整修中…為了期刊的婚宴議題…所以會館會關閉一週…而我想要你聯繫所有國際科學計畫的參加者們，請他們取回本來的作品，因為僅有獲勝者的作品會持續在第三建築物中展示…還有確認回絕所有私人企業的邀約…天文館在接下來的六個月都被訂走了…而且…要替所有面試者重新排定日期至6月1日，在婚宴期刊拍攝後的兩個禮拜…還有將所有履歷都帶到我的辦公室…我會很快的看過並與人事經理一一過濾，確保我們有最佳的聘僱…這就是你今天下午的工作…

試題中譯與解析	
95. Who might be the speaker? (A) Science Project participants. (B) an assistant responsible for various errands. (C) HR managers. (D) **the superintendent.**	95. 説話者可能是誰？ (A) 科學計劃的參加者。 (B) 負責不同類型差事的助理。 (C) 人事經理。 (D) **天文館的主管。**
96. When could be the date of the wedding photoshoot? (A) June 1. (B) during the renovation. (C) **May 18.** (D) six months before the interview.	96. 婚宴拍攝的日期可能是哪天？ (A) 6月1日。 (B) 在裝修的期間。 (C) **5月18日。** (D) 面試的前六個月。
97. Which of the following is not the task given by the speaker? (A) to phone the project participant. (B) **to discuss details with HR managers.** (C) to arrange another time for the interview. (D) to turn down the further reservation.	97. 下列哪一項並非説話者所給予的任務？ (A) 致電給計劃的參與者。 (B) **與人事經理討論細節。** (C) 安排其他的面試時間。 (D) 拒絕進一步的預約。

答案：95. D 96. C 97. B

解析

- **第95題**，這題在聽完後，説話者最有可能是有權力並發號施令者，故答案要選**選項D**。
- **第96題**，從reschedule the date for all interviewees to June 1, two weeks after the wedding issue is shot得知，婚宴拍攝最可能的日期會是5月18日，故答案為**選項C**。
- **第97題**，這題的話要注意細節的部分，説話者自己才要跟人事經理談論細節，而不是發配給聽者的工作項目，故答案要選**選項B**。

Questions 98-100 refer to the following news report

Best Clothing is shutting down four international shops and cuts 5,000 staff in a month, a move that makes the employee totally unprepared...and an employee who prefers to remain anonymous told us that he still has four kids to raise...while it seems depressing and discouraging...the CFO of the company claims that he has already made a job hop and gets signed by another retailer...and he is not even on the chopping block...he said that after knowing deficits and a lack of funds from other potential investors...he kind of knew that the company is doomed and it is really unlikely that they will get the government bailout...this is Cindy James at the Best Clothing entrance...

問題98-100請參閱下列新聞報導

倍斯特服飾店正關閉掉四家國際性的店而且在接下來的一個月內裁員5000名員工，此舉讓員工毫無準備...而一位偏好維持匿名的員工告訴我們他仍有四個小孩要養育...而這聽起來似乎是令人感到沮喪且氣餒的...公司的財務長宣稱，他已經決定跳槽且被另一家零售商簽走了...而他甚至不在裁員名單上頭...他說在得知赤字和缺乏其他潛在的投資客的資金時...他有點知道公司命數已定了而且公司真的不太可能會得到政府的金援...這是辛蒂 ·詹姆士，在倍斯特服飾的入口處...。

98. What can be inferred about the current status of the employee? (A) **jobless.** (B) employed. (C) fully prepared. (D) anonymous.	98. 可以從公司員工現在的狀態中推測出什麼？ (A) **失業的。** (B) 受雇的。 (C) 充分準備的。 (D) 匿名的。

99. Why does the CFO say, "he has already made a job hop"? (A) to confirm the layoff news is true. (B) to consolidate the company's faith in him. (C) **to demonstrate that he has other option.** (D) to show his work ethics.	99. 為什麼財務長要說「他已經跳槽了」？ (A) 以確認裁員的新聞是真實的。 (B) 以鞏固公司對他的信念。 (C) **以顯示他還有其他選擇。** (D) 以展示他的工作道德。
100. What does "on the chopping block" mean? (A) on the breaking news. (B) on the board meeting. (C) on a cutting board. (D) **on the list of downsizing.**	100.「在裁員名單上頭」指的是什麼？ (A) 在新聞快訊中。 (B) 在董事會會議中。 (C) 在切菜板上。 (D) **在縮減人力清單上頭。**

答案：98. A 99. C 100. D

解析

- **第98題**，這題是推測題，從聽力段落中可以得知，這些人是被解雇的，也就是意謂著是失業的，故答案要選**選項A**。
- **第99題**，財務長講這句話有很多原因，也可能是炫耀等等或他早想到這步，也可能是選項C，表示自己在公司營運不佳的情況下還是有其他選擇的，故答案要選**選項C**。
- **第100題**，這個俗諺等同於肉在菜刀板上了，也是常用的裁員等的隱喻，或是用於部門要砍掉多少人，故答案為**選項D**，在裁員的名單上。

模擬試題（一）

PART 1

1. D	2. C	3. C	4. A	5. C	6. B			

PART 2

7. A	8. B	9. C	10.C	11.A	12.A	13.B	14.C	15.C	16.B
17.B	18.C	19.A	20.C	21.B	22.B	23.C	24.C	25.C	26.A
27.B	28.B	29.C	30.C	31.B					

PART 3

32.A	33.C	34.B	35.C	36.B	37.D	38.D	39.B	40.D	41.B
42.C	43.D	44.B	45.C	46.C	47.B	48.B	49.D	50.B	51.D
52.B	53.A	54.C	55.C	56.D	57.D	58.A	59.B	60.A	61.D
62.A	63.C	64.B	65.A	66.B	67.C	68.B	69.C	70.A	

PART 4

71.D	72.D	73.C	74.C	75.C	76.B	77.B	78.D	79.B	80.D
81.C	82.D	83.C	84.D	85.B	86.C	87.C	88.D	89.B	90.D
91.B	92.D	93.C	94.B	95.D	96.B	97.C	98.A	99.B	100. C

模擬試題（二）

PART 1

1. B	2. B	3. B	4. C	5. A	6. A

PART 2

7. C	8. A	9. C	10.B	11.C	12.B	13.B	14.C	15.B	16.C
17.C	18.B	19.C	20.B	21.B	22.C	23.A	24.A	25.A	26.A
27.C	28.C	29.C	30.C	31.B					

PART 3

32.B	33.B	34.C	35.C	36.B	37.D	38.C	39.D	40.A	41.B
42.C	43.D	44.B	45.B	46.D	47.D	48.B	49.D	50.B	51.C
52.B	53.B	54.B	55.D	56.D	57.C	58.C	59.B	60.B	61.B
62.D	63.B	64.D	65.B	66.D	67.C	68.B	69.D	70.D	

PART 4

71.C	72.B	73.C	74.C	75.B	76.C	77.C	78.D	79.B	80.D
81.D	82.D	83.B	84.D	85.C	86.C	87.A	88.D	89.C	90.A
91.D	92.C	93.C	94.C	95.B	96.D	97.B	98.A	99.B	100. D

模擬試題（三）

PART 1

1. A	2. B	3. D	4. C	5. A	6. D			

PART 2

7. B	8. C	9. A	10.C	11.B	12.B	13.B	14.C	15.C	16.A
17.C	18.C	19.C	20.C	21.B	22.A	23.A	24.A	25.A	26.C
27.C	28.C	29.B	30.B	31.A					

PART 3

32.D	33.C	34.B	35.B	36.C	37.D	38.A	39.D	40.A	41.C
42.A	43.C	44.B	45.A	46.B	47.B	48.C	49.D	50.D	51.C
52.D	53.B	54.B	55.D	56.C	57.D	58.C	59.D	60.B	61.C
62.A	63.B	64.D	65.D	66.C	67.C	68.A	69.D	70.C	

PART 4

71.C	72.D	73.B	74.A	75.C	76.A	77.C	78.D	79.D	80.C
81.D	82.B	83.C	84.C	85.A	86.D	87.C	88.A	89.D	90.D
91.C	92.D	93.A	94.D	95.D	96.A	97.D	98.D	99.B	100. B

模擬試題（四）

PART 1

| 1. A | 2. D | 3. B | 4. A | 5. A | 6. C | | | | |

PART 2

7. A	8. A	9. C	10.B	11.B	12.B	13.B	14.B	15.B	16.C
17.B	18.B	19.A	20.C	21.C	22.B	23.A	24.A	25.B	26.C
27.C	28.B	29.A	30.B	31.B					

PART 3

32.B	33.B	34.B	35.A	36.D	37.A	38.C	39.D	40.D	41.C
42.C	43.A	44.C	45.D	46.B	47.B	48.A	49.B	50.B	51.B
52.A	53.D	54.B	55.C	56.D	57.D	58.D	59.C	60.C	61.A
62.B	63.D	64.C	65.B	66.D	67.B	68.A	69.C	70.B	

PART 4

71.D	72.D	73.B	74.B	75.C	76.D	77.D	78.C	79.C	80.A
81.D	82.A	83.D	84.B	85.A	86.D	87.C	88.A	89.B	90.B
91.D	92.B	93.C	94.C	95.C	96.D	97.B	98.D	99.C	100. D

模擬試題（一）

模擬試題（二）

模擬試題（三）

模擬試題（四）

模擬試題（五）

模擬試題（五）

PART 1

1. D	2. B	3. D	4. C	5. D	6. C				

PART 2

7. C	8. B	9. B	10.B	11.B	12.B	13.A	14.C	15.B	16.B
17.C	18.C	19.C	20.C	21.C	22.C	23.B	24.B	25.B	26.C
27.B	28.B	29.C	30.B	31.B					

PART 3

32.A	33.D	34.B	35.C	36.B	37.D	38.B	39.B	40.C	41.C
42.A	43.C	44.D	45.C	46.C	47.B	48.C	49.D	50.B	51.C
52.D	53.A	54.D	55.C	56.D	57.D	58.B	59.D	60.A	61.A
62.D	63.C	64.D	65.D	66.B	67.D	68.B	69.C	70.A	

PART 4

71.A	72.B	73.C	74.D	75.A	76.D	77.C	78.D	79.A	80.A
81.B	82.A	83.D	84.B	85.D	86.D	87.D	88.C	89.A	90.B
91.C	92.A	93.D	94.D	95.D	96.C	97.B	98.A	99.C	100.D

Note

國家圖書館出版品預行編目(CIP)資料

新制多益聽力滿分：神準5回全真試題＋解題策略 韋爾著-- 初版. -- 新北市：倍斯特, 2020.04 面； 公分. --（考用英語系列；22）
ISBN 978-986-98079-4-4（平裝附光碟片）
1.多益測驗

805.1895　　　　　　　　　　109004058

考用英語系列 024

新制多益聽力滿分：神準5回全真試題+解題策略（附MP3）

初　　版　　2020年4月
定　　價　　新台幣580元

作　　者　　韋爾
出　　版　　倍斯特出版事業有限公司
發 行 人　　周瑞德
電　　話　　886-2-8245-6905
傳　　真　　886-2-2245-6398
地　　址　　23558 新北市中和區立業路83巷7號4樓
E - m a i l　　best.books.service@gmail.com
官　　網　　www.bestbookstw.com
總 編 輯　　齊心瑀
封面構成　　高鍾琪
內頁構成　　菩薩蠻數位文化有限公司
印　　製　　大亞彩色印刷製版股份有限公司

港澳地區總經銷　　泛華發行代理有限公司
地　　址　　香港新界將軍澳工業邨駿昌街7號2樓
電　　話　　852-2798-2323
傳　　真　　852-3181-3973